Heritage of Power

EMPIRE OF THE LEGACIES ACADEMY
BOOK TWO

WRITTEN BY AWARD-WINNING AUTHOR

SUSAN HODDY

Heritage of Power—**Empire of the Legacies Academy**

First edition published in Australia in 2025

Text copyright © Susan Hoddy 2025

ISBN
978-0-9756370-3-6

Front cover image and book cover design is created by Ammonia Book Covers
Editing by Debbie Phillips and Deb Klanfar from DP Plus
Formatting by Debbie Phillips from DP Plus
Printed by Ingram Spark, in Dandenong South, Victoria, Australia 3175

Susan's website https://susanhoddy.com/

A catalogue record for this book is available from the National Library of Australia. www.nla.gov.au

CHARACTERS IN THE STORYLINE

Hawk Ironclaw (Griffin)

Sully Valerith (half Griffin, half Lepidoptera Vampire, Fae)

Garrick Ironclaw (Stormclaw Aerie, Griffins' leader)

Elara Ironclaw (Griffin)

Rhydian Ironclaw (Griffin)

Drakon Ironclaw (Griffin)

Zephyrion Ironclaw (Griffin)

Rimmer Ironclaw (Griffin)

Cambray Ironclaw (Griffin)

Aelvric Ironclaw (Griffin)

Eryndor Ironclaw (half Griffin, half Warlock)

The Griffin Soldiers: Draven, Kael

Elsie Brookton (Griffin)

The Lepidoptera Vampires:
Queen Talitha, Princess Violette, William, Grayson, Michael, Brock, Renee, Danielle, Stephen, Sharina, Shepherd, Christian, Kelan, Samantha, Samuel, Kiplin

Adrian Lachance (Warlock)

Stjernefrída (Mother Goddess of the stars)

Kura (Grandmother of Stjernefrída)

Alessia (Stjernefrída's daughter)

Fae:
Elyndra, Aevyressa, Myrrathen, Thalara, Adeline, Summer, Xanthia

Albinus Giordano (Human)

Eight cloaked councillors in Glittertind

Shadow Dweller in the ancient forest

A Serpentine Creature in the ancient forest

Three Guardians of the River of Whispers:

Guardian of the River's Source

Guardian of the River's Flow

Guardian of the River's Destination

Vindthorr (God of Storms)

Valdyrós (Spirit Griffin in the Realm of Shadows)

Pyros (Bear)

PLACES IN THE STORYLINE

Bagnolet, France
Olden Fjord, Norway
Wadi Tiwi, Oman
Muscat, Oman
Mibam Waterfall, Oman
Glittertind, Norway
Sentosa Island, Singapore
Corsica, France
French Alps, France
Cowaramup, Western Australia

CHAPTER ONE

As the sun began to filter through the mist-wreathed mountains, which reflected on the clear surface of the waters of Olden Fjord, a glimmer of the morning's first light sauntered through the window into Hawk's bedroom and flitted across Sully's face. Feeling recharged from the best damn sleep she'd had in weeks, Sully opened her eyes, sat up, and fluffed her pillows. Leaning against the headboard, she looked out at the imposing yellow-and-orange skyline, and the calming ocean water of Olden, and wondered what the day would bring. Most mornings, her first thought was of Hawk.

Hawk ... I wonder where you are, and if you are okay? thought Sully. She breathed a heavy sigh.

Pulling the covers back, she stood tall and rolled her shoulders. *Mmm, that feels better.* Twisting this way and that, Sully stretched her arms toward the ceiling and walked over to the window seat. As she sat down, she noticed that there were many Lepidopteras from her coven, which included her adoptive father, William, leader of the Gramaze Lepidopteras, standing on the grass area below, along with Garrick, leader of Norway's Griffins, and some of his family and soldiers. All were dressed in battle gear. They were waiting near a bluey-green shimmering portal, as Garrick addressed them.

Wonder what's going on? thought Sully, with a furrowed brow. She listened in on the conversation below with her Lepidoptera hearing abilities.

* * *

"Right … gather around everyone, and listen up," said Garrick, authoritatively, as he stood next to William.

They all did as they were instructed.

"Today, our mission is to retrieve the sacred Golden Chalice, which is an important historical artifact to our Griffin culture. It is currently situated in Wadi Tiwi in Oman," said Garrick, looking around at each of their faces. "When we arrive at Muscat via this portal," he pointed to the shimmering portal wall, "there will be a point of contact waiting for us, and they'll be able to transport us via road to Wadi Tiwi. From there we will need to find the Golden Chalice. I do have some intel on where the chalice is being held, but I am not sure if it is a hundred percent correct, because it has been many centuries since it was taken there, and no one has seen it in all that time, that we know of."

"How far is it from Muscat to Wadi Tiwi?" asked William.

"It is about one-and-a-half hours' drive, and there will be some canyons to climb and water pools to navigate, before we arrive there. Now … as all of you know", he looked around at each of their faces again, "Eryndor has escaped the councillors' jail cells in Glittertind, and he has Hawk and others under his mind control. If we come across them in Oman, our mission will be to bring Eryndor and the other prisoners back to Norway, so that they can be placed back in the Glittertind cells forever. If they don't come with us quietly, then they die. As for Hawk …" Garrick raked a hand through his short hair and sighed. "William and I will deal with Hawk. Am I making myself clear?"

They all shouted 'yes'.

"Right … get your weapons ready, and let's go," instructed Garrick. He turned and walked toward the shimmering portal with his sword drawn.

Sully watched everyone follow Garrick and William into the portal, and the portal close.

I wonder why Garrick said that they all would be driving by road from Muscat to Wadi Tiwi? That doesn't make sense when they could portal there instead. Portal would have been quicker, I would have thought!

"They have to be extremely careful when they arrive via portal," said Elara, who had been standing in the doorway, listening to Sully's thoughts. "They can't use any magic or cultural powers while they are traveling from Muscat to Wadi Tiwi."

Sully jumped when she heard Elara's voice. Turning, she said, "Why?"

"If others, particularly Eryndor, detect any form of our families' powers, they'll be alerted to the chalice's location, which we must prevent," stated Elara.

"That makes sense," said Sully, walking over to sit on the bed.

"How are you this morning, my dear?" asked Elara, as she walked into the room.

"Better, thank you," said Sully.

"I was thinking …" she sat next to Sully. "I think you should return home to Bagnolet. There is not much you can do here now and, besides, if anything changes, I will let you know; especially if Hawk returns."

"Oh, right! Do I have to?" queried Sully, as she looked into Elara soulful eyes.

"No, you don't have to, but I think you need to get back to some sort of normality, my dear, don't you?"

Sully took a deep breath in and exhaled. "I would prefer to stay here. Is that okay?"

"No, it's not okay, Sully," said her adoptive mother, Renee, as she walked into the room. "I think you have spent enough time here in Olden Fjord and it's time to get back home."

Sully frowned. "But …"

"There are no buts here. Pack your things. We leave in five minutes. Elara and I will meet you downstairs, and then you and I can portal back home to France." Renee stood her ground in front of Sully.

"Yes, Ma'am," Sully replied, following her instructions without hesitation. With her shoulders slumped forward and her eyes averted to the floor, she sauntered over to the bathroom that was connected to Hawk's room to gather her toiletries, and closed the door.

* * *

"Thank you for coming so quickly, Renee," said Elara. She had rung Renee earlier that morning to discuss Sully, and how they were going to keep her safe.

"You're welcome. I appreciated the call, Elara. It is about time Sully came home, anyway. And it's not doing her any good moping here, waiting for Hawk."

"I agree. Let's go downstairs and wait for her there," said Elara.

Renee nodded and followed Elara down the stairs to a spacious waiting room, that was adorned with European-style furnishings.

* * *

Sully quickly grabbed her toiletries and placed them into her beauty bag. As she looked into the large mirror, tears overflowed onto her cheeks and she silently sobbed.

Oh, Hawk, where are you? I wish you would return. Wiping away the tears with the palms of her hands, she took a deep breath in, then out. *I just hope you are still alive.* Casting one final glance in the mirror, she tried to compose herself, hoping to conceal any sign of her tears from Renee and Elara, before she opened the door.

CHAPTER TWO

The gateway to the portal became visible as it opened in Muscat with a powerful whoosh, resembling a blend of water and clouds.

Garrick stepped through first and was confronted by irate brown bears, upright on their hind legs, angrily roaring in his direction. Swiftly, Garrick raised his hand into the air, signaling for everyone who was traveling with him to pause.

Everybody immediately halted in their tracks as they noticed the enormous brown bears, and patiently waited for further instructions, positioned behind Garrick.

"Pyros!" called Garrick, recognizing a familiar face among the pack, as he secured his intricately designed sword in its sheath on his back.

"Yes," Pyros growled softly, his bear-like cadence lingering even as his body reshaped into human form, moving purposefully toward Garrick.

Garrick watched on as all the other bears lowered themselves onto all fours with a fluid and powerful movement.

The bears kept watch as Pyros approached Garrick.

"Garrick … it has been years, my friend. What brings you to the shadowed woods of Muscat?" Pyros inquired, his gaze focused on the soldiers Garrick had stationed behind him. He held his forearm out for Garrick to clasp.

"We are here to retrieve one of our artifacts," said Garrick, as he firmly grasped hold of Pyros' forearm. "We need safe passage to Mibam Waterfall. Are you and your pack able to provide that for all of us?" Garrick gestured to everyone behind him, and then held out a black pouch.

Pyros nodded once and accepted the pouch from Garrick, deftly pulling the drawstring. A gleam of excitement sparkled in his eyes as he discovered a piece of gold bullion within. "Of course, my friend." Pyros turned to his pack and said, "Organize transport." He waved them away authoritatively.

The brown bears, without hesitation, turned and ran toward the gravel roadway.

"You do realize that the track through to Wadi Tiwi, then to Mibam Waterfall is a long one and is fraught with many hidden dangers, Garrick?" asked Pyros.

"Our path may be long and treacherous, Pyros, but we are prepared for the challenges it holds. We will proceed with caution, and our readiness will guide us through any hidden dangers," stated Garrick, as he watched a large military-style, canvas-covered truck pull up on the edge of the roadway.

"Excellent. Then we will navigate the path together, and determination will see us through whatever challenges lie ahead, my friend," said Pyros. He turned around and watched his men alight from the truck and open the back canvas. "Looks like we are ready to go."

"Right!" said Garrick.

Everyone ... get in the back of the truck. This will take us to Wadi Tiwi, then Mibam Waterfall, thought Garrick to his men.

Do you feel as though you can trust these creatures, Garrick, thought William Gramaze.

Time will tell, my friend. Time will tell, replied Garrick telepathically, as he ushered his family and soldiers into the truck.

With caution, William and his Lepidoptera family walked toward the rear of the truck, jumped in and settled into their seats.

* * *

The truck rumbled along the road, its engine echoing through the quiet surroundings of Wadi Tiwi. The air was still, broken only by the occasional chirping of birds or the rustle of leaves in the breeze. The narrow, rock-lined back streets and hairpin corners demanded careful navigation from the truck's driver, who skillfully maneuvered through the winding terrain.

As the journey continued, small villages emerged, clinging to the mountainsides like patches of civilization against the rugged backdrop. The houses, with their traditional architecture, seemed to blend seamlessly with the natural landscape. Time appeared to move at a slower pace in this remote region, as if the mountains themselves guarded the tranquility of the area and its people.

The truck pressed on, passing by these settlements that looked like scenes frozen in time. The looming Rocky Mountains in the background added a sense of grandeur and mystery to the landscape. Each hairpin turn revealed a new vista, showcasing the beauty of a place where the quietude of nature and the simplicity of village life coexisted in harmony.

As the truck continued its journey, the echoes of its engine resonated against the rocky cliffs, creating a symphony of sounds that reverberated through the eerily quiet surroundings. The road to Wadi Tiwi and further was not just a physical journey, but a passage through a serene and timeless realm, where the charm of the mountains and the stillness of the villages painted a picture of a world untouched by the hustle and bustle of modern life.

* * *

Their bodies lurched sideways as the truck came to a stop on the roadway.

"Where exactly are we?" inquired William, casting a questioning gaze at Pyros.

"Mibam Waterfall," said Pyros, standing. "Come!" He signaled for everyone to alight from the truck.

"Where to from here, William?" asked Shepherd Mornington, the newest member of the Gramaze Lepidoptera family.

"Garrick will be advising us on our mission," said William, standing next to Shepherd.

Shepherd nodded as he listened to William's words, and found himself filled with a sense of anticipation and determination, ready to face whatever challenges lay ahead with the support of his newly found family and the Ironclaw Griffin soldiers. He guessed that the mission ahead was very important, and having someone with Garrick's worldly expertise would undoubtedly enhance their chance of success.

"Gather around, everyone," said Garrick, his voice steady and filled with authority. "Our mission is of the utmost importance, and success depends on each and every one of you playing your part. Is that understood?"

They all nodded in agreement.

Garrick's presence commanded respect, and his words carried a weight of experience that resonated with everyone, as they huddled together in Wadi Tiwi, creating a cocoon of concentration and focus.

Garrick went on to outline the details of the mission, providing insights, strategies, and highlighting potential obstacles. Everyone absorbed Garrick's words with rapt attention, the gravity of the situation starting to sink in. The quiet surroundings seemed to amplify the significance of their task, making every word from Garrick even more impactful.

"Remember … do not use your powers or abilities here. We don't want to alert anyone to our whereabouts," cautioned Garrick, glancing at each of them.

Garrick's prudence hung in the air like a silent command and everyone nodded in understanding. Each member met his gaze with a solemn expression, acknowledging the importance of keeping their capabilities under wraps.

* * *

Under the scorching sun's relentless rays, everybody followed Pyros down the winding two-hundred-and-seventy or so narrow concrete steps, that were flanked by limestone boulders and vibrant green date palms, as well as banana and papaya trees. As the waterfall and the turquoise-colored, crystal-clear, spring-water pool below emerged into view, it revealed a paradise waiting to be discovered, a sight that none of the Griffin or Lepidopteras had expected.

Hmmm, this looks like the place the councillors disclosed to me when we were in Glittertind, thought Garrick, as he looked over the cliff's edge. *Now all I need to do is find the cave where the chalice, forged with ashes from past ancient Norwegian Gods, is hidden.*

"Drakon, Zephyrion, you will come with me. Draven and Kael, you will stay with the Gramaze coven," said Garrick.

All the Griffins nodded in compliance.

Garrick jumped off the limestone cliff into the water pool below and waited for the two sons he'd tasked with this particular mission to join him.

Keep your wits about you everyone, thought William, as he stood guard alongside his six family members, while Garrick and two of his sons went to retrieve the ancient chalice.

CHAPTER THREE

With a desire to be anywhere but at the academy, Sully sat on the slatted wooden bench near the river, gazing out over the gentle current of the Seine. It had been weeks since Sully had last seen Hawk, who was still under the mind control of Eryndor, which had been evident on the operations room satellite feedback she had watched. He was still all she could think about, and not even her training, or any life experiences so far, had prepared her for the overwhelming emotions she had for Hawk. Whether it was the Lepidoptera within her, or their Griffin connection, she couldn't be certain. But one thing she was sure of was her feelings for Hawk.

Without a word spoken, Samuel placed his hand on Sully's shoulder. "How's it going, Sis?" He had heard her thoughts from far away and knew she needed someone to talk with.

Sully jumped. Turning, she noticed her adoptive brother, Samuel, standing behind her. Wiping her tearstained cheeks, her voice husky, she asked, "Has something happened?"

"No! I just thought I would come and see how you're doing," said Samuel. He sat next to her on the wooden seat and placed his arm around her shoulders.

Sully leaned into him and placed her head on his shoulder. "Do you think Hawk will ever return to the academy?"

"I would like to hope so, Sis."

"I still feel our connection, but it is intermittent," said Sully, as she looked out across the river. "So, I know he is alive."

"Oh, right!" said Samuel, who hadn't even realized that Sully could feel this deep connection to Hawk.

"I … I wish he was here," said Sully, as she slowly pulled away from Samuel.

"Yeah, same here," said Samuel, gazing at her shattered demeanor. "Have you checked in with Brock lately, to see if he has come across any live satellite feeds of Hawk?"

"Yes, daily. But I haven't checked in with him today, though. He seemed too busy when I went in to see him around lunchtime, so I decided that I would check back later," Sully explained.

"We could go and see if he is free now, if you like."

"I'm sure he has better things to do than search for Hawk, don't you think?"

Rising from the seat, Samuel said, "Come on, I am sure he won't mind. Let's go," he pulled Sully up off the seat.

"Okay!" said Sully, eagerly. Her face lit up with a radiant smile.

They ran toward the Gramaze mansion, with Lepidoptera speed.

* * *

With their backs to the glass sliding doors of the operations room, Brock and Kiplin heard the doors open and turned to see Sully and Samuel walking in.

"Hey, guys … what are you both up to tonight?" asked Kiplin, who was spending time with Brock to delve into the technical aspects of explosive detonation.

"We thought we would come by and see Brock, actually. We wanted to inquire if there were any updates on Hawk," Samuel explained.

"Ah, right!" said Kiplin.

"Evening, Sully and Samuel," greeted Brock. "I have some time now, if you want to take a seat." He gestured toward some chairs at the long table behind him. Brock turned his attention to the computer and pressed the search keys to look for any pictures of Hawk worldwide that might have surfaced since his last search.

"I'm sure he will be found, and soon," said Kiplin, looking at Sully. He had been missing his roommate, too.

"I hope you're right, Kiplin. Eryndor seems to have a tight grip on Hawk and at this stage I don't foresee him breaking free from the mind control," said Sully, her brow furrowed with worry.

"Guys ..." interrupted Brock. "It looks like the satellite *has* collected some data on Hawk's whereabouts." His fingers flew over the console with preternatural precision, manipulating the satellite's controls and locking onto the coordinates until the blurred landscape snapped into crisp, sharp clarity.

Sully swiftly jumped out of her seat and rushed over to Brock. As she stood beside him, she said, "That's Hawk. I would know that face anywhere." She watched the screen carefully and noticed that in every feed of Hawk he was always with others, never alone. "Fuck, they are all still under Eryndor's mind control. See!" She pointed to their eyes. "Look at their white, glazed-over eyes."

"Hmm, you're right. But what you're not seeing from the footage is it seems Hawk is deliberately trying to draw attention to himself from the cameras at each location they visit," Brock explained, scrutinizing the satellite feed more closely. "It's like he wants us to follow him."

"Yeah, it does seem that way," said Kiplin, watching the screen. "But why?"

"Maybe it's an attempt to lead us to him so we can bring him back home," Samuel suggested, attempting to make sense of the situation. "But even that doesn't add up. While Hawk is under mind control, it's not as if he can shake it off," he added, expressing his confusion.

"Do you know where he is?" asked Sully to Brock.

"It looks like he has been in a few countries. China, Japan, Korea and even Vietnam. But he is currently in Singapore. That's Keppel Harbour, and the cable cars that take you over to Sentosa Island." Brock pointed to the iconic landmarks on his computer screen. *Hmm, I wonder why Eryndor has been sending his ghostly eyed lackeys to all of these countries? I need to report this to Violette and see what she would like our family to do, or whether she wants to leave it up to Elara to sort out Hawk and the others.*

"So now we know where Hawk is, we can go and rescue him, right?" Sully inquired, expressing a desire to take immediate action.

"No, I'm afraid not," said Brock, looking at Sully. "I will need to speak with the Head Chancellor first, before we take any action."

Sully's lips thinned and her nostrils flared as she drew a deep breath inward, clearly frustrated with Brock's response. "There's always a roadblock." Sully walked toward the glass sliding doors.

"Sully, wait," yelled Samuel, as he watched her walk out of the operations room.

However, Sully was in no mood to wait. With Lepidoptera speed, she ran out of the Gramaze mansion and toward the Seine River, at the back of the property.

"Go after her, Samuel. Maybe you can calm her down," said Brock.

"I'll come with you," offered Kiplin.

"Thanks, Kiplin. Let's go, before she does something she regrets," said Samuel.

"I'll catch up with you later on, Brock, for some more training, if that's okay?" said Kiplin, looking at Brock.

"That's fine, Kiplin. Take your time," said Brock. He watched Samuel and Kiplin walk out of the operations room.

CHAPTER FOUR

She doesn't look too happy, thought Elsie, as she hovered in the sky above Sully and watched her run along the riverbank. "Hey, Sully … wait up."

Tears welled in Sully's eyes as she gazed toward the night sky, where she spotted Elsie. She then witnessed her descent, observing as Elsie gracefully landed in front of her, and retracted her large Griffin wings and claws.

"Are you okay?" asked Elsie.

"Yeah, I'm fine," said Sully, wiping her tearstained cheeks with the backs of her hands.

"What's happened? And don't tell me nothing." Elsie leaned in and gave Sully a friendly hug.

The tears came freely as Sully hugged Elsie back. "I just wish that Hawk was here," sobbed Sully.

"Everything will work out. Try not to worry too much," said Elsie, as she gently rubbed Sully's back in a soothing manner.

Sully pulled away from their embrace and said, "I hope so."

"What has bought all this on, anyway?" asked Elsie.

"Brock found Hawk in Singapore, of all places, and he said that we can't go and rescue him until he speaks with the Head Chancellor. By the time they talk about it, and speak with Elara as well, Hawk will be gone."

"For Gods' sake … I can't see why you have to wait. That is ridiculous," said Elsie, placing her hands on her hips.

"You should have seen Hawk on the satellite feed … he looked miserable and overwhelmed with everything. All I want to do is go and get him and bring him back. Is that too much to ask?" Frustration and concern were evident in Sully's voice.

"Oh, I am so sorry, roomie." Elsie spotted Samuel and Kiplin walking toward them. "Here come Samuel and Kiplin, maybe they can help," said Elsie, gesturing to them walking up behind Sully.

"Humph, I don't think so," said Sully, as she rolled her eyes.

"You okay, Sis?" asked Samuel, as he and Kiplin came to stand in front of them.

"What do you care?" asked Sully, angrily.

"Don't be like that, Sully. You know we care," said Samuel.

"Then why don't you help her rescue Hawk?" asked Elsie, as she glanced at both Samuel and Kiplin. "I thought we were all friends here, and as far as I know, friends help friends. Am I right?"

"Our hands are tied. You know we shouldn't disobey the Gramaze coven. And I don't want to be kicked out of the academy," said Kiplin, his brow furrowed.

"I don't think that will happen, especially if Samuel and Sully come with us to rescue Hawk. After all, what could they do besides reprimand us and take away our privileges," stated Elsie. "So, what do you say, boys? Are you with us or not?"

With a pleading expression, Sully turned her gaze from Samuel to Kiplin. "Can you help us, pleeeease?" Sully implored them.

Samuel looked to Kiplin and twitched his lips, then breathed a deep sigh.

What do you think, my friend? thought Samuel to Kiplin only.

Fuck it, why not! Hawk is our friend, too, and I for one am sick and tired of sitting around doing nothing about his disappearance and betrayal, thought Kiplin to Samuel.

Me too. Let's do this, thought Samuel to Kiplin.

"Okay ladies, we're in," stated Samuel, as he looked from Sully to Elsie.

"Awesome! Thank you, Samuel, and you too, Kiplin," Sully exclaimed with enthusiasm. However, her excitement quickly gave way to sadness when she realized that there was no quick way to get to Singapore. It would take at least fourteen hours to fly there, and she had no way of knowing if Hawk would still be there.

"What's the matter? asked Elsie. "You don't seem too happy about this?" asked Elsie.

"Unless we can portal to Singapore, it will take at least fourteen hours to get there by plane, and I think Hawk will have disappeared by then, don't you?" stated Sully.

"Shit … I never thought of that," said Elsie.

"I think I may know someone who could help us," said Samuel. "Give me ten minutes and I will get back to you." He ran off toward the academy.

I hope you are still in Singapore by the time we get there, Hawk. I wonder how we are going to break the mind control that Eryndor has over you, thought Sully, contemplating the challenge ahead.

* * *

"So we are in agreement, Elara?" questioned Head Chancellor Violette, standing in the operations room, as they communicated via video link.

"Yes, I think it would be best for you and your coven to retrieve Hawk from Singapore. I currently have limited soldiers and family here, only enough to protect me and our country. But please … take every precaution to ensure Hawk isn't harmed, or worse yet, killed," urged Elara.

"I give you my word," said Violette, sensing a mother's love for her child. "I will chat to you later on this evening when we have Hawk in hand. Goodbye!"

"Thank you, Princess. I do appreciate everything you are doing and undertaking for my family. Goodbye!" said Elara.

Violette pressed end on the call and turned to Brock. "I want you to organize some of the legacies at the academy to come with us tonight. I do not want Sully or Samuel to come with us, but maybe Kiplin, Elsie and a few others would be great. I will organize for Adrian to create a portal to take us all to Singapore. Call the rest of our coven and instruct them to return home to protect our Queen while we are away. Are we clear?" stated Violette.

"Yes, Princess. But … I have one question," said Brock, hesitantly.

"And that is?" asked Violette, authoritatively.

"You have not been on a mission for years. What makes you think that it is okay for you to leave the Gramaze mansion, especially without William's or the Queen's permission? You are next in line to the throne, and we don't want anything happening to you. And we don't even know where Eryndor is at the moment, let alone the resistance Hawk and Eryndor's helpers will create. I think you will be safer here, don't you?" queried Brock. He gulped hard.

"I don't need their permission. Just do as I ask, Brock," stated Violette. She walked away from him and through the glass sliding doorway.

I had better let Sire know what is going on here, thought Brock as he picked up his mobile to call William Gramaze.

"Yes, Brock," said William, as he answered the call.

"Sire … we have a bit of a problem here," said Brock.

"I already know. Queen Talitha has been listening to the chatter around the mansion and has called me. We have decided to let the Princess go to Singapore on this mission. Michael and Grayson will be returning from Oman to protect Violette while she is in Singapore. Violette just doesn't know it yet. In the meantime, and while she is away from the mansion and academy, I want you to keep an eye on her every movement in Singapore. Keep the satellite feed on her twenty-four-seven until she returns. Understood?" asked William commandingly.

"Yes, Sire," said Brock. Hearing the phone click and the line dropping out, he realized that William had hung up.

CHAPTER FIVE

"Drakon, Zephyrion, I need both of you to stand guard here at the mouth of this cave, while I venture deeper into the caves to retrieve the chalice." Garrick gestured toward the cave entrance, partially filled with turquoise-colored water. The cave featured limestone walls and round boulders that had been shaped by the pressure of water over thousands of years.

"Yes, Sir," they both said together, as they watched Garrick jump into the water.

Wading through the waist-high water, Garrick found that as he progressed deeper, the cave began to narrow, and the water deepened until it reached just below his chin.

I'm certain, based on the councillor's memories, that this is the place where the chalice is kept. But where is it? thought Garrick, as he surveyed his surroundings.

Time seemed to stand still, as a sudden current, more powerful than any he had faced before, pulled Garrick beneath the water's surface. While he fought to resurface, Garrick caught a glimpse of a shiny object, glistening in the distance. As he swam toward the glimmering object, his curiosity intensified. The water seemed to conceal both mystery and danger, but the allure of the shining object propelled him forward. When he reached the shimmering object, he realized it was a magnificent, ancient chalice adorned with intricate designs, which was placed inside an ancient-looking book. The waters around him seemed to resonate with an otherworldly energy as he reached out to grasp the artifact. However, as his fingers touched the surface of the book, a sudden surge of power coursed through him. Like an ancient scroll, it unlocked forgotten memories and revealed a hidden purpose. Now armed with newfound knowledge, Garrick faced a choice that would not only impact his destiny, but also the fate of his family, his country, and the world.

Securing the ancient book within his jacket, Garrick was suddenly struck by a powerful jolt, thrusting his world into darkness. Unconscious, his limp Griffin body drifted to the water's surface.

As Drakon and Zephyrion stood guard and observed the illuminated watery caves ahead of them, their attention was drawn to Garrick, who was now face down in the water. Rushing to his side, they quickly turned him over.

"Father," Drakon yelled, delivering a forceful slap to his father's face in an attempt to rouse him, while Zephyrion kept Garrick suspended above the water.

Garrick remained unresponsive.

Drakon, moving with the speed of a Griffin, swiftly pulled Garrick to the edge of Mibam Waterfall, and up onto the large limestone rocks.

Delivering another forceful slap, Drakon and Zephyrion anxiously awaited any sign of Garrick stirring. The echoes of the impact resonated in the air as Drakon assessed their father's reaction, hoping for a flicker of consciousness to break through the persistent stillness.

"If you do that again, your life won't be worth living," declared Garrick, his eyes opening with a sharp intensity. Confusion painted his expression as he questioned, "What happened?"

"We are not sure, Father. It appeared as though the water illuminated from below, and then we noticed your body floating on top of the water," explained Drakon.

"Right!" Garrick sat up, surveying his surroundings with a mixture of bewilderment and concern. "I have the chalice. Let's get the fuck out of here."

Drakon and Zephyrion exchanged glances, their brows furrowing in shared concern.

"Father … what are you talking about?" queried Drakon.

Garrick felt for the ancient-looking book that he had tucked into his jacket, then pulled his jacket open, only to discover the book was missing. "Fuck!" He raked a hand through his hair. "I must have dropped it. You both stay here, and I will go back and get the chalice," said Garrick.

"I don't think you are in any sort of state to be able to do that, Father," said Drakon, expressing concern for Garrick's well-being.

"I'm fine," Garrick asserted, attempting to stand but finding himself unable to do so.

Sire … Draven and I will go, thought Kael. He and Draven had been listening in on Garrick's conversation from above.

"I think that may be a wise decision," said Garrick, as he watched both of his soldiers dive from the cliffs above to the waters below.

Within minutes, both Draven and Kael had returned, and in Kael's hand was the ancient book with the chalice inside. "Let's get this topside!" said Kael, eager to get the artifact back to Olden Fjord.

Both Drakon and Zephyrion, not having seen anything like this artifact before, looked on in amazement at its ancient beauty.

"Let's go, Draven and Kael," said Garrick, noticing that his two soldiers had successfully retrieved the chalice.

Drakon and Zephyrion assisted Garrick to his feet, gently guiding him off the rocks, and offering their arms for support around his back.

* * *

As the Griffins and Lepidopteras reached the truck that would take them back to Muscat—where Adrian the Warlock awaited to portal them all back to Norway, a familiar figure suddenly appeared before them.

Stopped in their tracks, everyone swiftly retrieved their weapons of choice from sheaths and stood to attention, waiting for what would happen next.

"Ah, Father … and you have company. How delightful," Eryndor remarked, dripping with sarcasm.

Garrick, who needed assistance from Drakon and Zephyrion to walk, lifted his head and glared at Eryndor. He recognized that, in his current condition, he was in no shape to confront his adopted son, the Harbinger of Shadows.

"What do you want, Eryndor?" Draven demanded, his stance defensive, as he and Kael positioned themselves protectively in front of Garrick.

"What is rightfully mine," declared Eryndor. He turned his gaze to Kael and, with a single wave of his hand, lifted the ancient book with the chalice inside into the air and into his shadowy hands. "Ah, my beauty, I finally have you."

As the ancient artifact found itself in the clutches of Eryndor, the atmosphere crackled with an unsettling energy and everyone looked on with a mix of concern and determination. Eryndor's malevolence cast a shadow over the scene, but Shepherd Mornington was undeterred, and readied himself for the impending confrontation with the Harbinger of Shadows.

"Humph, rightfully yours, that's a joke, Eryndor! What a crock of shit!" stated Rimmer, another of Garrick's sons, mocking him. "You seem to think you can take whatever you want, whenever you want. Well … not this time." He clenched his hand into a fist, and thrust a lightning bolt at Eryndor's chest.

Eryndor clutched at his chest and dropped the ancient book to the ground. "You will pay, brother!"

As the intense scene unfolded, Shepherd, now a member of the Gramaze coven, received a telepathic instruction from William. In his mind, William directed Shepherd to retrieve the ancient book and ensure its safety. Shepherd obeyed instantly.

"It is you who will pay, Eryndor," said William Gramaze, who was now towering over Eryndor with his sword drawn. "You will pay with your life."

As William thrust his sword down toward Eryndor's neck, Eryndor clicked his fingers and in an instant he vanished.

"What the—!" exclaimed William, frustration evident in his voice, as his sword dug into the ground. "That fucker must have at least a thousand lives."

"Get in the truck, everyone," commanded Zephyrion. "We need to get back to Olden before Eryndor returns. We are stronger there."

In agreement, they all did as Zephyrion instructed.

* * *

Eryndor and his militant lackeys lay in wait around the next bend in the road, perched atop a mountain, with rocket-propelled missile launchers aimed at the truck.

Garrick ... you either hand over the chalice, or everyone dies, thought Eryndor, his menacing intentions echoing in Garrick's mind.

Everyone heard Eryndor's command and readied themselves for the attack.

"Pyros, stop the truck!" yelled Garrick urgently.

Everybody surged sideways as Pyros brought the truck to an abrupt stop. The air was filled with a sense of tension, heightened by the surrounding mountains that seemed to close in, creating a natural amphitheater for the impending confrontation with Eryndor and his minions.

Drakon and Zephyrion assisted a still-weak Garrick out of the truck. Despite being a Griffin, his ability to heal himself had not yet kicked in, leaving him vulnerable to the injury sustained previously at Mibam Waterfall. The urgency to find cover and regroup with their allies hung heavily in the air, as the chaos unfolded around them.

Here is your first warning, Father, thought Eryndor, as the first missile hit the side of the mountain near them, exploding in a burst of fiery chaos, scattering debris and dust in its wake. The ominous sound of the explosion reverberated through the mountainous terrain, signaling the beginning of the perilous encounter. *There won't be another!*

As everyone swiftly disembarked from the truck, William placed his finger over his lips and shook his head. The silent gesture signaled for Garrick not to answer and urged everyone else to maintain absolute silence. The urgency of the situation demanded discretion and the group, now on high alert, followed William's unspoken command with a heightened sense of caution.

You were warned, Father, thought Eryndor, who signaled for his minions to fire the next missile, and this time it struck the truck with a deafening explosion. The mountainside echoed with the successive blasts as another missile followed, intensifying the mayhem.

Within minutes of the last missile exploding, Eryndor and his glazed-eyed minions portaled over to the truck. As they lifted the tattered canvas cover off the truck, they were surprised to find not a soul in sight.

"Fuck!" Eryndor turned around and scoured the countryside for any sign of life. But there was nothing. "Where are they?" His shadowy hands clenched into fists and his nostrils flared in anger. The unexpected disappearance of their targets left Eryndor and his minions baffled, and the rugged landscape provided no clues to the sudden vanishing act of their adversaries, or the chalice.

CHAPTER SIX

The tropical climate and high humidity, coupled with the consistent heavy rainfall, took Sully, Samuel, Elsie and Kiplin by surprise as they came crashing through the portal onto the shores of Sentosa Island, Singapore, with a bang. The abrupt change in weather added an unexpected element to their arrival. However, the secluded beach where they landed provided a relatively quiet and hidden spot, allowing them to regroup without drawing immediate attention to themselves.

"Shit … we need to find cover," Sully urged her brother and friends, pushing herself up from the wet sand. Their clothes clung to them, soaked through, while rain streamed down their faces, plastering their hair to their skin. The urgency in Sully's voice made it clear that they needed to escape the relentless tropical downpour.

* * *

"Thank the Gods for that," said Sully, looking at Samuel, Elsie and Kiplin as they sheltered under a large tree. "Never expected this."

"Yeah, me neither," said Elsie, contemplating the state of her wet wings, and pondering whether they would expand or even allow her to fly in their drenched condition.

"Where are we?" queried Kiplin, as he looked out to the harbor. He had expected to land on the Singapore mainland.

"It looks like we are on Sentosa Island. I believe it's a ferry ride or cable car across Keppel Harbour, which takes you back to the Singapore mainland." Sully pointed to the ferry and cable cars visible in the distance.

"Oh, right. So … what is our plan?" asked Kiplin.

"Find Hawk, and get the hell out of here. When Samuel and I checked the satellite footage, back home in Bagnolet, this is exactly where Hawk was. Not sure if he is still here, but I am sure we will be able to find him, if he is," replied Sully.

"What makes you say that?" enquired Elsie, as she watched the rain cease, as if it were a shower being turned off in a bathroom.

"The bonded connection I have with Hawk allows me to sense or communicate with him if we are in the same country, as long as he doesn't deliberately block me," explained Sully, also noticing the rain has stopped. "Let's get out of these wet clothes and see if we can find him."

The group nodded in agreement, as they were eager to get back to Bagnolet before anyone knew they were missing.

* * *

Dressed in black leathers, with her Grikohr sword securely sheathed on her back, Violette stepped out of the portal alongside other supernaturals from the academy. "Listen up!" Her gaze swept across their silent faces as she waited for their attention.

"Our mission tonight is to find Hawk, nothing more. Just remember that he is under Eryndor's mind control, so he will not recognize any of you, or willingly come with us. Once you've located him, report to me, and I will then take the lead, ensuring his safe return to Bagnolet. Am I making myself clear?" asked Violette, her words carrying a sense of authority and purpose, as she looked each of them in the face.

In unison they all said, "Yes," and slightly bowed to the Princess of the Lepidopteras.

"Right … you already have your mission parameters, so off you go. Remember, keep in contact at all times," Violette instructed. She watched the nine legacies, all of whom had been at the academy for a year or more, and had plenty of training, walk off in groups of three, then she continued on by herself to look for Hawk.

* * *

"Doesn't she realize how dangerous it is here on Sentosa Island without guards? For fuck's sake, she hasn't even been on a mission, let alone fought someone in a battle, for over twenty years. When is this woman going to learn?" Michael vented his frustration to Grayson, irritated by his life partner's audacity and stupidity.

"Women … I can never figure them out, man!" said Grayson.

"Let's maintain our distance but ensure we don't lose sight of Violette. And, most importantly, we don't want her knowing we are here to protect her," said Michael.

"Agreed!" said Grayson, as they followed Violette. He, too, knew how annoyed Violette would be if she found out they were following her for protection.

* * *

"Thanks for the dry clothes, Samuel," said Sully, as she walked out of the public toilets at the Outpost Hotel, Elsie beside her.

"Yeah, thanks!" said Elsie, shrugging on a short-sleeved jacket. "Where's Kiplin?"

"You're both welcome. Kiplin is actually checking if the hotel has any spare rooms available, just in case we have to stay tonight," said Samuel, who had already changed into dry clothes and had been waiting by the infinity pool area for everyone to return.

"Oh, right!" said Elsie, her brow furrowed. "But I thought it was too risky to stay in Singapore for more than a day?"

"It is, but we certainly need a backup plan, in case we can't find Hawk. We don't want a repeat of what happened when we arrived earlier, do we?" said Samuel, with his hands on his hips, recalling the downpour of rain, and how they all got soaked. "Here comes Kiplin now." He watched Kiplin walking toward them. "How did you go?"

"Yeah, good," said Kiplin, who was now dressed in white jeans, a white long-sleeved T-shirt, with a short-sleeved burgundy shirt over the top. "Actually, the receptionist is a Lepidoptera, and she has put a hold on a room for us, just in case we need it tonight."

"Wow … that's lucky!" said Sully.

"Yeah, I thought she looked familiar. She was at the academy last year, and I remember having some classes with her," said Kiplin.

"Anyway, back to our mission. Have you been able to get hold of Hawk yet?" Samuel asked Sully.

"I tried when I was getting changed. But there was nothing. In the meantime, I think we should pound the pavement and see if we can find him," said Sully, hopeful that they would be able to bring Hawk back home to Bagnolet.

"I think we would be safer scouring Sentosa from the rooftops, don't you?" asked Samuel.

"Yeah, good idea," said Kiplin.

"Well, what about if Elsie and I do the rooftops and you guys hit the pavement," said Sully.

"Not a bad idea, Sis. We could probably cover more ground that way. However, I would like to emphasize that we all stay in touch with each other while we are separated," said Samuel.

"That's a given," said Elsie, looking at Samuel.

Sully nodded yes. "Catch up with you both later on," said Sully. She grabbed Elsie's hand, "Let's go." They leapt onto the rooftop of a nearby building and began their search for Hawk.

* * *

The moon hung high in the ink-black sky as Sully and Elsie gracefully leaped from one rooftop to another, the rhythmic tapping of their footsteps echoing through the silent night. Dressed in dark attire, their figures blended seamlessly with the shadows, making them nearly invisible.

As they landed on another rooftop, Sully's sharp Lepidoptera vision caught a glimpse of a figure in the distance. "There he is," she whispered to Elsie, her voice carrying a sense of urgency, as she pointed in his direction.

Hawk was oblivious to their presence and moved with an uncanny speed.

"Hey, Hawk!" Sully called out. But her words seemed to dissipate in the night air. He didn't acknowledge her; instead, he quickened his pace and disappeared into the labyrinth of rooftops.

Without hesitation, Sully and Elsie followed in hot pursuit. The humid wind rushed past them as they navigated the urban jungle, their agile movements keeping them on Hawk's trail. The chase led them through narrow alleys and over makeshift bridges between buildings, then back to the rooftops.

"Hawk, stop!" Sully's voice cut through the night air. To her surprise, he turned his head in acknowledgment, but his eyes, once a deep, soulful brown color, were now glazed over in an eerie, unnatural white.

Hawk came to a sudden halt, his silhouette stark against the cityscape.

Sully and Elsie approached cautiously, hoping to discern the cause of his erratic behavior.

"Help me," pleaded Hawk, breaking free momentarily from the mind control imposed by Eryndor, as Sully and Elsie approached him.

Sully noticed his eyes had changed back to normal. "Come with us. We can help you."

With his hands either side of his head, he shook his head vigorously, attempting to dispel the lingering influence. In a moment of clarity, he said, "I only have a few seconds. I can't seem to shake this." He shook his head again. "Please, forgive me," begged Hawk. However, the respite was short-lived as the mind control swiftly tightened its grip once again. Without warning, his eyes glazed over, reclaiming him once more, and he sprinted away.

Sully's senses heightened as she watched him try to disappear into the shadows.

Samuel, Kiplin, we've spotted Hawk. He's on the move. Head toward the eastern side of the island, Sully relayed telepathically, her voice steady despite the urgency of the situation.

We will be there in a few minutes, thought Samuel.

As Sully and Elsie continued the pursuit, the cityscape blurred beneath them. The distant lights of Singapore's skyline cast an ethereal glow on the rooftops. Undeterred, Sully and Elsie maintained their focus on the chase, their determination unwavering as they aimed to reach Hawk and safely return him to Bagnolet.

As the pursuit intensified, Samuel and Kiplin swiftly joined Sully and Elsie on the rooftops. The moonlight illuminated the determined expressions on their faces as they seamlessly integrated into the chase. Following Hawk across the urban landscape, the group moved with synchronized precision, their footsteps echoing through the quiet night.

However, as they navigated the labyrinth of rooftops, Hawk's movements became increasingly elusive. He seemed to melt into the shadows, leaving his pursuers momentarily disoriented.

"We've lost him," Sully announced.

Undeterred, the team continued their search, weaving through the maze of structures. In the end, their perseverance led them to a surprising discovery: a pile of discarded clothes, near a long clothesline.

Elsie's brow furrowed, when she realized that these clothes looked like the ones Hawk had been wearing. "Are these Hawk's clothes? Why would he leave them behind?"

Sully examined the abandoned attire. "I think he has stolen some clothes from this line." She gestured to the abandoned pegs that had been discarded on the rooftop. "Maybe he's trying to throw us off. Let's stay alert as he might still be nearby."

The night air hung heavy with uncertainty as they pondered the mysterious turn of events.

As the pursuit continued, Hawk's appearances became increasingly sporadic, like a wisp of smoke evading their grasp. The rooftop quartet pressed on, navigating the urban maze with determination, but eventually Hawk vanished into the depths of the night, slipping into hiding.

CHAPTER SEVEN

"Where do we go from here?" inquired William, walking side by side with Garrick out of a portal and into Garrick's Olden Fjord office, followed by their family and soldiers.

"Now that we possess the chalice, obtaining the Fae's Golden Ring is the next step. Though, it shouldn't pose much difficulty," remarked Garrick, who had now fully recovered from his injuries.

"Yes, but first we must extract the chalice from the book," Elara, interjected, having caught wind of the conversation as she entered the office. "Have the councillors provided any information on who the potential candidates are for this extraction?"

"No, the councillors haven't provided that information, but I do have a contact. However, I have been considering whether it might be more prudent for us to refrain from extracting the chalice, at this point," suggested Garrick.

"Why?" queried Elara.

"Because we can't risk Eryndor getting hold of the chalice once we extract it from the book," declared Garrick.

"I never thought of that!" said Elara, her brow furrowed, as she recalled the telepathic conversation she'd had with Garrick earlier about Eryndor and the attack in Oman. "Who are we going to use to extract the chalice from the book, anyway?"

"According to our mythology, the Mother Goddess of all the stars, Stjernefrída, is the one we will need for the extraction," said Garrick. "I have already spoken with her telepathically, and she is willing to help."

"You say that we need the Fae's Golden Ring. So, where is it kept?" asked Elara.

"We will need to visit the Fae's kingdom. But as you know, they are located in another realm, which is quite a trek to get to from here. We can only portal some of the way, and then once we enter their realm, our magic is limited," said Garrick.

"It looks like you will be needing my family and I to help with this next mission, am I right?" queried William to Garrick.

"On the contrary, my friend," Garrick sat on the corner of his office desk and folded his arms over his chest. "While the Fae's realm poses dangers for Griffins, I am confident that once I elucidate our purpose to Elyndra, the Queen of the Fae's kingdom, she will be inclined to assist us. But thank you for the offer."

"Very well. We'll bid you farewell, my friend. Reach out if you need assistance; otherwise, travel safely, and best of luck on your mission," expressed William, extending his hand for a forearm handshake with Garrick.

"Thank you, William. I'm grateful for all the support you and your family have offered," replied Garrick, reciprocating the forearm handshake with William.

"Yes, thank you, William. Your alliance and assistance mean a great deal to us," said Elara, as she looked upon his face with respect.

"You're welcome!" said William. He turned to his family. "Time to return home, Lepidopteras. Adrian, open a portal."

Adrian effortlessly opened the portal with a wave of his hand.

"Let's go," said William. The Lepidoptera Vampires walked toward the entrance and passed through.

* * *

"Aelvric, I require you to reach out to your contacts in the Fae Kingdom and ascertain whether it's acceptable for us to pay them a visit," instructed Garrick, his gaze shifting from the closing portal to his son.

"Yes, Sir," replied Aelvric. He turned and walked toward the doorway.

"Right … I need each of you to prepare our kingdom for the potential return of Eryndor. By now, he probably realizes that we are alive, and will soon come back to try to steal the chalice," declared Garrick, scanning the room and meeting the gaze of each individual. "Well, what are you waiting for, begone."

They all nodded and rushed toward the doorway, united by a single purpose: to save their kingdom and protect their leader from the Harbinger of Shadows.

* * *

Shepherd, Stephen, Christian and Kelan walked out of the portal and watched the edges shrink inward, until it became a pinpoint, before vanishing, giving the impression of the gateway closing in on itself.

"Where is William?" queried Shepherd, his brow furrowed.

"Weren't William and Adrian behind us?" questioned Kelan.

"Fuck, where are they?" asked Christian, as his eyes scanned the backyard of the Gramaze coven mansion.

"Let's head to the operations room and see Brock. I'm sure he'll be able to help us sort this out," said Stephen. They ran with urgency, using their Lepidoptera Vampire speed, toward the mansion.

"Brock," uttered Stephen, his voice carrying a note of concern, as he entered through the glass sliding doors, accompanied by Kelan, Christian and Shepherd.

Brock turned to see the four Lepidopteras entering the operations room. "What can I do for you?"

He proceeded to read their confused thoughts.

"Shit! I don't know where William and Adrian are," stated Brock. "Maybe they're on another mission? Give me a minute." Brock turned his chair around, pressed the number one button on the operations room phone console, and waited for William to answer.

Seconds seemed like minutes, as the five Lepidopteras waited patiently for William to connect; but it went straight to message bank.

"William! It's Brock. Where the fuck are you? Call me back," said Brock, his voice laced with concern.

Time seemed to stand still, as the five Lepidoptera coven members waited for the call back. But there was nothing, even after ten minutes had passed.

Usually, the protocol was to ring back within minutes.

Brock pulled up the satellite footage of the portal opening in Olden Fjord, watching who entered, and then the portal closing, before switching to the portal in Bagnolet at the mansion, watching who exited. As he meticulously examined the recordings, he discerned that the closing portal displayed an unusual pattern, distinct from Adrian's typical creations. "Guys ..." Brock directed their attention to the screen on the wall of the operations room. "Take a look at this."

The perplexed expressions on the faces of each Lepidoptera revealed their uncertainty; they had no clue what they were looking at.

"The closing portal ... it looks different," stated Brock, pointing to the screen.

"So, if it's different, what does that mean?" asked Stephen.

"It could mean two things. Firstly, Adrian could have created another portal to take him and William somewhere else, or ... they could have been intercepted by someone else and taken hostage."

"Shit … how are we going to figure this out?" questioned Shepherd, who was anxious to find his new leader.

"I believe if William and Adrian had gone on another mission, they would have informed us, don't you think?" said Renee, as she walked into the operations room. She had been tuned into their mind-chatter and was well aware of the unfolding situation.

"Yes, I was thinking the same," said Brock.

"And that's not our only issue right now. I've discovered that Samuel, Sully, Kiplin and Elsie have also disappeared. We can't seem to locate them anywhere on the academy grounds, their dorms, or at the mansion. What the hell is going on?" expressed Renee, her concern deepening.

"First things first; we need to look for William and Adrian," insisted Brock. "Then we will look for the others."

CHAPTER EIGHT

"Hawk looked disturbed, didn't he? I mean his eyes, they were—how do I say it?—hollow," stated Elsie, as she sat next to Sully on the queen-size bed at the Outpost Hotel.

Sully nodded in agreement. "Yeah, and I am a bit worried that we will never be able to release him from the mind control that Eryndor has him under. Every time I see him, he tries, but to no avail. Eryndor is a lot stronger than Hawk," said Sully. She breathed a heavy sigh.

Elsie placed her arm around Sully's shoulders and pulled her in close. "I am sure everything will work out, in the end. You'll see!"

"I hope you're right, Elsie," said Sully.

They both jumped when they heard a knock on the room's interconnecting door.

"Can we come in?" asked Samuel, his voice muffled through the wooden door.

"Yes, come in," said Sully, as she and Elsie stood up.

"You decent in there?" asked Kiplin, as he opened the door.

"Yes, come in, you idiot," said Elsie.

"You both look refreshed after your showers." He noticed their wet hair and how they were dressed in white robes. "Would you like to get room service for dinner, or …?" asked Samuel, as he looked from Sully to Elsie.

"Sounds good. I am starting to get hungry," interrupted Elsie.

"Yeah, okay. But where are we going to get blood from?" queried Sully. Her Vampire appetite was starting to show, as her sharp teeth protruded through her gums.

"We already have that sorted," said Kiplin, looking at Sully. "There is some in our bar fridge. I think my friend—you know the receptionist who attended the academy last year—well, I think she put some in there for us."

"Awesome. That was kind of her," said Sully. "I must remember to thank her."

"Yeah," said Kiplin, who'd already had his share of blood prior to coming into the girls' room.

"I was thinking, perhaps after dinner, we could go and search for Hawk, again. What do you think?" asked Samuel. He looked from Sully to Elsie to Kiplin for approval. "Have you heard from him, or have you been able to sense him, Sully?"

"I keep seeing flashes of what he's doing, but he doesn't communicate with me. Not yet, anyway. But it does seem like he has others working with him who are always by his side. So maybe that's why he doesn't talk with me, but shows me instead. Just guessing," explained Sully.

"Hmm, could be. Do you see any street signs or some sort of landmark, so we can find him again?" asked Samuel.

"Not yet," said Sully, shaking her head. "I will let you know if I do."

"Okay, well in the meantime, why don't we get some room service," said Samuel.

"Sounds good," said Elsie.

"Yeah, and I might take you up on that blood, Kiplin," said Sully.

"No probs. Come with me," said Kiplin, as he walked toward the open doorway that connected their rooms.

* * *

Report! thought Violette, authoritatively to the nine legacies.

There was only silence.

I said, report, thought Violette, heatedly, as she jumped from rooftop to rooftop. But she only heard the sound of the traffic and people below.

Fuck ... why aren't they answering? thought Violette. She pulled her mobile phone out of her pocket and dialed the operations room.

"Yes, Princess ... how can I help?" answered Brock, who was always on call at the Gramaze operations room.

"I haven't heard from the nine legacies, and I can't seem to locate them. Can you please have a look at the satellite feed and see if they are okay."

"Give me five minutes and I will get back to you, Princess," said Brock.

"Thanks, Brock," said Violette. She pressed the end button on her phone and continued her search for Hawk and the nine legacies.

* * *

Brock reviewed all the satellite data for Singapore, starting from the moment Violette and the legacies arrived, until Violette contacted him.

She is not going to be too happy about this, thought Brock, as he raked a hand through this hair and sat back in the chair. Following his investigation, he contacted Violette to inform her of his discoveries.

"Yes!" Violette answered.

"Princess, we have a problem. It looks like Hawk and his gang of entranced henchmen kidnapped the nine legacies. From watching the satellite feedback, they were knocked unconscious, then they were picked up in a white van. I have followed the van to the wharf in Singapore, where it looks like the legacies' limp bodies were placed into a shipping container. They haven't been moved from there since. So, I am surmising that they are still inside. What would you like me to do?" asked Brock.

"Has everyone returned from the Oman mission?" inquired Violette. "I need to know who would be able to portal in to help rescue the nine legacies."

"Yes and no," responded Brock, hesitantly.

"Which one is it?" questioned Violette.

"Well …" Brock's voice lingered too long.

"What is going on? What aren't you telling me, Brock?"

"William and Adrian never returned. We don't know where they are, either."

"Fuck! What about the others?"

"All returned, except for Michael and Grayson, Princess," said Brock. He swallowed hard, knowing what was about to come next.

"What does that mean? Michael and Grayson aren't accounted for?" questioned Violette, heatedly. She was worried about her life partner, Michael, the most.

There was tense silence on the line. Brock didn't know what to tell her.

"I asked you a question, Lepidoptera, and I expect an answer," stated Violette. She then watched Michael and Grayson drop in front of her. They had been listening in on the conversation.

"They are …" Brock began, but Violette interrupted.

"Yes, I see. They are watching over me. Humph!" Violette shook her head and took a deep breath. *I should have guessed.* "So, what is being done about William and Adrian, who are still missing?"

Brock explained about how William and Adrian never came through the portal, and that he was still scouring through satellite images worldwide, in a quest to locate them.

"Right! Keep me informed on this. And in the meantime, I want to know if the shipping container is moved before I, or should I say, we, arrive," directed Violette, casting a glance at Michael and Grayson.

"Yes, Princess," said Brock.

Violette abruptly hung up her mobile phone and placed it into her jacket pocket. "What the fuck, Michael, oh and you, Grayson." She shook her head at them.

"We were instructed to follow you, by the Queen herself. It's for your protection," said Grayson.

"Protection! Humph! I don't need protection. I can look after myself," shouted Violette.

Michael walked toward her. "We know you can take care of yourself, Violette. We have seen you in action, remember. What you fail to understand is that our coven can't afford to lose you. You do know how important you are to not only our coven, but to me as well, don't you?" asked Michael, in a calm manner.

His comforting demeanor and words soon soothed her angry mind. "I just get so frustrated with all this. I haven't been outside the perimeter of the Gramaze mansion for years, and now I find out that I am being followed." A deep sigh escaped her lips. "Sorry, babe, I don't mean to take it out on you. It's just, well, I feel utterly useless sometimes, that's all," Violette admitted.

"No need to apologize, sweet girl. I can see why you would feel that way." Michael pulled Violette in close to his chest to comfort her. "However, we currently face a more pressing issue that demands our full focus—the nine legacies."

Violette pulled away from their embrace. "Yes, you are correct. I am surmising you and Grayson overheard the conversation that I had with Brock, so let's get going."

"We sure did. Did Brock send you some coordinates on your phone?" enquired Grayson.

Violette retrieved her phone from her pocket and checked for messages, finding Brock's message providing her with the location of the container that was holding the nine legacies.

* * *

In a matter of minutes, Violette, Michael and Grayson reached the brightly illuminated and securely fenced boundary of the shipping yards at Keppel Harbour. Huddled behind the bushes defining the perimeter, they observed numerous containers being loaded onto ships by overhead cranes.

We need to find that specific container, she thought to Michael and Grayson. *Brock's information is our best lead. Let's move carefully and try to stay unnoticed*, Violette added, watching the bustling activity in the shipping yard.

Both men nodded in agreement.

The rhythmic sounds of machinery and the occasional foghorn echoed through the air, as they navigated through the shadows, avoiding workers and security personnel. Inching closer to the containers, their eyes scanned the numbers and labels for the one mentioned by Brock.

As they drew nearer, a sense of urgency filled the air, then Violette's phone vibrated with a new message. "It's Brock," Violette looked from her phone to Grayson and Michael. "He's providing additional details about the container's distinctive markings. Oh, and it looks like we have some backup coming to help us."

Adjusting their course accordingly, guided by the crucial information that Brock supplied, every step felt like a calculated risk. As they moved through the shipping yard, Violette, Michael and Grayson exchanged silent glances, and their shared determination pushed them forward. The night held a tense stillness as they approached the potential location of the container with the nine legacies inside.

Looks like the container is guarded, thought Michael, spotting some of Eryndor's glaze-eyed creatures, with their swords drawn.

We will wait for backup, thought Grayson to Michael and Violette. Within seconds of saying this, Grayson heard footsteps. Turning, he observed three familiar members of his coven making their way toward them.

Thank you for coming, thought Violette, as she looked at each of their faces.

Stephen, Violette's brother, Shepherd and Kelan bowed their heads to the Princess and waited for instructions.

Looks like we have company, thought Shepherd when he spotted four of Eryndor's minions. His brow furrowed when he recognized a familiar face, someone he had thought was dead. *What the ...?*

What is it? thought Michael, looking at Shepherd.

I'm sure that is Albinus Giordano. He pointed to a man with gray hair. *I thought he was dead.*

You mean, Xanthia's father? thought Violette. She cast another glance at the glazed-eyed man.

Yes! thought Shepherd.

Well, that is a turn up for the books, thought Grayson.

Our mission parameters have changed, thought Michael.

What would you like us to do, Princess? asked Shepherd. Being new to the Gramaze coven, he was eager, and stood ready to assist with any situation that might arise during this extraction.

Rather than beheading these creatures, we will apprehend them and detain them in the cells beneath the Gramaze mansion in Bagnolet, thought Violette, looking at them all. She then proceeded to provide specific instructions to each member of her Lepidoptera coven on how she would like to handle this volatile situation.

CHAPTER NINE

With the Lepidoptera Vampire power of illusion on his side, Grayson made himself visible to the four mind-controlled minions standing guard by the container.

"Sire!" exclaimed Albinus, as he bowed to the creature he thought was the Harbinger of Shadows, Eryndor.

The other three minions mimicked the gesture, convinced that Eryndor stood before them.

"Sheath your weapons," instructed Grayson.

The four minions obediently did as they were told.

As soon as they had done so, the Gramaze Lepidopteras, who had Vampire speed and swiftness on their side, had the four minions bound and gagged on the ground.

Pulling her phone out of her pocket, Violette called Brock.

"Yes, Princess," Brock answered.

"I want you to arrange for Adrian to open a portal and transport four of Eryndor's minions back to Bagnolet. Have them held in the cells until I return," Violette instructed.

"Yes, Princess."

Violette ended the call, slid the phone into her jacket, and turned to Shepherd and Kelan. "Take them back to the Gramaze mansion," she ordered.

"Yes, Princess," acknowledged Shepherd, as he watched a portal open up in front of them. He lifted two minions from the ground and escorted them through the portal. Kelan followed suit with the other two.

As the portal continued to stay open, Violette waved her hand once more, causing the doors of the container to swing open. The dark interior revealed nothing. Violette frowned and approached the doorway. "Where are they?"

Michael and Grayson walked into the darkened container and with their Lepidoptera night vision inspected the floor and walls.

"There's nothing here!" declared Michael. He and Grayson proceeded to run their hands along the walls of the shipping container before retracing their steps back toward the doorway.

Violette pulled her mobile phone from her jacket pocket and dialed the Gramaze mansion operations room.

"Yes, Princess," answered Brock.

"The nine legacies are not in this container. Search the satellite footage and get back to me. I want to know where they are, NOW," ordered Violette.

"Yes, Princess," said Brock. He hung up the phone and searched the satellite footage.

Within minutes he called back.

"Well?" asked Violette.

"They have not left the container. Are you sure they are not inside?" questioned Brock.

"Yes, I am sure …" Her brow furrowed in response to his doubt about her judgment. "Wait … what is that?" asked Violette, as she looked into the container with her Lepidoptera night vision. "I'll get back to you Brock." She hung up her phone and ran at Vampire speed toward the back of the container and used her strength to boot the back wall open. What she found was a concealed section, revealing the bodies of the nine legacies. "Fuck!" Violette ran over to their still bodies and checked to see if they were alive.

Michael, Grayson and Stephen joined her in the container.

"They're alive … thank goodness! Let's get them back to Bagnolet," declared Violette, as she felt for each of their pulses.

"What about Hawk?" asked Grayson.

"He will have to wait. The legacies are more important and are our number one priority at the moment," stated Violette.

"If you are in agreement, Michael and I can stay and continue to look for Hawk," said Grayson.

Violette breathed a deep sigh and thought about it for a few seconds. "I will get you and Michael to help me with the extraction of the legacies, and then you can return and look for Hawk."

"Okay!" said Grayson.

Michael nodded in agreement.

With a wave of her hand, Violette thrust the shipping container toward the open portal, eventually landing in the Gramaze mansion car park in Bagnolet.

* * *

Sully placed her empty cup, which previously had blood in it, down on the coffee table, and as she relaxed back on the lounge, her mind was thrust into a scene of mayhem. With her eyes staring straight ahead, she realized she was seeing through Hawk's eyes.

Hawk! Where are you? Sully thought to him, as she tried to locate a sign or some sort of landmark to pinpoint his location.

As she watched the scene play out, where some of Eryndor's glazed-eyed creatures were killing innocent people and taking their souls, Sully realized that this was the reason they were in Singapore. To gather souls for Eryndor to eat, to make him stronger.

Hawk ... show me a sign, thought Sully.

Her consciousness then shifted to another scene where a young Griffin sat on a toilet, only to be abruptly pulled through the bowl and pipe bend, ultimately meeting his demise and having his soul extracted. The relentless series of scenes continued, depicting various acts of killing and soul-taking. But in all of the scenes it wasn't Hawk who killed these people or took their souls, it was always the other glazed-eyed minions Eryndor had working for him.

Elsie, who was sitting on the lounge with Sully, looked over at her roommate and wondered what she was thinking, witnessing a distant glare, and her frowning, then smiling. "Sully!" Elsie placed her hand on Sully's leg.

At first Sully didn't acknowledge Elsie, she just continued to stare into what seemed like space. Every now and then frowning, then smiling.

"Sully!" said Elsie, louder, shaking her.

"Hmm … what?" said Sully, as her thoughts came back into the hotel room.

"Are you okay?" asked Elsie. "You seem off with the pixies, roomie."

"Yeah, I'm fine. I keep seeing visions from Hawk, that's all. He seems to be giving me snippets of where he is and what is happening. I haven't recognized any landmarks, though," said Sully.

There was a knock on the interconnecting door. "Can we come in?" yelled Kiplin, through the door.

"Yeah, all good, Kiplin," shouted Sully.

"You girls ready to go and look for Hawk?" asked Samuel.

"Yes," said Sully, standing.

"Sure," said Elsie.

"Let's blow this joint," said Kiplin, walking toward the door.

"Any idea where to start, Sully?" asked Samuel.

"I'm not sure. From the images and scenes that play out in my mind every now and then, Hawk seems to be showing me the same area," said Sully.

"What sort of things is he showing you?" asked Samuel.

"Well … it's hard to describe. They look like trees, but with lights, and there seems to be an interconnecting bridge from one tree to another," Sully explained. She shrugged her shoulders.

Kiplin pulled out his mobile phone and typed in, *Ten best things to do and see in Singapore.* As he scrolled through the many pictures of the Singapore attractions, he came across one that looked like the one Sully was trying to describe.

"Is this it?" asked Kiplin, holding the phone up in front of her.

Sully took the phone from Kiplin and looked at the picture. "Yes, that's it. It's called the Supertree Grove, and it's in the Gardens by the Bay."

Elsie came and stood next to Sully to have a look. "Wow … that's beautiful."

"Well, at least we now have a starting point. How do we get there?" Samuel asked.

"It says we can catch a cable car over Keppel Harbour to the Singapore mainland, and then it's approximately six kilometers on foot to the Gardens by the Bay," said Sully, looking at the screen's directions.

"Let's get going. The sooner we find Hawk, the sooner we can take him back to Bagnolet," stated Samuel. They all followed Samuel out the door and into the elevator.

We're coming, Hawk, we're coming, thought Sully.

Oh, no, you're not, thought Eryndor to himself, as he listened in on Sully and Hawk's thoughts.

CHAPTER TEN

It had been a few months since her father, Albinus Giordano, had died and, despite a growing sense of comfort in a house full of Vampires, the absence of her father continued to weigh heavily on Xanthia's heart.

"Xanthia!" Danielle called out, as she walked into Xanthia's bedroom.

"I'm in here," hollered Xanthia from her bathroom.

"Morning … are you nearly ready?" asked Danielle, as she leaned on the doorframe and watched Xanthia put her hair up into a ponytail.

Danielle had been asked by her sister, Princess Violette, to make sure Xanthia was taken care of, and that she made it to her new school safely.

"Almost," replied Xanthia, who was dressed in the Lycée International high school uniform. "I need to get my jacket and bag, and then I will be ready." She smiled at Danielle and headed from the bathroom to her bed, where the jacket and bag awaited.

"Being that this is your first day, are you nervous?" asked Danielle, remembering her first day, twenty years ago, at Lycée and how anxious she had felt.

"A bit," said Xanthia. She held her shaky hands out.

"You will be fine; I know you will. You're a strong-willed girl, and I am sure you will make new friends easily enough." Danielle gently wrapped her hands around Xanthia's and used her Lepidoptera abilities to not only calm her nerves, but also to clear her mind.

"Thanks, Danielle. You're a good friend," said Xanthia, embracing her calming touch.

"You're welcome. Well … we had better get going. We don't want to be late for your first day at Lycée," said Danielle, as she released Xanthia's hands. She watched Xanthia put her jacket on.

Xanthia smiled, picked up her bag from the bed and slung it over her shoulder. Together they proceeded out the door and down the marble staircase.

Wonder what all the commotion is about? thought Danielle, hearing a lot of chatter around the house, as they descended the stairs.

Albinus Giordano is here, thought Christian to Danielle.

What? Are you sure? thought Danielle. She gulped hard.

Yes! But you can't let Xanthia know, yet, thought Christian.

Why? questioned Danielle. *She deserves to know her father is alive.*

Well, he isn't exactly alive. Eryndor has turned him into one of those glazed-eyed creatures, and Princess Violette is trying to work out how to break the mind control, thought Christian.

Shit, really? thought Danielle. *Don't worry, I won't say a word. Poor Xanthia …*

Yeah, I know, and just when she was starting to get back on track, too. Poor girl, thought Christian. *I have to go, chat later.*

Okay!

"Danielle … everything alright?" asked Xanthia, as she watched the concerned expression on Danielle's face.

"Yeah, all good," lied Danielle. "Let's get a move on, hey!" She ushered Xanthia toward the double front doors, where a limousine was waiting out front to take them both to the Lycée International high school.

* * *

"Enter!" exclaimed the Lepidoptera Queen, when she heard a knock on her door.

With a profound sense of reverence, Princess Violette stepped into the Queen's room, which was nestled in the depths of the Gramaze mansion's basement. Bowing her head with genuine humility, she gracefully sank to the ground on one knee, her every movement resonating with deep respect.

"Rise!" commanded Queen Talitha. "What can I do for you, Violette?"

"Thank you for seeing me, my Queen," said Violette, as she rose to a standing position. "I … I wanted to ask if you knew anything about Warlocks and their mind control?"

"Why do you ask?" queried Talitha.

"We have a situation … well, it's not a situation exactly, but …" She didn't get to finish her sentence.

"Spit it out, Violette," interrupted Talitha. "I haven't got all day."

"Yes, Ma'am. We have a human who is being mind-controlled by a Griffin. But not just any Griffin … he is also a Warlock and the Harbinger of Shadows, and extremely powerful."

"Right! And why are we getting involved in this?" questioned Talitha.

"The human I am speaking of is Xanthia's father, and we captured him when I was in Singapore. He is currently under mind control and in our coven's cells," said Violette.

"Have you spoken with Garrick, who is leader of the Griffins?"

"Yes, Ma'am. He was utterly useless," Violette confessed, swallowing hard.

"Leave it with me, Violette. I will handle this," declared Talitha. She let out a deep sigh and gestured for Violette to depart, sweeping her hand in the air with an unmistakable intensity.

Violette bowed her head and said, "Yes, my Queen."

Standing in solitude, Talitha watched intently as the door slowly closed, her mind already unraveling the intricate web of possibilities. She was determined to free Albinus from the relentless grip of the mind control that bound him.

With a wave of her hand, Lepidoptera Vampire Queen Talitha stood before a shackled human, who was ensnared by the malevolent influence of Eryndor's mind control. The air was thick with a palpable darkness and the echoes of distant whispers hinted at the insidious power that had taken hold of the unfortunate human.

"Albinus Giordano, what say you?" probed Talitha. Her regal presence exuded a timeless elegance, as she hovered above the ground and observed the entranced human with a mix of concern and unwavering determination.

Albinus lifted his head and his glazed eyes met Talitha's gaze unflinchingly. "Fuck. The. Hell. Off. I serve Eryndor, and Eryndor alone. You won't extract anything from me." Eryndor's influence was a force to be reckoned with, his tendrils reaching into the deepest recesses of Albinus's mind.

"Humph, we will see," said Talitha, knowing that breaking the shackles of such control required not just magical prowess, but a mastery of the arcane.

With a flick of her hand, Talitha conjured an ancient book, bound in leather and as black as the midnight sky. The pages, adorned with cryptic symbols, held the secrets of forbidden spells and incantations. As she leafed through the pages, her eyes landed upon a passage that spoke of breaking psychic bonds.

Positioning herself in a strategic stance, Talitha began to recite the incantation, her voice resonating with a melodic yet commanding cadence. The atmosphere crackled with a mixture of ancient magic, and the potent energy that fueled the undead Queen's essence.

By the blood that flows through night,
Within shadows, deep and tight,
I command the chains to break,
Free this mind, no more to take.

The chamber pulsated with a subdued energy and Albinus, who was caught in the throes of Eryndor's control, twitched as the mystical forces began their delicate work.

As Talitha extended her hands toward Albinus, her fingertips emitted a soft, ethereal glow. With each gesture, she directed the arcane energies to unravel the threads of mind control that Eryndor had woven. The room seemed to hold its breath, anticipating the crucial moment when the influence would finally yield.

As the last remnants of Eryndor's control began to dissipate, Albinus's eyes flickered, lucidity returned, and the oppressive darkness lifted, replaced by a newfound clarity and awareness. "Where am I?" Albinus frantically questioned Talitha, his eyes darting around the dimly lit underground cell, panic etched across his face.

"You are in Bagnolet, France … my home," explained Talitha.

"Why have you brought me here?"

"To save your life. More importantly, what do you remember?" asked Talitha, as she unshackled Albinus from his chains with a flick of her wrist.

Albinus rubbed his head, "Not much. The last thing I can recall is when I was being held at gunpoint in my workplace. It's all a bit of a blur." Albinus closed his eyes and rubbed his temples.

"Come …" Talitha held out her hand for Albinus to take.

Albinus opened his eyes and instinctively moved backward, intimidated by the regal radiance emanating from Talitha. "What manner of being are you?" he stammered, fear palpable in his voice, mixed with a hint of awe.

"We can talk about that later." Talitha listened to his frightened and bewildered thoughts, recognizing that Albinus wasn't currently receptive to the idea of incorporating Vampires into his reality. "Let's get you upstairs and settled into a room." She proceeded to project calming thoughts into his mind.

"Yes, Ma'am," said Albinus. As he placed his hand in hers, she led him toward the cell door, which she promptly flung open with a wave of her hand. In a dazed state, he continued to walk beside her up the stairs.

Christian, Kelan ... I need you to look after Albinus, make sure he gets some rest. He has been through a lot, thought Talitha. Her regal power demanded obedience, as she and a fatigued Albinus approached the top of the stairs.

Christian and Kelan appeared and nodded in unison, understanding the gravity of their task.

"Albinus, you're in good hands," Christian said with a reassuring smile, gently leading him toward a bedroom. Kelan followed closely, prepared to help if needed.

Albinus glanced between Christian and Kelan, his expression dazed as he allowed them to guide him to a room in the Gramaze mansion. "Thank you," he murmured softly.

CHAPTER ELEVEN

"Wow! That's absolutely amazing," exclaimed Elsie, her face glowing with excitement. She gestured toward the Supertree Grove in the distance, as the cable car descended into Singapore, providing a captivating view of Gardens by the Bay. Never before had she seen anything quite like it.

"Yeah, it sure is beautiful," said Sully, catching a glimpse of the light show.

Samuel breathed a heavy sigh and rolled his eyes in frustration as he looked at the glass building that was looming ever so close. They needed to find Hawk, and return to Bagnolet, before anyone noticed them all missing. Having to deal with the consequences of William's wrath loomed over him like a storm he was eager to avoid.

Hopefully you are still in Singapore, Hawk, thought Kiplin, as he folded his arms over his chest.

Are you still at the Gardens, Hawk? thought Sully to Hawk.

There was no answer from Hawk, nor had she received any visions from him since they had left the hotel on Sentosa Island.

The cable car glided smoothly into the Harbour-Front Station and the group disembarked, their excitement for the Singapore adventure overshadowed by the urgency of finding Hawk. The air was thick with anticipation as they made their way through the bustling station, their eyes scanning the crowd for any sign of Hawk. But he was nowhere to be seen.

Where are you, Hawk? Show me, thought Sully to Hawk, anxiety gripping her heart.

There was only silence, and no visions.

"Let's go," urged Samuel, motioning toward the exit, as he led the way to the MRT station. He was set on reaching the Supertree Grove in Gardens by the Bay, finding Hawk, and getting back home to Bagnolet as soon as possible.

As they stepped onto the MRT platform, a shiver ran down Samuel's spine, an inexplicable feeling that something sinister loomed.

Kiplin's gaze darted around, his instincts on high alert, too.

Do you feel that? thought Sully to Samuel. The hackles on the back of her neck stood up, and a sense of unease set in.

Yeah. I would say we are close to finding him, thought Samuel to Sully, as he watched the train approach the platform.

As the train came to a halt in front of them and the doors slid open, they were taken aback by the multitude of passengers spewing out of the train, and the number of people still within. Boarding the carriage, they had to squeeze in tightly and hold on, as the doors quickly sealed shut, and the train accelerated forward at a rapid pace.

* * *

Exiting the MRT, Sully, Samuel, Kiplin and Elsie approached the Supertree Grove, their surroundings bathed in the ethereal glow of the illuminated structures.

Suddenly, a flicker of movement caught Sully's attention. There, on the edge of the grove, she caught a glimpse of Hawk. He seemed disoriented and had a vacant look in his eyes.

"Hawk!" Sully called out, her voice echoing in the night.

Samuel, Sully, Kiplin and Elsie quickened their pace to try and catch him, but before they could reach him, an otherworldly portal materialized behind Hawk and a dark figure emerged: Eryndor, the malevolent Harbinger of Shadows. The cheesy grin on Eryndor's face was unmistakable as he seized Hawk and disappeared into the portal.

Shock and determination flashed across the faces of Samuel, Sully, Kiplin, and Elsie.

"We can't let him get away!" Kiplin exclaimed, his eyes narrowing in resolve.

"We're not leaving without him. Let's go!" Samuel exclaimed. He sprinted toward the still-open portal.

Kiplin, Sully and Elsie joined hands and in unison they followed Samuel into the unknown, ready to face the challenges that awaited them in the dimension where Eryndor had taken Hawk. Their mission had taken an unexpected turn, and their quest to rescue Hawk had become more perilous than ever.

* * *

"Where do we go from here, Princess?" asked Grayson to Violette, as he, Michael and Violette emerged from the portal near the Gardens by the Bay.

"Brock has informed me that Hawk has been spotted in there," Violette replied, pointing toward the Supertree Grove.

With his eyes scanning the area as he walked out of the portal that Violette had created, Michael noticed some familiar faces. "Shit ... is that Samuel, Sully, Kiplin and Elsie? What are they doing here?" he exclaimed.

Violette and Grayson looked in the direction he was pointing.

"Fuck, and it looks like they're stepping into a portal," said Violette, her voice laced with urgency. She sprinted with Vampire speed toward the portal, with Michael and Grayson close behind her.

As the portal closed with an ominous hum, it left the Supertree Grove in eerie silence.

"Oh no you don't," declared Violette. With determination etched on her features, and her superior Vampire abilities surging within her, she extended her hands and commanded the portal to reopen.

The ground rumbled as the portal reopened with a whoosh, casting a brilliant glow against the night sky.

Violette's gaze shifted from Michael to Grayson, determination gleaming in her eyes. "I wasn't sure that was going to work, but let's move!" she exclaimed, her voice ringing with urgency.

The three Lepidopteras stepped into the portal with a single purpose: to locate Sully, Samuel, Kiplin and Elsie and get them to safety. Their resolve was unwavering as they vanished into the swirling vortex, driven by the urgency of their mission.

* * *

"Where are we?" asked Elsie, as she walked out of the portal, alongside Sully, Samuel and Kiplin.

"I don't know," Kiplin replied, his senses on high alert as he scanned the surroundings for any sign of danger. Every rustle of the leaves, every whisper of the wind, seemed amplified in the eerie silence that enveloped them.

"You have entered the Fae Kingdom," a voice ringing with a melodious tone chimed, as a Fae woman emerged from behind a tree. With her high-pitched voice and light purple hair that seemed to emit a soft glow, she was a vision of ethereal beauty amidst the enchanted surroundings.

Startled by her presence, Sully, Samuel, Elsie and Kiplin unsheathed their swords, the metallic gleam of their blades catching the light as they stood poised for battle. Tension crackled in the air, uncertainty hanging thick between them.

The Fae woman's delicate features contorted with fear. With a flutter of her iridescent wings, she lifted herself gracefully above the ground, hovering just out of their reach. Her movements were fluid, almost ethereal, as she sought refuge in the safety of the air.

Kiplin, recognizing the fear in the fairy's eyes, lowered his sword slightly, his stance softening. "We mean you no harm."

The Fae's wings shimmered like spun silk, as she hovered hesitantly, her eyes darting between the four beings before her. "Please," she pleaded, her voice trembling. "I … I didn't mean to startle you. I'm just … afraid."

With a silent agreement, Sully, Kiplin and Elsie lowered their weapons, extending a gesture of peace toward the frightened creature before them.

"What is your name?" asked Kiplin, who was fascinated by her glowing beauty.

"Adeline."

"What is this place?" queried Samuel, as he gestured toward the mystical woods that were now illuminated by Adeline.

"You are in the Fae Kingdom," said Adeline again, gracefully lowering herself to the forest floor.

"Right!" said Samuel, his brow furrowed, as he tried to take in where they were. "So … did you see two others who entered through the same way we came in?"

Adeline nodded slowly, her expression troubled as she recalled the sinister figure and the young man it had captured. "Yes," she replied with a gulp, the memory weighing heavily on her.

"Which way did they go?" questioned Samuel.

"They went through the forest opening, over there," Adeline explained, as she pointed to a tree-lined archway that beckoned from the depths of the forest. "But I would advise you to be careful if you go through there."

"Why is that?" asked Samuel.

"There is evil up ahead," stated Adeline, her tone grave, hinting at the dangers lurking beyond the serene facade of the forest. "I can take you another way, if you like."

"What trickery is this? First you warn us, then you want to show us another way. Why should we follow you?" Sully demanded, her sword held firmly in front of her, while her other hand rested assertively on her hip.

Samuel placed his hand on Sully's sword and gently lowered it. "Sully, I understand your concern, but let's hear her out," Samuel urged, his voice calm yet persuasive. "We're in unfamiliar territory and Adeline might have valuable information that could help us navigate through these woods."

Sully hesitantly nodded in agreement.

A sly grin tugged at the corners of Adeline's lips as she observed the group's hesitation. *Humph, I have you now*, she thought to herself, confident in her ability to guide them according to her own hidden agenda.

"Would you like me to show you the way?" asked Adeline, her voice gentle and reassuring.

"Thank you, Adeline That would be great," said Samuel, not knowing you should never say *Thank You* to a Fae, because it would mean you are indebted to them.

Adeline smiled warmly at the four inexperienced supes, her light purple hair glowing softly as she hovered above the ground with a flutter of her wings. "Follow me," she beckoned, her demeanor exuding confidence and trustworthiness.

Without hesitation, the four young supes followed the fairy into the woods.

CHAPTER TWELVE

As the portal spat them out with a forceful jolt, Violette, Michael and Grayson tumbled onto a large grassy area. The impact sent them sprawling, their bodies rolling and tumbling until they finally came to a stop.

"Where in the hell are we?" exclaimed Violette. Groaning, she pushed herself up, shaking off the disorientation that clouded her senses. Blinking against the sudden brightness of their surroundings, she scanned the area, taking in the eerie-looking trees that loomed at the far end of the grassy expanse.

Michael and Grayson rose to their feet, their expressions mirroring Violette's confusion and apprehension.

"I can't be sure, but I think we are in the Fae realm," said Grayson, taking in the surroundings. He had only ever been to the Fae Kingdom once previously. The landscape seemed to stretch endlessly before them, devoid of any signs of life, except for the strange, gnarly trees that stood like silent sentinels in the distance.

Violette's Lepidoptera senses tingled with unease as she took in their surroundings. "Something about this place feels off. It's as if we've stumbled into a realm untouched by time," stated Violette.

"You are correct," chimed a melodic voice, as a Fae woman seemed to materialize out of thin air.

When Michael and Grayson caught sight of the red-haired fairy, they sprang into action, swiftly positioning themselves in front of Violette. With practiced fluidity, they drew their swords, ready to guard their Princess with unwavering determination.

"State your business here," commanded the fairy.

Violette, who was dressed in black leathers, stepped between Michael and Grayson, placing herself squarely in front of them. With a firm yet composed demeanor, she sought to defuse the escalating tension. "We don't want any trouble here," she stated, her gaze steady as she addressed the fairy. "I am Princess Violette of the Gramaze Lepidoptera coven, and these are my soldiers, Michael and Grayson."

"Ah, Vampires. I am Summer. Why are you here?" she asked.

"We followed four of our kindred here through a portal. Do you know where they are?" asked Violette.

"Hmmm, let me see," murmured Summer, her eyes momentarily clouding over as she tapped into the Fae grapevine. In a matter of seconds, her gaze cleared, returning to its usual state. "Yes, I believe they are here," she confirmed, a thoughtful expression crossing her features. "Apparently tracking through the forest with a sister Fae, Adeline." She pointed to the edge of the green grass area.

"Are we permitted to enter the forest?" asked Violette, her tone earnest as she sought a swift resolution to their quest.

"Yes, but I can't guarantee your safety," said Summer sincerely.

"That's okay. We are grateful for your warning," said Violette. She turned to Michael and Grayson, "You lead the way."

With determination in their steps, they all made their way toward the forest, prepared to face whatever challenges lay ahead.

Summer grimaced at them as they walked by her.

* * *

"It seems like we have been walking for a few hours. How much further, Adeline?" Elsie's voice carried a hint of weariness, tinged with anticipation and a touch of impatience.

There was no response from the fairy, who flew ahead of them, her form a fleeting silhouette against the backdrop of the forest canopy.

"Adeline, did you hear me?" asked Elsie.

"I heard you," Adeline's voice rumbled, deep and husky, sending shivers down their spines. When she turned around, she was suspended in the air and had undergone a sinister transformation. Her once-radiant appearance shifted into that of a dark Fae, with ebony hair cascading around her, pixie ears twitching with malevolence, and a foreboding aura enveloping her form.

The four young supes swiftly drew their swords from their sheaths, their stances poised and ready, as they stood side by side and waited for whatever Adeline might unleash upon them.

"You will pay for entering our Fae Kingdom," stated Adeline, her voice carrying a menacing undertone as she remained suspended in the air.

"It is you who will pay, Fae," Grayson interjected, his tone firm and unwavering, as he jumped out from behind a tree. Drawing upon his Lepidoptera powers of illusion, he wove a web of confusion in Adeline's mind, disorienting her momentarily. With determination blazing in his eyes, Grayson focused all his strength, channeling it into a powerful force that brought Adeline down to her knees before him.

Sully, Samuel, Kiplin and Elsie turned to see Michael and Princess Violette standing behind them.

Shit, now we're in trouble, Sully thought to Samuel, her heart sinking as she contemplated the impending trouble they were in, unsure of what would unfold next.

"You will take us to your Queen," said Grayson, as he held Adeline firmly on the ground, his knees pinning her delicate wings. With an impassive glint in his eyes, he pressed the cold edge of his iron sword against her neck and sneered.

"And if I don't?" asked Adeline, as she struggled beneath him.

With a predatory gleam in his eyes, Grayson seized Adeline by the wrist, dragging her toward a towering oak tree. "Time to teach you not to mess with a Lepidoptera, Adeline," he scoffed, his grip unyielding as he forced her against the rough bark of the tree.

Adeline met his gaze with steely determination, her chin held high despite the chill from the blade that grazed her skin. "You think this will scare me? Your iron may sting, but it will never break me," she declared, her voice carrying an unwavering resolve.

A flicker of frustration flashed across Grayson's face, but he quickly masked it with a facade of indifference. "We'll see about that, Adeline," he growled, his grip tightening on the hilt of his sword as he held it against her throat.

But before he could make another move, Adeline's eyes blazed with raw magic, tendrils of light spiraling from her fingertips and engulfing the sword in a shimmering barrier. With a swift motion, she broke free from his grasp, flipping gracefully to her feet as the iron sword clattered uselessly to the ground. "You won't get away with this," she spat, her voice laced with defiance even as her wings trembled with unease.

Ignoring her protests, Grayson swiftly produced a length of iron chain from his cloak. "Oh, but I will, my dear," he taunted. A unfriendly smirk twisted his lips, as he used his Lepidoptera Vampire speed to wrap the iron chain around her slender form, securing her tightly to the tree.

Adeline winced as the iron bit into her flesh, her breath hitching with the effort to remain composed. "You think your iron can hold me? Then you underestimate the power of the Fae," she retorted, her eyes blazing with a fierce determination even in the face of captivity.

"Grayson, release Adeline," Summer interrupted, her authoritative voice cutting through the tension, as she materialized seemingly out of thin air.

"Humph, you are not my boss, Fae," interjected Grayson. Even though he was taken aback by her sudden arrival, he remained undeterred by her appearance.

Summer's ethereal form radiated a faint, iridescent red glow as she approached them, and her expression darkened with displeasure at the sight of Grayson holding Adeline in iron chains against the tree. "Grayson!" she chided, her voice carrying a melodic but stern tone, "Release Adeline at once. Your use of iron is an affront to our kind." With each word, tiny motes of light seemed to flicker around her, reflecting her growing irritation.

Michael and Violette pushed the four younger supes behind them and raised their swords defensively in front.

Keep behind us, instructed Violette, telepathically to the four young supes.

Sully, Samuel, Kiplin and Elsie waited with growing unease, as the tension in front of them continued.

"Just let Adeline go and I'll escort you all to speak with the Queen of the Fae Kingdom," stated Summer.

"As I said earlier, Summer, we don't want any trouble here. Take us to your Queen," Violette requested firmly.

"Yes, Ma'am. As soon as he lets Adeline go," replied Summer, as she looked from Violette to Grayson.

Grayson snapped the chains binding Adeline and watched her crumple to the ground.

Summer swiftly flew with her shimmering Fae wings to Adeline's side and knelt beside her. "Are you alright, Sister?" she inquired with concern, gently lifting Adeline's chin to assess her condition.

"Yes, I'm fine," stated Adeline, whose body was weak from the cold iron chains.

"Let's get you up, Sister," said Summer, wrapping her hand around Adeline's back and helping her to stand.

As Adeline stood up, she felt the Fae healing powers of Summer pulsate through her body. "I will remember your kindness," she murmured gratefully, feeling strength returning to her limbs and wings.

"Come … this way," directed Summer to everyone, her voice gentle yet authoritative, as she continued to assist Adeline to walk.

The six Lepidopteras, along with Elsie the Griffin, moved cautiously behind Summer and Adeline as they ventured deeper into the kingdom's enchanted forest. The air was thick with tension; the swaying trees were alive with the hum of Fae magic. A sense of unease prickled through the group—whether it was the forest's ancient power or the unknown dangers that lay ahead, they couldn't be sure. Elsie's sharp eyes darted between the shifting shadows, while the Lepidopteras exchanged wary glances, their instincts on high alert.

CHAPTER THIRTEEN

Elyndra, Queen of the Fae Kingdom, greeted Eryndor with a discerning smile. "Ah, there you are, Eryndor. I've been anticipating your return to my realm," she remarked, her voice carrying the weight of an ancient Irish accent that had wisdom and regal authority. She rose from her throne, which was crafted from wood, intertwined vines adorned with shimmering crystals and delicate blossoms. Its organic design blended seamlessly with the enchanted surroundings, exuding an aura of natural majesty and mystical elegance. "Who do we have here?" She motioned toward Hawk, her emerald-green eyes fixed on him as he struggled against Eryndor's grasp, his attempts to break free proving futile.

"No one of importance," remarked Eryndor, dismissively.

Elyndra sensed a celestial energy that unmistakably marked the divine nature of a Griffin. "If I'm not mistaken," she mused, lightly tapping her chin with her index finger and thumb, "This presence ... it's that of a Griffin, isn't it?"

"You are correct."

"Why have you brought trouble to my Kingdom?" questioned Elyndra, as she walked toward Eryndor and Hawk.

"To keep him away from his family."

"I am sensing that he is *your* family," observed Elyndra, now standing in front of Eryndor.

"You are correct. I have taken him for leverage over my mother and father," Eryndor admitted, his tone revealing a calculated strategy. "Is there a cell or cage within the Fae Kingdom where I can keep him captive?"

Elyndra looked into Eryndor's dark sunken eyes and thought about it for a few seconds. "I don't usually get involved in family squabbles." Her eyes narrowed with suspicion. "But I will make an exception, just this once." She placed her celestial hand on Hawk's forehead and watched as he wilted into Eryndor's embrace. "Follow me!"

Eryndor trailed behind Elyndra as they approached a wooden cage that mysteriously materialized and swayed gently in midair. Its intricate latticework and aged timber bore witness to craftsmanship of another time, while tendrils of ivy embraced its corners, hinting at its connection to the enchanted surroundings. With a wave of her hand, Elyndra lowered the cage to the ground and its door swung open. Gesturing toward it, she indicated for Hawk to be placed inside.

Following her instructions, Eryndor placed Hawk within the cage. As he closed the door, he slid the bolt across to secure it shut. He then observed as Elyndra effortlessly, with a wave of her hand, lifted the cage back into the air. Despite its seemingly fragile appearance, there was an undeniable aura of magic about the cage that kept it aloft, casting dappled shadows on the ground below.

Elyndra turned gracefully, her flowing robes trailing behind her as she made her way back to her throne. The fabric, woven from shimmering threads of moonlight and shadow, draped elegantly around her form, adorned with intricate Celtic knot motifs that seemed to pulse with ancient power. Her attire, a reflection of her regal stature, bore hues of midnight blue and deep purple, accentuating her ethereal beauty.

As she approached her throne, Elyndra's sisters, Aevyressa, Myrrathen and Thalara, stood in attendance, their own attire echoing her regal elegance. Aevyressa wore robes of deep crimson, her fiery presence unmistakable even in the subdued light of the Fae Kingdom. Myrrathen's garments shimmered with iridescent hues, mirroring the ever-changing colors of a raven's feathers, while Thalara's attire reflected an earthy warmth, adorned with motifs reminiscent of the forest floor. Together, they exuded an aura of power and mystique, a formidable trio alongside the Fae Queen.

The three sisters' expressions held a mixture of reverence, anticipation, and perhaps a hint of curiosity, as Elyndra reclaimed her seat upon the throne. Their eyes followed her movements with a combination of respect and deference, acknowledging her return with an unwavering loyalty that spoke of their deep bond as sisters and fellow rulers of the Fae Kingdom. There was an air of anticipation, as if they waited for Elyndra's next command or decision, ready to offer their support and counsel as needed.

"I am grateful for your help, Elyndra," Eryndor expressed with a respectful nod.

"You are most welcome. I will recall the favor one day, and you will repay me, I am sure," Elyndra replied, her voice carrying a hint of anticipation, and the weight of a future debt.

"Well, I shall take my leave for now. I'll return later to collect the boy," Eryndor stated, his body hovering above the ground with an ethereal grace.

"I'm sure you will," said Elyndra, sarcastically.

Eryndor gave Elyndra a curt nod before turning away. As his gaze drifted upward, he noticed another wooden cage beside Hawk's, this time containing another familiar figure—his brother Aelvric. Eryndor's brow furrowed as he pondered: *What is he doing here? And what does Elyndra want with him? This had better not interfere with my future plans, otherwise there will be consequences.*

He spun around to confront the Queen, but Elyndra and her sisters had vanished without a trace. The only thing that remained was an unsettling silence, broken moments later by a melodic voice that drifted through the air like a poison.

"When you return, you will be mine," it whispered, the words dripping with icy menace. Elyndra's laughter followed, haunting and sickening, echoing into the distance before fading away.

Oh, well, it's not as if they can escape, and this place is secure enough to keep them right where I want them. Humph. Elyndra may be a snake, but for now, she serves her purpose, Eryndor thought, glancing up at Aelvric and Hawk. *I really do need to find that damn chalice. That is my number-one priority at the moment, above all else.*

Without another word, Eryndor snapped his fingers. A portal tore through the fabric of the Fae Kingdom and he stepped through, leaving the haunting laughter to fade into the void.

* * *

"Our Queen awaits through that opening," Summer announced, her voice carrying a melodic tone as she gestured toward a towering tree with a grand entrance at its base, beckoning the group forward.

"Right!" said Violette, her gaze sweeping over the magical landscape.

"We will be on our way," said Summer, as her delicate wings began to flutter.

The group watched as Adeline and Summer gracefully ascended, disappearing into the depths of the forest with an air of enchantment.

Violette turned to Sully, Samuel, Kiplin and Elsie. "You four will stay here, behind the trees and out of the way, while I discuss our safe passage back to Bagnolet." Her voice carried authority as she addressed the four legacies.

The four young supes nodded in agreement, and watched Grayson, Michael and Violette walk through the base of the hollowed-out tree.

Stay vigilant as we converse with the Fae Queen, Grayson cautioned Michael and Violette silently, as they strolled side by side beneath the towering canopy toward Elyndra, who sat upon her throne radiating regal authority.

"Ah, who do we have here?" asked Elyndra, as she looked with contempt at the three Vampires standing before her.

"I am Violette, and these are my soldiers, Grayson and Michael," stated Violette, gesturing to both of them. "May I know your name?"

"I am Elyndra, Queen of the Fae Kingdom, and these are my sisters—Aevyressa, Myrrathen and Thalara." She gracefully gestured to each one.

Violette nodded in their direction to recognize their presence.

"Why have you ventured into my Kingdom?" Elyndra inquired with authority, harboring reluctance toward the presence of Vampires within her realm.

"Firstly, I am sorry for this intrusion; this was not our intention."

"You have not answered my question!" snapped Elyndra, standing.

Aevyressa, Myrrathen and Thalara moved to Elyndra's side, representing a formidable shield against any threat that may come their way.

"We are here to collect a Griffin," Grayson stated firmly, his stance confident and resolute, conveying determination and purpose.

"And why do you think we have a Griffin here in the Fae Kingdom?" questioned Elyndra.

"We followed two Griffins through a portal and ended up here. We are sorry for the intrusion, but ...," said Grayson. He was interrupted, before he could finish.

"You say two Griffins. What are their names?" asked Elyndra.

"Hawk and Eryndor," Grayson said sharply, one hand resting on the hilt of his sword, the other planted firmly on his hip. "Where are they?" His tone was cold, his patience thin. He had no interest in the lies and trickery the Fae Queen was infamous for.

"Eryndor … yes. I have spoken with him. Hawk … why is that name familiar to me?" said Elyndra, sarcastically.

"Sister, he is the one …," said Aevyressa. She was interrupted, before she could finish.

"Be quiet, foolish woman," said Elyndra, as she sealed Aevyressa's lips shut with a wave of her hand.

"What is the meaning of this?" Grayson demanded, his voice cutting through the air like a blade.

"You would be wise not to meddle in matters that do not concern you within my Kingdom," Elyndra asserted with a tone that tolerated no argument.

"We mean you no disrespect, Elyndra," Violette interjected, her voice a soothing balm aimed at defusing the escalating tension, aware of the potential consequences if matters spiraled out of control. "Our sole aim is to acquire Hawk, and then secure a safe passage back to France. Can you provide this?"

"The safe passage, indeed. But Hawk? No!" Elyndra declared. With a snap of her fingers, she summoned Hawk and Aelvric to appear.

Violette, Grayson and Michael turned around to see Hawk and Aelvric, both imprisoned within floating cages.

Michael and Grayson drew their swords from their sheaths and held them out front.

"Release them!" demanded Grayson, his nostrils flared with frustration.

In response, Elyndra flicked her hand toward Grayson and Michael, effortlessly disarming them, as their swords clattered to the ground.

"You dare threaten me?" Elyndra bellowed. With a wave of her hand, she incapacitated both Grayson and Michael, causing them to crumple unconscious to the forest floor.

"Stop!" Violette shouted, afraid of what would happen next.

Elyndra regarded Violette with a disdainful glare, her contempt unmistakable in her piercing gaze.

"You promised safe passage to France. Is this still an option?" Violette inquired, her brow furrowed with genuine concern.

"Hawk!" Sully's voice echoed through the forest as she emerged from behind the trees, her urgency palpable. "Please … let him go. I beg of you."

"Sully … stop!" Samuel's voice rang out, filled with urgency, as he sprinted after her, trailed closely by Elsie and Kiplin.

With a wave of her hand, Elyndra halted the four young legacies in their tracks, suspending them in midair, so that their feet barely touched the ground, effectively immobilizing them. "Ah, I see there are more of you." She looked to Violette for answers.

"They are young, and inexperienced. Please forgive their impudence," Violette pleaded, uncertainty evident in her voice as she attempted to reason with the Fae Queen. "All we desire is a safe passage back to France."

"Begone then," Elyndra commanded, her patience exhausted with this intrusion into her Fae Kingdom. With a flick of her hand, she summoned a ring of mushrooms to encircle the seven supes, and then a portal materialized and the group was abruptly thrust into its depths.

"Good riddance," Elyndra muttered, her gaze lingering on the closed portal. "Now … let's awaken these two Griffins and uncover their intentions," she declared, determination flashing in her eyes.

CHAPTER FOURTEEN

The air crackled with energy as the seven travelers emerged from the Fae Queen's portal, which was alive with swirling colors shifting between fluorescent blues, pinks and purples that pulsed with magic. Landing with a thud upon the cobbled streets of a picturesque village, Violette, Grayson, Michael, Sully, Samuel, Kiplin and Elsie staggered, momentarily disoriented, yet grateful for their safe return from the Fae Kingdom.

Grayson shook his head, attempting to shake off the dizziness from the portal journey. "Is everyone alright?" he asked, concern etched in his voice.

One by one, they all nodded.

Samuel, ever the vigilant one, scanned the area for any signs of danger, his hand resting on the hilt of his sword. "It seems quiet. Where are we?" he murmured, his voice low and edged with caution.

"This looks like Corsica," Michael remarked, scanning their surroundings.

"I think you're right, Michael," said Grayson, spotting the Corsican Moors Head emblem on a nearby flag.

"So, we are in France?" questioned Violette, taking in the aroma of freshly baked bread that wafted from nearby bakeries, mingled with the scent of blooming flowers.

"Yes, Princess," replied Grayson.

"Right! Then let's return home," Violette said, extending her hands forward and conjuring a shimmering portal. She knew it was imperative to safely escort Sully, Samuel, Kiplin and Elsie back to Bagnolet.

"But what about Hawk?" Sully questioned, her brow furrowed with concern.

"We will send someone to get Hawk and Aelvric later. Right now, my priority is to get you four back to Bagnolet," answered Violette.

"But we can't just leave them there," Sully protested.

"You will do as you are told, Sully. In fact, the four of you have a lot of explaining to do once we are back in Bagnolet," Violette asserted firmly. She locked eyes with each of them, as she placed her hands on her hips.

"Yes, Princess," said Sully. She breathed a heavy sigh and lowered her head in respect.

Samuel, Kiplin and Elsie lowered their eyes and bowed their heads in Violette's direction. They were well aware that challenging her was not an option.

"Let's go!" commanded Violette, waving everyone toward the portal she had created.

Michael and Grayson led the way, with everyone else following closely behind.

* * *

A few days had passed since the disappearance of William and Adrian, and with no word from them, Queen Talitha, the head of the Lepidoptera Vampires, summoned Brock, Violette, Michael and Grayson to a meeting.

As they entered the operations room at the Gramaze mansion, their expressions reflected a mix of concern and anticipation. They took their seats at the long mahogany table, with their attention focused on Queen Talitha, who stood at the head of the room with an air of authority.

"Now that you four are here," Talitha began, her voice carrying a weight that commanded attention, "I want to discuss the disappearance of William and Adrian. What do you all know so far?"

"I have been in contact with Pyros in Muscat, and he advises that there has been no sign of William or Adrian there," said Grayson.

"I have been in contact with Garrick in Olden Fjord, and he advised that William and Adrian have not turned up there, either," said Violette.

"There is no chatter on the streets, and I am wondering if they are even still alive," said Michael, raking a hand through his short brown curly hair.

"And you, Brock—what have you found?" asked Talitha, turning to Brock.

"Not much, I'm afraid," said Brock, who was now sitting at the operations room computer, and had been previously been scanning satellite feed daily, for facial recognition of William and Adrian worldwide. "The only thing that I did come across, which was strange and out of the ordinary, was a shimmering wall out in the Atlantic Ocean, just near Norway."

"Hmm … not much then," remarked Talitha, considering the information carefully. "Well at least I know William is still alive, as I can feel the Lepidoptera connection we have. As for Adrian, I am not sure."

"I could contact the council of Warlocks and inquire if they have any information on Adrian," Violette suggested, her brow creased with concern.

"I've already pursued that avenue, my dear; unfortunately, it yielded no results," Queen Talitha replied, her voice carrying a trace of disappointment.

The group fell into a tense discussion, brainstorming and exchanging ideas in a desperate attempt to formulate a plan to locate William and Adrian. The room buzzed with urgency, every word spoken charged with determination. Suddenly, the steady hum of Brock's computer was shattered by a sharp, insistent beep.

All eyes snapped toward the screen as Brock spun around, his fingers flying over the keyboard with practiced speed. His focused expression faltered, replaced by one of astonishment.

"Queen … I believe we may have found them," Brock announced, his tone urgent, yet laced with hope.

Without hesitation, the group rushed to crowd around the monitor.

"Look—there," said Brock, pointing to William and Adrian on the screen.

"How recent is this satellite feed, Brock?" Queen Talitha inquired, her voice tinged with urgency. "And where the hell are they? This place looks familiar."

"It's in real time," stated Brock, turning to her. "I'm not too sure where they are, but the satellite feed does have coordinates. Hang on, I'll type them into Google Maps and that will give me their location," he turned to his computer and punched in the coordinates.

"Well …?" questioned Queen Talitha, impatiently.

"It's saying the Palace of Versailles. What would they be doing there?" replied Brock, his brow furrowed, as he continued to scrutinize the satellite feed pictures. "Actually, it seems like they are trapped inside the mirrors in this room. But that doesn't make any sense, my Queen."

"Ah … yes. I see," said Talitha, remembering the Galerie des Glaces, more commonly known as the Hall of Mirrors, one of the most famous rooms in the Palace of Versailles. "How in the hell did they get in there? And more importantly, what is stopping them from leaving?"

Heads up, Lepidoptera! We have located William and Adrian. I need anyone who is not currently on patrol to get their weapons ready and prepare for action. We rendezvous in the backyard in ten minutes, Queen Talitha projected her thoughts to her Lepidoptera family in France, her mental command carrying a sense of determination and urgency.

"Brock, I need you to remain here and monitor the Palace of Versailles closely," commanded Talitha, her voice firm with authority. "Liaise with only myself,

Grayson and Michael regarding any change in William or Adrian's whereabouts."

"Yes, my Queen," Brock responded obediently. He turned back to his computer, ensuring that the satellite feed remained live and ready for any updates on William and Adrian's movements.

"Grayson, Michael, let's move!" declared Talitha, her tone leaving no room for argument. "You stay here, Violette," she directed firmly.

Violette sighed heavily but complied with a nod. She understood the gravity of obeying the Queen's orders, and dared not challenge them, mindful of the potential consequences.

Keep our Queen safe, at all costs, coven, thought Brock to every Lepidoptera going on the mission. For he knew what the broader consequences would be, and also what it would mean to them personally to lose Talitha.

The whole Lepidoptera coven murmured telepathically at once, *you can count on us!*

Talitha smiled, knowing that everyone had her back, as she ventured toward the backyard to undertake and control this mission. *Thank you, Brock!*

Michael and Grayson trailed behind Talitha as she led the way out of the operations room and into the backyard of the Gramaze mansion.

CHAPTER FIFTEEN

Confusion clouded Albinus's mind as he jolted upright in the dimly lit room, his breath quickening at the unfamiliar surroundings. *Where am I?* The thought echoed sharply as he leaned back against the headboard, his racing heart thudding in his chest.

"You are at the Gramaze mansion," responded Christian, his voice breaking the silence as he listened to the human's thoughts.

With a start, Albinus turned to find Christian seated near the doorway, his presence unexpected.

Christian approached the bed and positioned himself at the foot, his demeanor calm and reassuring. "I am Christian," he gestured toward himself. "You are safe here, Albinus," he added, his voice steady and comforting.

Albinus's heart continued to race as he posed his questions to the blond-headed, six-foot-tall male in front of him. "Safe! Where exactly am I? What country?"

"Bagnolet, France. You are at the Gramaze mansion, Sir," Christian replied, his accent Italian.

Gramaze mansion? thought Albinus, his brow furrowed. *Well at least I am still in France.*

"Can I get you anything? Food or water?"

"I'm a bit thirsty," said Albinus, realizing his mouth was a tad dry. "Could I get a drink of water?"

"Next to you," Christian indicated the glass of water next to Albinus on the bedside table.

Albinus glanced at the glass, and then back to Christian. "Thank you," he said, reaching out to grasp the glass, and taking a large gulp of water to refresh his parched palate.

"You're welcome. When you are feeling up to it, there is a bathroom through there," he pointed to a doorway on the left-hand side of the room. "Feel free to take a shower and freshen up," he offered warmly.

"Thank you," replied Albinus, as he placed the glass back on the bedside table.

"I can organize some food, too, if you like," offered Christian.

"Thank you, Christian. You are very kind," said Albinus.

"So that's a yes?"

Albinus nodded in agreement.

"Great! I will leave you to freshen up, and come back with some food," stated Christian.

"Thank you!" Albinus replied again. He watched Christian head toward the doorway and close the door on his way out.

No sooner had the door clicked shut, than Albinus pulled the quilt from his body and quickly jumped out of bed. Walking toward the window, he gently tugged at the curtains and was surprised to see a breathtaking sight: a sprawling backyard adorned with a grand swimming pool, lush green lawns, vibrant gardens and an elegant gazebo. Upon noticing several individuals enjoying the outdoor space, he thought, *my chances of slipping away unnoticed are slim, so it looks like I am trapped here*. Making his way toward the bathroom, he couldn't shake the nagging thought, *I wonder why I am here?* His mind raced with cynical suspicions, imagining yet another opportunist seeking access to his place of work, the ammunition warehouse. *Typical*, he thought bitterly. Switching on the bathroom light, Albinus was taken aback by the sheer opulence of the room, and noticed that some clean clothes awaited him on the vanity.

* * *

"Hi, guys, what are you both up to?" Violette inquired as she entered the Gramaze kitchen, settling onto one of the stools at the white marble island bench.

"I've just dropped Xanthia off at Lycée International School this morning. It's her first day, today, Sis," replied Danielle. She took a sip of her cup of blood.

"Okay. I bet she was nervous," stated Violette, remembering hers and Danielle's first day, back twenty years ago, when they moved from the United States to France.

"A little. But I soon helped her with that."

"That's good. What about you, Christian? Have you been out on a mission overnight?" asked Violette.

"Nah, I've been standing guard in Albinus's room overnight, making sure he's alright. Actually, I'm just waiting for Lamiae to prepare some food for him," said Christian, looking from Violette to Lamiae.

"Oh, right. How's he doing?" asked Violette.

"Yeah, okay, I suppose. He's a bit scared. But that's to be expected," Christian replied, his expression reflecting a hint of concern.

"Has Albinus asked about his daughter yet?" asked Violette.

"No, not yet. When are we going to tell Xanthia that her father is alive?" enquired Christian.

"I spoke with the Queen about Xanthia and Albinus earlier this morning, and she informed me that given Albinus is no longer under Eryndor's mind control, or a threat to us, I can let Xanthia know her father is alive," Violette explained.

"I'm sure that they both will be thrilled with this news," replied Christian.

"Yeah, I agree. I wonder if they'll choose to stay here, or if they'll opt for their own place?" questioned Danielle.

"Good question. Time will tell, I suppose," said Violette, as she walked over to the fridge to retrieve a cup of blood.

"Here you go, Christian. I'm sure Albinus will appreciate this," Lamiae said, setting a tray with a hearty plate of roast beef, complete with gravy and vegetables, in front of him.

"Thanks, Lamiae. I'm sure he will," said Christian, standing. "I had better get this to him before it gets cold. Catch you all later." He gave his life partner, Danielle, a quick kiss on her cheek, picked up the tray and headed for the doorway.

"What are your plans for the day, Sis?" Danielle asked Violette.

"Since I wasn't asked to join the mission to rescue William and Adrian, I was thinking of checking in on the nine legacies and see how they're faring, since their return from Singapore," Violette replied.

"Do you need some help?" queried Danielle.

"That would be great. Are you free now?"

"Sure," said Danielle, standing. "Are they here or at the academy?"

"Since they've all recovered well from their ordeal, I sent them back to the academy," Violette explained. She finished the last bit of blood from her cup and placed it in the sink. "I think I'll just summon them all to the conference room at the academy and check in on them there."

"Okay! I'm ready when you are," said Danielle.

"Thanks, Danielle. I appreciate your help," said Violette.

* * *

"Knock, knock," Christian announced as he pushed open Albinus's bedroom door and stepped inside. Receiving no response, he proceeded further into the room. Observing the closed bathroom door and the sound of running water, he gently set the tray of food down on the queen-size bed, before retaking his seat beside the doorway.

A few minutes later a refreshed and dressed Albinus cautiously opened the bathroom door. Turning the bathroom light off, he made his way to the bed, where he noticed the inviting tray of food. "Mmm, smells good," he murmured to himself. Settling onto the bed, he reached for the knife and fork, ready to indulge in the meal. As he took his first bite, he became aware of Christian's presence, seated near the doorway.

"Thank you," said Albinus to Christian.

"You are welcome. Is there anything else I can get you?"

"No," said Albinus, as he continued to cut into his food.

"How are you feeling, now that you've had a shower and are in some clean clothes?"

"Better, thank you."

"Do you think you will feel up to a bit of a chat later?" questioned Christian.

Here we go ... the real reason why you have me here, thought Albinus.

Hmm, I wonder what he thinks I want from him, pondered Christian, who had used his Lepidoptera Vampire abilities to listen in on Albinus's thoughts.

"Yes! What did you want to discuss?" questioned Albinus.

"Your daughter, Xanthia."

Albinus gulped hard and tears sprang to his eyes at the mention of his daughter's name. "Where is her body? I want to give her a proper burial."

Christian carried the secret of Xanthia's survival like a stone lodged against his heart, its weight pressing heavier with every breath. He watched Albinus, who at this stage was still blind to the truth, and felt the conflict inside him twist sharper. *I wish I could tell him, but this isn't my call.* The thought gnawed at him as his gaze softened, tracing the worn lines of a father who had no idea his daughter was still alive.

Violette ...

Yes! thought Violette telepathically, as she approached the academy with Danielle.

Can I tell Albinus that Xanthia is alive, mind-thought Christian

Yes, but be mindful that he did see her dead at Boardman's residence, thought Violette. *So, he may not believe you.*

Right! Leave it with me, thought Christian.

Christian raked a hand through his blond hair. "I have something to tell you, Albinus."

"What?" queried Albinus. He placed his knife and fork down on the plate in front of him and gulped hard.

"Xanthia is alive." Christian walked over to the foot of the bed.

Albinus's brow furrowed deeply at the mention of his daughter being alive. "But … I thought … she was dead. I saw it with my own eyes."

"Yes, but what you didn't see, was our Lepidoptera family and one Griffin, who brought Xanthia back to life," explained Christian.

Albinus swiftly hopped off the bed and locked eyes with Christian. "What sick twisted trickery is this? How dare you!" he demanded.

"This is not a trick, Sir. Sit, and I will explain," commanded Christian.

Albinus swallowed hard and his heartbeat quickened, as he sank onto the bed. As he pushed the food tray away, tears began to well in his eyes.

Christian approached the doorway, retrieved the chair, and placed it in front of Albinus, before taking a seat.

"What I am about to tell you cannot be repeated to anyone. Do I make myself clear?" Christian's tone was firm, his expression serious. He was adamant about keeping the existence of the supernatural world hidden from humans.

"Yes!" nodded Albinus, eagerly.

"Listen carefully. Do you remember when Tassone Boardman kidnapped you?" Christian showed Albinus a picture of Tassone, which he had on his phone.

"Yes!" Albinus's lips thinned in frustration when he saw the picture, then remembered Xanthia lifeless body on the basement floor.

"What do you remember happened after that?"

Albinus wiped the tears from his eyes. "After he killed my daughter and I gave that bastard the code to the ammunition warehouse, he struck me down and rendered me unconscious," said Albinus, remembering the blow to his head. "After that, nothing."

Christian searched Albinus's mind to see if he was telling the truth.

"Right ... that explains it. After you were knocked unconscious, Boardman brought you, along with the ammunition, back to his home in France. From there, you were kidnapped and shipped off to Singapore. That is where we found you."

"Right, but that doesn't explain what you said about my Xanthia, though," stated Albinus.

"Sorry, I got off track. So ... a few of my family found your daughter, and we brought her back to the Gramaze mansion. And when she arrived here, my family helped bring her back to life."

"But how?" asked Albinus, trying to comprehend it all.

"We are not human," explained Christian.

Albinus paused, his mind racing to process the new information. He glanced at Christian, his brow furrowing in confusion. "Oh, right! You said Lepidoptera; what are they?" His voice held a mix of curiosity and uncertainty, clearly trying to make sense of the unfamiliar term. The mention of it had sparked something in him, but he couldn't quite grasp its meaning.

"Vampire, and there are many other supernatural creatures in France, too. But it was a Vampire and a Griffin who helped to save your daughter," said Christian, watching the shock on Albinus's face.

"Where is Xanthia? I want to see her," asked Albinus, tears filling his eyes once again.

"I believe she is at school, at the moment. Apparently, she has been enrolled at Lycée International School," said Christian.

"School! So, she doesn't know that I am alive, either?" asked Albinus, trying to make sense of it all in his mind.

Christian shook his head. "She thinks you died in an explosion. Our leader, William Gramaze, and his wife, Renee, took Xanthia in and have looked after her for you, Sir," stated Christian.

"I cannot believe this …" Albinus murmured, his voice a mixture of awe and disbelief. "I mean, I do believe what you've told me, but … well … I suppose it doesn't matter what I believe. When can I see my Xanthia?" His words were rushed, full of emotion, and his face broke into a wide, uncontainable smile, stretching from ear to ear. There was a spark in his eyes, revealing a glimmer of hope that had been absent for far too long.

"She should be here within the next couple of hours. Our family car will collect her from school and bring her back here."

"I can't thank you enough," He grabbed hold of Christians hands and held them both tight. "What can I do to repay you and your family for your kindness?" he asked sincerely.

"You are kind, but nothing, Sir. We are more than happy to help you and your daughter," Christian replied warmly. "You just need to remember to keep our secret, that is all."

"I definitely will. You have my solemn promise," replied Albinus.

CHAPTER SIXTEEN

As the limousine cruised along the freeway, Xanthia sat with her schoolbag and books beside her, gazing out the window. Her first day at a new school had been a break from the confines of the Gramaze mansion. The rush of passing cars blurred into a mosaic of colors, but Xanthia's mind was elsewhere. The day's classes had left her brain feeling fried and foggy, overwhelmed by the influx of new information.

"How was your first day?" asked Danielle, as she listened to Xanthia's thoughts.

"Exhausting, but good," replied Xanthia, as the limousine pulled up in front of the Gramaze mansion wrought-iron gates, set in a high limestone brick wall with electric wire along the top. Xanthia watched as the driver punched in a code on the keypad located outside. When the gates opened inward, they drove along a winding, white pebblestone driveway, flanked by manicured green lawn and colorful gardens on both sides. When the house came into view, it too was made of large limestone blocks, with a black gabled roof and double door windows with balconies.

I wish my father were here, so I could tell him about my day. I miss him so much, Xanthia thought, as the tears welled in her eyes.

Danielle, who was sitting next to Xanthia in the limousine, placed her hand over Xanthia's and said, "I have something to show you when we get inside. But first, I need you to go have a shower and find some comfortable clothes to wear." Danielle smiled sweetly at Xanthia.

Xanthia nodded in agreement, as the car came to a stop at the front double door entrance.

"I'll come and get you from your room in a little while," said Danielle, as they alighted from the car and walked inside.

"Okay. I'll see you soon," replied Xanthia, as she walked up the white marble staircase.

* * *

Christian ... are you ready? Danielle's thoughts resonated in his mind.

Yes! Christian replied.

We will be there in five, thought Danielle.

"Knock, knock," Danielle called out, as she stood in front of Xanthia's closed bedroom door.

"Come in," Xanthia called out from behind the door.

Opening the door, Danielle noticed that Xanthia had all of her schoolbooks scattered across her bed. "Wow ... is that your homework from today at Lycée?"

Xanthia nodded. "Yep." She glanced at the books spread out on her bed "I really need a desk for my studies. Do you think William and Renee will purchase one for me?"

"I think there should be one already here somewhere. I will check it out and let you know."

"Thanks, Danielle."

"No problem. Are you ready to come and have a look at something with me?" asked Danielle.

"Sure, what are we going to look at?" enquired Xanthia.

"It's a surprise!" Danielle answered.

"Surprise ... I love surprises. Give me a minute, I need to give my hair a quick brush, then I'm all yours," replied Xanthia, as she walked toward her bathroom doorway.

Danielle nodded and waited for Xanthia to return.

"So ... what is this surprise?" asked Xanthia, as they walked out of her bedroom and down the staircase.

With a confident smile, Danielle replied, "You'll see, and I'm quite certain you'll adore it," She gently tugged Xanthia's hand as they made their way through the house.

Xanthia smiled and followed Danielle through the house.

Stopping at the back glass sliding doors, which led out onto a large gazebo area, Danielle turned to Xanthia and said, "Now … what you're about to see is real, so don't think that you're dreaming. Okay?"

"Okay!" said Xanthia, excited to see what it was.

"Let's go," said Danielle. She placed her arm around Xanthia's shoulders and pulled her toward the gazebo.

As they neared the gazebo, Xanthia noticed Christian and waved. She really liked the friendship she had formed with Christian, especially as he had recently taken on the role of teaching her self-defense techniques against malevolent forces and evil.

Christian returned her wave with a warm smile, gesturing for her to come closer. With each step, Xanthia's anticipation heightened. However, her excitement shifted to disbelief as she noticed another figure standing beside Christian; a man with gray hair, his back turned to her.

Frozen in her tracks, Xanthia's mind raced with confusion and disbelief. With cautious steps, she approached the man, her breath caught in her throat.

As she drew closer, the man turned, revealing weathered features softened by a mix of shock and longing. Their eyes locked and, in that moment, time seemed to stand still.

"Father?" Xanthia's voice trembled with emotion, disbelief mingling with hope.

Tears glistened in Albinus's eyes as he reached out, pulling her into a tight embrace. "Xanthia, my dear daughter," he whispered, his voice thick with emotion.

Overwhelmed with a flood of emotions—joy, relief, and a lingering sense of disbelief—Xanthia clung to her father, her heart overflowing with love and gratitude for this unexpected reunion. The weight of uncertainty lifted from her shoulders as she held on to him, cherishing the moment she had believed to be impossible.

Danielle and Christian stood on the sidelines and watched Xanthia and Albinus's emotional reunion and smiled.

Our good deed for the day is done, thought Danielle to Christian, as she held his hand.

Sure is. Let's leave them to enjoy the moment, thought Christian.

Thank you, Danielle and Christian, thought Xanthia, as she watched them walk away. She knew, from previous experience, that they would be listening to her thoughts.

Danielle and Christian exchanged a knowing glance before raising their hands in acknowledgment, silently conveying that they'd heard Xanthia's thoughts.

CHAPTER SEVENTEEN

The crystal chandeliers swayed as a portal materialized within the grandeur of the Hall of Mirrors, nestled within the opulent confines of the Palace of Versailles.

Queen Talitha, who was dressed in her regal robes, walked out of the portal, side by side with seven members of her coven, all brandishing their drawn swords.

"Find them!" commanded Talitha. She stood poised beside the gaping portal, anticipation coursing through her veins, awaiting the response of her family.

"Over here!" Kelan's voice echoed urgently as he spotted William and Adrian ensnared behind a mirror's reflective surface. He watched William frantically gesturing, his lips moving, yet only muffled sounds reached his ears through the barrier of the mirror.

Queen Talitha floated gracefully toward Kelan, her regal presence captivating all, compelling everyone to merge at the spot.

Can you hear me, William, thought Talitha to the leader.

Yes. Thank fuck you have found us, thought William.

Stand back and I will get you both out of there, thought Talitha.

William quickly moved Adrian, who was injured, aside and observed with awe as his Queen conjured a shimmering portal that bridged the gap between the Hall of Mirrors and the space behind the mirror where they were ensnared.

As the mirror opened, William picked Adrian up off the ground and the Queen summoned William and Adrian forward, positioning them directly before her.

"What is wrong with him?" inquired Talitha, her gaze falling upon Adrian the Warlock, as the portal closed behind them.

"I don't know, my Queen. But whatever it is, Adrian seems to be worsening with each passing moment," replied William, his voice tinged with concern, as Adrian fell unconscious in his arms.

"Lay him on the floor," said Talitha, noticing that there was not one mark or bloodstain on Adrian.

William quickly did as he was instructed.

The seven Lepidopteras swiftly formed a protective circle around William, Adrian and Talitha, shielding them from potential harm.

Queen Talitha knelt beside Adrian, her expression a mix of determination and compassion. Gently, she placed her hands over his body and her fingertips started to glow with a soft, ethereal light. With a focused intensity, she delved into the depths of Adrian's affliction, seeking to mend the wounds that marred his flesh and soul. As her healing magic flowed, a serene aura enveloped them, suffusing the air with a sense of tranquility.

But Adrian remained unconscious, his breathing shallow and labored, his body seemingly untouched by the efforts to heal or rouse him.

Talitha's heart sank as she realized the severity of the situation. Her powers were usually so reliable, but this time they faltered.

"Why isn't this working?" William asked Talitha.

Talitha shrugged her shoulders. "I'm not sure."

A ripple of unease swept through the gathered Lepidopteras as they sensed their Queen's struggle.

"Let's return to Gramaze mansion and I will do some more healing on him there," commanded Queen Talitha, her voice tinged with urgency as she gestured toward the already open portal.

With determination, William carefully lifted Adrian into his arms, carrying him toward the beckoning portal that would transport them back to safety within the walls of Gramaze mansion.

In solemn silence, the rest of the group followed Queen Talitha through the portal, their expressions a mixture of concern and determination as they prepared to face whatever lay ahead.

* * *

Violette ... come to Adrian's room, NOW! thought Queen Talitha to her daughter, as she walked out of the portal.

Yes, my Queen, thought Violette. She ran at Vampire speed through the Gramaze mansion to her foster father's room.

Upon reaching the upper level of the mansion, Violette was met by the sight of William, Grayson and Michael standing in the doorway. "What's happening?" she exclaimed, pushing past them with urgency. Her breath caught in her throat as she laid eyes on her father's unconscious body, now resting on a four-poster bed.

"Shit ... what's happened to him?" asked Violette, as she knelt next to his bed and placed her hand under his.

"We are not too sure, my dear. I need you to assist me to heal him," said Queen Talitha, looking from Violette to Adrian.

"Yes, my Queen," said Violette. She placed both hands over Adrian and started to chant, along with Talitha, an ancient Buddhist healing ritual, which they chanted over and over.

> *Ong, Ma, Lee, Bae, Mae, Hong.*
> *Ong, Ma, Lee, Bae, Mae, Hong.*
> *Ong, Ma, Lee, Bae, Mae, Hong.*

The room was bathed in a soft, soothing light, emanating from the combined energies of their powers. The walls shimmered with a faint, ethereal glow, casting intricate patterns of shifting colors across the space, as Violette and Talitha continue to chant.

William, Grayson and Michael stood in the doorway, their expressions a mixture of awe and reverence as they witnessed the incredible power of the Queen and Princess at work. Their eyes widened in amazement as they observed the ethereal glow suffusing the room, and they exchanged silent glances, wordlessly acknowledging the magnitude of what they were witnessing.

The air crackled with energy, charged with the potent magic being wielded by Talitha and Violette. William, Grayson and Michael remained rooted to the spot, unable to tear their gaze away from the scene unfolding before them.

In that moment, they realized the true extent of the Queen and Princess's abilities, and a newfound respect and admiration swelled within their hearts. They stood in silent wonder, humbled by the sight of such formidable power being used for the greater good.

As Adrian's body hovered weightlessly above the bed, Violette and Talitha continued their chanting, their voices weaving together in a harmonious melody of healing magic. With each verse, the energy surrounding them intensified, swirling around Adrian's form like a protective cocoon.

Then, in response to their combined efforts, a serene calm washed over the room, permeating the air with a palpable sense of tranquility. Talitha and Violette's chanting gradually faded into silence and, with a final gentle motion, Adrian's body slowly descended, settling back onto the bed with a featherlight touch.

The room seemed to sigh with relief as the healing process came to its conclusion. Talitha and Violette exchanged a knowing glance, their eyes reflecting the satisfaction of a task well done, as they watched Adrian open his eyes.

"Where am I?" asked Adrian, as he sat up and leaned against the headboard.

"My home!" stated Talitha, standing. "How do you feel?"

"Good, I think?" said Adrian. "A bit foggy, though." He rubbed the right side of his head.

"That is to be expected," Talitha reassured him.

"So … what happened, Adrian?" asked Violette, as she sat on the bed next to him. "One moment you and William were in the portal returning home, and the next you both were trapped inside the Hall of Mirrors."

"When William and I entered the portal with the intention of returning home, a sudden surge of dark energy engulfed us, diverting our intended path. Instead of arriving safely, we found ourselves inexplicably transported to the Hall of Mirrors in France," Adrian recounted.

"I would wager that this was Eryndor's doing," William remarked, as he walked over to the bed with Grayson and Michael.

"I believe you're right," Adrian concurred, nodding at William.

"I'm just relieved you're alright, my friend," William expressed sincerely.

"Me too." Adrian turned his gaze toward Talitha and Violette, expressing his gratitude, "Thank you for healing me."

"You're welcome. However, what I'm curious about is what caused your illness in the first place. I've encountered a lot of dark magic in my long life, but it took the combined efforts of both of us to bring you back from near death, Adrian," Talitha's voice carried a tone of concern.

"If this was Eryndor's doing, then I surmise that his dark magic has grown immensely powerful. We must exercise greater caution from now on," Adrian concluded, his tone filled with gravity.

"I agree, and I believe it's imperative that we go and visit Garrick and Elara to delve deeper into this matter, and to ascertain Eryndor's whereabouts. We must confront this fucker head-on," William asserted.

"I agree, but are you sufficiently recovered for such a mission, William?" Talitha inquired, her concern evident. She sensed through their Lepidoptera connection that he was weakened from abstaining from blood for a few days.

"Yes, I'll be fine, my Queen. I just need some sustenance, and then I'll reach out to Garrick and Elara to discuss our next steps regarding Eryndor," William assured Talitha.

"Great! Well, I might return to my chambers, as I am feeling exhausted from all the healing I have performed. Keep me up to date with any developments," stated Talitha.

"Yes, my Queen," said William, dutifully. He watched her walk toward the doorway.

"I think that I might get some rest, too," said Violette, suddenly feeling drained from the healing she had performed on Adrian. She leaned into Adrian and gave him a hug. "I'm glad you're going to be okay."

"Thanks, Violette. You go and get some rest and we can catch up later on," said Adrian.

"Come on," Michael interjected, standing next to the bed, and extending his hand toward Violette.

Violette looked up at her life partner, smiled, and took his hand.

CHAPTER EIGHTEEN

"Come on Garrick, pick up," urged William, seated at his office desk, with his mobile phone pressed to his ear.

However, there was no response, only Garrick's voicemail greeting.

William attempted two more times, but each time was met with the same voicemail recording. *Hmm, that's strange*, William thought to himself.

Brock, pull up Olden Fjord on the satellite feed. I need to know what's happening there. I'll be there in a moment, William said telepathically.

Yes, Sire, thought Brock, who was seated in the operations room at his computer.

"Anything happening in Olden Fjord?" William demanded, as he burst into the operations room, through the glass sliding doors.

"Unfortunately … yes. Have a look," Brock replied, gesturing toward the computer screen mounted on the wall.

William witnessed the mayhem and carnage before his eyes. "Shit!"

Heads up Lepidopteras! Gather in the operations room, immediately, William commanded mentally.

Within moments, every male and female Vampire not currently on assignment, appeared before William and Brock in the operations room.

"Right, quiet down everyone," demanded William, looking around the room at each member of his coven. "Brock, bring up the images you have of Olden Fjord."

"Yes, Sire," said Brock. He turned back to his computer keyboard and repositioned the satellite feed to show the coven members the devastation and destruction that had been caused by Eryndor and his glazed-eyed creatures.

A collective murmur of disbelief filled the room.

"I need you all to get your weapons ready, and to meet me in the backyard in ten minutes. Violette, where are you?" William scanned the room for her.

Standing at the back of the room, obscured by taller Lepidopteras, Violette raised her hand in the air. "Here!"

William directed his gaze toward her, prompting the other Lepidoptera to make way. "I will require you to create a portal to transport all of us to Olden Fjord," stated William.

"Yes, Sir. Do you require me to come on this mission?" enquired Violette.

William paused for a moment, considering her question before responding. "Once you have created the portal, I then want you to take over from Brock. I require the satellite feed to be kept live. We don't want any surprises."

"Yes, Sir," said Violette, knowing what was required of her.

"Brock, you will be coming with us today. We are going to need all hands on deck," said William.

"Yes, Sire," replied Brock, his eagerness to participate on any mission evident.

Without exchanging another word, the coven members swiftly dispersed from the operations room, running at Vampire speed toward the weapons room arsenal.

* * *

As William and his coven members materialized at the edge of Olden Fjord, a scene of utter devastation unfolded before them. Smoke billowed from charred remnants of buildings, mingling with the mist that cloaked the rugged landscape. The air was thick with the pungent scent of burnt wood and scorched earth.

William's eyes widened in horror as he took in the extent of the destruction. Houses that had only just been repaired lay in ruins, crushed beneath fallen trees and rocks. The once-tranquil waters of the sound churned angrily, evidence of flooding caused by Eryndor's chaotic rampage.

Brock stepped forward, his expression grim. "This is worse than we anticipated, Sire," he said, his voice heavy with sorrow.

William clenched his fists, his anger simmering beneath the surface. "This is the second time that Eryndor has caused all of this destruction. He will pay for what has transpired here," William vowed, his voice laced with determination.

As they moved deeper into the devastated landscape, they came across the bodies of those who had fallen victim to Eryndor's rampage. Some lay motionless on the ground, while others floated in the murky waters of the sound. The magnitude of the destruction was beyond comprehension, leaving them grappling with the enormity of the tragedy before them.

"We need to help the survivors, and get this place cleaned up," William declared, his voice firm, as he looked around at each of his coven. "Go!" He waved them away with his right hand.

With a sense of urgency, William watched some of his coven members set to work, using their supernatural abilities to search for survivors and provide aid where they could. Amidst the destruction and chaos they remained a beacon of hope, determined to rebuild and restore peace to Olden Fjord and the Griffins.

"Michael, Grayson and Brock … you will come with me. I need to find Garrick and Elara. Let's go!" commanded William.

The four of them ran toward the once-majestic stone castle, which was perched proudly on the rugged cliffs overlooking Olden Fjord, but that now bore the scars of a brutal assault. Its towering walls, once impenetrable, were marred by cracks and crumbling battlements, evidence of the relentless onslaught it had endured. Smoke billowed from charred remnants of towers and turrets, mingling with the mist that shrouded the sound. Flames licked hungrily at the castle's stone facade, casting an eerie glow against the darkening sky.

With their swords drawn, the four Lepidopteras entered the castle's courtyard; they found it littered with debris and rubble, and remnants of defensive barriers that had been destroyed in the chaos. Broken weapons and armor were strewn about, discarded by defenders, and fallen combatants' bodies were everywhere.

"Shit!" said Michael, as he looked around at the destruction. "Where do we start?"

"Let's go inside. We need to find Garrick and Elara," instructed William. He walked toward the entrance, and Grayson, Michael and Brock followed.

William leaned on the wooden door and tried to push it open, but it wouldn't budge. "What the hell!" He pushed against the door with his Lepidoptera strength and this time it opened slowly.

"Holy mother of hell," stated William, as he stepped through the doorway, his eyes widening in shock at the sight that greeted him. Half of the once-stalwart castle's walls lay in ruin, their stones scattered like fallen soldiers. The roof had crumbled inward, a chaotic jumble of broken timbers and shattered tiles now littering the ground. Dust hung thick in the air, swirling in the beams of faint moonlight that filtered through the gaps in the decimated structure.

"What the fuck went on here? This looks like a war zone," said Grayson, looking around at the scene set before him.

"Sire ... where do we start?" asked Brock.

"We need to stay together, and search room by room for Garrick and Elara. We are stronger in numbers if

Eryndor and his creatures appear. Understood?" queried William, looking at each of them.

They all nodded yes.

"Alright, let's move," instructed William.

William, Grayson, Michael and Brock hurried through the debris-strewn halls, their hearts heavy with dread as they searched for any sign of their comrades, Garrick and Elara.

"Garrick! Elara! Can you hear us?" yelled William, his voice echoing through the crumbling corridors.

As they listened for any response amidst the groans of shifting stone, suddenly a faint cry reached their ears.

"Over here! Help!" yelled Garrick.

Following the sound, the group scrambled over fallen beams and masses of debris until they reached a section of collapsed wall. There, beneath the rubble, they spotted the outstretched hand of Garrick, barely visible in the darkness.

Without hesitation, the group sprang into action, working together to clear away the rubble and free their trapped friends. Dust filled the air as they worked tirelessly, their movements fluid and relentless.

After what felt like an eternity, they finally uncovered Garrick and Elara, their faces streaked with dirt, but alive.

"Thank the Gods, you're both okay," exclaimed Brock, his voice filled with concern.

Garrick and Elara blinked up at their four rescuers, their expressions a mix of exhaustion and relief.

"I thought we were done for," said Elara, her eyes shining with tears, as Brock helped her up.

"Thank you," murmured Garrick, his voice hoarse, as William helped him stand.

"You're welcome, my friend. What has happened here?" queried William.

"Eryndor … that's what happened. He and his underlings showed up here a few days ago, wreaking havoc and leaving nothing but destruction in their wake," explained Garrick. He turned to survey his once-beautiful city through the crumbled wall of the castle, shaking his head in dismay.

"Why didn't you call us to come and help, my friend?" asked William.

"We didn't have time. Eryndor appeared out of nowhere with his creatures and, as you can see, they've destroyed our city. It all happened so fast," stated Garrick.

"Did he get what he came for?" asked William.

"No. I told him that I wasn't going to hand the chalice over to him," said Garrick.

"Probably our biggest mistake. Because Eryndor told us that if we didn't release the chalice to him, he would destroy our Kingdom; and he did," said Elara, gesturing to the war zone that surrounded them.

"Do you still have the chalice safely stored somewhere?" asked William.

"Yes, but it's not here in Olden. Thank the Gods. We moved it to a safe place that only a true Griffin can open. In other words, only Elara and I can open," stated Garrick.

"Right! Do you know if Eryndor and his creatures are still in Olden?" asked William.

Shaking his head, Garrick said, "I don't know. We have been trapped under that rubble for at least two days." He gestured toward where they had been entombed.

"I don't understand, my friend. Why couldn't you and Elara use your Griffin abilities to fight Eryndor, or at least escape from under the rubble?" William enquired, his brow furrowed with concern.

"We are not sure," replied Garrick, a note of frustration creeping into his voice. "The only explanation we can come up with is that Eryndor somehow drained our abilities."

"Sounds like he has gotten a lot stronger since we last saw him," said Grayson.

"He certainly has. The Twin Icefire Blades have bestowed upon him an immense amount of power. Imagine what he would be like if we handed over the chalice;

unstoppable, that's for sure," Garrick remarked, his voice laden with concern.

"So, how are you both feeling now? Have your abilities returned?" asked William, as he looked from Garrick to Elara.

"I can feel a tingling sensation coursing through me, so my abilities feel like they are returning," said Elara. She extended her hand and effortlessly shifted a large piece of stone wall from one side of the room to the other.

Garrick mirrored her action, placing his hand forward and effortlessly moving a long wooden table, rubble strewn across its surface, across the room. "Yes, mine have returned too."

"Great!" exclaimed William. "Well, let's go and see if we can assist your Kingdom's people in restoring some semblance of normalcy back into their lives.

"Sounds like a plan. Thank you, Gramaze family. We are heavily in your debt," said Garrick, gratefully.

As they made their way out of the crumbling castle, their spirits buoyed by their reunion, they knew that they would confront whatever challenges lay ahead together, their alliance stronger than ever before.

CHAPTER NINETEEN

"Morning, Renee," greeted Sully as she approached her under the expansive patio outside.

"Good morning, dear girl. How are you this morning?" asked Renee, her Swedish accent apparent.

"I'm okay … can I speak with you about Hawk?" asked Sully, standing in front of Renee.

"Of course. Sit down, dear girl," said Renee, patting the seat next to her.

"Thank you!" Sully gulped hard and sat next to Renee.

"What would you like to know about Hawk?" asked Renee.

"When is someone going to rescue him from the Fae Kingdom? I mean … it's been over five days since I last saw Hawk, and goodness knows what has happened to him," pleaded Sully, her voice filled with urgency and concern. "Let alone Aelvric."

Renee placed her hand over Sully's and said, "We are currently waiting for the Fae Queen, Elyndra, to accept our request to visit. Once she has done so, then we can go and speak with her about the release of Hawk and Aelvric."

"But that could take forever. I am not prepared to wait that long," said Sully, pulling her hand away from Renee's with a mixture of frustration and determination.

"Unfortunately … we don't have a choice." Renee looked into Sully's mind and listened to her thoughts about Hawk.

"What do you mean, we don't have a choice? We always have a choice, it's just not a high priority for some. I bet if it was William in there, the Gramaze coven wouldn't even hesitate or ask for permission from Elyndra to visit the Fae Kingdom. Who does that woman think she is, anyway?" Sully exclaimed, her frustration palpable.

"You need to calm down, Sully."

"Don't tell me to calm down," Sully retorted, rising to her feet. "If it was your life partner who was held by the Fae, wouldn't you do everything you could to save him?"

"Yes … but …" Renee was interrupted by Violette, who had overheard the whole conversation.

"Sully … you will cease speaking to Renee this way, and return to the academy, NOW!" commanded Princess Violette.

"But …"

"There are no buts here. What you fail to see is the whole goddamn picture here. We are trying to get Hawk and Aelvric out, but it's not easy dealing with the Fae Queen. She is a formidable monarch who you don't want to mess with. Am I making myself clear?" exclaimed Violette, with her hands on her hips.

"Yes, Ma'am," replied Sully, averting her eyes and taking a deep breath. Sully knew better than to argue with Princess Violette.

"Off you go!" Violette dismissed Sully with a wave of her hand. Following the recent events in the Fae realm, Violette was resolute in withholding any additional information from Sully that might jeopardize the upcoming mission.

Sully walked away from Renee and Violette, disheartened.

* * *

"Has there been any word from the Fae Queen yet?" Renee asked Violette, once Sully was gone.

"Yes, we heard from her this morning. She granted us permission to visit, but she specified that only three of us can attend the meeting in the Fae Kingdom," explained Violette.

"So, who will be going?" asked Renee.

"I don't know yet. Queen Talitha is making that decision," said Violette.

"I've heard that Elyndra can be pretty ruthless," stated Renee.

"You are correct. Elyndra's actions are guided by her own motives. So, it will be interesting to see what motive she has for granting our kind a visit to her Kingdom." She shook her head. "Despite her elegance and grace, there is an underlying sense of danger surrounding her, a reminder that she is not to be trusted and is unpredictable," said Violette, remembering her recent unplanned visit to the Fae Kingdom.

Violette ... attend my chambers, NOW! Queen Talitha's command echoed in Violette's mind.

Yes, my Queen, thought Violette.

"I must go, Renee. Queen Talitha has summoned me for a meeting," Violette informed Renee.

"Okay! Keep safe, my dear. Catch you later on," said Renee. She watched Violette walk toward the mansion.

* * *

When Violette arrived, she noticed that Queen Talitha's door was open. Inside the Queen's chambers she observed that William and her sister, Danielle, were already seated at the table. "Knock, knock. May I come in?"

"Enter, Violette," ordered Queen Talitha, looking up at the doorway. She watched Violette close the door. "Sit! We need to discuss how we are going to deal with the Fae Queen."

"Yes, my Queen," said Violette, taking her seat at the round table.

"Right, now that we're all gathered ..." Talitha's deep blue eyes looked around the table at each of their faces,

"I've made a decision regarding who will attend the meeting in the Fae Kingdom with Elyndra. It will be myself, Danielle and William. Violette, I understand your desire to join us, but I need you here to safeguard the Lepidoptera lineage. Elyndra can be quite challenging to negotiate with, and if the meeting takes a wrong turn she may pose a serious threat to us."

Violette sighed heavily, but complied with a nod.

Danielle and William also nodded yes.

"Does she know why we're coming for a visit?" asked Danielle, tucking a strand of blonde hair behind her ear.

"She's aware that we want to discuss Hawk and Aelvric, nothing more," replied Talitha.

"Do we need to dress formally, or in our battle attire, and what about weapons?" inquired Danielle, absently fidgeting with the golden ring on her finger, which her mother had left her when she'd passed away.

"Unfortunately, Elyndra has said no weapons are to enter her Kingdom. She has actually invited us to a morning tea with the Fae, so I would say we will need to dress appropriately for the occasion," explained Talitha.

"Humph, what I have on now," William indicated to his sleek leather jacket over a black T-shirt, paired with black denim jeans. "This is what I will be wearing."

"That will be fine, William," said Talitha, with a nod of approval. "I have a gown for you to wear, Danielle."

"Thank you, my Queen," said Danielle, gratefully.

"So, what's the plan when we arrive in the Fae Kingdom, besides a morning tea?" asked William, his tone reflecting curiosity and readiness for action.

"Basically, our plan is to ask for the return of Hawk and Aelvric, on behalf of Garrick and Elara. Additionally, while we're there, we aim to gather any information that Elyndra might have about Eryndor's plans," explained Talitha.

"Right! When do we leave?" asked William.

"Tomorrow morning, around nine o'clock," said Talitha.

"Why are we even bothering to reason with this bitch? Wouldn't it be better to simply rescue Hawk and Aelvric now, instead of wasting time with this morning tea? She could still refuse us, and that's not something I'm inclined to be patient about," William stated, his tone expressing frustration and intolerance.

"I don't like this any more than you do. We're left with no alternative, William. Rushing in there won't guarantee we find Hawk or Aelvric, and we mustn't forget that the Fae can't be trusted," declared Queen Talitha, who'd had a few dealings with the Fae over her long lifetime.

William nostrils flared as he took a deep breath in, then out, and tried to calm himself. "Yes, my Queen."

"Do our abilities still work in the Fae realm?" asked Danielle.

"Indeed, they do, Danielle. That's why I'm not concerned about going unarmed. Your abilities are one of the reasons I selected you to join us in the Fae Kingdom, along with your Fae heritage," Queen Talitha explained.

"Oh, I see," Danielle responded, shifting her gaze from Talitha to Violette. "But what if Elyndra refuses to release Hawk and Aelvric? How do we proceed without jeopardizing our relationship with the Fae?"

"If it comes to that, I will handle the situation," Queen Talitha stated firmly. "I will require both you and William to be prepared for anything that might happen while we are there. That's all!"

Danielle nodded in agreement.

"Who is creating the portal for transport to the Fae realm tomorrow morning?" asked Violette, uncertain whether she or Queen Talitha would take on that task.

"Elyndra," stated Queen Talitha.

"Oh, right," said Violette, raising her eyebrows.

"Do you think that is wise, letting her create the portal?" asked William, his brow furrowed with concern.

"It's a precarious situation to be in, to say the least. We must proceed with utmost caution. The Fae are not to be trusted, especially when it comes to matters of crossing realms. Their intentions are often veiled in secrecy, and their alliances can shift like shadows," said Queen Talitha.

"I agree. We must be vigilant and be prepared for any unforeseen consequences, and rely on our own instincts to navigate this journey safely," stated William.

"We will meet tomorrow morning in the backyard, and proceed with the plan to portal to the Fae realm at nine o'clock," Queen Talitha announced with authority. "Now, if you don't mind, I need some time to prepare. You may leave my room now."

Danielle nodded respectfully and pushed her chair back. Standing, she walked toward the doorway and waited for Violette and William.

William nodded in agreement. "Good night, my Queen."

"Good night, my Queen," Violette added.

William, Violette and Danielle quietly exited the room, leaving Queen Talitha to her thoughts and preparations.

CHAPTER TWENTY

Dressed and ready for what the day might bring, Violette walked over to her bedroom window and drew back the curtains. As she glanced down into the Gramaze back lawn area, suddenly a vivid and mesmerizing electric blue colored portal began to materialize before her eyes, pulsating with energy.

Who is that? Violette wondered, observing two young women emerge from the portal. They appeared almost regal, one adorned with light purple hair and the other with cascading red locks. She also noticed their Fae wings. *Ah ... that looks like Adeline and Summer, from the Fae Kingdom.*

Adeline and Summer had never visited the human world before, and as they fluttered around, examining intricate details, experiencing everything with childlike curiosity, they were captivated by its beauty, which evoked a range of positive and enchanting responses that reflected their magical and ethereal nature.

"Adeline, Summer ... stand guard beside the portal," Queen Elyndra said telepathically with a commanding voice, through the opening of the portal. She knew that the two young fairies would be distracted from the main objective of their assignment.

Hearing Elyndra's voice, both fairies quickly gathered their thoughts and stood either side of the portal, waiting for the three Lepidopteras to arrive.

Violette watched on with curiosity and smiled.

"Knock, knock," said Danielle, standing in Violette's doorway.

Violette turned and said, "Morning, Sis. How are you this morning?"

"Good, I think," said Danielle, entering her bedroom. "What are you looking at?"

"These two," said Violette. She gestured with her hand for Danielle to come have a look.

Danielle walked over to the double door windows and gazed down at the lawn area. "Wow … aren't they pretty?" She watched their intricately patterned butterfly-like wings shimmer with every movement.

"They sure are. But … don't be fooled by their charm; Fae can be unpredictable and manipulative. Remember that when you are in the Fae realm today," said Violette.

"I will. Thanks for the heads-up, Sis," said Danielle, appreciative of the reminder.

"Are you feeling nervous?" Violette inquired, sensing that something was troubling Danielle.

"A bit. It's … well, because I'm half Fae, I'm wondering what will happen when I arrive in the Fae realm." Danielle explained. "Will Elyndra recognize my Fae heritage?"

"I don't believe Elyndra is aware of your Fae heritage at this point, but I suspect that Talitha may hold this knowledge as a trump card, if you catch my drift. However, I'm confident that everything will turn out alright," reassured Violette. She gently placed her hand on Danielle's arm, utilizing her calming Lepidoptera abilities to soothe her sister's mind.

"Thanks, Sis. I hope so," said Danielle.

Danielle … William, it's time to go, mind-thought Queen Talitha.

"Our Queen is calling me. I need to go, Sis. I will catch up with you when we get back from the Fae Kingdom," said Danielle.

Violette leaned in to hug Danielle. "Stay safe."

"I will," said Danielle, hugging her back.

* * *

"Adeline, Summer, lead the way," said Queen Talitha, gesturing toward the Fae-created portal.

They both nodded once and walked into the portal.

Keep your wits about you, Lepidopteras, thought Queen Talitha, as she, William and Danielle entered the portal to the Fae realm.

To their surprise, as they walked out of the portal, Queen Talitha, William and Danielle were greeted by a majestic Fae realm, where the air was filled with a soft, iridescent glow, casting a gentle, ethereal light over everything.

They stood in a lush meadow, decorated with vibrant, exotic flowers in hues unseen in the human world—glowing blues, purples and pinks that seemed to emit their own radiant light. The emerald-green grass beneath their feet was soft and sparkling with tiny dewdrops like scattered jewels.

In the distance, towering trees grew, twisted, silver-trunked birches and majestic oak branches stretched toward the sky, their leaves shimmering in hues of gold and crimson.

Streams of crystal-clear water flowed gently through the landscape, cascading down miniature waterfalls and forming sparkling pools that reflected the colors of the surrounding flora. Dragonflies and butterflies with wings like stained glass flitted among the flowers, adding to the sense of enchantment.

"Welcome!" said Queen Elyndra. She gestured toward her kingdom.

"Thank you, Elyndra," said Queen Talitha, surprised by the surroundings.

"Wow ... your kingdom is truly beautiful, Queen Elyndra," exclaimed Danielle, her eyes taking in the enchanting surroundings.

"Thank you," replied Elyndra with a slight smile, her gaze lingering on Danielle. A sense of intuition stirred within Danielle, as she felt a hint of unease when the portal closed behind them. "Come!" Elyndra gestured toward a long wooden table and chairs, which had already been set up for their morning tea.

William nodded in her direction and they all walked toward the table.

Elyndra took her seat at the head of the table, her presence commanding and regal. She observed as the three Lepidopteras took their places near her, their expressions a mix of curiosity and respect.

Queen Talitha, William and Danielle watched with fascination as the other fairies gracefully presented a delightful assortment of treats on three-tiered stands. The spread included delicate elderflower cupcakes adorned with edible flowers, petite pixie-sized sandwiches filled with cucumber and cream cheese, and mushroom tartlets in flaky pastry, glistening with savory goodness.

Amidst the mouthwatering display, the fairies also poured cups of Fae blossom tea, its aromatic steam carrying hints of blossoms and woodland herbs.

Queen Talitha couldn't help but smile, outwardly displaying warmth and gratitude toward Elyndra for her gracious hospitality. However, inwardly, she harbored a lingering sense of caution and wariness, knowing better than to fully trust the enchanting Fae around her.

Elyndra looked over at Danielle and her eyes were immediately drawn to the golden ring adorning Danielle's finger. "I believe you possess something that rightfully belongs to the Fae Kingdom, my dear," Elyndra declared, her voice commanding and firm as she addressed Danielle directly.

"It was handed down to me from my mother, when she passed away," Danielle replied, fully aware of what Elyndra was referring to.

"Ah, so you are Fae then?" questioned Elyndra.

"Yes, Queen Elyndra; part Fae and part Lepidoptera," replied Danielle.

"I see … so, born Fae, but then turned Vampire. How dare you!" Elyndra exclaimed, her tone filled with disgust and disapproval at the revelation.

Queen Talitha pushed her chair back forcefully, causing it to tip over as she rose to her feet. "You will not address my family in such a manner. We will be leaving now," she declared firmly, her voice carrying a tone of authority and determination.

"Humph!" stated Elyndra, her smirk lingering.

Calm yourself, Talitha, thought William, standing. He was feeling a bit nervous due to the confrontation between the two Queens, and worried about the potential consequences or tensions arising from their heated exchange.

Despite feeling grateful for Queen Talitha's defense, Danielle rose to her feet and addressed Queen Elyndra directly. "What you don't know is that over twenty years ago, I was drugged by the Debauched, and that's how I became part Lepidoptera and part Fae. If it weren't for Queen Talitha and William, I wouldn't even be alive. So don't you say 'How dare you!' to me, because this is no one's fault besides the Debauched."

"Well … I beg your pardon. I apologize," Elyndra said, her tone softening slightly in response to Danielle's explanation. "May I have a look at your ring, my dear?"

Danielle turned her gaze toward Queen Talitha, her eyes seeking reassurance and guidance, *Should I let her see it?*

Yes, but be careful, Queen Talitha thought in response, her voice echoing in Danielle's mind.

Danielle approached a still-seated Elyndra and held her hand out for Elyndra to view the Fae ring.

Elyndra pulled Danielle's hand forcefully toward her to examine the ring closely.

Queen Talitha nostrils flared. "We will be going!" she declared firmly.

"Wait! I thought you came here to discuss other issues," stated Elyndra, rising from her seat.

"I wouldn't waste my time," Talitha replied as she turned away from the table, indicating her resolve to leave. Danielle and William flanked her either side.

"So … you're saying you don't want to talk about the two Griffins." Elyndra waved her hand to reveal the suspended cages holding Hawk and Aelvric, before everyone's eyes.

"I have no use for these two Griffins. As I said, we will take our leave, now," stated Talitha.

Danielle and William looked at each other with concern.

"Wait! I will swap the two Griffins for the Fae's Golden Ring," said Elyndra.

"That ring is a family heirloom. And Danielle will not be passing it to you or anyone else. Do I make myself clear, Elyndra?" said Talitha, firmly. "Come, Danielle and William."

Waving her hand gracefully, Talitha conjured a portal to transport them back to Bagnolet. As the three Lepidopteras stood at the entrance of the portal, Talitha gestured with her hand, causing the cages holding Hawk and Aelvric to be swiftly pulled from the air and into the portal. Before Elyndra could react or respond, Talitha, William and Danielle stepped into the portal, and with another wave of Talitha's hand the portal closed behind them.

"You will pay, Lepidoptera! You will pay!" shouted Queen Elyndra in frustration, as she watched the portal close.

Turning to Adeline and Summer, Elyndra said, "Find Eryndor! We need to let him know what has happened here."

CHAPTER TWENTY-ONE

In the aftermath of Eryndor's destructive rampage throughout their domain, Garrick and Elara, accompanied by a few of their powerful Griffin sons, gathered to assess the damage and begin the arduous task of restoration once again.

"Fuck, what a mess," said Garrick, as he raked a hand through his graying blond hair and looked around at the destruction throughout his kingdom.

"You're not wrong, Father," said Zephyrion.

"Let's get this chaos sorted," commanded Garrick.

"Yes", the Griffin sons all cheered loudly.

Cambray summoned lush greenery to reclaim the castle's grounds, weaving vines and roots to stabilize the structure. His brother Drakon gathered swirling winds to lift fallen debris and clear paths.

Meanwhile, Rhydian commanded tides to bring forth stone and coral from the ocean depths, shaping new foundations for damaged buildings. And Rimmer infused the soil with vitality, encouraging rapid growth to rebuild gardens and orchards.

As the Griffins worked in harmony, their parents bolstered the restoration efforts with their own elemental powers. Garrick channeled his celestial energy to mend fractured walls and roofs. Elara reached deep into her core, drawing forth precious metals and gemstones to embellish the renewed structures.

Days passed, marked by the tireless efforts of the Griffin family. Slowly but surely the castle began to rise from its ruins, transformed by the magic and determination of Griffins alike. Villagers gathered to witness the miraculous rebirth of their homes, awed by the power and unity displayed before them.

Well done, everyone. Garrick thoughts echoed throughout the Kingdom, as he looked around proudly.

Amidst the newly restored surroundings, the Griffins shared a moment of quiet satisfaction. Their collaborative spirit had transformed devastation into renewal, forging a lasting sense of camaraderie among them.

Garrick felt his phone vibrate in his pocket. Retrieving it, he noticed it was William Gramaze calling. "Hello, my friend."

"Morning, my friend. How are you going with the cleanup and repairs? Do you need any assistance?" asked William over the phone speaker as he sat at his office desk.

"No, we should be okay from here. But thank you for the offer. We've just about cleaned up the mess and destruction that Eryndor left behind. The castle took a beating, but we've repaired the damage. We're focusing on restoring the villagers' homes at the moment," replied Garrick.

"I am relieved to hear that, my friend. Any rumors circulating about Eryndor's whereabouts?" William inquired.

"None! We've tightened security just in case. How's everything in France? Any fallout from Eryndor's antics reaching your way?" asked Garrick.

"We've been fortunate here. No direct impact, but the news of Eryndor's havoc has put everyone on edge," replied William.

"I don't doubt that. My people feel the same here," said Garrick.

"I, for one, am glad that you didn't hand that chalice over to Eryndor. It could have led to disastrous consequences for all of us," stated William.

"Agreed!"

"Well, I must be going, Garrick. If you need any assistance with the repairs in Olden, please don't hesitate to ask," offered William.

"Thank you, William. I appreciate the offer. Take care, my friend. Chat again soon," replied Garrick.

"You too, Garrick. Stay safe, and let's hope for calmer days ahead," said William.

* * *

As William hung up his phone, he heard a huge explosion. *What the fuck was that?* Running at Vampire speed, he exited his office and headed toward the operations room.

Every other Lepidoptera at the Gramaze coven heard the explosion, too, and also headed toward the operations room to see what or who had dared to cause any problems for them.

"Brock, what is going on?" demanded William, as he ran through the sliding doors of the operations room.

"It looks like Eryndor is trying to break through our wards," said Brock, studying the grounds' security camera feed.

"What does this fucker want?" asked Grayson, storming into the operations room, with Michael by his side.

"I would say he wants Hawk," answered Queen Talitha, walking through the sliding doors.

"I reckon you could be right. Brock, get Garrick on the phone and tell him what is happening. I want him and Elara here, NOW! With our help, they can deal with their rogue son," demanded William.

"Yes, Sire," said Brock, picking up the operations room phone and dialing the number.

William turned around to see another eight Lepidopteras, including Princess Violette, behind him. "Talitha, Violette, we may need you both to hold our wards up while Eryndor continues his onslaught."

"Not a problem," stated Violette, her nostrils flared.

"Come on, Violette, let's work together on this," said Queen Talitha. She grabbed Violette's hand and they ran out of the operations room, toward the back of the Gramaze house, where Eryndor was situated with his glazed-eyed minions.

"The rest of you," William looked around the room at his family, "I want you all suited up and weapons ready. Go!"

They all nodded in agreement and sped off toward the weapons room.

"Sire, Garrick is on the line," Brock announced, handing the phone over to William.

William took the phone from Brock and held it up to his ear. "Garrick … you need to portal to our home. Your son, Eryndor, is causing trouble here. Heads will roll if he breaches us and the academy."

"We will arrive shortly, my friend," Garrick assured. He then ended the call and swiftly contacted his Griffin family to coordinate backup.

William slammed the phone down on its cradle. "Brock, keep an eye on that fucker. And let me know if he breaches our wards and the perimeter," commanded William.

"Yes, Sire," Brock replied calmly. He turned back to his computer screen, observing Eryndor's relentless attempts to break through the wards with each forceful slam, which vibrated the grounds within.

William ran at Vampire-like speed out of the operations room and toward the rear of the Gramaze mansion. As he reached the outside, he observed the shimmering of the invisible wards with each powerful strike from Eryndor. "Fuck!" He raked a hand through his brown hair and watched with growing concern, knowing that it wouldn't be long before Eryndor breached the wards.

William ... the legacies are taken care of, thought Violette, as she turned to see William standing behind them. *I have instructed the councillors to contact my father, so that they can portal out of here to somewhere safe.*

Thank you, Violette, thought William, as he came to stand next to Talitha and Violette, his sword drawn.

"How are we doing holding him out?" William asked Talitha as he watched Eryndor trying to break down the wards with his Harbinger of Shadows abilities.

"So far, okay. I'm not sure how much longer we can hold him off, though," replied Talitha.

William watched on as Talitha and Violette continued to extend their hands out front and focus their energy. Shimmering barriers and protective shields materialized, forming a formidable defense against the approaching threat.

"You will not stop me," yelled Eryndor from the other side of the wards. He sneered as he continued his onslaught to manipulate the elemental energies of the wards.

"You will stop this attack, Eryndor, or you will regret it," shouted William, his voice full of authority and warning.

"It is you who will regret ever crossing me, Vampire," yelled Eryndor.

Suddenly, the sky above the Gramaze mansion and academy darkened, and a deep, commanding voice echoed in Eryndor's mind. "Eryndor, enough!"

Startled, Eryndor paused mid-attack and looked up. Descending from the darkened sky were Garrick and Elara. Their presence filled the air with a palpable aura of authority and ancient power.

Garrick's voice resonated in Eryndor's mind again, cutting through the chaos. "Cease this madness, Eryndor. Your actions have consequences beyond your understanding."

"Eryndor, remember who you are, and where you come from. This path leads to destruction, not glory," said Elara, her voice gentle, yet firm.

Although Garrick and Elara knew from past experience that negotiating with Eryndor was futile, they still had to try—anything to prevent him breaking down the wards and causing destruction.

"I will not be stopped," Eryndor's voice reverberated with anger and determination. "I will show you all the power I possess!" His eyes glowed with a malevolent energy as he defiantly confronted his parents.

Before Eryndor could cause any more destruction, Garrick and Elara swooped down from the sky, landing gracefully in the Gramaze backyard beside Talitha and Violette, Talitha having tweaked the wards, allowing them safe passage onto the property. Without hesitation, Garrick and Elara combined their strength to erect powerful barriers and wards. These defenses, fortified by the unique abilities of the Lepidoptera Vampires, pulsed with energy, designed to contain and repel the surge of Eryndor's dark powers.

Eryndor soon realized that he would not be able to defeat them together. "You will pay dearly for your alliance. I will return!" yelled Eryndor defiantly. With a sharp click of his fingers, he disappeared as swiftly as he had appeared, leaving behind a lingering sense of foreboding.

Garrick shook his head in dismay as he watched Eryndor disappear, feeling a mix of anger and disappointment toward his son for embracing a path of darkness, and inflicting harm upon others.

"I am deeply sorry for the trouble that Eryndor has caused here today, William," Garrick said, his voice heavy with sincerity.

William placed a hand on Garrick's shoulder and said, "You have nothing to be sorry about, my friend."

"On the contrary … I think we do, and I think it's time we, as a family, deal with our son," said Elara, looking from William to Garrick.

"And how are you going to do that?" asked Queen Talitha, dubiously.

"Good question!" said Elara, as she shrugged her shoulders. "He has caused us nothing but pain and destruction, and I certainly don't know where to go from here."

"Maybe this is something you can talk about with your council in Glittertind?" queried Queen Talitha.

"I think you might be right there," stated Garrick. "We can certainly try."

"We are happy to help, when required. But … I am warning you both," Talitha looked from Garrick to Elara, "If your son poses any threat to my family, then I will have no hesitation in retaliating against him; even if that means killing him."

"I totally understand, Talitha. Elara and I have been trying to come up with a solution to Eryndor and his evil ways for years, and there just doesn't seem to be one. So, if that is what it takes to stop him …" He bowed his head in shame.

"Unfortunately, as parents of supernatural creatures, we have to make these decisions every now and then. I don't like it either, but sometimes it's necessary," said Queen Talitha, remembering the times she has had to kill some of her own kind, who had turned into Debauched Vampires.

Each Lepidoptera and Griffin stood around in silence and listened to what was being discussed, knowing full well the consequences of what would happen to rogue creatures.

"On a brighter note, I have some good news for you both," Talitha looked from Garrick to Elara. "I have brought back Aelvric and Hawk with me from the Fae Kingdom. The only problem is, they are still under Eryndor's mind control. I will be working with them in the next couple of days to try and free them of this," explained Talitha.

"What … Aelvric is under mind control, too? How did this happen?" asked Garrick, his brow furrowed. "We sent him to the Fae realm, to speak with Queen Elyndra about acquiring the Fae's Golden Ring."

"Oh, right. I believe William did tell you that he, Danielle and I went to the Fae realm to retrieve Hawk. You're aware of that, correct?" Queen Talitha clarified.

"Yes, we were aware that you were going to rescue Hawk, but not Aelvric. Actually, that does help to explain why Aelvric didn't return after a few days. We just assumed that it was because time moves slower in the Fae realm relative to Earth," explained Garrick.

"Queen Elyndra, who I fear is in cahoots with Eryndor, had them imprisoned in cages, which were suspended in the air. Being under mind control, they didn't stand a chance of escaping," explained Queen Talitha.

"Typical Fae; you can never trust them. Thank you for bringing our sons back safely. We really appreciate it. You say it will be a few days before they can return home?" asked Elara.

"You're welcome, my dear. And yes, I need to perform a ritual spell on them, to bring them out from under the mind control Eryndor has over them," said Queen Talitha.

"Is this something we can help with?" asked Elara. She gestured to Garrick and herself.

"I am afraid not, but thank you for asking," replied Queen Talitha. "We will contact you when Aelvric and Hawk are ready to return to your home."

"Thank you, Talitha," said Garrick.

"You are most welcome. And thank you both for coming to help with the situation here today. We are stronger together when it comes to Eryndor. Well, if I'm not needed, I will return to my chambers. I am feeling a tad weak from using my powers to try and protect our home and the academy. So, I will bid you both farewell," said Queen Talitha.

"Goodbye, Talitha," said Elara.

Garrick bowed his head to Talitha and smiled.

"Violette, you will join me in my chambers," commanded Queen Talitha.

"Yes, my Queen," said Violette, rushing over to Talitha's side. Linking their arms, they walked side by side toward the Gramaze mansion. Violette was also weary from helping to protect her family today, and was glad to be going inside to recuperate.

"Do you need a portal home, or are you able to conjure one yourselves?" William asked Garrick and Elara.

"Thanks, William, we should be okay to get home by ourselves," replied Garrick.

Elara placed her hand out front and a portal opened in front of them.

"Thank you for coming," said William, as he looked from Garrick to Elara. "I will be in touch about your sons."

"No problem," said Garrick.

William watched them walk into the portal and the portal close.

"Right, let's get to the operations room and find out where Eryndor went. That bastard is going to pay for what has transpired here today," said William to Grayson and Michael.

"Yes, Sire," they both said together, and followed William inside.

CHAPTER TWENTY-TWO

Chained to the cold concrete floor of the Gramaze coven's dungeon, Hawk and Aelvric found themselves ensnared in more than just physical bonds. The dimly lit chamber echoed with their attempts to break free from the forbidding shackles that held them fast. Both were still under the influence of Eryndor's mind control, and their thoughts were not entirely their own.

Hawk's usually sharp eyes were clouded with a distant longing for not only Sully, but also his home. "We must find a way out of here, Aelvric. I can't stand another moment under Eryndor's control. My mind feels fogged, and chained to Eryndor's will."

"I hear you, Hawk. We must resist, and break free from Eryndor's hold," Aelvric urged, his voice tinged with defiance. "I too miss the open skies, and our home in Olden Fjord."

In the depths of the dungeon, where shadows danced ominously against the walls, their whispered conversations held a glimmer of hope; a determination to reclaim their minds and their destinies from the clutches of Eryndor's mind control, even if only for fleeting moments, filled Hawk and Aelvric with a profound sense of empowerment.

"Someone's coming," whispered Aelvric, hearing the lock on the cell door unlock.

Hawk and Aelvric watched as Queen Talitha and Violette walked into the dungeon and came to stand in front of them.

"Ah, good, you're both awake," Queen Talitha remarked, her gaze shifting from Hawk to Aelvric.

"What do you want with both of us," Aelvric questioned, his eyes momentarily glazed over again.

"I don't want anything from either of you. In fact, it is you who will require our help," Queen Talitha replied calmly, her expression unreadable in the dim dungeon light.

"I doubt that! Where is Eryndor?" asked Hawk, his eyes glazing over. "And why are we chained up here."

Queen Talitha read their minds and realized that Hawk and Aelvric were oblivious to their location, and the reasons behind their captivity.

With a flick of her hand, Talitha conjured the ancient book, which previously had helped to break Albinus's mental bonds with Eryndor. Flicking through the pages, she located the spell.

Taking up a strategic stance, Talitha and Violette clasped hands and they began chanting the incantation. The atmosphere crackled with a blend of ancient magic and the potent energy imbued with the essence of the undead Queen and Princess.

> By the blood that flows through night,
> Within shadows, deep and tight,
> I command the chains to break,
> Free these minds, no more to take.

The dungeon thrummed with a subdued energy and Hawk and Aelvric, who were ensnared by Eryndor's control, felt a faint spasm rippled through them as the mystical energies commenced their careful work. Talitha and Violette's fingertips emitted a soft, ethereal glow, and with each gesture, they directed the arcane energies to unravel the threads of mind control that Eryndor had woven.

As the last fragments of Eryndor's control began to dissipate, lucidity returned to Hawk and Aelvric.

"Welcome back!" said Violette, watching the oppressive darkness lift, and be replaced by a newfound clarity and awareness.

"Head Chancellor?" stated Hawk, recognizing Violette's face from the academy.

"How are you feeling?" asked Violette.

"Still a bit foggy, but okay," replied Hawk.

"Where the hell are we?" asked Aelvric, looking around at the dimly lit dungeon.

"You are in Bagnolet, France … my home," explained Talitha.

"Why are we shackled?" asked Aelvric.

Talitha clicked her fingers to unshackle them both from their binding chains. "For your own safety."

Both Griffins rubbed their wrists and rose to their feet.

"Do you both remember what has been transpiring, since you have been under mind control from Eryndor?" asked Talitha.

"Some of it," replied Hawk, remembering back to when Eryndor first appeared in Saint Lucia.

"Nothing! The last thing I remember is going to visit the Fae Kingdom," said Aelvric.

"Well, it seems you have a lot to catch up on. Do you both feel up to traveling by portal home to Olden Fjord?" asked Talitha.

"Yes, that is fine with me. The sooner, the better," stated Aelvric, enthusiastically.

"If it is okay with you, Head Chancellor, I would like to return to the academy," said Hawk.

"That is okay with me, but I am sure your parents won't agree," said Violette.

"Right now, I don't care what they want. I need to see Sully. She is alive, right?" Hawk gulped hard.

Violette nodded yes and smiled. She knew from experience what it felt like being away from your life partner, and how much you longed for not only their touch, but their scent too.

"Let's get you sorted with a shower, clean clothes and some sustenance, first," said Talitha. "Come this way!" She gestured toward the cell doorway.

Hawk and Aelvric followed Queen Talitha out the door and up the concrete stairs, to the Gramaze coven household, and Violette followed closely behind.

* * *

As Hawk walked into the bathroom, he wasted no time in shedding his clothes, discarding them to the floor. Naked and unburdened, he stepped into the warm embrace of the shower.

Closing his eyes, he lost himself in the rhythm of the spray against his skin. The hot water cascaded down his back, and seemed to soothe his mind, and the steam enveloped him, leaving him feeling like he was in a private sanctuary within the tiled walls.

Just as he began to relax into the ritual of cleansing his body, a voice suddenly pierced through that tranquil moment.

Hawk! The voice that echoed in his mind was insistent and dark.

Hawk eyes quickly flitted open and he looked around the bathroom, unsure if he had imagined it. Turning off the water, his senses were suddenly heightened. The bathroom was silent except for the faint patter of droplets from the shower. Wrapping a towel around his waist, Hawk stepped out cautiously, his bare feet meeting the cool tiles.

"Who's there?" he called out, his voice echoing slightly in the tiled space.

No reply came. He glanced around, the steam thinning to reveal a bathroom that seemed empty and ordinary. But then, as if from the shadows, the voice spoke once more.

Join me, Hawk, the voice urged. *Together, we can wield unimaginable power.*

"No, I will never join you," Hawk replied defiantly, realizing it was Eryndor calling him. "I will not succumb to you, Eryndor." Hawk clenched his fists. He remembered all too vividly the havoc Eryndor had wreaked, and the lives he had destroyed, the pain he'd inflicted. Hawk could not allow himself to be a pawn in Eryndor's dark game any longer.

Hawk, Eryndor's voice whispered, now a chilling presence in his mind. *You cannot hide forever. The world awaits our reunion.*

Get the fuck out of my head, Eryndor, thought Hawk.

Hawk swiftly changed into fresh clothes and stormed out of the bathroom, refusing to let fear or coercion control him. As he left the bathroom behind, the memory of Eryndor's haunting voice still lingered, a constant reminder of the danger that lurked in the shadows. Hawk knew he had to stay vigilant, to steel himself against the darkness that sought to consume him. But he was determined, come what may, that he would not yield to Eryndor's malevolent call.

"You are safe here, Hawk," said Violette, as she walked toward him. She had also heard Eryndor's mental intrusion directed at Hawk. "Eryndor can't get to you while you're protected by the wards."

"Thank you, Head Chancellor. I appreciate everything you are doing to keep me safe," Hawk expressed gratefully. "Has Aclvric returned to Olden Fjord yet?"

"Yes. And I have spoken with your parents and they are happy for you to stay at the academy; that's if you still want to," queried Violette.

"I would really like that. Thank you. Do you think it would be possible for me to slip back into training the younger legacies?" enquired Hawk. He previously had enjoyed this, and it had given him a sense of purpose in life.

"Of course, Hawk," Violette replied with a warm smile. "We would be delighted to have you back in the training sessions with the younger legacies. Your expertise and guidance will be invaluable to them."

"Great! Am I allowed to visit Sully?" asked Hawk.

"Certainly! I believe she is currently downstairs in the kitchen. Come on, I will show you where it is," said Violette.

"Thanks!" replied Hawk, excited at the prospect of seeing his life partner again.

"Come this way," gestured Violette.

Hawk smiled and followed her down the stairs to the back of the house.

* * *

"Thanks, Lamiae, but I'm not that hungry," said Sully, pushing the plate of pancakes away from her.

"Everything alright, my dear?" queried the cook.

"I'm a bit concerned about Hawk, that's all," replied Sully, who was sitting at the kitchen island bench, with her back to the doorway.

"No need to worry, my dear," Lamiae reassured, motioning for Sully to turn around.

Sully turned in her swivel seat and found Hawk standing in the doorway, "Hawk!" She ran over to him and placed her arms around him. "I have missed you."

"And I've missed you, too," Hawk replied, his voice filled with longing and affection. As he held her close, he gently lifted her chin, drawing her face closer to his and tenderly kissed her lips, conveying his deep feelings in that intimate moment.

As Sully pulled away slowly, she gazed into Hawk's bourbon-colored eyes and smiled. "Let's go out to the backyard. We can probably get some privacy there."

He nodded, placed his hand in hers and they walked out of the kitchen, to the covered area in the backyard.

Lamiae smiled as she continued to clean the kitchen benchtop. *Young love ...*

CHAPTER TWENTY-THREE

"It's so good to finally be able to speak with you, without Eryndor in my head, or the mind control taking over," said Hawk to Sully, as they sat on the outdoor double chair beneath the patio's shade.

"I didn't think I was ever going to see you again," stated Sully, as she placed her hand in his. "How are you feeling?"

"I'm okay," answered Hawk, as he tucked a lock of Sully's deep red hair behind her right ear, his eyes tracing every contour of her face.

"Truthfully?" asked Sully, reading his thoughts.

"It's Eryndor. I'm a bit worried that he will be able to break through the wards and come for me. I … I don't want to be controlled by him ever again," Hawk confided, his tone tinged with concern and vulnerability.

"Don't worry, Eryndor can't break the wards that are currently up around the Gramaze property. Violette has assured me of this. You are safe here, Hawk," Sully reassured, running her left hand down the side of his face, her gaze fixed lovingly on his endearing eyes.

"But, for how long? I think Eryndor has a lot more reach than we have anticipated." Hawk took a deep breath and sighed.

"What makes you say that?" asked Sully.

"Earlier, when I was in the shower, Eryndor managed to enter my thoughts and speak to me," Hawk admitted with a sigh. "I just can't seem to break free from his influence."

"Shit, really?"

"Yeah. The Head Chancellor told me that she heard Eryndor talking to me, but she said not to worry about him, as he can't get to me while the wards are up. Still, I'm starting to have doubts," Hawk admitted, his tone reflecting a mix of uncertainty and apprehension.

"I'm sure she knows what she's talking about. After all, she is the Lepidoptera Princess, with formidable abilities, and quite capable of giving Eryndor a run for his money, if you know what I mean," said Sully.

"I hope you are right. I just wish Eryndor would stay out of my head. It's like he thrives on my misery. I wish I knew how to stop the mind-chatter he imposes on me," said Hawk, the frustration evident in his voice.

"I'm sure he will eventually give up, especially when he can't physically get to you," stated Sully.

"Anyway …" Hawk took a deep breath in, then out, "I wanted to apologize."

"For what?" asked Sully, her brow furrowed.

"For punching you and knocking you unconscious at Olden Fjord. You can't imagine how much that ate me up inside. But please believe me when I say I wasn't in control of my actions at that time," Hawk pleaded, his eyes searching hers for forgiveness and understanding.

"Hawk, I already knew that," Sully said, watching his face with empathy. "I could feel it in our connection. And believe me when I say—if you ever do that again, you'll be the one on the ground, not me." She looked at Hawk with a serious expression before breaking into a smile, letting him know she was only teasing.

"Humph!" Hawk smiled and leaned in to kiss her tender lips.

As Sully kissed him back, she felt a sense of relief, knowing that her life partner was safe, and here with her.

* * *

"Come!" said William, hearing a knock on his closed office door. As it opened, he watched Albinus and Xanthia walk through the doorway toward him.

"We were wondering if you are free for a chat?" queried Albinus, now standing in front of William's desk, with Xanthia by his side.

"Take a seat," said William, gesturing to the two chairs in front of his desk. "What's this about?"

"Firstly, I wanted to thank you and your family for looking after Xanthia, while I have been gone. And for helping me to return to Xanthia. I am forever in your debt, Mr. Gramaze," stated Albinus.

"You're welcome. But, please, call me William. We are all on a first-name basis around here. Was there something else?"

"Yes," Albinus hesitated for a moment and continued. "If you are in agreement, I would like to take Xanthia back to our home in Paris," stated Albinus.

"You are both free to leave whenever you want to, and I am sure you're both wanting to get back to some sort of normality," said William, looking from Albinus to Xanthia. "But there is something you need to know."

"What's that?" asked Albinus.

"After your … supposed passing, your estate was liquidated to settle outstanding debts. It was a regrettable situation, and unfortunately there is nothing left of your home or belongings," replied William.

Albinus's brows furrowed in disbelief. "Everything … gone?" he repeated softly, as though saying it out loud might make it less true. A shadow of loss settled over him, and for a brief moment he looked as though the foundation of his identity had been shaken.

"I'm afraid so," William replied, his tone sympathetic. "But please understand, we did what we could to ensure Xanthia's well-being. She has been under our care ever since."

"He is telling the truth, Father. The day I went to collect my clothes and things from the house, the debt collectors were already there taking everything, and there was a for sale sign out the front," explained Xanthia.

Albinus nodded slowly, at the realization that everything he had worked so hard for was gone. "I see …"

"We may not have our old home or some of our possessions, but at least we are together, Father," Xanthia's voice was soft but resolute.

"Yes, I agree, my child," said Albinus.

"You are welcome here, Albinus. Consider this your home for as long as you need," said William.

"I appreciate your offer of hospitality, William. If this mansion is indeed our refuge for now, then we will make the most of it. Thank you," said Albinus, with a mixture of gratitude and concern in his eyes. "So … would I be right in assuming that I can't return to my place of work, either?"

"Correct. They think you have passed. In fact, everyone thinks you are deceased. We will need to look at getting you a new identity, if you ever feel the need to leave us," stated William.

"Oh, right!" said Albinus, now coming to realize the implications of what life ahead of him and Xanthia would be like, if they left the Gramaze mansion.

"In the meantime, I will arrange for one of our family members to procure clothing for you that meets your specific preferences," offered William.

"You are most gracious. But what can I do to repay your kind gesture?" asked Albinus.

William pondered how best to integrate Albinus into the Lepidoptera Vampire coven's operations. He believed in utilizing each individual's strengths to benefit the coven as a whole. "I understand you have experience in the ammunition industry. While our needs differ somewhat, your skills could be quite useful to us in other ways. I could offer you a position within our operations. Your knowledge of weaponry and defense mechanisms could be adapted to suit our unique needs here at the Gramaze mansion."

Albinus listened intently, intrigued by the prospect of contributing in this unfamiliar world. "Maybe!"

"Of course, we also have a variety of other tasks that may be more aligned with your interests and abilities. For instance, maintaining our grounds and overseeing various aspects of our estate could be well within your capabilities," added William.

Albinus nodded thoughtfully, considering the possibilities before him. The idea of utilizing his skills in a new, supernatural context intrigued him.

"Additionally, we have technical aspects of our operations that require attention. If you are proficient with computers or technology, that could also be an area where you could contribute significantly. We value the unique perspective you bring," William concluded, his tone reassuring.

Albinus nodded gratefully, and his mind raced with thoughts of this unexpected opportunity. While the world he once knew had vanished, a new chapter beckoned, a chance to adapt, contribute, and perhaps find purpose once more, within the enigmatic world of the Lepidoptera Vampire coven.

"Together, we can find a role that suits you best and allows you to thrive within our coven; that's if you end up staying with us," stated William, leaning back in his chair.

"Thank you, William. What you're offering is a lot to take in. May I have a few days to think about this, and get back to you on my decision?" Albinus replied, his voice reflecting a mix of gratitude and contemplation.

"That will be fine, Albinus. And in the meantime, enjoy the time with your daughter," said William, standing. He looked from Albinus to Xanthia.

Rising to her feet, Xanthia mouthed the words *Thank you* to William and offered a warm smile.

William nodded in acknowledgment.

Albinus rose to his feet and extended his hand toward William, offering it for a handshake.

Shaking his hand back, William bid them farewell and then watched them walk toward the doorway.

136

CHAPTER TWENTY-FOUR

Since Garrick and Elara had returned to Olden Fjord from Bagnolet, things had been quite busy with the rebuilding of their Kingdom, and there had been no sign of Eryndor in the last few days.

Where are you, Eryndor, and what are you planning? thought Garrick, as he stood in the bay window of his office, looking out over the starlit night skies that illuminated the inky waters of Olden Fjord.

Garrick and Elara ... you are summoned to our chambers, thought a councillor from Glittertind.

Elara, who had also heard the request from the councillors, burst through the wooden door of Garrick's office, leaving it wide open, and rushed over to him. "Are you ready to go, Garrick?"

"Yes, my love. Let's get this sorted out, once and for all," replied Garrick with determination. He placed his hand in hers and, within seconds, they were standing at the limestone rock formation, waiting for the secret passage to the Glittertind council chambers to open.

Place your hand on the rock, they heard a deep voice say.

Garrick and Elara both did as they were instructed and watched the door-sized hole open inward.

Come ...

As Garrick and Elara walked inside, the door closed behind them, and the moon shining in above them lit up the chambers. The narrow passageway ahead of them had limestone rock walls lined with the skulls of all the sacred Griffins who had gone before them.

Keep moving ...

Garrick and Elara quickly navigated the corridor that was bordered by rows of limestone rock cells, each one empty of prisoners behind its open bars and windowless walls, all thanks to their son's successful efforts in aiding their escape.

When they reached the end of the passageway, there was a round, open room in front of them, where all the councillors were standing.

Sit ...

One of them indicated to a seat, which was on a limestone wall beside them.

Garrick and Elara did as they were instructed.

Why have you requested a meeting with us?

The councillor's spectral maw did not move, but you could plainly hear one of them speak in a deep commanding voice to Garrick and Elara.

"We wanted to speak with you about our son, Eryndor," replied Garrick.

Yes ...

"Each time we cross paths with Eryndor, he seems to be getting stronger, so how are we going to stop our malevolent son?" asked Garrick, as he looked at each of the eight cloaked councillors.

The councillors communicated telepathically, while Garrick and Elara waited patiently for an answer.

He is to be stopped at all costs, even if it means eliminating him. And we are sure you both know what the solution is. Do we need to spell it out for you, Garrick and Elara?

"We understand what needs to be done, but what remains unclear is how we will accomplish it. Eryndor has grown significantly stronger than before," Elara responded.

Our patience is running thin. Just deal with him ... Was there anything else you wanted to know?

"Have you hidden the chalice, and is it safe?" asked Garrick. "I mean, we went to a lot of trouble to get that artifact."

Of course it's safe. How dare you question us. This meeting is over. Begone, NOW!

He waved his hand toward the entrance.

The earth under them rumbled, and dust from the limestone formations rained down on them. Garrick grabbed hold of Elara's hand and they ran toward the entrance of the councillors' chambers.

As Elara looked behind her, she watched each councillor, one by one, huddle together, and form one body.

When they reached the secret doorway, Garrick and Elara placed their hands on the wall, and the limestone rock opened for them to escape.

"Well, that was a bloody waste of time. Let's get the hell out of here," said Garrick to Elara. He clicked his fingers for their return to Olden Fjord castle.

"What should we do about Eryndor?" Elara asked Garrick, as they materialized back in the castle office.

"It's certainly a challenging dilemma. Banishment to hell risks his return, and imprisonment has proven ineffective as he always escapes. It appears, as the council suggested, that our only viable solution is to eliminate him."

"I'd hoped we wouldn't reach this point. The last thing I want is to be the one who takes Eryndor out—but what choice do we have? Maybe someone else he pushes too far will deal with him. If not, it's going to be on us," stated Elara, shaking her head.

Elara and Garrick heard a knock at the office door.

"Come!" said Garrick.

"Sire … you have a visitor," said the soldier, standing to attention.

But before Garrick could ask who the visitor was, she burst through the doorway.

"Get out of the way, soldier," said Stjernefrída, Mother Goddess of all the stars, who was dressed in a flowing gown made of the finest midnight-blue silk, which shimmered like a thousand stars. She pushed the soldier aside and walked toward Garrick and Elara.

"What can we do for you?" asked Garrick, as he watched the Goddess walk toward them.

"I believe we have some business to discuss," stated Stjernefrída, coming to stand in front of Garrick and Elara. She placed her hands on her hips, the movement drawing attention to the bodice of her dress, which accentuated her divine figure.

Leave us, soldier, thought Garrick.

The guard nodded toward Garrick and closed the door behind him.

"Please, have a seat, Stjernefrída," Garrick said, motioning toward a comfortable lounge area.

"What would you like to discuss with us?" asked Elara, taking a seat on the lounge across from Stjernefrída.

"I see the Golden Chalice has been moved. What prompted this change?" asked Stjernefrída.

"The Glittertind councillors thought that it would be best kept safe with them," replied Garrick, sitting next to Elara.

"You haven't answered my question!" stated Stjernefrída, her brown eyes searching their faces.

Elara gulped hard and looked at Garrick.

"Our son, Eryndor, is attempting to obtain the chalice for malevolent purposes. He already possesses the Twin Icefire Blades, and we are determined to prevent him from acquiring any more sacred objects," replied Garrick.

"And you think that the chalice is safe with the councillors?" questioned Stjernefrída.

"We think that this will be the last place that Eryndor will look for it. And besides yourself and the councillors, Elara and I are the only ones who know the chalice is in Glittertind," said Garrick.

"Right! Am I correct in surmising that the chalice is still inside the mystical book?" queried Stjernefrída. She pushed a thick strand of her black hair behind an ear, as she remembered the spell she had cast many years ago, to conceal the Golden Chalice inside of the book.

"Yes, Goddess, you are correct," answered Garrick.

"And what are your intentions for Eryndor?" asked Stjernefrída, picturing the Harbinger of Shadows in her mind.

"At this point, we have no choice other than to eliminate him." The weight of this decision hung heavy upon Garrick's shoulders, casting shadows across his troubled expression. Contemplating the notion of extinguishing his adopted son's life tugged at the deepest recesses of his conscience, prompting a cascade of conflicting emotions to surge within him. Memories of his promise to Eryndor's dying parents—his vow to protect the boy and watch over him—surfaced without warning, a bitter reminder that now cut deeper than any blade.

"I understand," remarked Stjernefrída, acknowledging the difficulty of making such a decision.

"This is not something we *want* to do, but something we *must* do to keep our world safe from destruction, Stjernefrída," Elara said, her brow furrowed.

"I agree! Did you know that Eryndor and Elyndra are working together to acquire the chalice?" queried Stjernefrída.

Garrick turned to face her. "We knew that Eryndor had been to see Elyndra, but we didn't know she was now helping him. I am not surprised, especially as Fae can be quite tricky and deceitful."

"I believe, from the rumors, that Eryndor has promised Elyndra limitless power, and access to other realms, if she helps him to acquire more artifacts," stated Stjernefrída.

"We cannot allow them to succeed," Garrick declared, determination flashing in his eyes. "We must thwart their plans at any cost, for the sake of our world and all who inhabit it."

"I agree! We will do whatever it takes to stop them, even if it means facing them in battle," stated Stjernefrída, rising to her feet. "Do you have the resources to stop them, though?"

"Yes. We now have many allies who are willing to help us," replied Garrick.

"Great. I think we need to come up with a plan—just in case Eryndor returns or, worst-case scenario, he finds me and forces me to help him extract the chalice from the book," said Stjernefrída.

"Good idea," said Elara, standing. "I think if we could possibly pool our resources, then we may have a chance to defeat Eryndor and Elyndra."

That night, Garrick, Elara and Stjernefrída convened in solemn council, their minds entwined in the hope of devising a plan—though none of them were certain it would be enough to stop Eryndor and Elyndra's malevolent schemes.

CHAPTER TWENTY-FIVE

Several weeks had passed since Hawk's return to the academy. Among the echoes of recent turmoil, a semblance of tranquility had begun to settle. Despite Eryndor's relentless attempts to breach the protective wards and reclaim Hawk, the academy had stood firm, and its defenses were unyielding.

Amidst this newfound stability, Hawk resumed his duties with renewed vigor, dedicating himself once more to the mentorship of the academy's young legacies. With each passing day, he nurtured their burgeoning talents, guiding them along the path of mastery.

"That will be all for today, everyone." said Hawk, his authoritative voice echoing throughout the training chamber, commanding attention from the twelve young legacies gathered before him. As his gaze swept over each of them, he observed a mixture of exhaustion and determination reflected in their expressions.

With a sense of purpose, the twelve young legacies dispersed, acknowledging his authority with respect, and headed for the showers.

Hawk carefully placed his Khopesh sword on the wall. As he gazed around the training and combat room, he noted the banners emblazoned with the academy's crest, and historical artifacts from various eras. The room exuded an air of reverence for the past. The scent of leather and a faint tang of polished metal mingled in the air, hinting at the countless hours of training that had previously taken place within the walls.

"Care to share?" Violette interjected. She had been observing Hawk for a few moments, and couldn't help but notice his guarded demeanor against any telepathy.

Hawk turned to see Violette standing behind him and grinned. "Good morning, Head Chancellor. Actually, I enjoy training the young legacies. Every time I step into the training room, I feel alive, knowing that I have the opportunity to shape these young warriors into something greater. It's not just about teaching them how to wield a sword or defend themselves, it's about instilling in them the values of honor, courage and discipline. Seeing their growth, their determination, it fills me with a sense of fulfillment that I can't quite put into words."

"I'm glad you have found your niche, Hawk. It's clear that you pour your heart into what you do, and the results speak for themselves. They're lucky to have you as their mentor," said Violette.

"Thank you, Head Chancellor," Hawk acknowledged respectfully. "Is there anything I can assist you with this morning?"

Violette gestured toward the doorway.

Hawk spotted his parents standing in the doorway and smiled. "Mother, Father!" he exclaimed warmly, bowing in respect to them, as they walked toward him.

"Rise, Son," said Garrick solemnly, his voice carrying the weight of authority and paternal warmth.

Hawk did as he was instructed. "Why are you here?"

"We need you to return home with us," answered Elara.

"I understand your wishes, but I don't want to return to Olden yet," stated Hawk, firmly.

Elara's brow furrowed in concern, while Garrick's expression remained unreadable.

"I have found my path here at the academy. I am learning invaluable skills, not just in combat, but in leadership and honor. I believe I have a duty to fulfill, not only to myself but to our people and the academy. I wish to continue my training here, to become the best warrior I can be," stated Hawk.

There was a moment of tense silence as his parents absorbed his words. Hawk held his breath as he waited for their response.

"We have had nothing but good reports about your progress, my son. And today we have witnessed your dedication to training the younger legacies, which has reaffirmed our belief that you've matured significantly. However, we need you to return home," said Elara, gently.

"Returning to Olden Fjord now would mean abandoning all that I have worked for, all that I have become. My deepest desire is to honor you both, to carry forward our traditions and principles. However, I genuinely believe that staying here to further my training is the most effective way to do that," Hawk asserted, meeting their gazes with unwavering sincerity. "Please, have confidence in my decision-making. Trust that I am following the path that aligns best with our family's values."

"Son, we only want what's best for you. If your heart lies here, then we will support your decision," replied Garrick, his eyes reflecting both pride and understanding.

"Thank you." Relief flooded through Hawk as he embraced his parents. He was grateful for their understanding and support. Though the road ahead would be challenging, Hawk knew he was where he belonged, at the academy, forging his own destiny. "And to be honest with you both, I think I would be a lot safer here, than Olden, where Eryndor can easily mind control me."

"You could be right there, Hawk," interrupted Violette, who had been standing on the sidelines listening to the conversation. "We are more than happy to have Hawk stay with us."

"Thank you, Princess Violette," said Garrick.

"Yes, thank you, Head Chancellor," said Hawk.

"Well, if there is nothing else, could I offer you some morning tea?" asked Violette.

"That would be lovely, dear," said Elara. She turned to Hawk and said, "We will see you again, Son, before we leave." She leaned in to give him a hug.

"Yes, Mother," said Hawk, hugging her back. As he pulled away, he looked at Garrick and placed his hand out front. "Father!"

Garrick shook his hand and smiled, knowing that their son, who was next in line for the throne, was finally starting to mature, and that their decision to send him to the academy had been a good choice.

"Come this way." Violette gestured toward the doorway.

Garrick and Elara followed Violette toward the back of the house, through the tunnels, and to the Gramaze residence.

* * *

Sully, who has been exercising and training in another part of the training and combat chambers, watched her life partner, Hawk, walk into the room, position himself under the chin-up bar, discard his shirt to the floor, and start training. The sight of his strength and determination, combined with the physical exertion and the display of toned muscles, stirred a powerful attraction within her.

Like what you see? teased Hawk, who had been listening to Sully thoughts.

What's not to like? thought Sully playfully. She smirked at him as she continued to do her leg squats.

Are you free later on? thought Hawk, as he pulled himself up and down on the chin-up bar.

I have another class in a few minutes, but I might be able to catch up with you just after lunch. Would that work with your schedule? thought Sully.

Sounds great. I miss you, babe. What about if we meet in the cathedral tower? asked Hawk.

It's a date. I'll see you later, replied Sully telepathically, as she walked toward the open doorway. Since Hawk had returned to the academy and resumed his training with the young legacies, Sully hadn't spent much time with him. *I miss you, too.*

Hawk's gaze shifted toward the open doorway, and a smile formed on his lips as he spotted Sully returning his smile, before she passed through the doorway.

CHAPTER TWENTY-SIX

Sire, Eryndor is outside our front gates, again. What would you like me to do? asked Brock, telepathically, as he continued to monitor the security cameras outside the Gramaze mansion.

I will be there in a few seconds, replied William, as he ran at Vampire speed toward the operations room.

"That fucker just doesn't give up, does he?" stated William, as he walked through the glass sliding doors and stood next to Brock at his computer.

"He seems to be chanting some sort of ritual. What would you like to do?" asked Brock.

"We need to get rid of this fucker, once and for all," declared William authoritatively, as he watched the monitor up on the wall.

"Sire, that looks like some of the legacies from the academy." He pointed to the screen. "What the hell are they doing at the front gate and, for that matter, how did they even get from the academy to the mansion grounds?" asked Brock, watching the young legacies stop in front of the gate.

"There …" said William, pointing to the screen. "Look at their glazed-over eyes … they are under mind control. How in the hell did that happen?" He raked a hand through his hair. "We have wards up to stop this. Verify that they are still up."

Brock did as he was instructed.

* * *

"Enter!" commanded the Lepidoptera Queen, when she heard a knock on her door.

Princess Violette stepped into the Queen's room, which was nestled in the depths of the Gramaze mansion's basement. With genuine humility, she bowed her head and gracefully lowered herself to one knee, every gesture resonating with profound respect.

"Rise!" commanded Queen Talitha. "How can I help, Violette?"

"Do you feel that something has changed?" asked Violette.

"Can you be a bit more specific," replied Talitha, her brow furrowed.

"The atmosphere around the house … it's changed somehow. It's as if we're suddenly vulnerable, exposed. I can't quite put my finger on it. Do you sense it too?" Violette inquired.

Queen Talitha closed her eyes and listened for the familiar sounds that usually came from the house. However, all she encountered was silence, instead of the usual hum. As the realization sank in, her eyes opened wide. "The wards are down. Quickly, come with me." Talitha extended her hand toward Violette, clasping hers firmly as they instantly transitioned to the operations room through a portal.

Hearing a whooshing sound behind them, William and Brock turned to find Talitha and Violette standing behind them.

"William, the wards are down," stated Talitha, her brow furrowed with concern.

"We gathered as much, my Queen," said William.

"We are vulnerable in this state. What are you doing about it and how did this happen?" Talitha demanded.

William pointed toward the operations room computer screen. "This is how."

Talitha's nostrils flared at the sight of Eryndor walking through the wrought-iron bars of the gate. "How did this happen?"

"We don't know yet. But I am about to find out," stated Brock.

"Wait! What are those nine legacies doing at the front gate?" asked Violette, recognizing them from the academy. "They are the same ones we found in that shipping container, in Singapore. What the hell is going on?" She looked to Talitha, William and Brock for answers.

"Eryndor has them under mind control, and I would say that the legacies helped him penetrate our wards," replied Brock.

Lepidopteras, heads up! We are in Protect Mode: we have a breach. I want everyone to create a surrounding barrier around the mansion and academy, NOW, commanded William telepathically, to all the Gramaze Vampires at the mansion, and currently out on missions.

Within seconds, all Lepidoptera Vampires, including, William, Talitha, Violette and Brock, surrounded both the home and academy like a dark, swirling mass. Their presence cast a shadow over the surroundings, and their figures loomed tall and menacing as they formed a perimeter around the buildings and the grounds, with their weapons drawn. The air was thick with an eerie silence, and their eyes glinted with anger and the anticipation of facing the enemies who dared breach the confines of their home and the academy.

"Where has Eryndor gone?" asked Talitha, standing next to William and looking around. "I don't see him anywhere!"

"No idea!" stated William.

Grayson, Michael, Kelan and Stephan, your task is to locate Eryndor. Start by searching the academy. I suspect he's after Hawk. And be careful, because he is more powerful than ever. As for the rest of you Lepidopteras, you will refrain from harming the nine legacies. However, the minions accompanying Eryndor through our gates are fair game, and they are to be exterminated, commanded William telepathically.

All present nodded in agreement with their leader's instructions.

Violette and I will assist the nine legacies, and then join the search for Eryndor, Queen Talitha communicated telepathically.

Renee, Sharina, you will accompany our Queen and Princess, ensuring their safety, commanded William.

Understood, William, Renee thought, acknowledging him.

Yes, Sire, thought Sharina.

William watched the four of them rush toward the nine legacies.

Brock ... I need you to get the Brussels and London leaders on the phone and ask them to send reinforcements for us, commanded William.

Yes, Sire, thought Brock, taking his mobile phone out of his pocket to call them.

William took his own phone out of his pocket and dialed Garrick's number.

"Yes, William!" said Garrick, abruptly answering his phone.

"Eryndor is here causing trouble and he has breached our wards. Get your butt here, NOW!" ordered William.

"Fuck! We will be there in a few minutes, my friend," Garrick assured. He ended the call and quickly contacted his Griffin family to coordinate backup for the mansion and academy.

William ended the call and slipped the phone into his pocket. Gazing ahead, he observed his Lepidoptera family engaging with Eryndor's glazed-eyed minions, each one attempting to eliminate the threat. With a sigh, he ran a hand through his tousled brown hair, the weight of responsibility evident in his expression.

"Sire … Joseph and Vincent have both said that they are sending soldiers to help us," said Brock, turning to William.

"Great!" William exclaimed, observing two portals that quickly materialized before him. From within emerged soldiers, each with their weapon of choice drawn as they walked out. William recognized them all immediately.

Lepidopteras … thank you for coming. I want you to guard both the mansion and the academy. If anyone attempts to breach our defenses, eliminate them, William commanded mentally, scanning each of their faces.

In unanimous agreement, they all nodded and swiftly dispersed equally toward the mansion and academy.

How are you going, Talitha? thought William.

We have taken the mind control off the nine legacies and are now headed to the academy with them, thought Queen Talitha.

Don't worry, William, Eryndor won't get past all of us, thought a confident Princess Violette, as she, Talitha and the nine legacies ventured into the tunnels of the Gramaze mansion that led to the academy.

Thank you. But be careful, all of you. And keep in contact, thought William.

We will, replied Violette, walking through the tunnels.

"Let's go, Brock. The family needs our assistance," William declared, his eyes fixed on the ongoing battle involving his Vampire coven.

Brock nodded in agreement, and they sprinted with Vampire speed toward the conflict ahead.

* * *

"Ah, young love. Isn't it beautiful?" Eryndor remarked sarcastically, upon discovering Hawk and Sully in the cathedral tower.

As Eryndor's voice broke the serene moment, Sully and Hawk's expressions shifted abruptly from blissful intimacy to startled surprise. Their eyes widened and they pulled apart, their features registering a mix of shock and confusion. The sudden intrusion, and Eryndor's sarcastic tone, created an instant sense of unease and apprehension.

"How in the hell did you breach the wards?" questioned Sully, her tone abrupt, as she stood to attention.

"That's for me to know, girly, and you to not find out," teased Eryndor, as he walked toward them.

Hawk pushed Sully behind him. *Stay behind me!* "What do you want, Eryndor?"

"I think you know the answer to that question, brother," replied Eryndor, cynically. "Now … either you come with me quietly, or I kill her."

"Why are you doing this?" asked Hawk, shaking his head.

"Enough of the chitchat … we will be going, little brother," commanded Eryndor, his tone firm and devoid of empathy. With a swift gesture, he placed his hand on Hawk's forehead, and Hawk was suddenly one of Eryndor's glazed-eyed minions once again.

"Stop!" screamed Sully at Eryndor, her voice filled with desperation as she attempted to push him away.

Eryndor merely scoffed, his expression cold and indifferent. With a flick of his pointer finger, he cast a forceful gesture, hurling Sully against the stone wall of the cathedral tower. The impact rendered her unconscious, her body slumping to the ground in a motionless heap.

Sully! screamed Hawk internally.

"Let's blow this joint," Eryndor remarked, his tone dripping with contempt. He then placed his hand on Hawk's shoulder and with a swift motion they vanished through a portal, reappearing at the outside perimeter of the Gramaze mansion.

* * *

"Sully!" exclaimed Grayson, when he found her unconscious body on the ground. He picked her up in his broad, muscular arms and walked toward the Gramaze tunnels.

Violette ... are you nearby? thought Grayson.

Yes, Grayson. We are in the tunnels, headed toward you, thought Violette, sensing him.

I have Sully with me, and she is unconscious. I need your healing power, thought Grayson, as he continued through the tunnels at Vampire speed. Soon enough he was standing in front of Talitha, Violette, Renee and Sharina.

"Place her on the floor," instructed Violette.

Grayson knelt down and carefully placed Sully on the floor of the tunnel.

Violette knelt beside them and placed her healing hands over Sully's body. Within seconds Sully opened her eyes.

"Sully … are you alright?" asked Violette.

Sully nodded yes, but screwed her face up as she reached for the pain that was on the right-hand side of her head.

Violette placed her hand over the same spot and healed her head.

"Thank you," said Sully, sitting up.

"You are welcome." Violette searched Sully's thoughts and memories, as she helped her stand. "Eryndor did this?

Sully nodded yes in agreement.

"Where did he take Hawk?" asked Violette.

"I don't know. The only thing I remember is Eryndor turning Hawk into one of those glazed-eyed monsters again," replied Sully, her brow furrowed

"We must return to the mansion," stated Queen Talitha, when she heard a telepathic message from William. "It looks like we are too late; William is telling me that Eryndor has Hawk, and that our family haven't been able to stop him."

"Shit!" said Violette. She knew that Garrick and Elara where not going to be happy that their boy, who was next in line to the throne, had been taken by Eryndor once again.

CHAPTER TWENTY-SEVEN

Eryndor abruptly pushed Hawk through the opening of the portal, causing him to stumble onto the deck of the ship that he was using for his headquarters.

"Where is the Golden Chalice, Hawk?" questioned Eryndor, as he floated above the deck.

"I don't know," Hawk stood to attention, with his eyes averted, as Eryndor came closer to him.

Eryndor grabbed Hawk by the throat and pushed him up against the ship's mast. The thick ropes and woven rigging that dangled like serpents from above, cast intricate patterns against the backdrop of the night sky. With his face only inches from Hawk's, he threatened, "You had better be telling me the truth, otherwise I will have no choice but to kill your bitch." Eryndor pushed Hawk to the ground and sneered.

"I … I swear, I have told you everything I know. Please, spare her. Sully is blameless in all of this," pleaded Hawk, his innocent side showing for a fleeting moment, before the glazed-eyed creature within took over his mind once more.

Eryndor's lips curled into a sinister smile, his eyes glinting with malice as he loomed over Hawk. "If you've spoken the truth, perhaps she will be spared … for now! Tell me this, then, who do I need to reach out to in order to extract that damn chalice from the book?"

"Her name is Stjernefrída, Master," Hawk responded, his voice tinged with deference.

"And where might we find this Stjernefrída lurking?" Eryndor inquired, with a tone that hinted at both impatience and intrigue.

"She resides within the depths of the ancient forest," Hawk explained, his voice steady but tinged with caution.

Help! pleaded Hawk, from the depth of his mind, as the glazed-eyed creature, who had returned, took over completely.

"Get your scrawny body downstairs, NOW!" commanded Eryndor, who had heard Hawk's cries for help.

Hawk obeyed his instructions, in fear of what Eryndor would do to him.

Eryndor turned away from Hawk, his towering figure casting a menacing silhouette against the horizon. As the first hints of dawn began to streak across the sky, a cruel smirk played across his lips, his gaze fixating on the rising sun as if challenging its authority. In that moment, an unsettling aura of power emanated from him, casting a shadow of dread.

Hmm ... luckily, I know a Shadow Dweller that lurks in the ancient forest. I'm sure he will be able to help me find this Stjernefrída, thought Eryndor.

* * *

Garrick, Elara and their soldiers materialized from their portal's shimmering vortex. As they stepped onto solid ground, their presence was met by William, who stood before them, alert.

"Where do you need us?" asked Elara, as she looked around the front lawn area of the Gramaze mansion, at all the decapitated bodies lying lifeless everywhere.

"You are too late. Eryndor has taken Hawk," stated William.

"Are you joking? It couldn't have been more than five minutes since you phoned us," Elara questioned.

"Unfortunately, no, I'm not joking. Once Eryndor breached our wards, it only took him a few minutes to find Hawk, and then he vanished with him," William stated solemnly.

"How did this happen?" Garrick inquired, his voice heavy with concern and disbelief.

"Eryndor had assistance from some of the younger legacies at the academy. Somehow, he ensnared them under his mind control, and showed them through his mind's eye how to dismantled the wards for him." William sighed heavily. "I demand to know what action you intend to take regarding Eryndor. Look at the mess he has left behind," William declared, sweeping his hand toward the grim scene of fallen bodies strewn across the front yard of the Gramaze mansion.

"William, I offer my apologies for the chaos and devastation that Eryndor has brought upon your home and people," Garrick began, his tone grave yet resolute. "I assure you, we will not let his actions go unchecked. I intend to personally address this matter and ensure that justice is served. Eryndor's betrayal will not be tolerated, and we will do everything in our power to rectify the damage he has caused."

"Your apology is appreciated, though it cannot mend the loss we've suffered," William replied, his voice tinged with sadness and frustration. "But your commitment to accountability and justice is noted. We must act swiftly to contain the damage and prevent further harm. Let us work together to confront Eryndor, and restore peace to our community."

"Agreed!" Garrick declared, extending his hand in a gesture of solidarity toward William. "Our alliance is steadfast, my friend. I pledge to devote all my efforts to heal the wounds inflicted by Eryndor's treachery."

"Thank you," William replied, clasping forearms with Garrick. "What shall we do with those who have fallen?"

He gestured solemnly toward the lifeless bodies strewn across his front yard.

"We will return them to Glittertind," Garrick replied with resolve. "The fallen soldiers will receive the honor they deserve, but for those who chose escape from the Glittertind cells, their remains will be cremated, and their spirits released to the winds."

William nodded in agreement and observed Elara conjure a portal. With a wave of her hand, Elara guided the fallen warrior's bodies through the ethereal gateway.

"After I've tended to our fallen comrades, I'll reach out to you to strategize," Garrick declared.

"I look forward to discussing this further," said William.

With determination etched upon their faces, Garrick, Elara and their soldiers strode purposefully toward the shimmering portal.

Talitha ... have the wards been reinstated? asked William telepathically, as he watched the portal close.

Yes! came Talitha's swift response, her mental voice brimming with assurance as she confirmed the wards had indeed been restored.

"Grayson, Michael, I want you to make sure there are no more glazed-eyed creatures hiding anywhere on the grounds or at the academy. We don't need any further surprises," instructed William to his second-in-command, and third-in-command, who were standing beside him.

"Yes, Sire," they both said together. They immediately set off on their mission.

William strode purposefully toward the Gramaze mansion, his steps echoing with determination, as he made his way back to the operations room to confer with Brock.

* * *

As Eryndor stepped out of the portal, he observed an ancient forest that stretched endlessly before him. Its towering trees cast long, dancing shadows that seemed to whisper secrets of ages past. Moss-covered rocks littered the forest floor, and tangled roots snaked across the ground like ancient guardians. Shafts of golden sunlight filtered through the dense canopy, dappling the forest floor with patches of light.

Confidently he floated along the winding path, his presence casting a sinister aura that seemed to amplify the darkness around him. He knew he was nearing the home of the Shadow Dweller, a being of great power and ancient knowledge.

As he ventured deeper into the heart of the forest, the air grew thick with an oppressive energy and crackled with dark magic. The sounds of the forest seemed to bend to his will, the rustling of leaves and the creaking of branches echoed his approach.

At the center of a clearing bathed in an eerie green light stood the Shadow Dweller, his form shifting and twisting like smoke in the wind. His eyes gleamed like twin orbs of obsidian, as he watched Eryndor with a mixture of curiosity and suspicion.

"Shadow Dweller," Eryndor called out, his voice echoing through the stillness of the forest. "I seek your wisdom. I seek Stjernefrída."

The Shadow Dweller inclined his head, acknowledging Eryndor's power with a subtle nod. "I know why you have come," he murmured, his voice a whisper that sent shivers down Eryndor's spine. "But the path to Stjernefrída is fraught with peril. Are you prepared to face the darkness that lies ahead?"

Eryndor's lips curled into a malevolent smile, his eyes burning with a fierce intensity. "I am," Eryndor replied, his voice a low growl that seemed to reverberate through the very depths of the forest. "Whatever challenges await, I will conquer them."

The Shadow Dweller regarded him for a long moment, his gaze piercing through the veil of shadows that surrounded them. "Very well … follow the path deeper into the heart of the forest. There you will find the answers you seek. But beware, for not all who wander into the darkness emerge unscathed."

With a final nod, the Shadow Dweller faded back into the shadows, leaving Eryndor alone once more in the ancient forest. With a sense of grim determination, Eryndor set off into the depths of the forest, his dark power pulsing with anticipation. For he knew that the path to Stjernefrída would be treacherous, but he was prepared to embrace the darkness and emerge victorious.

CHAPTER TWENTY-EIGHT

As Eryndor ventured deeper into the ancient forest, the dense canopy overhead cast eerie shadows, and whispers seemed to echo through the trees. He moved with purpose, his eyes ablaze with determination to find Stjernefrída, the elusive guardian of the sacred chalice. Along his path he encountered mystical creatures and spirits, each with a tale to tell and a warning to heed.

"Who dares tread upon these sacred grounds?" hissed a serpentine creature, its emerald scales glinting in the speckled sunlight.

"I seek Stjernefrída," Eryndor declared, his voice dripping with malice. "Tell me where she hides and I might spare your existence."

The creature recoiled, sensing the evil darkness that emanated from Eryndor. "Stjernefrída dwells beyond the River of Whispers," it hissed. "But beware, for she is guarded by spirits more ancient and powerful than you can imagine."

"Humph!" Undeterred, Eryndor pressed onward, his path fraught with obstacles and whispered warnings. As he neared the River of Whispers, three ethereal beings materialized from the mist, their eyes gleaming with ancient wisdom.

"You seek Stjernefrída?" they murmured in unison, their voices like the rustle of leaves. "She is the keeper of secrets, the guardian of that which you desire."

"Yes! Tell me where to find her," Eryndor demanded, his patience wearing thin.

But the spirits only shook their heads solemnly. "Stjernefrída will not be found by those who seek to do harm," they whispered. "Her loyalty is unwavering, her resolve unbreakable. You must tread carefully, for the consequences of your actions will echo through the ages."

As the three spirits faded into the shadows, another voice chimed in from the depths of the forest. "Stjernefrída dwells beyond the River of Lost Souls," a creature with glowing eyes whispered, its form a shimmering apparition.

Eryndor's lips curled into a malicious smile. "And what awaits me there?"

The creature hesitated before answering. "Only those who prove themselves worthy may pass. Beware, for the guardian tests all who seek her."

With a snarl of frustration, Eryndor pressed on, his heart consumed by darkness and his mind set on vengeance. He would find Stjernefrída, whatever the cost, and claim the chalice as his own.

Humph! If she dares to defy me, I will unleash hell upon her, and all she holds dear, thought Eryndor.

* * *

As Eryndor continued on his journey, it led him to the banks of the River of Whispers, where the air hung heavy with the weight of forgotten secrets and lost souls. Its waters flowed dark and silent, mirroring the starlit sky above. Across the river, nestled among the towering trees, lay the realm where Stjernefrída was said to dwell.

With measured steps, Eryndor approached the water's edge, his gaze unwavering as he surveyed the mist-shrouded shores. He could sense her presence, a flicker of ancient power hidden amidst the wilderness. "Stjernefrída," he called out, his voice carrying across the stillness of the night. "I know you're here. Show yourself."

For a moment there was only the sound of rustling leaves and the gentle murmur of the river. Then a figure cloaked in moonlight emerged from the shadows, her eyes ablaze with a primal wisdom that seemed to pierce Eryndor's very soul.

"You dare to seek me out, Eryndor?" Stjernefrída's voice was like the whisper of the wind through the trees, soft yet laden with an unyielding strength.

"I seek what is rightfully mine," Eryndor replied, his tone dripping with disdain. "The chalice belongs to me and I will stop at nothing to claim it."

Stjernefrída regarded him with a mixture of pity and defiance. "The chalice is not yours to possess," she said, her gaze unwavering. "It is a relic of power, meant to safeguard the balance of the realms. In the wrong hands, it could bring about untold destruction."

Eryndor scoffed, his anger flaring like a tempest within him. "I care nothing for your petty concerns," he spat. "Tell me where the chalice is, or suffer the consequences."

But Stjernefrída remained unmoved, her resolve unbroken. "I will not yield to your threats," she declared. "The chalice is hidden where no darkness can penetrate, and where only the pure of heart may tread."

Enraged, Eryndor lunged forward, his hand outstretched to seize her. But before he could reach her, the River of Whispers roared to life, its waters rising up to form a barrier between them.

"Enough!" Stjernefrída's voice echoed across the river, commanding and final. "Leave this place, Eryndor, or face the consequences of your greed."

Seething with frustration, Eryndor retreated. His fists clenched in impotent rage and the darkness within him churned like a stormy sea. The defiance of Stjernefrída fueled the fire of his determination, promising a reckoning that would shake the very foundations of the forest.

"Mark my words, Stjernefrída, you will face the consequences of your defiance," Eryndor declared ominously. With a snap of his fingers, a portal materialized, offering him a swift escape.

I don't think so, evil one, thought Stjernefrída, as she watched the portal close.

"Who was that dweller of evil?" Kura inquired, as she shuffled to stand beside Stjernefrída. Despite her age, Kura's steps were steady but slow, supported by a sturdy walking stick that she leaned on for balance.

"No one of any importance, Grandmother," replied Stjernefrída, calmly.

"Why did he demand the chalice?" asked Kura.

"For some nefarious purpose, I suspect. However, he won't succeed in locating the sacred chalice; measures have been taken to ensure that," replied Stjernefrída confidently.

"Be careful, my child," murmured Kura tenderly. She rested a weathered hand on Stjernefrída's cheek, offering a gentle smile to her granddaughter. Kura had been the one to look after Stjernefrída when her parents had passed away, many years ago.

"You have nothing to worry about, Grandmother. Our people and the sacred objects are secure," reassured Stjernefrída with confidence. "Come on. Let's get you back to the cabin."

With a smile exchanged between them, Kura and Stjernefrída strolled back to their cabin, their arms intertwined in a display of their close bond.

Approaching their rustic cabin, Stjernefrída and Kura observed the creeping vines and moss draping over the roof, which resembled a lush blanket. Yet, a peculiar feeling unsettled Stjernefrída as they neared. Stepping onto the small porch, she tightened her grip on Kura's arm, sensing something amiss.

"Is everything alright, dear?" Kura inquired, noticing Stjernefrída's sudden tension.

"I'm not sure," Stjernefrída murmured. She swung open the cabin's front door and ushered Kura inside, guiding her to an armchair near the crackling fire, where she settled her down gently.

"Ah … you have returned. How good of you," stated Eryndor, sarcastically, as he stepped out of the shadows, near the shelves that were lined with relic books and trinkets from distant lands.

Stjernefrída turned to see Eryndor, who was now standing on the woolen rug. "You are not welcome here, Eryndor. Leave … before I call on the guardians," commanded Stjernefrída.

"I'm afraid they won't be of much use to you. I've rendered them powerless against my illusions and distractions," Eryndor replied, with a chilling certainty.

"Guardians!" Stjernefrída called out urgently.

But there was only the crackling of the fire echoing through the room, a solemn reminder of their solitude.

"You will leave our cabin, evil dweller!" shouted Kura defiantly, as she rose to her feet.

With a flick of his hand, Eryndor silenced Kura, sealing her mouth shut, and exerted a force that pushed her back into her seat, rendering her powerless to speak or resist.

"Leave my grandmother alone." With determination blazing in her eyes, Stjernefrída attempted to distract Eryndor by flinging the room's furniture at him, with a flick of her wrist. But to her dismay, he simply waved them away effortlessly. It became evident that she was no match for the malevolent force that stood before her.

"Now … you will hand over the sacred chalice. Otherwise, your grandmother will die," said Eryndor.

"I don't have it," stated Stjernefrída, firmly, her resolve unwavering.

Kura's eyes widened in fear and she fought against her invisible restraints, in a desperate attempt to break free from her seat.

"If you don't have it, then where is the chalice?" queried Eryndor, his tone laced with impatience.

"I can't say," replied Stjernefrída.

Don't tell him anything, thought Kura to Stjernefrída.

"Can't or won't?" Eryndor twisted his wrist, cutting off Kura's air supply.

As Kura began to lose consciousness, Stjernefrída's hand shot into the air. "Stop!" she yelled.

Eryndor smirked and lowered his hand. "Now … where is it?"

Stjernefrída remained silent, as she looked at Kura's pleading eyes and furrowed brow, wondering what to do.

"Answer, or your family dies, bitch," stated Eryndor, firmly.

"I won't let you harm anyone else. The chalice is hidden where it will remain safe from your grasp," said Stjernefrída.

"Then you leave me no choice," said Eryndor, as he flicked his wrist and made Kura lose consciousness.

"Grandmother!" cried Stjernefrída, kneeling down beside her. She placed Kura's withered hand in hers. Turning to Eryndor, she said, "What have you done?"

"She is only unconscious," replied Eryndor, with contempt.

Torn by fear and anguish, Stjernefrída knew she had no choice but to embark on the perilous quest to retrieve the chalice—if only to buy some precious time. Rising to her feet, she met Eryndor's gaze. "I will travel to where it is situated, as long as you spare my grandmother's life and leave us in peace."

Eryndor quickly seized Kura from the armchair into his arms. "You have one week, bitch. Otherwise, you will never see your precious grandmother again." With a flick of his wrist they vanished into the night, leaving behind only echoes of his wicked laughter.

"Shit!" Stjernefrída took a deep breath. "Guardians, I need your help, please," she yelled.

CHAPTER TWENTY-NINE

The three mystical guardians, who were cloaked in flowing robes that seemed to shimmer and shift like the surface of the river, instantly appeared before Stjernefrída.

"Finally!" exclaimed Stjernefrída, glancing at each of the three guardian's faces, which were veiled in wisps of mist that obscured their features. She shook her head in disappointment. "Where have you been? Your presence was sorely needed when that malevolent intruder darkened our doorstep and abducted Kura." She sighed heavily.

"We deeply regret our failure to protect you and your grandmother from Eryndor's deceitful schemes. Our senses were clouded by Eryndor's illusions and we were unable to see through his deception until it was too late," replied the Guardian of the River's Source, who held a staff carved from the wood of one of the ancient trees that line the riverbanks, etched with runes of power and protection.

"Eryndor was too powerful for us, Goddess," stated the Guardian of the River's Flow. His eyes gleamed with an otherworldly wisdom, with depths seemingly endless, that were like pools of liquid silver reflecting the secrets of the creation.

"We are seeking help from other powerful mystical spirits, enchanted creatures and any allies within the realm, to aid us if this happens again," said the Guardian of the River's Destination. On his brow rested a circlet of twisted vines and delicate blossoms, woven with shimmering pearls that seemed to glow with an inner light.

"I don't want to hear excuses. It should go without saying: as guardians of the River of Whispers, your foremost responsibility is to ensure the safety of this mystical river. Each of you pledged to me many moons ago to safeguard its secrets for eternity," stated Stjernefrída, authoritatively.

Each guardian lowered their head with respect and the room was filled with silence.

"Do you think there may be a possibility of retrieving Kura, without handing over the chalice to Eryndor?" asked Stjernefrída.

"It's highly unlikely, Goddess. But perhaps we could devise a plan to create a diversion, which would allow us to infiltrate Eryndor's domain, and rescue Kura without relying solely on the chalice. It won't be easy, but with careful planning and coordination, it might be our best chance," replied the Guardian of the River's Source.

"Hmmm, that sounds like a good plan, but … there is just one problem with that … we don't know where Eryndor is holed up at the moment, and I am sure Eryndor and his minions won't hand over Kura without a fight," stated Stjernefrída. She walked over to the fireplace and watched the dancing flames.

"Indeed, locating Eryndor's exact whereabouts poses a challenge," replied the Guardian of the River's Source, furrowing his brow in thought. "And you're right, Goddess, Eryndor won't relinquish Kura willingly. However, we do possess the knowledge of Eryndor's past haunts and patterns. We could conduct reconnaissance, gather intelligence, and track any suspicious activities in known areas of his influence. As for the confrontation, we must be prepared for a battle, if necessary. Our strength lies in unity and strategy. Together, along with other allies, we can overcome even the most formidable adversaries."

"I agree! So, who are these additional allies you speak of?" asked Stjernefrída.

"Eryndor's parents, Garrick and Elara. And I am sure that they will know of others who can offer us assistance, Goddess," stated the Guardian of the River's Source.

"Then proceed and return with your findings," commanded Stjernefrída decisively.

"First, we will need to discuss with you, Stjernefrída, a potential reconnaissance strategy, and contingency plans to locate Eryndor and rescue Kura," said the Guardian of the River's Source.

* * *

"Where do we stand on locating the Cauldron, Hawk?" Eryndor inquired.

"I believe, from a reputable source, it lies within the Citadel of Shadows, which is situated in the French Alps," replied a glazed-eyed Hawk.

"Well, what are you waiting for, brother? I require the Cauldron of Chaos to orchestrate a catastrophic Armageddon that I aim to bring upon the world, and claim fame for," Eryndor smirked, relishing the idea of the havoc he was proposing to unleash.

"How will I get to the French Alps, let alone the Citadel of Shadows, Master?" asked Hawk, his mind cluttered by Eryndor's control. "I don't even know where this is in the world." He lowered his head in respect.

Eryndor clicked his fingers and a map appeared in his left hand. "Here." He handed the map to Hawk. "Once you arrive by portal, which I will create for you, you should be able to find the Citadel with this map."

Hawk took the folded map from Eryndor and spread it out on the deck. Carefully he traced his fingers over the map, his eyes following the intricate lines and symbols, until he pinpointed his destination.

"Do you have a clear understanding of how to find the Citadel now?" Eryndor asked, looming over Hawk.

"Yes, Master," stated Hawk, as he looked up at Eryndor. He quickly folded the map and stood to attention.

"Great!" Eryndor said with biting sarcasm. He snapped his fingers, and a shimmering portal crackled to life before them. "Now, begone—and don't return without the Cauldron. And remember," he added, narrowing his eyes at Hawk, "you'll need to remain in human form. No flying. We wouldn't want anyone sensing your Griffin powers." With a casual flick of his hand, Eryndor shoved Hawk toward the portal and watched him impassively step inside.

Good help is hard to find these days, thought Eryndor, as he contemplated his next move.

* * *

Hawk stepped into the shimmering portal and felt the familiar tug of magic as it transported him from the hidden ship to the heart of the French Alps. Emerging into the crisp, cold air, he found himself surrounded by towering, snowcapped peaks and dense, shadowy forests. The landscape ahead of him looked not only breathtaking, but treacherous.

Hmmm, a perfect hiding place for the Citadel of Shadows, thought Hawk.

With determination etched on his face, a glazed-eyed Hawk began his arduous search through the rugged terrain, navigating steep inclines and narrow, winding paths, through the eerie silence of the mountains, that only added to the sense of foreboding. Guided by the ancient map given to him by Eryndor, and the occasional cryptic sign, Hawk was driven by the urgent need to acquire the Cauldron of Chaos for his Master.

* * *

After two days of relentless searching, Hawk came across a secluded valley, where the imposing silhouette of the Citadel loomed against the horizon, its dark stone walls a stark contrast to the pristine white of the surrounding snow.

At last, I've found you, Hawk thought triumphantly.

A surge of determination pulsated through him as he tucked the map securely into his jacket pocket. With purpose in his stride, he made his way toward the Citadel, each step resonating with a mix of anticipation and resolve.

"Who dares to enter the Citadel?" asked a deep, dark voice when Hawk reached the building.

Hawk was suddenly stopped in his tracks. Looking around, he couldn't see a soul in sight, only the exterior of the Citadel of Shadows, which was adorned with ominous gargoyles, twisted sculptures and other macabre embellishments, that exuded a sinister appearance.

"I am Hawk," he declared, standing proudly. "I have come to collect the Cauldron of Chaos from within."

"Turn back, Griffin. For beyond these gates lies only darkness and despair. The Citadel of Shadows welcomes only those who are prepared to embrace the darkness within. Once you step across this threshold, there is no turning back, as the darkness within will consume you, and your soul will be lost to the shadows forevermore."

You obviously don't know Eryndor, then! thought Hawk.

"Your warning is acknowledged, but my path remains unchanged," stated Hawk, as he walked toward the metal gates, which had carved ornate patterns resembling snarling beasts and twisted faces, giving the impression that the gates themselves were alive with malevolent intent.

"You have been warned. Darkness awaits you!" said the deep voice.

It can't get any worse than what is happening to me now, thought Hawk.

As Hawk entered the gates, a chilly wind seemed to emanate from within, carrying muffled whispers of dark secrets and ancient curses. The air hung thick with the scent of decay, while the distant echo of howling winds and dripping water reverberated through the encroaching darkness. Stepping forward, Hawk noticed the walls suddenly burst into flickering torchlights, which cast an eerie glow that illuminated the tunnels that winded and twisted like the labyrinthine passages of a nightmare. Their walls were made from ancient stone that bore the marks of untold centuries.

Where the hell is this cauldron? thought Hawk, as he ripped a torch from the wall and continued on through the citadel.

Each tunnel he ventured down had signs of ancient rituals and arcane ceremonies, with altars and sacrificial pits hidden in the darkest recesses. Strange symbols adorned the walls, their meanings lost to time, while the occasional glimpse of movement in the shadows hinted at unseen entities that watched and waited.

As the tunnels gave way to vast chambers shrouded in perpetual gloom, Hawk came across the chamber where the Cauldron of Chaos was located. It was a place of profound darkness and malevolent power. Here, the air thrummed with an otherworldly energy, and the very fabric of reality seemed to warp and twist, as the forces of light and darkness collided.

When Hawk dashed toward the Cauldron of Chaos, he was suddenly hurled backward, landing heavily at the doorway. "What the fuck was that?" he exclaimed, rising to his feet and retrieving his dropped torch from the ground. Casting a wary glance around the chamber, he searched for any sign of what, or who, had sent him flying, but there was no soul in sight. Once more, he attempted to advance, only to be met with the same result.

How in the hell am I going to manage to not only reach the cauldron, but also get it back to the ship? Hawk wondered, his frustration mingling with a creeping sense of fear. As he observed the cauldron's massive, dark metal frame, adorned with ancient runes and intricate carvings, he realized that it would take a monumental effort to move or transport something of such immense size and weight back to the ship.

Eryndor! I've located the Cauldron of Chaos, thought a glazed-eyed Hawk, to his master.

Excellent! thought Eryndor, hearing Hawk's mind-chatter. *Are you ready to portal with it to our home?*

No, Master. I can't seem to get near it. Some sort of force is blocking me, thought Hawk. He swallowed hard and waited for Eryndor's reaction.

Eryndor, who had sensed Hawk's distress through their telepathic connection, materialized beside him. "What seems to be the issue?" he inquired, his voice a low, ominous murmur.

Hawk jumped at the sound of Eryndor's voice, and his heart raced, as he turned to face his master. "I've attempted to approach the cauldron, twice, but it seems to repel me. I can't get anywhere near it," he confessed, his voice tinged with frustration and apprehension.

"It may be because only someone with a dark heart can get near it," said Eryndor. He walked toward the cauldron with his hands outstretched, and a ripple in the air began to form. "Follow me, brother."

Hawk obeyed Eryndor's instructions, falling into step behind him as they approached the cauldron.

"She's a beauty, isn't she?" stated Eryndor, as he rubbed his bony hand on the cauldron's blackened metal surface and felt its power surge through him.

With a wave of his hand, Eryndor summoned a swirling portal, its dark energy crackling as it opened, ready to transport himself, Hawk, and the cauldron back to the ship.

"Let's go," commanded Eryndor, as he gestured for Hawk to enter the portal.

Hawk nodded and walked toward the portal.

Eryndor commanded the cauldron to enter the portal. As the formidable artifact's three sturdy legs lifted into the air, he observed that each one was intricately carved with the likeness of twisted, snarling beasts, their mouths agape in eternal menace. Smirking, Eryndor strode confidently into the shimmering portal.

CHAPTER THIRTY

"Stjernefrída!" called the Guardian of the River's Source, who stood outside Stjernefrída's home, flanked by the other two guardians of the river.

Stjernefrída, who was dressed in a suit of armor crafted from enchanted river stones and hardened leather, adorned with intricate carvings depicting flowing water and swirling currents, providing both protection and flexibility in combat, swung open her door. "Yes!"

"We've discovered Eryndor's current whereabouts," said the Guardian of the River's Source. "Our sources tell us that he is visiting the Nexus of Realms."

"Right! What makes you think he is still there, besides your sources?" asked Stjernefrída.

"We believe he is after an artifact that can only be acquired in that realm," replied the Guardian of the River's Source.

"What artifact?" asked Stjernefrída, impatiently.

"We have heard it's the Ethereal Nexus Amulet, Goddess," said the Guardian of the River's Flow.

"I wonder what he would need this artifact for?" asked Stjernefrída, her brow furrowing.

"We believe this mystical artifact can be used as a conduit, and is capable of combining the powers of objects," replied the Guardian of the River's Flow.

"Right!"

What are you up to, Eryndor? thought Stjernefrída to herself.

"Does he have Kura with him?" queried Stjernefrída.

"We don't believe so, Goddess. However, once Eryndor returns to the human realm, which can only be done via a portal, we'll be able to detect him, and track him to Kura's location," responded the Guardian of the River's Destination.

"That's if he returns to where he has Kura held captive, right?" questioned Stjernefrída.

"You are correct, Goddess. This is our only option at the moment," said the Guardian of the River's Destination.

Stjernefrída furrowed her brow in thought. "We need to be prepared for any possibility. If Eryndor returns through the portal, we must act swiftly. I want you three to ensure that our tracking spells are ready, and fine-tuned to pick up even the faintest trace of Eryndor's presence."

"Understood, Goddess," replied the Guardian of the River's Destination. "I'll have our best mages working on it immediately."

Stjernefrída's eyes hardened with determination. "Good! We must thwart Eryndor's plans and rescue Kura. Prepare your teams and I will await your signal of Eryndor's return."

"Yes, Goddess."

Stjernefrída watched the three guardians turn and walk into the ancient forest.

Time to call in some help, thought Stjernefrída. She pulled her mobile phone out of her pocket and dialed Garrick's number.

* * *

"Evening, Goddess," said Garrick, answering his phone on speaker. He looked at Elara with a questioning brow. "Everything alright your way?"

"Not really, Garrick. My Grandmother, Kura, has been taken by your son, Eryndor, and he has told me that if I don't hand over the Golden Chalice to him, then my grandmother will die."

176

"You haven't handed it over to Eryndor, have you?" Garrick asked, his tone dismissive, not even acknowledging Kura's kidnapping. The very thought of Eryndor possessing the Golden Chalice sent a chill through him. He knew it would unleash chaos across the world.

"No, I haven't. Not yet!" She shook her head in disbelief at Garrick's arrogance.

"Stjernefrída, this is Elara ... I am sorry our son is causing you so much trouble. What can we do to help?"

"Thank you, Elara. This is why I have contacted you and Garrick. We are currently monitoring the whereabouts of Eryndor and apparently he is in the Nexus of Realms, and is hunting for the Ethereal Nexus Amulet. Once he returns to our realm, we are hoping he will lead us to Kura. In light of this, I will need allies to help us. Are you willing to join us?"

"Of course we are happy to help! When do you require us to come, Goddess?" asked Elara.

"At this stage, I'm not sure," replied Stjernefrída. "The guardians are monitoring the situation. When they confirm Eryndor's return, they will follow him and hopefully he will lead us to Kura. Once we have more information, I will contact you and request your assistance," stated Stjernefrída.

"Certainly! In the meantime, would it be acceptable for two of our soldiers to come and provide you with protection?" Elara inquired.

"Thank you, Elara and Garrick, I am most grateful."

"It's the least we can do, Stjernefrída. You wouldn't be in this situation if it wasn't for our son," added Elara.

"We will send Draven and Kael to guard you, Goddess. Give them about twenty minutes to arrive via portal," said Garrick.

"I will be on the lookout for them. Thank you. I must go now to inform the guardians of their arrival, and prepare the forest for a potential threat. We'll talk soon," said Stjernefrída, bidding them a farewell.

As Garrick pressed the button to end the call, he looked at Elara and said, "I think that we would be wise to call in some reinforcements."

"Yes, I think you're right, Garrick. Let's give William Gramaze a call and see if he can assist us," said Elara. "What I am most concerned about, though, is why our son is trying to obtain the Ethereal Nexus Amulet."

"Yes, and with a magical artifact that powerful in his hands, the balance could tip drastically in his favor," replied Garrick, folding his arms across his chest. "We need to find out exactly how he plans to use it—and stop him before it's too late."

"We'll know soon enough, I'm sure," stated Elara, as she dialed William Gramaze's mobile and placed their phone on speaker.

* * *

"Guardians, show yourselves!" commanded Stjernefrída, impatiently. With a snap of her fingers the three cloaked guardians appeared before her, inside her cabin.

"Yes, Goddess!" said the Guardian of the River's Source.

"Have you found Eryndor? Or more importantly, my grandmother?" demanded Stjernefrída, with her hands on her hips.

"Eryndor is in the Fae Kingdom, but it doesn't appear that Kura is with him," replied the Guardian of the River's Source.

"What is Eryndor doing in the Fae realm?" questioned Stjernefrída, her brow furrowing.

"We are not sure, Goddess. But it does seem that he has made allies with the Fae Queen, Elyndra," said the Guardian of the River's Destination.

"Right! So where is my grandmother?" asked Stjernefrída, impatiently.

"We are not sure, yet," admitted the Guardian of the River's Destination.

"What do you mean, yet? We need to find her, NOW!"

The Guardian of the River's Destination sighed heavily. "When you summoned us, we were lying in wait, in the Fae realm, heavily hidden in the mystical forest. We were waiting to see if we could gather some information on Kura's whereabouts."

"This is ridiculous. We only have one week before that monster, Eryndor, kills my grandmother." She sighed deeply. "While you have been gone, I have enlisted two of Garrick and Elara's soldiers, Draven and Kael, to help guard me and our realm—they should be here soon," stated Stjernefrída, pulling her phone from her pocket. "I'll call Garrick and Elara to see if they can also assist you with the search in the Fae realm for Kura."

Each guardian nodded respectfully in agreement.

"Yes, Goddess," said Garrick, answering his phone. He placed it on speaker so Elara could hear.

"Is it possible for you provide some assistance with the search for Kura, in the Fae Kingdom?" asked Stjernefrída.

"Yes. Is that where our son is holding Kura captive?" asked Elara.

"We don't know. But what we do know is that Eryndor is currently there, and it looks like he is forming some sort of alliance with the Fae Queen," replied Stjernefrída.

"Humph, that doesn't surprise us," said Elara, shaking her head.

"If you give us a few minutes, we will portal with Draven and Kael to your cabin, Goddess," said Garrick.

"Thank you, Garrick and Elara. I appreciate your kindness. See you soon!" said Stjernefrída. She ended the call and turned to the three guardians. "Garrick and Elara are on their way to help you search for Kura in the Fae Kingdom, and Draven and Kael will be traveling with them to help guard our realm."

The three guardians nodded in agreement once again.

* * *

Within minutes a shimmering blue portal appeared in front of Stjernefrída's cabin, and out walked Garrick, Elara and their two soldiers.

"Thank you for coming," stated Stjernefrída, who had been waiting on her cabin's front porch. "My guardians will show you the way to the Fae realm, while I stay here to protect the ancient forest." She gestured toward them.

"Okay," said Garrick looking at the three guardians. "Draven and Kael will stay here to guard you, while we are away." He looked from Stjernefrída to Draven and Kael, who were still standing to attention.

Draven and Kael nodded in respect and agreement.

"Lead the way, guardians," commanded Garrick.

They nodded and walked toward the ancient forest, with Garrick and Elara following closely behind.

Stjernefrída watched them until they disappeared from view, then returned to her sitting room inside the cabin, while Draven and Kael took their positions outside on the porch, standing guard by her doorway.

Hopefully, they'll find Grandmother before Eryndor tries to kill her—because I won't be giving him the chalice, thought Stjernefrída, her gaze fixed on the dancing flames in the fireplace. *I can't just sit here and do nothing. Waiting around to learn the outcome is unbearable. I need to be doing something—anything. Maybe there's more I can uncover at Glittertind. There has to be a way to help.* She sighed deeply.

With a snap of her fingers, Stjernefrída conjured a portal, transporting herself to the base of Glittertind, where the chalice was hidden, to consult with the councillors.

CHAPTER THIRTY-ONE

Stjernefrída stepped out of the portal in front of the limestone rock entrance of the Glittertind council chambers.

May I enter? thought Stjernefrída to the councillors.

Place your hand on the rock. She heard a deep voice say.

Stjernefrída did as instructed and watched the door-sized hole open inward in front of her.

Come ...

Stjernefrída stepped inside and the door closed swiftly behind her, leaving a moonlit passage ahead to navigate. She took a deep breath to steady her heart.

Keep moving ...

She walked toward the limestone rock walls, lined with the skulls of ancient Griffins who had shaped history, and eventually arrived at the councillors' chambers. The interior of the chamber was dimly lit by flickering candles, casting shadows on the faces of the councillors. They sat in a semicircle, their eyes sharp and their expressions solemn, as she entered.

Sit ...

One of them indicated a seat, which was on a limestone wall in front of the councillors.

Stjernefrída did as she were instructed.

Stjernefrída, what brings you to the council of Glittertind?

"Esteemed councillors," she bowed her head slightly to each of them. "I come seeking the Golden Chalice."

Murmurs spread among the councillors.

One of the councillors raised a hand, and the room fell silent.

The Golden Chalice is a sacred artifact, protected by our ancestors and guarded by our traditions. Why do you seek it?

"It cannot fall into the hands of evil," Stjernefrída replied. "Dark forces are rising, and the chalice is their target. With its power, they could corrupt and control our lands—even the spirits of the Griffins."

What makes you think you can protect it better than we can?

Stjernefrída took a deep breath, her voice steady and filled with conviction. "I do not come to claim it for myself, but to safeguard it. I have communed with the spirits in the sacred grove—through flame and wind, they guided me here. They trust me to protect the chalice with my life. It must be kept moving, hidden from those who would use it for harm. I am but a vessel to ensure its safety."

Your words are strong, Stjernefrída. But words alone do not prove your worthiness. We know the chalice is hidden within a book, protected by enchantments that only you can break. What do you offer us in return for such a treasure?

Stjernefrída met their gazes. "I offer my service, my loyalty, and my life. I will do whatever it takes to keep the chalice safe. And if I fail, I will return to face your judgment—whatever the cost, even if it means my life."

All the councillors exchanged glances, their faces unreadable. The silence stretched, thick with tension.

Your resolve is clear, Stjernefrída. But we must test your spirit. Prove to us that you are guided by the ancestors. Prove that you are not swayed by the same darkness that seeks the chalice.

Stjernefrída nodded, understanding the gravity of the challenge. "What must I do?"

One of the councillors rose from his seat, his eyes piercing into Stjernefrída's soul. *You will enter the Realm of Shadows, where the spirits of the dead Griffins reside. Speak with them, seek their guidance. If they deem you worthy, we will grant you the chalice.*

The air grew cold, and Stjernefrída felt a shiver run down her spine. Yet, she stood firm. "If this is what I must do, then I will enter the Realm of Shadows, and return with the blessing of your ancestors."

One of the councillors raised his hands toward the ceiling, and the other councillors began to chant, their voices merging into a haunting melody. The air around Stjernefrída shimmered and the council chambers faded away, replaced by a misty, ethereal landscape. Stjernefrída was now in the Realm of Shadows, the final test standing between her and the chalice.

* * *

Stjernefrída found herself standing at the edge of a vast expanse, shrouded in twilight. The Realm of Shadows was both eerie and beautiful, with mist swirling around her feet, and shadowy figures moving in the distance. She could feel the presence of the dead Griffins, their energy palpable in the air.

Taking a deep breath, Stjernefrída stepped forward, her footsteps silent on the ethereal ground. She knew she had to seek out the spirits, to gain their blessing and prove her worthiness. As she walked, the shadows seemed to part before her, guiding her deeper into the realm.

All of a sudden, a figure emerged from the mist, tall and imposing. It was Vindthorr, the God of Storms. His eyes glowed with an intense light as he regarded her.

"Stjernefrída," Vindthorr's voice was like the rumble of distant thunder. "Why do you walk in the Realm of Shadows?"

Stjernefrída bowed her head respectfully. "I seek the blessing of the ancestors to protect the Golden Chalice. Dark forces aim to claim it, and I have vowed to keep it safe."

The Griffin's gaze bored into her, searching for any hint of deceit. "Many have claimed such intentions. What makes you different?"

"I am guided by the spirits, and I have pledged my life to this cause. I seek not power, but the preservation of balance, and the protection of our people," stated Stjernefrída.

From within the shadows, other figures began to materialize: Griffins and spirits of legendary warriors. They surrounded Stjernefrída, their presence both intimidating and awe-inspiring.

"She speaks the truth," a voice whispered, echoing through the realm. It was Valdyrós, the Griffin known for being cunning and brave. "I feel her heart is pure."

The spirits murmured in agreement.

"Very well. If you are to protect the chalice, you must understand its power and responsibility. We grant you our blessing. But know this: the path ahead will be fraught with danger. Stay true to your purpose, and you will succeed," stated Vindthorr, solemnly.

Stjernefrída felt a surge of energy as the spirits bestowed their blessing upon her. The Realm of Shadows began to fade, and she found herself back in the sacred chambers of Glittertind, the councillors' chants still echoing in her ears.

The councillors watched her return, their eyes filled with a mix of awe and respect.

You have done what many could not. The chalice will be entrusted to you once again.

One of the councillors stepped forward, holding an ancient, leather-bound book. The book was carefully wrapped in a piece of flax cloth, woven with intricate patterns that told stories of their ancestors. The natural fibers gave the package a sense of timelessness and reverence, reflecting the sacred nature of its contents. With a solemn nod, the councillor handed it to Stjernefrída.

The fate of many rests in your hands. Guard it well.

Stjernefrída accepted the package, unwrapping the flax cloth to reveal the book. Nestled within its pages, bathed in a soft, ethereal glow, was the Golden Chalice. The room seemed to hold its breath as the ancient artifact was brought into view. "I will protect it with my life," she vowed, knowing that her journey was only beginning.

CHAPTER THIRTY-TWO

Emerging from a portal into the Fae Kingdom, Garrick and Elara crept through the dense, enchanted forest. As they walked along, their forms shifted with the dappled light filtering through the canopy. The air was thick with magic; the very atmosphere hummed with the energy of the Fae. Moving silently through the forest, their Griffin presence was masked from the keen senses of the Fae Queen, Elyndra, and her subjects.

From their vantage point behind a cluster of ancient oaks, they watched Elyndra, the Fae Queen, who stood regal and commanding in the center of a clearing, surrounded by her people, and before her stood a dark figure who they knew all too well—Eryndor.

I wonder what Eryndor has promised the Fae Queen, for her to help him? thought Garrick to Elara. *Elyndra doesn't help anyone but herself and her Kingdom, unless there is something in it for her.*

I agree! Shit, Garrick, look, thought Elara, pointing toward the sky.

Garrick's eyes narrowed as he spotted Kura, the ancient spirit and grandmother of Stjernefrída. She was trapped in a cage of glowing light, suspended high above the ground, her otherworldly form shimmering with a faint blue aura. The sight of her captivity ignited a fierce protective instinct within Garrick.

"They've made a mockery of her," Elara whispered, her voice tinged with sorrow and anger. "I don't think we will be able to negotiate with Elyndra, as she clearly is aligned with Eryndor. So how will we be able to rescue Kura?"

Garrick nodded in agreement. "I think it's time to contact William Gramaze and ask him and his Vampire coven to come and help us."

"I think you are correct!" Elara replied.

At the mention of the Vampires, the Fae Forest seemed to grow darker, as if in anticipation. With a silent nod, Elara extended her hands, her fingers brushing the forest floor. The earth responded to her touch, sending a ripple of energy through the roots and trees, which send a silent summons to William Gramaze and his coven in France.

Moments later, a shimmering portal appeared before them, swirling with dark hues. From the portal emerged eight formidable Lepidoptera Vampires and four legacies from the academy, their presence commanding and enigmatic. William Gramaze, their leader, stepped forward, his eyes gleaming with a blend of curiosity and readiness for what lay ahead.

"Thank you for coming, William," said Garrick, greeting him with a handshake.

* * *

Sensing a disturbance in her Fae Kingdom, Elyndra shouted, "Who dares to enter my realm uninvited?"

"We have come for a purpose that transcends our borders, Queen Elyndra," declared William Gramaze, his voice firm and unwavering. He strode toward her, and his coven and the Griffins followed suit close behind him, their eyes sharp and their stances prepared for whatever might unfold.

Shit ... mother and father! What do they want? "I'm out of here, Elyndra," declared Eryndor, snapping his fingers to open a portal. Within seconds he had vanished.

"Cowardly fool," Queen Elyndra spat, her disdain evident as she watched him disappear.

Elyndra sisters—Aevyressa, Myrrathen and Thalara—stood alongside Queen Elyndra, embodying a formidable force. Their gazes remained steady and unwavering, silently promising committed protection. Meanwhile, other Fae skirted the area, sensing the tension in the air.

"And that purpose is?" questioned Elyndra to William.

William's eyes then flicked to the floating cage and his expression hardened into one of fierce determination, his formidable nature evident in the tight set of his jaw.

"Ah … what business is this of yours?" queried Elyndra, as she came to stand in front of William, Garrick and Elara.

"You will release Kura to us, NOW!" demanded William.

"What happens in my Kingdom is none of your concern. In fact, it's time for you to leave, NOW!" commanded Queen Elyndra, her voice laced with authority. With a wave of her hand, she attempted to force everyone in front of her to the ground. Yet, to her astonishment, not one of them budged.

"Let me be quite clear, Elyndra … you will hand Kura over, otherwise suffer the consequences. Your choice!" stated William, his voice carrying a weight of finality.

Aevyressa, Myrrathen and Thalara stood resolutely in front of Elyndra, forming a protective barrier. Despite being powerful and on her own ground, Elyndra noted the unexpected strength of their presence—but she refused to show any sign of weakness.

The Lepidopteras, Griffins and legacies drew their weapons of choice from their sheaths, their movements synchronized as they stood back-to-back, a formidable force ready for whatever was about to transpire.

With her head held high, Elyndra surveyed the clearing, her keen eyes assessing the situation. It was clear they were outnumbered, but she refused to show any sign of weakness.

As tension thickened in the air, a charged silence settled over the clearing, broken only by the rustle of leaves and the faint hum of magic. Elyndra's gaze flickered between

William and his allies, her expression unreadable, her mind calculating.

With a graceful yet deliberate movement, Elyndra raised her hand, signaling for her sisters and the encircling Fae to hold their positions. The Fae warriors, their features etched with determination, tightened their ranks, ready to defend their Queen against any threat.

William's eyes narrowed, his stance unyielding, as he faced off against Elyndra. "You have a choice, Elyndra," he reiterated, his voice firm.

Elyndra's lips curled into a subtle smirk, a glint of defiance shining in her eyes. "You underestimate the power of the Fae, William," she replied, her voice carrying an edge of warning. "We do not yield to threats."

As the standoff dragged on, a sudden rustle echoed through the forest, followed by the emergence of a figure from the shadows. It was Stjernefrída, the Goddess whose grandmother, Kura, was held captive.

Stjernefrída stepped forward and her presence commanded attention. "Elyndra, this conflict between Eryndor and myself does not concern you," she said, her voice resonating with authority. "Release Kura, or face the wrath of not only the Lepidopteras and Griffins, but also the entire pantheon."

Elyndra's expression flickered, a hint of uncertainty crossing her features. She knew the weight of Stjernefrída's words, and the power she wielded as a descendant of the divine. With a subtle nod, she signaled to her sisters and surrounding Fae to stand down. She then commanded the cage containing Kura to descend from the sky, and watched its ethereal glow dim as it touched the forest floor.

"Thank you, Queen Elyndra. We are most grateful!" stated Stjernefrída, as she watched the cage open.

Danielle, see to Kura's health, instructed William telepathically.

Yes, Sire, thought Danielle. She sheathed her sword and rushed over to where Kura lay unconscious. Tearing the cage sides off, she knelt beside Kura and placed her hands over her body and started to heal her. Within moments Kura opened her eyes.

The tension in the clearing dissipated, replaced by a sense of cautious peace, as everyone watched on.

"Where am I?" asked Kura, as she sat up.

"In the Fae Kingdom," replied Danielle. "How are you feeling?"

"A tad groggy, my dear," stated Kura, wondering how she'd even got there. "Can you help me up?"

Standing, Danielle assisted Kura up off the cage floor.

"Keep hold of me, my dear. I may fall," murmured Kura, as she looked into Danielle's soulful eyes.

Danielle smiled and held her close. "Don't worry, I have you."

"Now that you have retrieved what you came for," Queen Elyndra gestured toward Kura, "you will leave my Kingdom," she commanded.

"Thank you for your cooperation, Elyndra. We trust you'll make wiser choices regarding our son, Eryndor, in the future," stated Garrick as he conjuring a portal.

"Humph! Begone," commanded Queen Elyndra, her gaze steely as the portal opened. She turned to her sisters. "Let's leave. I've had my fill of this for today."

Aevyressa, Myrrathen and Thalara fell into step behind Elyndra as she led the way toward the depths of the Fae forest. Each sister emanated an aura of silent determination, their eyes sharp and vigilant as they moved with purpose through the ancient trees. Together, they disappeared into the verdant shadows, their presence a formidable force amidst the whispering foliage.

As William stepped into the portal alongside Garrick, Elara and Stjernefrída, he cast a solemn glance back at the Fae Kingdom. "I don't believe this will be our last visit to this realm," he remarked, his voice tinged with a sense of foreboding.

"I fear you may be correct," stated Stjernefrída, as a shadow passed over her features. She knew all too well the impending threat that loomed over them, the inevitable confrontation with Eryndor and the dark forces he commanded. It was only a matter of time before their paths would cross once again, and the true test of their resolve would begin.

CHAPTER THIRTY-THREE

Draven and Kael stood in a defensive stance, weapons drawn, as they watched a portal open. Eryndor stepped out and walked into the ancient forest, headed straight toward them.

What does this fucker want? thought Draven, turning to Kael.

Not sure! thought Kael, as he and Draven walked toward Eryndor.

"Where is Stjernefrída?" Eryndor demanded. With a flick of his wrist, Eryndor used his malevolent powers, suspending Draven and Kael in the air, and their swords dropped to the ground.

Draven and Kael struggled to breathe, writhing helplessly, as they tried to answer.

Eryndor released his grip, sending Draven and Kael tumbling to the ground in a heap. "Well?" he urged.

Despite their efforts to catch their breath and rise, Eryndor effortlessly exerted control with a flick of his hand, pressing them against an ancient tree, as he stood directly in front them.

"I will only ask once more … where is Stjernefrída?" questioned Eryndor.

Draven and Kael chose not to respond, but instead gave a steely defiant expression. As their jaws clenched and their eyes narrowed with a simmering rage, their bodies tensed and their muscles coiled, ready to spring into action if given the opportunity. Maintaining a resolute silence, Draven and Kael refused to give Eryndor the satisfaction of a response.

"Your disobedience only hastens your demise." Eryndor's voice echoed with dark satisfaction. Using his malevolent powers, he stretched their bodies against the tree's surface, until they could stretch no further.

Draven and Kael faces became distorted as they screamed in pain, until they were rendered unconscious.

As Eryndor watched their bodies crumple to the ground, he sneered. "That's what happens when you dare challenge me." He walked toward Stjernefrída's cabin, surveying the surroundings with a menacing glare.

"Stjernefrída … show yourself," demanded Eryndor, as he stood on the front porch, in front of the door.

There was no answer.

With a flick of his wrist, Eryndor flung the door open, shattering it from its hinges. As he walked inside, the cabin was quiet and only the wood from the fire crackled. "Stjernefrída … show yourself."

Again, there was only silence.

As Eryndor moved about the cabin, not knowing that Stjernefrída was on her way back from the Fae Kingdom, he tore through the cabin, toppling furniture and shredding her belongings in frustration.

Where the fuck are you, bitch?

As the echoes of his rampage faded within the cabin, leaving an eerie silence in their wake, Eryndor felt a subtle, yet undeniable, energy signature pulsating from somewhere within the cabin. With a chilling determination, he homed in on the elusive source, scouring every corner of the cabin, until his gaze fell upon the floorboards. A wicked grin twisted his lips as he realized what lay below. With a swift motion, he tore up the floorboards, revealing a hidden chamber beneath. There, nestled among the shadows, lay the coveted chalice, concealed within the pages of an ancient tome. With a triumphant laugh, Eryndor reached in to claim his prize, knowing that its power would soon be his to wield. However, as his hand delved into the hidden chamber beneath the floorboards, he suddenly recoiled in shock, feeling an intense heat sear through his fingertips as if the very air itself had turned against him.

"Argh, fuck! What sorcery is this?" exclaimed Eryndor, in frustration and agony.

After the initial shock, Eryndor quickly regained his composure. "Such feeble attempts to thwart me will not succeed. I will have what is rightfully mine." Hissing through clenched teeth as he examined his injured fingertips, he was determined to overcome this unexpected obstacle.

With fierce resolve, Eryndor summoned the full extent of his dark magic to overcome the barrier thwarting his grasp of the chalice. Pouring his malevolent energy into the hidden chamber, he sought to shatter the protective enchantments that stood between him and his coveted prize. Nothing would deter him from claiming the power he so ardently craved.

With a triumphant smirk, Eryndor cautiously extended his bony hands into the now-vanquished hidden chamber, the remnants of protective magic crackling at his touch. Slowly and deliberately, he wrapped his fingers around the ancient book containing the chalice, feeling its weight and power resonate through his skeletal frame. With a steady, calculated motion, he withdrew the book from its hiding place, relishing the moment as he finally claimed the object of his relentless pursuit.

Two down, one to go! thought Eryndor, as he held the book close to his chest.

With a click of his fingers, he created a portal to carry him back to the hidden ship.

* * *

Stjernefrída and Danielle helped a frail Kura step out of the portal and onto the banks of the River of Whispers. The guardians, Lepidopteras and legacies followed closely behind, as the portal closed behind them.

Sensing that something was amiss in her realm, Stjernefrída placed her hand in the air and everyone stopped behind her. "Danielle, can you take care of my grandmother?" asked Stjernefrída.

"I will guard her with my life, Goddess," replied Danielle, placing her arm around Kura's back.

"Be careful, my child," said Kura, looking at Stjernefrída. She too, had sensed that something had gone on in their realm since she had left.

"Yes, of course, Grandmother," replied Stjernefrída. She ran toward her cabin. *Guardians, please accompany me!*

The three guardians did as they were asked, while everyone else waited.

"Shit … Draven, Kael," Garrick exclaimed, spotting their unconscious bodies on the ground near the cabin. He dashed over to them.

"William, can we use your healer?" asked Garrick, as he knelt next to Draven and Kael.

"Danielle!" called William.

"Give Kura to me, Danielle," said Elara, walking over to them.

"Thank you," said Danielle, leaving Kura with Elara. She rushed over to Draven and Kael's sides, placed a hand on each of their chests, and tried to heal their internal wounds. As Danielle concentrated, a warm, soft light began to emanate from her hands, enveloping Draven and Kael. Slowly, their breathing steadied and after a few tense moments, their eyes fluttered open.

"How are you feeling?" asked Danielle to Draven and Kael, as she looked from one to the other.

Draven let out a weak groan, "Good, but sore."

Kael managed a faint smile, "Okay, but a bit weak."

"Let's get you both up," stated William, placing his hands out front for them to take.

* * *

As Stjernefrída approached her cabin, she noticed that the door had been blown to smithereens.

"Stand back! You wait here, Goddess. We will check the cabin first," stated the Guardian of the River's Source.

Stjernefrída nodded and waited on the porch for their return.

The three guardians stepped inside the cabin and checked each room for the source of the threat, but found nothing, except for a scene of mess and destruction.

"You are fine to enter, Goddess," said the Guardian of the River's Source, who was standing in the doorway.

"Thank you," replied Stjernefrída. As she walked past him into the cabin, she was shocked and overwhelmed to find the chaos before her. Furniture had been overturned and torn apart. Cushions were shredded, their stuffing spilling out like entrails. As she walked in further, she noticed that the kitchen had shattered glass and broken dishes scattered across the floor, and the refrigerator door was left hanging ajar, so that its contents spoiled and were dripping. Walking in further, she found the bedroom's mattresses were slashed open, and her clothes were strewn everywhere, as if a wild animal had rampaged through the place. The walls bore deep, angry gashes, and dark, ominous symbols drawn in an unfamiliar substance, which suggested a malevolent presence had been inside her cabin.

Shit! The chalice. The thought hit Stjernefrída like a bolt of lightning. She had hidden it under the floorboards—but had she been gone too long? She ran toward the living room and approached the spot where she had hidden the chalice. Her heart sank when she noticed the floorboards had been pried up and scattered, leaving a gaping hole in the floor. Anxiously, she dropped to her knees and peered into the cavity, her stomach twisting as she saw that the hiding place was empty.

Stjernefrída felt a hand touch her shoulder, and as she looked up she found Garrick was standing beside her. "I have really fucked up, this time," stated Stjernefrída.

Garrick brow furrowed. "What was in this hole, Goddess?"

Stjernefrída gulped hard. "The Golden Chalice."

"What … I thought it was still with the councillors at Glittertind, for them to take care of it and keep it safe?" questioned Garrick.

"It was … but … I," Stjernefrída shook her head, "I retrieved it from them, and promised that I would be able to keep it safe. What have I done?"

The gravity of the situation hit Garrick like a ton of bricks. "Who do you think in your realm would have taken it? Who knew it was here?"

"No one in my realm would have taken it, and I was the only one, besides the councillors, who knew it was here," replied Stjernefrída, standing. "This is Eryndor's doing. I can feel his malevolent presence has been here."

"Eryndor … I think you could be right, Stjernefrída," stated Elara, who had been standing behind them, listening to their conversation.

Stjernefrída turned to Elara and said, "He left a trace behind. I can feel it still clinging to the walls."

Elara glanced between Stjernefrída and Garrick, and shook her head. "Garrick, we must devise a plan to stop Eryndor's relentless defiance. With two sacred artifacts already in his possession, it's only a matter of time before he acquires the final one. Gods help us if that happens."

"I agree," stated William Gramaze, who had been listening in on the conversation, as he walked into the room. "This has now become a global threat. I think that we should all work together, along with other allies, to put a stop to Eryndor, once and for all. Are you prepared for what outcome may arise, Garrick and Elara?"

"We are going to have to be, aren't we!" stated Garrick. This was the last thing he wanted. He had vowed to Eryndor's parents that they'd keep him safe, not hunt him down.

"Eryndor has caused too much pain and destruction—we have to stop him," said Elara. "We tried to save him, Garrick, but he's crossed too many lines. If stopping him means ending his life … we'll have to find a way to live with it."

"Then we are in agreement?" questioned William, as he looked from Garrick to Elara.

Garrick hesitated, a flicker of guilt in his eyes, then gave a slow, reluctant nod.

Elara's gaze dropped briefly to the floor before she met William's eyes and nodded in agreement.

"At the moment, I think that our top priority must be ensuring Stjernefrída's safety," explained William, raking a hand through his hair. "Since you are the only one who can extract the chalice from the book, Eryndor will likely target you and try to use your grandmother as leverage again. We've reinforced the wards at our home and they should keep Eryndor out, and protect both you and your grandmother. So, I believe it would be wise for you to come with us, to our home in Bagnolet."

"I must agree. That would be perfect, as Eryndor won't suspect that the Goddess is in France," stated Garrick.

"Thank you, William Gramaze. Your kindness will be repaid one day," said Kura, standing in the doorway.

"That won't be necessary," replied William. He turned around and inclined his head respectfully to Kura. "My family and I are only too happy to help, where needed."

Kura smiled and inclined her head to William.

"We need to get moving … you never know when Eryndor will return. Especially when he realizes that he can't retrieve the chalice from the book," stated Stjernefrída.

"Don't worry about here, Goddess. We will clean this mess up, for when you and Kura return, and keep the rivers safe," said the Guardian of the River's Source.

"Thank you, guardians. But if Eryndor returns, you must contact me, and please … don't take any chances. I don't want anything happening to any of you," said Stjernefrída. She looked upon each of their faces with respect.

They all nodded in agreement.

"Let's move!" Stjernefrída walked toward the doorway, placed her arm around Kura's back, and helped her walk out into the ancient forest. Extending her hand, she focused on the familiar magic signature of the Gramaze estate, that she had been to once before. The portal shimmered open, revealing a path to transport them to Bagnolet.

CHAPTER THIRTY-FOUR

"Ah, a wondrous sight ... such a beauty," murmured Eryndor, gazing at the chalice, which was nestled within the book's pages. "Now ... let's get you out of there." His fingers attempted to penetrate the pages and retrieve the chalice, but they merely skimmed over the surface, unable to breach the magical barrier. *So, it is true: Stjernefrída really is the only one who can extract the Golden Chalice.* He tried again, this time more forcefully, but with the same outcome. "Fuck ..." he snarled. "The bitch must have put a spell on the book."

Hawk, get your butt down here, NOW! thought Eryndor, standing on the lower deck of the ship, where the two sacred artifacts, were hidden, along with the Ethereal Nexus Amulet and the Cauldron of Chaos.

Hawk appeared within minutes in front of Eryndor. "Yes, Master."

"How do I retrieve the chalice out of this book?" asked Eryndor.

"I believe that there is only one who can retrieve it," replied Hawk, trying to remember the history his mother had taught him years previous.

"And who might that be?" demanded Eryndor.

"I have told you before, its Stjernefrída," replied Hawk.

"You had better not be lying to me, Hawk," stated Eryndor. He tried to delve into Hawk's mind for the information but found nothing else.

"Aww, shit." Hawk clutched the sides of his head, agony coursing through him, as Eryndor's intrusion into his memories intensified. The pain was excruciating, each probe deeper into his mind sending waves of torment through his entire being, until Eryndor finally released him. "I'm not lying."

Hmm, who can I ask for help? Perhaps Elyndra? Eryndor mused, with a sinister gleam in his eyes. *She might be able to conjure a spell for this. Besides, she owes me a favor, and I am in need of the Fae's Golden Ring. It's a perfect opportunity for a win-win,* he thought, with a wicked grin curling his lips.

"I want you to guard these artifacts with your life, Hawk," demanded Eryndor.

"Yes, Master!" replied Hawk, inclining his head in compliance.

Eryndor clicked his fingers and disappeared from sight.

Hawk had read Eryndor's thoughts, so he knew he was headed to see the Fae Queen, to ask for help.

Sully, help me, please, thought Hawk, as his mind cleared from the mind control. *Sully!*

Hawk ... where are you? thought Sully, when she heard his cry for help.

Somewhere in the deep oceans. I'm not sure. Help me, please. I can't seem to get out from under this mind control that Eryndor has on me, thought Hawk, as he grabbed the side of his head.

I will find you! thought Sully.

No, you won't, bitch. Fuck off, and leave us alone, thought a glazed-eyed Hawk. The mind control Eryndor had over him had returned, and the real Hawk felt himself being pushed down deep inside.

* * *

Sully slammed her fist down on the mattress. "Fucking bastard! You will pay dearly one day, Eryndor. I promise."

"Are you okay?" Elsie asked, waking up to her roommate's threat.

"Hawk just contacted me, while he was in and out of mind control. He wanted me to come and get him, but he didn't know where he was. He only knew that he was out in the ocean somewhere," replied Sully, as tears sprang to her eyes.

Elsie quickly got out of bed and sat next to Sully. Leaning against the headboard, she suggested, "We should report this."

"What are they going to do? We don't even know where he is," stated Sully. She wiped the tears that had spilled onto her cheeks.

Elsie placed her arm around Sully and pulled her in close. "Everything will be alright, Sully. I am sure of it. At least you know Hawk is still alive."

"I just want him back, that's all. But it seems that is too much to ask," said Sully, leaning on Elsie's shoulder.

"Why don't we get dressed and go and see the Head Chancellor. We need to let her know that Hawk has contacted you and I am sure she will be able to help us," said Elsie.

"Okay," said Sully. With the wards currently up, Sully didn't know what else she could do, other than to speak with Head Chancellor Violette.

* * *

"Come!" commanded Head Chancellor Violette, looking up from her paperwork to the doorway.

"Good morning, Head Chancellor," said Sully, as she walked in with Elsie, leaving the door behind them open. "I, we, were wondering if we could take up some of your time, to chat about Hawk?"

Violette glanced at her phone for the time, and said, "I can give you five minutes. Otherwise, you will have to wait until my meeting with the Gramazes is over. Take a seat." Violette gestured to the two seats in front of her office desk. "What would you like to talk about?"

"Hawk has been telepathically chatting with me this morning. He asked me to help him escape … but he wasn't sure where he was being held. He said something about being out in the ocean, but didn't know where," replied Sully, her eyes pools of unshed tears. "Is there anything you can do to help find him?"

"I'm afraid not. Until we can get a definite location, then it's out of my hands. We can't waste resources at the moment, looking for a needle in a haystack. And don't even think about going to look for him yourselves." Violette looked forbiddingly from Sully to Elsie. "Just so you know, the wards have been tightened around the academy and the Gramaze mansion and grounds, because we have two dignitaries staying with us, and we can't afford for Eryndor, or anyone else, to get past the wards and kidnap them."

"I understand," said Sully. She took a deep breath in and out to steady her anxiety.

"If Hawk contacts you again, try to get more information from him on his whereabouts, or try to see what he is seeing. This may lead us to him. I know this is hard, being that he is your life partner, but this is out of our hands at the moment." Violette looked at her phone and spotted the time. "I have to go to this meeting. But like I said before: don't even try to go looking for Hawk. The wards we currently have up are not very kind to flesh or feathers."

"Yes, Head Chancellor," said Sully, standing.

"Thank you for seeing us, Head Chancellor," said Elsie, also standing.

"You are welcome. Keep me informed if anything changes," Violette stated, rising from her seat. She retrieved a manila folder brimming with papers from her desk and followed the two young supes to the doorway. "Take care, ladies!" Violette waited for the two girls to leave, then she ran at Lepidoptera Vampire speed down the corridor, which led her to the interconnecting tunnel that joined the academy and the Gramaze mansion.

* * *

"I knew that would be a waste of time," said Sully, as she walked down the corridor with Elsie to their room.

"Sorry, Sully. I know how much you want to find Hawk. At least we tried," stated Elsie, as they reached the doorway of their dorms room. "Would you like to go and get some breakfast?"

"Nah … I might go for a walk. I need to clear my head," replied Sully.

"Did you want some company?" asked Elsie.

"No," said Sully. She leaned in to give her best friend a hug. "Thank you for asking."

"That's okay. Are you going to be alright?" asked Elsie, as she returned the hug.

"I think so. I just need some time alone," said Sully, pulling away from their friendly embrace.

"Well, if you need me, you know where to find me," stated Elsie.

"Thank you. I'll catch you later," said Sully. She smiled at Elsie and walked toward her favorite place: the river.

"Yep, see ya!" Elsie watched Sully walk away, as she opened the door to their dorm room.

* * *

The glass sliding door to the operations room at the Gramaze mansion opened and Violette walked into the room with her life partner, Michael, finding everyone else seated and waiting for them. The room was filled with an air of anticipation, the soft hum of magical wards resonating in the background.

William Gramaze stood at the head of the table. His presence commanded attention and, as Violette and Michael took their seats, he began to speak.

204

"Right, now that everyone is here, let's get this meeting started," said William, his voice smooth but authoritative. "We have important matters to discuss concerning our current guests—Stjernefrída and her grandmother, Kura. As you are aware, extra wards are up around the building, providing us with an initial layer of protection. However, we must consider additional measures to ensure their safety."

William paused, letting his gaze sweep across the room, ensuring he had everyone's full attention before continuing.

"We stand as guardians not only of our kind but also for those who seek our protection. Let us ensure that our actions reflect the seriousness of this duty. Now, let's proceed with finalizing these plans."

A murmur spread through the room and everyone nodded in response.

"We need to establish some internal security protocols. I propose assigning a personal guard to Stjernefrída and Kura, ensuring they are accompanied at all times. Furthermore, we should implement a rotation schedule for our patrols, both inside and outside the mansion, to keep our security unpredictable. Violette, I want you to oversee the schedule and ensure that we have continuous coverage. No gaps, no oversights."

Violette nodded and made a mental note. "I'll coordinate with everyone to make sure it's airtight. What about the security of their rooms? Should we enhance the protection there as well?"

"Absolutely!" William replied with a nod. "We should reinforce the wards around their rooms and install additional monitoring devices. Any suspicious activity, no matter how minor, must be reported immediately. We cannot afford to take any chances."

"What about potential threats from within?" Michael asked. "Do we have a system in place to vet staff or new legacies—to make sure there are no infiltrators among us? Even with the reinforced wards, we can't risk another incident like before, when Eryndor controlled those nine legacies and breached our defenses."

William's expression hardened. "A valid point, Michael. I will personally oversee a thorough background check of all staff members and legacies. Trust is essential, but vigilance is paramount. We must be prepared for any eventuality.

"Now, beyond magical defenses, we need to consider physical security. I've arranged for discreet patrols around the perimeter. Additionally, we should be prepared for any attempts to breach our wards and lines of defense," stated William.

"I've also coordinated with our Lepidoptera covens across the globe and the Griffins, to be on standby," stated Grayson, William's second-in-command. "In the event of a situation we can't handle, such as a breach of our wards, they will be ready to assist."

"Excellent!" replied William.

With that, the room buzzed with a renewed purpose, everyone ready to take on their roles in safeguarding the dignitaries under their care.

William looked around the room one last time. "Alright," William concluded, "Let's get to work."

As everyone dispersed, William noticed that Violette and Michael remained behind. "Was there something you both needed to discuss?" asked William.

"Yes, William. We wanted to speak with you about Sully and Hawk," replied Violette. "It seems that Hawk is still able to contact Sully telepathically. This can only mean one thing: that he is still near France."

"You are correct. Did he give her any indication on where he was?" asked William.

"Apparently Hawk told Sully that he didn't know where he was, but that he knew he was out in the ocean somewhere. I was thinking that if he is in the ocean, that would mean he is close by, somewhere in either the Atlantic Ocean or the Mediterranean Sea," replied Violette.

"I think you are correct. I will have Brock scour the Atlantic Ocean and the Mediterranean Sea via satellite and let's see what he finds," said William.

"Would it also be beneficial to let Garrick and Elara know, because they could send some of their people to search the oceans as well?" queried Michael.

"Good idea. I will get in contact with them and let them know. Hopefully we can find not only Hawk, but also Eryndor and his glazed-eyed minions, and the sacred artifacts," stated William.

"Great! Thanks, William. Do you mind if I let Sully know what is going on? She is desperate to get her life partner back safely," said Violette.

"That will be fine. But I want you to make it quite clear to Sully that she is not to leave the protection of the wards around the academy and Gramaze mansion. We don't want her going off half-cocked, or trying to find a way around the wards, while we are protecting Stjernefrída and Kura. Am I making myself clear?"

"Yes, Sire," responded Michael, who was William's third-in-command.

"I have already spoken with Sully about this very point, this morning. But I will reiterate it to her, again, when I catch up with her," replied Violette.

"Now that is sorted, was there anything else you wanted to discuss?" asked William.

"No, that is all. We will leave it with you and get on with the protection and guarding of the two dignitaries," said Violette, standing.

"Thank you for your time, Sire," said Michael pushing his chair back.

"Anytime!" said William.

William watched Violette and Michael walk through the glass sliding doors.

CHAPTER THIRTY-FIVE

The air shimmered with an ominous hue as Eryndor, the Harbinger of Shadows, stepped through the portal into the realm of the Fae Kingdom. His presence cast a dark shadow over the vibrant landscape, sending shivers down the spines of the creatures that dared to observe him.

At the heart of the enchanted forest, amidst the whispering trees and dancing sprites, stood the palace of the Fae Queen, Elyndra, adorned with intricate carvings and bathed in an ethereal light. When Eryndor approached the palace, his eyes gleamed with a hunger for power, as he crossed the threshold into Elyndra's domain.

Inside the grand hall of the palace, adorned with flowers and glowing crystals, Elyndra waited for him upon her throne of ivy and moonlight. Her beauty was otherworldly, her gaze sharp and knowing, as she regarded the Harbinger of Shadows with a mixture of curiosity and caution.

Keep quiet, my people, we don't want Eryndor knowing that Kura has been rescued, said Elyndra telepathically to her subjects.

"Eryndor," greeted Elyndra, her voice like the rustle of leaves in the wind. "To what do I owe the pleasure of your visit?"

"I come seeking your assistance, in a matter of great importance," replied Eryndor, his voice a low rumble that seemed to echo through the chamber.

Elyndra arched an eyebrow, though her expression remained serene. "And what might that be?"

"I require the Golden Chalice," Eryndor stated bluntly, his eyes narrowing with intensity. "The one hidden within the pages of this ancient book of spells. I need it extracted." He held the book up in front of him for Elyndra to see.

Elyndra's lips curved into a subtle smile, though her eyes betrayed no hint of warmth. "Ah, the chalice," she mused, tapping her chin thoughtfully. "A powerful artifact indeed. And why, pray tell, do you need it?"

Eryndor's gaze grew steely. "That is none of your concern," he replied icily. "I require it for my own purposes."

Elyndra's lips curled into a knowing smile, though her eyes betrayed no hint of her true intentions. "Right, I see," she mused, her voice dripping with feigned innocence. "Yes, I can retrieve it for you. But such a task requires delicate handling. The enchantment bindings are intricate. It will take some time."

A flicker of suspicion crossed Eryndor's features, but he pushed it aside for the moment. "Very well. But I will not wait long. And there is another matter—the Fae's Golden Ring?" he pressed, his tone expectant. "You promised it to me, yet I have not seen it."

Elyndra's expression shifted, a shadow passing over her features. "Ah, yes," she replied smoothly, though her words held a hint of evasion. "Unfortunately, we do not possess such a ring. However, I know where one may be found."

Eryndor narrowed his eyes, sensing the deception woven within Elyndra's words. "You assured me you would deliver it. Do not trifle with me, Elyndra."

"The ring is elusive, but I know where it can be found. A place of great peril, but worth the risk for one of your prowess," stated Elyndra.

"Do not deceive me, Elyndra. I will tolerate no treachery," said Eryndor.

"Trust me. Our goals are aligned, are they not? Retrieve the ring, and the chalice will be yours as well," said Elyndra, as she leaned in closer to him.

"Very well. But mark my words, Elyndra. Cross me, and you will regret it," said Eryndor, narrowing his eyes, suspicious but hopeful. He handed the ancient book to Elyndra.

"I wouldn't dream of it," said Elyndra, smiling sweetly, as she took the book from Eryndor. She placed her hand on her heart. "I will take good care of it, until you return."

You'll find nothing but shadows and lies in this realm, Eryndor. And the chalice will be mine to command, thought Elyndra.

"And what of the ring ... where can I find it?" questioned Eryndor.

Elyndra's eyes gleamed with calculated mischief as she prepared to divulge the location of the Fae's Golden Ring to Eryndor. "The ring you seek is in the possession of a unique being. Her name is Danielle, and she is a rare blend of Fae and Lepidoptera. She wears the ring on her finger, a keepsake given to her by her mother when she passed on twenty years ago. You will find her in Bagnolet. She lives with, and is protected by, the Gramaze coven of Vampires."

"Yes, I do know of this coven," stated Eryndor.

Not an easy feat, but doable, thought Eryndor to himself.

"You will leave us now, and I will contact you when we are ready for your return, Eryndor," stated Elyndra. With a nod of acknowledgment, Elyndra made her way toward a hidden alcove within the chamber. As she disappeared from view, Eryndor's gaze lingered upon her retreating form, a silent promise of retribution burning within his soul.

With a wave of his hand, Eryndor summoned a swirling portal. Stepping through, within seconds he reappeared on his ship's top deck, amidst the turbulent waves of the Atlantic Ocean. As the weight of Elyndra's unspoken promises and hidden betrayals hung heavily in the air, Eryndor pondered how he would be able to secure the ring from Danielle's finger.

* * *

As the door closed behind her, Elyndra walked down a seemingly endless corridor that was bathed in soft ethereal light, streaming through stained glass windows, which cast colorful patterns on the marble floor below. The arches overhead were intricately carved with scenes of Fae lore, depicting tales of magic, bravery and enchantment, and the ceiling was adorned with chandeliers made of crystal and vines, casting a soft, captivating light. Tapestries that lined the walls were woven with threads spun from moonlight and starlight, depicting scenes of Fae celebrations, mystical creatures, and ancient rituals. Along the length of the hall, pedestals displayed precious artifacts and magical relics, each pulsing with its own energy and history. Elaborate floral arrangements cascaded from golden urns, their petals shimmering with iridescence, releasing a delicate wildflower and earth fragrance that perfumed the air.

Reaching the library, which was situated at the end of the corridor, holding the ancient tome that had the chalice within, Elyndra made a beeline for the bookshelves that were filled with ancient scrolls, grimoires and books of magic. The shelves seemed to be never-ending, with ladders that had a will of their own, as they shifted along the expansive rows of knowledge.

As her fingers glided along each book's spine, Elyndra came across a book of ancient spells.

This one should have something in it to extract the chalice, thought Elyndra, taking it off the shelf. She placed the tome and the ancient spell book on the low table behind her, sat in the leather armchair, and started to flick through the pages for a spell.

* * *

Ah ... here it is. Looks like all I need to get is a piece of gold thread, a drop of dew and a sprig of sacred oak. I'm sure I have all of these, thought Elyndra. Standing, she walked over to her armoire, which was near the doorway, and rifled through the drawers for the ingredients.

Here we go, thought Elyndra, as she scooped up the three ingredients together, closed the drawer, and walked back to the table. Sitting in the armchair, she directed her fingers to read the castings and the incantation for the spell. *Seems easy enough. Right here we go ...*

Elyndra placed the sprig of sacred oak on top of the book, wrapped the gold string around the book, then sprinkled a drop of dew on top of it, and started to chant the incantation.

By moonlit glow and ancient tome,
reveal the chalice, its rightful home.
With words of power, I now decree,
unveil the hidden, set it free.
In this book, a secret lies,
bound by magic, unseen by eyes.

Threads of time and weave of fate,
I call upon thee, open the gate.
Golden threads and golden light,
guide my hand, make my vision bright.
From paper cage to open air,
let the chalice now appear.

Suddenly the golden string vanished and the ancient book, with the chalice inside, flew open. Its pages turned on their own, propelled by the invisible force of Elyndra's magic.

You are nearly mine! mused Elyndra as she smirked, contemplating the possibilities of her future.

As the pages turned faster and faster, they began to glow with an ethereal light. Symbols and illustrations leaped off the parchment, swirling in the air and forming a shimmering vortex. From within this vortex, a voice echoed, deep and resonant, reciting an incantation in an ancient language. The room trembled, and the chalice began to levitate, pulsing with a radiant energy. Elyndra reached out to grasp the chalice, but it slipped from her fingers and flew back into the book. The shimmering vortex began to close, drawing the chalice and the glowing symbols back into the pages. With a final flash of light, the book snapped shut, leaving Elyndra in a stunned silence.

Despite her initial confidence, Elyndra soon realized that the chalice was bound by enchantments far beyond her solitary power. Unwilling to admit defeat, she delved further into her vast library, searching forbidden texts and ancient scrolls for answers.

CHAPTER THIRTY-SIX

It had been two days since the Griffins, Lepidoptera Vampires and legacies had returned from the ancient forest and brought Stjernefrída and Kura back with them to the Gramaze coven's mansion, and everything seemed to be going to plan.

"Knock, knock," called Violette, standing outside of William's office doorway.

"Come!" stated William.

"Good morning, William. Do you have a minute?" asked Violette, as she walked toward him.

"Morning, Violette. What can I do for you?" replied William, gesturing for her to sit in the chair in front of his desk.

"I am wondering what is happening; you know, about finding Hawk. Sully keeps asking, and I told her I would personally come and find out."

"Shit … with everything that has been going on in the last couple of days, I have forgotten about Hawk. Fuck!" William raked a hand through his hair in frustration and shook his head.

"Is this something I can take on for you, William?" asked Violette.

"That would be most appreciated, Violette. I would start with Brock first, then ring Garrick," said William, standing. "Stick with our original plan that we discussed." He walked over to his office window, and peered out across the Seine River, at the back of his property.

Standing, Violette walked over to William and placed a hand on his shoulder. "Are you okay, William?"

William nodded, but didn't say anything.

They stood there for a few minutes, looking out over the river in silence.

"Is there anything else that I can help with? asked Violette.

"I'm sure you have enough on your plate, Violette. Thank you anyway!" said William, turning to her.

"You look troubled. What is going on?" questioned Violette. She tried to read his thoughts, but he had blocked her.

"Besides the usual Debauched Vampire problems—with their drugs, and bleeding people dry—keeping you and Queen Talitha safe …" He continued to look out the window, "And now, we have Stjernefrída and Kura to guard. It's just never-ending. I even have to deal with the mayor of Paris, who wants to come and visit us and chat about security. For fuck's sake, Violette. I just can't keep up."

"Well, why don't you delegate some of these things to someone else? There are others who are quite capable of taking on more, if you let them," Violette suggested, her concern evident. She stood in front of him and looked him in the eyes. "You need to off-load some of these things, before something goes unnoticed or amiss. And there are many Lepidopteras here who can step up to the plate, so to speak."

"Yes, I know you're right," stated William. "Why are you so levelheaded?" He smiled at Violette and leaned in for a hug.

Violette leaned into William's embrace, recalling a time, years ago, when he had shied away from affection. Over the years, she had taught him the importance of showing emotion and that, sometimes, even Vampires needed hugs.

"So …" Violette pulled away from his embrace and looked into his eyes, "What do you have on your list that I or others could take on?"

"I will show you," William gestured for Violette to follow him over to his desk. Picking up a small pad, he handed her the list.

Violette raised her eyebrows as she looked it over and thought about who would be suited for these types of tasks. "You could meet with the mayor today and see what he wants. That will be one big task sorted. I am sure he will have some kind of security problem going on with the other supernatural beings in the city. He always does when he comes to visit. And I can deal with the rest."

William shook his head and opened his mouth to speak.

"Nope! Don't even think about it," She held her hand up in the air. "I will be fine with everything else on this list, and you know it." Violette smirked.

"Yes, but …" said William, though he never got to finish his sentence before Violette interrupted.

"There are no buts!" Violette smirked again, and raised her left eyebrow, as she looked at his tired face. "I remember a time, not too long ago, when someone told me that I needed to learn how to delegate. Gee, I wonder who that was?"

William smiled, as his admiration for Violette increased, and he reflected on how far she had come since her parents' death and the discovery of her destiny as the Lepidoptera Princess, next in line to the throne. He placed a hand on her shoulder. "Yes, I do remember."

"She has you there, William," said Renee, smirking, as she walked into the room. She had been standing outside the doorway, listening in on their conversation.

Violette and William looked over at Renee as she walked into the room and stood next to her life partner.

Renee knew from her many discussions with William just how much he admired Violette, and thought of her as a daughter. She also knew that he would never let anyone else speak to him the way Violette did. As the Lepidoptera Vampire leader of France for many years, William had earned immense respect within the Vampire communities and businesses worldwide.

"I can also help with this list, Violette. Let's sit down and discuss how we could attack it," stated Renee.

"That would be most appreciated, Renee," replied Violette.

"Thank you, both of you," said William, as he looked from Renee to Violette.

"You're welcome, William. That is what family is for," Violette turned to Renee, "Shall we go to my office at the academy to mull over this list?"

"Good idea," said Renee to Violette. She turned to William and gave him a quick peck on the cheek and a hug. "See you later, my sweet man."

"You will …" replied William. *Thank you!*

"I will be in touch, William. See you later on," said Violette. She walked toward the doorway with Renee.

"Bye, ladies. Keep me informed," said William, as he pulled his mobile phone out of his pocket to call and speak with the mayor.

* * *

"Thank you for the offer of help, Renee. It's much appreciated," stated Violette, as they walked down the white marble staircase at the Gramaze mansion.

"It is my pleasure. Is there much to organize?" asked Renee, her Swedish accent apparent.

"Yes, there is." Violette handed the list to Renee. "But I think before we head to the academy, we should go and see Brock. I need to speak with him about Hawk," replied Violette.

"Right!" said Renee, as she took the list from Violette and looked it over. "No wonder William was stressed. Look at this list. He really needs to learn how to delegate."

"Agreed!" said Violette, as they arrived at the operations room and opened the sliding doors.

"Good morning, Brock," said Renee, walking toward him with Violette.

Brock, who was sitting at the computer, turned to see Renee and Violette now standing behind him. "Morning, ladies. What can I do for you?"

"Hawk has been in contact with Sully telepathically. He has said he is situated somewhere in the ocean, but he is not sure where. Is it possible for you to check on the Atlantic Ocean and the Mediterranean Sea via satellite, to see if we can find Hawk?" asked Violette.

"Sure!" stated Brock, turning back to his computer. "This may take minutes or hours, depending on where he is. When do you need to know by … I can get back to you when I find something, if that's alright?"

"We need this information as soon as possible, Brock. Just let me know when you find where he is, and then I can organize a reconnaissance mission," replied Violette.

"Yes, Princess. I'll contact you when I have something," Brock said, placing a picture of Hawk on the screen and zooming in on the relevant satellites. His computer resumed scanning through playback of Hawk's recent interactions—footage he hadn't yet reviewed, but had briefly lost track of over the past week.

"Thanks, Brock. We will leave you with it," said Violette, as she and Renee walked toward the sliding doors. Violette turned to Renee, "Next, we need to give Garrick and Elara a call."

"Okay," said Renee, as they entered the tunnel that connected the Gramaze mansion and the academy buildings.

* * *

When Renee and Violette opened the door to Violette's office at the academy, they found Sully asleep on the couch situated near the window.

She looks peaceful. Why don't we leave her to sleep and find somewhere else to chat, thought Violette to Renee.

Good idea ... poor girl, thought Renee to Violette.

Come on, follow me, thought Violette.

Closing the door to her office, Violette said, "I know Michael and Grayson are out on assignment at the moment, so we can use their office."

"Okay," said Renee, as she walked beside Violette.

"Here we go," said Violette, gesturing to the door on the right. She opened the door, and, to her surprise, found Michael and Grayson inside. "I thought you guys were on assignment?"

"We only just arrived back, had our showers, regrouped and were about to discuss the mission. What are you ladies up to?" asked Grayson.

"Oh, right! Renee and I needed to find a quiet place, where we could discuss a delegation plan for a few things that are requiring attention. We can go somewhere else, if you like," said Violette.

"Anything we can help with?" questioned Michael, looking at Violette.

"Four heads are probably better than two, so yes, that would be great," said Violette, walking into the room with Renee. She handed the list to Grayson.

"These are not ..." said Grayson, but he was interrupted by Violette.

She held her hand in the air. "Stop ... I know what you're about to say. But I told William that we—Renee and I—would take care of these things. So, let's sit down, mull over this list, and see if we can come up with a plan of attack," commanded Violette.

"Right ... okay then," stated Grayson, second-in-command to William. He knew better than to argue with the Princess.

Michael smiled, for he too knew not to mess with his determined life partner, and her mission.

"Now … let's get this sorted," stated Violette, sitting on a couch across from Grayson and Michael, with Renee sitting next to her. "First of all, I need to give Garrick and Elara a call to let them know that Hawk could be in the Atlantic Ocean or Mediterranean Sea and discuss how the Griffins can look for him. I am hoping that they will agree to send some of their soldiers or family to search for him."

"Good idea," said Grayson.

"Next … I think we should post a guard outside Talitha's room," said Violette.

"I like the way you are thinking, Princess," said Grayson.

"Well, I figure that if Eryndor does get past the wards, and tries to take either Stjernefrída or Kura, then he could also take our most prized possession, our Queen," said Violette.

"I believe William has already organized this, Violette," said Renee.

"I will check with him, and we can go from there," replied Violette. She made a mental note to contact William about it.

Over the next thirty minutes, the four Lepidoptera agreed on a plan of attack for William's list of duties, deciding who to send on each mission and how to execute them.

CHAPTER THIRTY-SEVEN

Princess ... do you have a moment? thought Brock telepathically to Violette.

I'm right here, thought Violette, as she walked through the doors to the operations room.

"Have you found him, Brock?" queried Violette.

"Definitely. Hawk is being held on a ship out in the Atlantic Ocean. Look at this," replied Brock, pointing to the screen.

"Where? Am I missing something? Because I don't see a damn thing," stated Violette, looking at the screen.

"Can't you see that shimmering wall?"

"No!" replied Violette, her brow furrowed. "Wait, yes, I see it. But I don't see the ship."

"Use your Lepidoptera vision and you will see it," stated Brock.

Violette looked at Brock and frowned, then back to the computer screen. Adjusting her vision, the ship then became clear. "Got it. I don't see Hawk, though."

"Give it a minute. He is on the top deck's mast. Up there, see," said Brock, pointing to the screen.

"Hmm, that does look like Hawk. Can you get any closer, so we can see his face?" asked Violette.

Brock nodded yes and zoomed in the satellite's view to show the face of the person on the mast.

"Yep, that is definitely Hawk," said Violette, recognizing his face. "Who can we send to rescue him?"

"I am not sure, Princess," replied Brock.

Violette felt her phone vibrate and retrieved it from her pocket. Being that she was now in charge of all sorts of daily tasks around the Gramaze mansion and the academy, she sure was busy, running from one job to another. "Yes!" she answered abruptly.

"Good evening, Princess. This is Garrick."

"Good evening to you, Sir. How can I help you?" asked Violette.

"After your phone call this morning, my soldiers and family launched a relentless search for Hawk, and our exhaustive efforts have borne fruit. We've located him in the vast expanse of the Atlantic Ocean," declared Garrick triumphantly.

"Terrific. Actually, it's funny you should ring now, because we have just found him, too, via our satellite feed," said Violette. She placed her phone on speaker for Brock to hear the conversation too. "I have Brock here with me, Garrick, and he can hear what you are saying. Go ahead!"

"As I mentioned, we've located Hawk. My team and I are mobilizing immediately to rescue him," Garrick declared with determination.

"Excellent! Let me know if we can be of any assistance, Garrick. Oh, and don't forget, we have the tools here to free Hawk from the mind control that Eryndor has him under," stated Violette.

"Thank you, Princess. We would appreciate your help with this. I was also hoping Brock would be able to keep an eye on things on and around the ship, while we get on board and rescue Hawk. Would this be possible?" asked Garrick.

Brock nodded yes to Violette.

"Yes, that will be fine. Brock will keep an eye on the satellite feed and will ring you if he sees anything that would impact your mission."

"Great … thank you, Princess," said Garrick.

"No problem. Keep us informed," replied Violette.

"We will keep in touch, Brock. Speak soon!" stated Garrick.

"Yes, Sir," said Brock. He heard the call end and looked at Violette. "Well, that was good timing."

"Sure was. Can I leave this with you to monitor?" She picked her phone up and placed it in her pocket.

"Yes, Princess. I will keep you up to date with what happens," said Brock.

"Great." Violette looked at her watch and breathed a heavy sigh. "I need to get moving. I have a meeting with Grayson, Michael and Renee to discuss a few things. Catch you later on. Call me if you need anything!" She walked toward the sliding doors.

"I will," said Brock, watching her walk out the room.

* * *

"Turn the engines off," commanded Garrick to Draven, as the fishing trawler neared the coordinates that Garrick had earlier typed into the GPS.

"Yes, Sire." Draven did as Garrick commanded, and the trawler eventually came to a stop, as it bobbed up and down in the rough Atlantic Ocean.

"Let's go! We don't want to draw attention by flying over the ship, so we'll swim to it instead." Garrick gestured for Draven, Kael, Zephyrion and Aelvric to follow him, then dove into the water.

Draven, Kael, Zephyrion and Aelvric nodded and dove into the rough seas.

Coming up on the inside of the shimmering wall, Garrick signaled for his soldiers and family to board the huge ship, via the metal anchor chain, which was embedded in the ocean's floor.

As the five Griffins boarded the ship, landing on the top deck, Garrick noticed that there was no one in sight. *I want this ship searched. No stone unturned ... you understand me?* thought Garrick.

The Griffins nodded in agreement. With their weapons of choice drawn, and working in pairs, Draven and Kael ran quietly down the left-hand side of the ship, while Zephyrion and Aelvric checked the right-hand side.

There is nothing and no one here, Sire, thought Draven, searching the cabins with Kael. *All is quiet. Looks like we have missed them.*

Same here, Father, thought Aelvric, as he searched the lower deck with Zephyrion. *What would you like us to do?*

Come back up to the top deck, thought Garrick, as he took his waterproof covered phone out of his pocket.

"Yes, Garrick. How can I be of service to you?" asked Brock as he answered his call.

"Have you been monitoring the vessel?" asked Garrick, who was wondering how Hawk had gotten off the ship without anyone noticing, especially as Brock had been keeping a close eye on the hidden ship via satellite.

"Of course. What seems to be the problem?" asked Brock, his brow furrowed, as he continued to watch the satellite feedback.

"There is no one here. Not a soul," stated Garrick.

"Shit, really … I don't understand, are you sure?" asked Brock, who was looking straight at Hawk standing on the top deck. "Hawk is still standing behind you, Garrick."

The hairs stood up on Garrick neck as he turned around, but no one was behind him. "I am telling you, Lepidoptera, there is no one here at all."

Brock's brow furrowed in disbelief. "Give me a minute, Garrick. I'll call you right back—I need to check the satellite feedback." He ended the call abruptly, his movements sharp and purposeful.

Brock logged into the satellite terminal to make sure it was working correctly. As his fingers deftly worked the keyboard, and he entered the coding pages, he noticed that a link had been inserted. *Fuck, what is that?* When he clicked on the link a video of Hawk on the top deck appeared, which was looping over and over. *Ah, that explains it.* Picking up his console phone, he called Garrick straight back.

"Garrick … you are too late."

"Yes, I know that. But where is Hawk. Is there anything on your satellite feedback on this?" demanded Garrick.

"Nothing. From what I can see, it looks like someone has tampered with the satellite terminal coding, corrupting it with a video that loops over and over. I would say that Eryndor knew we would be looking at the feedback, and that you were coming," stated Brock.

"For shit's sake! That fucking little bastard! "Garrick slammed his fist down on the side rail of the ship, making it split down the bow of the ship, and take on water. His angry voice echoed through the rough seas, as he ended the call and placed his phone in his jacket pocket.

Draven, Kael, Zephyrion, and Aelvric, let's get the fuck out of here. This ship is going down, thought Garrick, realizing what he had done, and what was about to happen.

With powerful sweeps, Draven, Kael, Zephyrion and Aelvric unfurled their wings and soared into the air, heeding Garrick's command.

Better luck next time, Father! thought Eryndor to Garrick telepathically.

I will catch you Eryndor and next time will be your last time on this earth, Garrick vowed. He unfurled his wings and launched into the sky, eyes locked on the ship as it split in half below him.

Eryndor's malevolent laughter filled the air. *Your threats don't scare me, Father. You'll never defeat me*, Eryndor taunted, his voice echoing over the waves.

Only silence filled the air, as Garrick flew with the others back to the fishing trawler. Landing, Garrick said, "Draven, take us back to Olden Fjord."

"Yes, Sire," said Draven.

* * *

As Brock deleted the embedded coding link from the satellite feed, he wondered what was currently happening onboard the vessel. Opening the satellite replay, Brock was astounded as he watched an angry Garrick slam his fist down and split the ship in two. "Fuck!"

Violette ... the mission to rescue Hawk didn't go well, thought Brock.

What happened? thought Violette, walking through the sliding doors.

"There was no one onboard the ship when Garrick got there," said Brock, turning around to face Violette. "And, believe it or not, bloody Eryndor tampered with the satellite coding, so that we had a video of Hawk that played over and over."

"For real! Wow ... Eryndor has gotten a lot smarter than we gave him credit for. Did you see where Hawk went, prior to this?" asked Violette.

"No, but I will keep searching," replied Brock.

"Thanks, Brock. Keep me updated, will you?" said Violette, as she walked toward the sliding doors.

Keep this between us, Brock. I don't want Sully knowing what has happened with Hawk, thought Violette, as she walked up the marble staircase to William's office.

Yes, Princess! thought Brock.

CHAPTER THIRTY-EIGHT

The sleek, black V8 Chevrolet Camaro hummed softly as it pulled up in the parking lot of Lycée International. As Danielle turned the engine off, her Lepidoptera blue eyes scanned their surroundings with a vigilant intensity.

"Wait!" instructed Danielle to Xanthia, as she placed her hand on top of Xanthia's to stop her exiting the car. "Something's not right."

Before Xanthia could react, a dark van with blackened windows screeched to a halt behind them. The doors burst open and four hooded figures with glazed eyes lunged toward them.

"Xanthia, looks like we have company!" Danielle stated, as she watched them surround the car.

Xanthia gulped hard and nodded in agreement. "What do they want?"

"I don't know, but I think we are about to find out," replied Danielle, who was looking for a way to escape.

Within seconds and without a word spoken, the glazed-eyed minions moved with an eerie coordination, grabbing the two girls from the car with surprising strength.

As Danielle tried to fight them off, she was stabbed in the neck with a sharp object that sapped her energy and strength, making her movements sluggish.

With her heart pounding in her chest, Xanthia tried to struggle, but her captors were relentless. "Danielle!" Xanthia cried out, her voice filled with panic, as one of the glazed-eyed creatures also stabbed her in the neck with a needle, making her sluggish, eventually rendering her unconscious.

Filled with determination and driven by her mission to protect Xanthia, Danielle attempted to use her Lepidoptera Vampire abilities to fend off their captors. However, she was also rendered unconscious, when the drugs finally kicked in.

"Get them in the van, before we have company, NOW!" shouted a glazed-eyed Hawk, who was in charge of the mission.

The three minions did as they were instructed and dragged both women into the van. Jumping in, they closed the side door and sped out of the parking lot.

* * *

"Ah, you're awake, my pretties" said Eryndor, sarcastically, as he walked toward them and watched their eyes flutter open.

"You won't get away with this," Danielle spat, her voice defiant, despite her weakened condition, when she realized who had taken them hostage.

Eryndor chuckled, a cold, hollow sound. "Oh, but I already have."

Xanthia's heart raced, and her mind was a whirlwind of fear and confusion, as she tried to comprehend, through the sluggishness, what was happening and why she was chained to the floor. She turned to Danielle and watched her trying to break the chains.

With his bony fingers, Eryndor pulled Xanthia's chin up to meet his gaze. "Still a bit groggy, I see." Xanthia tried to pull away from his grip, but Eryndor held her firm.

Danielle struggled against the chains that held her to the floor. "Let her go," she ordered, as she looked around the dimly lit room, which she realized was a cabin in a ship. The air was thick with the pungent scent of salt, mildew and rust—and something more sinister. She looked around for an exit.

"Not yet, my dear," stated Eryndor, smirking.

"What do you want, Eryndor?" asked Danielle.

"I'm glad you asked, my dear. I already have what I came for," said Eryndor, as he held up Danielle's gold ring in front of her eyes.

"YOU GIVE THAT BACK," shouted Danielle. "It's not yours to take!" Danielle vividly recalled the day she received the golden ring at the reading of her mother's will, and just how much she had loved its feel, let alone its Fae power.

"Ah, so you know of its power," said Eryndor, who had listened to her thoughts.

"I don't know what you're talking about," replied Danielle, struggling to free herself from the chains that held her. "That ring is a family heirloom, which has been handed down through the generations, and I want it back." Danielle glared at Eryndor with contempt.

Eryndor smirked, his eyes glinting with dark amusement. "Oh, Danielle, don't play coy. We both know the ring is more than just an heirloom. Especially as it comes from a Fae."

"You will pay dearly, Eryndor, if my family's heirloom is damaged in any way!" stated Danielle.

"Oh, it will be more than damaged, when I am finished with it. In fact, I intend to melt it down and use it for one of my spells. And I don't suppose you will be needing it anyway, as the world will be ending soon, and you and all the others will be departing this world," stated Eryndor.

"You fucker!" Danielle's eyes blazed with fury as Eryndor's words sank in. Her entire body tensed and she pulled harder against the chains, her muscles straining with the effort. Curling her fingers into fists, she glared at Eryndor with a look that could cut through steel. "You have no idea what you're doing, Eryndor. If you destroy that ring, you will doom us all. And if the world burns, I will make sure you burn with it." Her voice, when she spoke, was low and venomous, barely controlling the rage seething beneath each word.

"Believe me, my dear, I know exactly what I'm about to do," Eryndor stated, with a chilling smile. "Once you and your kind are wiped out, I'll be free to wreak havoc on other realms, too."

Danielle's rage reached a boiling point as Eryndor's words echoed in her ears. Her eyes flared with an intense, otherworldly light, and a surge of power coursed through her veins. With a primal scream, she pulled against the chains with all her might. The metal links groaned in protest, then snapped one by one, shattering like glass under her raw strength.

Freed from her bonds, Danielle lunged at Eryndor with blinding speed, her movements a blur of fury and determination. Eryndor barely had time to react as she slammed into him, the force of her attack driving them both to the ground.

"You will not destroy my world!" she hissed, her voice trembling with anger, as she tightened her grip, and her nails dug into his skin, leaving glowing trails of energy. Eryndor struggled beneath her, his own dark power flickering as he tried to counter her assault.

For a moment the two were locked in a deadly struggle, Danielle's wrath and strength pitted against Eryndor's dark magic. The air around them crackled with energy, the very ground beneath them trembling from the intensity of their clash.

With a snarl, Eryndor managed to summon a wave of shadowy energy, forcing Danielle back just enough to break her grip. But she was relentless, her eyes burning with an unyielding fire, as she used every ounce of her Lepidoptera strength and anger directed at the Harbinger of Shadows, determined to stop him at any cost.

With a swift, decisive motion, Eryndor unleashed a burst of dark energy. The force of the blast sent Danielle flying across the cabin, her body slamming into the cold steel wall with a sickening thud. She crumpled to the ground, gasping for breath, her strength momentarily drained.

Eryndor rose to his feet, brushing off the remnants of her attack with a cold smile. "You are strong, Danielle," he acknowledged, his voice dripping with malice. "But your anger makes you reckless."

"Humph, you should talk!" retorted Danielle.

He approached her slowly, his footsteps echoing ominously in the chamber. Danielle tried to rise, but pain and exhaustion held her down. Eryndor knelt beside her, gripping her chin, and forcing her to look into his eyes. "You should have known better than to challenge me, bitch."

With a flick of his wrist, the shadows obeyed Eryndor's command, binding Danielle to the floor once more, this time with even stronger chain.

Danielle's eyes burned with defiance, as she struggled weakly, her spirit unbroken despite her defeat. "You will pay for what has transpired here, Eryndor."

"Somehow, I think you are wrong," Eryndor declared, gesturing to the chains restraining Xanthia and Danielle. "You and your Fae friend will be the ones to pay. I'll make sure of it, Lcpidoptera."

Danielle frowned and wondered what Eryndor was talking about. "Xanthia is not Fae. Only I am, you fucking idiot."

Eryndor raised an eyebrow and smirked. "Interesting ..." He rubbed his chin. "So ... you don't know, do you?"

"What are you talking about?" demanded Danielle.

"Xanthia is Fae, and make no mistake, I am one hundred percent sure of my facts," stated Eryndor, glancing from Danielle to Xanthia.

Xanthia looked at Danielle, her brow furrowed. "I think I would know if I was this Fae he speaks of, wouldn't I?" She gulped hard.

He couldn't be right, could he? thought Xanthia, unsure what being a Fae even meant.

"Fae—or as they are more commonly known, Fairies—are both fascinating and formidable, and they embody the mystical and unpredictable nature of magic and the natural world," explained Danielle. She had been listening to Xanthia's muddled thoughts, and thought she would explain.

"Oh, right! What sort of magic or power do I have?" asked Xanthia.

"I don't know what you would have. Fae have many powers," replied Danielle.

"Enough of this chitchat," yelled Eryndor. "Now that I have what I came for, we are out of here." Eryndor clicked his fingers and a portal appeared in front of him. "Bye, ladies." He turned to Hawk, who was standing in a dark corner awaiting instructions from his master. *Kill these two bitches, get rid of their bodies, and join us later when the job is done.*

Yes, Master, thought Hawk. He bowed in agreement to Eryndor.

Come minions ... let's blow this joint, thought Eryndor, as he moved toward the portal's opening.

"Eryndor, stop," yelled Danielle, as she watched him walk into the portal. She then watched three other glazed-eyed creatures walk into the portal with Eryndor, and the portal close. "Fuck!" Danielle struggled against the chains that held her to the floor. As she fought the chains, she noticed Hawk stepping out from the shadows and into the moonlit cabin. "Hawk!" Her brow furrowed when she noticed his glazed eyes as he walked toward them, his sword drawn.

"Not today, bitch," stated Hawk, who was under Eryndor's malevolent mind control.

"Humph!" Without hesitation, Danielle called upon her Lepidoptera Vampire ability to alter someone's thoughts.

Hawk dropped his sword to the ground and clutched the sides of his head, hoping the pain and visions that Danielle was inflicting would stop. "Get out of my mind, bitch!" he shouted.

Danielle didn't listen, instead she kept up the intense pain and visions.

Within minutes, Hawk's eyes, that were once clouded with a sinister haze, gradually cleared, as he broke free from Eryndor's mind control. With his posture straightening and his expression shifting from twisted malevolence to his familiar, calm demeanor, he asked, "Danielle, Xanthia … where did you come from?" Hawk looked around the cabin and wondered where he was.

"You don't remember?" questioned Danielle.

"No, nothing! I think the longer Eryndor has me under his control, the less I remember," stated Hawk, as he noticed that they were chained to the floor. "Here, let me help you with those chains." He walked over and tore the chains off their wrists with ease. As a Griffin, Hawk had the power to break chains that another Griffin had manufactured.

"Thanks, Hawk," said Danielle, standing. She helped Xanthia up off the floor.

"Yes, thank you," said Xanthia, standing. "Can we get out of here?"

"You're welcome, young Fae," replied Hawk, as he placed his muscular arms around her back.

Hmm, even Hawk thinks Xanthia is a Fae. I will have to report this to William when we get back home, thought Danielle to herself.

"How are you feeling, Hawk?" asked Danielle, as she stood next to him.

"Not too good. My head hurts and my mind is fuzzy."

Danielle watched Hawk rub the sides of his head. "Are you okay to travel?"

"I think so. But I don't know how much longer it will be that I am going to be free from Eryndor's mind control.

In the past, it only seemed to last minutes, sometimes seconds, before Eryndor took control again." He shook his head in confusion, as his mind clouded over.

"Right. Well, we had better get moving," said Danielle to Xanthia and Hawk, as she picked up Hawk's sword from the ground and sheathed it on her back. "Hopefully we might be able to work out where we are."

Hawk seized Xanthia, one arm locked around her torso and the other gripping her neck, in a viselike hold. "Hand over the sword. We aren't going anywhere."

Oh shit. His eyes ... they have turned white again, thought Danielle, looking at Hawk's glazed stare.

"Calm down, Hawk," instructed Danielle, as she drew the sword and pointed it toward him. "Let Xanthia go."

"Hand over the sword, now, or this bitch dies," stated Hawk, holding Xanthia in a tight grip.

Xanthia began to scream, as Hawk's grip tightened on her neck.

Danielle called upon her abilities once more and inflicted maximum pain, and visions of being held over red-hot, steaming lava.

As Hawk felt the heat of the hot lava on his face, and witnessed it erupting in front of him, he released his hold on Xanthia.

Danielle grabbed hold of Xanthia and pulled her in close.

Xanthia placed her head on Danielle chest and sobbed hard. "What is wrong with him?" She glanced back at Hawk and watched his face distort.

"He is under Eryndor's mind control again. It's not Hawk who now stands before us, it's one of Eryndor's minions," stated Danielle, as she continued the visions in Hawk's mind.

Hawk dropped to his knees and screamed. "Help me, please!" He was then rendered unconscious.

"Is he dead?" asked Xanthia, nervously, as she looked at Danielle.

"No. He's unconscious. He'll be alright, I promise," replied Danielle.

"How are we going to get back home? We're going to die, aren't we?" Xanthia asked, desperation in her voice.

"Don't be silly, we are not going to die," replied Danielle. She smiled and pulled Xanthia in tight to try and calm her with her Lepidoptera power. "I am hoping we are still in France, because if we are, then I can contact the Gramaze coven to come and save us."

"You can do that?" questioned Xanthia.

Danielle nodded. "Give me a minute and I will try and connect to my life partner, Christian."

"Okay," said Xanthia, as she hugged Danielle in a childlike manner.

Christian! Christian ... can you hear me? thought Danielle.

Yes, my love. Where are you? thought Christian, not even knowing his life partner had been kidnapped.

I am not sure where we are. Xanthia is here with me ... and we have been taken by Eryndor and his minions, said Danielle telepathically.

Fuck! Are you both alright? asked Christian. He ran his fingers through his blond hair in frustration.

We are fine, and Eryndor has now gone. Hawk is here, too. Can you see if you can find us? asked Danielle.

Is there anything you can see outside for a landmark? asked Christian, his Italian accent apparent. He ran toward William's office.

Danielle walked over to the small window, which was located on the left-hand side of the cabin and looked out into the dark night sky. *We're in some kind of ship. I see mostly ocean, but there is some land nearby. Otherwise, nothing else.*

Okay. Leave it with me. Don't worry I will find you, my love, promised Christian, as he entered William's office.

Thank you. I love you, said Danielle telepathically.

"Everything is going to be okay. The Gramaze coven will be here soon," said Danielle to Xanthia, as she watched the tears spill over onto Xanthia's cheeks.

"I hope so," sobbed Xanthia, as she placed her head on Danielle's chest once again.

Out of the corner of her eye, Danielle noticed a pool of water slowly spreading across the floor and silently hoped her Lepidoptera family would find them soon.

CHAPTER THIRTY-NINE

"Sire," said Christian, as he approached William's desk. "Danielle and Xanthia have been captured by that fucking psychopath, Eryndor. And apparently Hawk is with them, too."

"What the hell … I wonder what that bastard will do next?" William exclaimed, rising to his feet. "Do you know where they are?"

"No, but according to Danielle, they're in a ship on the ocean, but near land," replied Christian.

"Let's go and see Brock. Maybe he can find them on the satellite feed," said William, walking toward the doorway. William knew from past experience that if a Lepidopteras life partner was in the same country, they could contact each other, so he knew that Danielle, Xanthia and Hawk wouldn't be far away.

"Yes, Sire," said Christian, as he followed William.

Heads up, Lepidopteras … Xanthia and Danielle have been captured by Eryndor and his minions. Hawk is with them, as well. I want Adrian, Stephen, Sharina, Michael, Violette, Grayson, Samantha and Kelan, to meet Christian and I, in the backyard in five minutes. Brock, I want you to search the satellite feed to see if you can find them in the Atlantic Ocean, but nearer to land, thought William telepathically to his family.

They all chanted, 'Yes'.

* * *

"Brock, what have you found?" asked William, as he walked through the sliding doors of the operation room, with Christian behind him.

"Nothing, so far, Sire," acknowledged Brock, continuing to look over the feedback, as William and Christian stood behind him, double-checking the screen.

"There, go back," stated Christian, pointing to the screen. "What is that?"

"It looks like a shimmering wall," answered Brock, as he positioned the satellite to have a closer look.

"Look closer … it looks like an old, abandoned ship behind that shimmering wall. I would say that is our starting point. Right, you stay here, Brock, and keep us informed. Let's go, Christian," commanded William. They ran at Vampire speed toward the sliding doors, and out to the backyard to meet up with their coven.

Violette had heard the mind-chatter in the operations room and had opened a portal to carry everyone to the abandoned ship. "Is everyone ready?"

They all nodded in agreement.

Thank you, Violette, thought William telepathically, as he approached the backyard with Christian and saw the shimmering blue-green portal already open.

You're welcome, thought Violette telepathically.

"Listen up, everyone," said William, as he stood in front of his coven, looking at each of their faces.

"It looks like Xanthia, Danielle and Hawk are on an abandoned ship, off the coast. And we don't know what to expect when we get there. We don't know if Eryndor is still hanging around, either, so keep your wits about you," stated William.

They all said, 'Yes'.

Violette, you will be staying here to guard the academy and Gramaze mansion, with Queen Talitha. I will call on your help, if needed, when we need to return via the portal, thought William.

Yes, William, thought Violette.

"Right … let's move," commanded William to his coven, as he walked toward the portal and his Lepidoptera family followed.

* * *

Danielle! thought Christian as he walked out of the portal, along with everyone else, including Adrian, Danielle's foster father and a Warlock.

Yes! said Danielle, telepathically.

Can you see us by the shoreline? asked Christian.

Danielle walked over to the small window and peered out. *Yes! I see you.*

Is Eryndor or anyone else on board the ship, thought Christian.

I don't think so. But could you hurry, because we are taking on water, fast, thought Danielle.

Shit … we will be there in a few seconds, my love, thought Christian.

"William, if we don't get there soon, they will drown," stated Christian.

"Yes, I heard the conversation." William turned to Adrian. "Can you create a portal to take us out to the abandoned ship?" He pointed to the ship off the coast.

"Of course," replied Adrian. He placed his hands out front and created the portal. "Go!" He was anxious to get his daughter back, and in safe hands.

"Sharina, Stephen, Samantha, I want you to stay here and guard the shoreline and keep Adrian safe. Everyone else, let's move," instructed William, as he walked into the portal and his coven followed.

* * *

Doesn't look like anyone is on board the ship, thought William to his coven, as he looked around. *Christian, contact Danielle*, instructed William.

Danielle, where are you? Christian called out telepathically.

I think we are in the bow of the ship, answered Danielle. *Hurry, we don't have much longer.* The water was lapping at her and Xanthia's chins, as they tried to stay afloat.

Just as she said this, Christian opened a doorway and appeared from above. "Give me your hands." He placed his hands in the water for both girls to take.

They reached up and grabbed hold of Christian's hands, and he pulled them out of the water to the top deck of the ship. "Are you both okay?" He looked from Danielle to Xanthia.

Danielle nodded yes.

"I'm freezing," Xanthia said through chattering teeth, shivering against the cool night air.

"Come here … I can warm you up. One of my specialties," joked Kelan.

"Go, you will be okay," Danielle said softly, giving Xanthia an encouraging look before heading over to Christian.

Xanthia hesitated, her cheeks flushing as she reluctantly made her way to Kelan, whom she recognized from the Gramaze mansion.

"Don't worry, I don't bite," said Kelan, as he held her close to his muscular chest, and used his Lepidoptera powers.

"Ah, nice and warm. Thank you!" said Xanthia.

"You're welcome," said Kelan.

"Where is Hawk?" asked Grayson to Danielle.

"Down there." She pointed to the water below.

Grayson nodded and dove into the water. With his Lepidoptera Vampire vision, he scanned the cabin. *Ah, there you are.*

Grayson swam into the cabin, his heart pounding—then froze. Hawk was there, suspended in the center of the flooded chamber, floating eerily still like a ghost. Unconscious ... but breathing.

Grayson quickly grabbed hold of Hawk and dragged him to the top of the cavity opening. "Michael, can you help me with him?" asked Grayson, holding Hawk's head above the water.

Michael pulled Hawk out of the water and laid him on the top deck.

Pulling himself up out of the water, Grayson knelt next to Hawk and felt his neck for a pulse. "He is alive."

"You will need to restrain him before he wakes. He is still under Eryndor's mind control," stated Danielle.

"Thanks for the heads-up, Danielle," said Grayson.

"Everyone ... good job. Let's head on home," said William.

Adrian, can you open a portal for us to get back to the shore? asked William, telepathically.

No problem, my friend, replied Adrian.

As the portal opened on the abandoned ship, in front of them, Grayson picked up Hawk, who was still unconscious, and walked with everyone else into the portal.

"Grayson, when we get back to our home I want you to chain Hawk up in the dungeon. I don't want him causing any trouble when we return," stated William.

"Yes, Sire," replied Grayson.

"Danielle ... I want a full report on how you and Xanthia were captured this morning by Eryndor," said William.

"Yes, Sire," replied Danielle.

"Xanthia ... how are you, my dear?" asked William, as he walked out the portal, which opened on the shoreline.

"I'm okay, I think!" replied Xanthia, her voice a bit shaky.

"I'm sure your father will be happy to have you back home," said William.

Xanthia smiled and nodded yes.

Violette, we have Danielle, Xanthia and Hawk. Open a portal to bring us home, William communicated telepathically, fully aware that only Talitha or Violette could open a portal back to the Gramaze mansion, due to the wards they had erected for protection.

Yes, William, thought Violette. She conjured a portal to bring them home.

* * *

"How are you feeling, my love," Christian asked Danielle as they finished getting dressed.

"I'm fine," replied Danielle, shrugging on her jacket. "Actually, I need to go and debrief with William."

"You have been through quite a bit today; would you like me to come with you?" asked Christian.

"No, I should be okay. It's only a debrief. But thanks for offering," replied Danielle. She leaned in to give her life partner a hug.

"Okay," said Christian, placing his arms around Danielle. "I am on guard tonight, at Talitha's doorway. So, if you need me, I am close by."

"Thanks, babe," said Danielle. She slowly pulled away from their embrace and looked into his brown eyes. "Maybe we can catch up later on?"

"Sounds like a plan. I suppose I had better get going," said Christian.

Danielle nodded and watched him walk toward the doorway. *Hmm, cute ass!*

I heard that, thought Christian to Danielle.

Danielle smiled and placed her mobile phone in her jacket pocket and headed toward the doorway.

* * *

"Come!" said William, hearing the knock on his open office door.

"Sire!" said Danielle, closing the door and walking toward him.

"Take a seat, Danielle," said William, gesturing to a chair in front of his desk. "I won't be a moment."

Danielle sat on the chair and watched William finish up with his paperwork.

"Right, let's get this debrief done," said William, placing a manila folder with papers inside into a tray behind him. "Tell me what happened, from the start."

Danielle relayed in detail the events of the day to William and watched the expression on his face change.

"That fucker … So, he not only took your mother's gold ring—you think he ordered Hawk to kill you both as well?" stated William frowning, his voice low with disbelief.

Danielle nodded slowly. "I can't be sure, but that's what it felt like. They blocked me—I couldn't read their thoughts. But their body language … it said enough."

"Eryndor needs an early grave, and I am just the Lepidoptera to do it. How dare he kidnap and threaten my family." He slammed his fist down on the desk. "I will be speaking with Garrick about Eryndor and Hawk this evening, and he had better get these two under control, otherwise I will deal with both of them. Hopefully Garrick will know why Eryndor wanted your Fae ring," said William, standing.

"Sire … that's not all, either." Danielle watched William walk over to the window. "I believe, but am not a hundred percent sure, that Xanthia is a Fae."

William's brow furrowed as he turned and said, "Hmm, who told you this?"

"Eryndor and Hawk. But I don't think Xanthia knew that she is Fae, because she queried me on what a Fae was," replied Danielle.

"Well, she knows now. I need to speak with her father about this. I wonder if he knows, but has never said anything," said William, walking back to the desk and taking a seat.

"Yeah, I've been wondering the same thing. But I think we're forgetting something—if Xanthia really is Fae, she and her father won't be safe outside our home. Maybe that's something you could bring up with Albinus, too. They need to understand just how powerful Fae abilities are to other supernaturals and how that makes them a target," stated Danielle.

"Yes, definitely. Also, I need to inform you that from now onward, I will arrange for two of our coven members to follow you in another car when you drop Xanthia off at Lycée International. Additionally, I will assign one of our coven to guard Xanthia, while she is at school each day," said William.

"Thanks, William. That would be greatly appreciated. I have no doubt Eryndor has more schemes in motion, so we'll all need to remain especially vigilant," stated Danielle.

"Yes, you are probably right. Was there anything else you wanted to discuss?" asked William, standing.

"No, Sire. Was there a mission or something you required me to do this evening?" queried Danielle.

"At this point, no. Maybe you could check on Xanthia for me?" asked William. "Let me know how she's doing?"

"Good idea!" said Danielle, standing.

"Right now, I need to go and have a chat with Albinus," said William, walking toward the doorway. He gestured for Danielle to walk with him.

Danielle followed William out of his office and down the marble staircase. "Chat to you later on, Sire." As they reached the landing, Danielle watched William walk toward Albinus, who was seated in the sitting room, with Xanthia by his side.

*　*　*

"Evening, Albinus, Xanthia," said William as he walked into the sitting room.

"Good evening, William." Albinus placed his hand out front to shake William's hand. "I wanted to thank you for rescuing my beautiful daughter."

"You are welcome, my friend," said William, shaking his hand. He looked from Albinus to Xanthia, who had her head on her father's shoulder. "Xanthia, would you mind leaving us, so that your father and I can have a discussion?"

"Yes, Sir." Xanthia looked up at William and smiled. "It's been a long day, so I might turn in for the night. Good night, Father." She kissed him on his cheek. "Night, Mr. Gramaze."

"Good night, Xanthia," said William.

"Night, sweetheart. I will see you in the morning," said Albinus. He leaned in and gave Xanthia a hug. "Sweet dreams!"

Standing, Xanthia walked toward the doorway, leaving Albinus and William to talk in peace.

William sat on the coffee table in front of the lounge Albinus was sitting on.

"What did you want to discuss, William?" asked Albinus.

"Have you made a decision yet, on if you and Xanthia are going to stay with us permanently?" queried William.

"I haven't, no. Why do you ask?" replied Albinus.

"I have found out some information this evening that I think you should be told. But I have the feeling you already know," stated William.

"What?" questioned Albinus.

"Did you know that Xanthia is Fae?" asked William.

Albinus gulped hard and took a deep breath. "Yes, I do know."

"Considering what we are—" he gestured to himself, "—why in hell didn't you let us know?"

"I'm sorry, William. It's not that I don't trust you or wanted to keep it a secret. It's … just … I promised

Xanthia's mother that I would not let anyone know. We have never discussed this with Xanthia, either, even though her mother was Fae. And I wasn't totally sure Xanthia was Fae. She hasn't, as yet, shown any sign of this. Can I ask how you found out?" stated Albinus.

"The creature that kidnapped Xanthia and Danielle, he confirmed it," replied William.

"So … does Xanthia know that she is Fae? Did this creature tell her?" asked Albinus.

"I'm afraid she does know, Albinus. And yes, it was the creature who kidnapped them who told Xanthia."

Upon hearing the news, Albinus sighed deeply and his shoulders slumped forward. "When she returned this evening she didn't say anything to me. I wonder what she is thinking? I must go and chat with her," said Albinus, standing.

"Before you go, there is one more thing that I want to talk with you about," said William, also standing.

Albinus's brow furrowed. "What?"

"I think that you need to consider your living arrangements. If Xanthia is Fae, she'll be vulnerable out there—and she'll need protection. Her powers would be incredibly valuable to other supernatural beings, which makes her a target for exploitation. The safest place for both of you is here at the mansion. We can protect you," explained William.

"Yes, I know you are right, and I have already considered this. I do thank you for the offer, but at this stage I just don't know. Would you mind if I take a few more days to process the implications of moving into your residence permanently?" asked Albinus.

"Take your time. As I have said before, you and your daughter are welcome to stay with my family and I permanently. Also, just so you know, I have organized for more security, and guards to look after Xanthia when she returns to Lycée International," said William.

"Thank you, William. I appreciate everything you are doing for Xanthia and myself." He placed his hand out front to shake William's hand again.

"You are welcome, my friend. I will chat with you more tomorrow, when things have settled down," said William, shaking Albinus's hand.

"Yes, for sure. I might go and see how Xanthia is doing. See you tomorrow," said Albinus. He walked toward the doorway.

* * *

"Knock, knock!" said Danielle, as she stood outside Xanthia's room.

"Come in," called Xanthia, sitting up in bed and turning her bedside light on.

"Hi, Xanthia. I thought I would come by and check on you," said Danielle, as she opened the door and walked into the room. "How are you?"

"I'm okay," lied Xanthia.

"That's good. I was wondering … would you like to know more about being Fae?" asked Danielle, as she sat on the bed. "You know that I am part Fae, don't you?"

"No, I didn't know that. I thought that you're a Lepidoptera Vampire," replied Xanthia.

"I am both. So … if there is anything you want to know about the Fae, I can help you there," said Danielle.

"Oh, right!" said Xanthia, her brow furrowed. "How do I know if I am turning into a Fae? I mean, so far, I haven't felt any different. I am wondering if I really am Fae."

"There's one way to find out." Danielle looked around Xanthia's room. "Ah … the glass of water you have on your side table. Watch what I can do with the water."

Xanthia observed as Danielle pointed her finger at the glass, causing the water inside to swirl. "Is that something I can do, too?"

"Yes, and more," replied Danielle. "You try it." She indicated to the glass. "Point your finger at the glass and try to swirl the water with your finger."

Xanthia did as Danielle instructed, but nothing happened. "See, I told you. I don't think I am a Fae."

"Try again … only this time, concentrate on swirling the water inside the glass with your mind," replied Danielle.

With a look of intense concentration on her face, Xanthia pointed her finger at the glass, and the water began to swirl in a circular motion. Smiling, she quickly looked at Danielle, and then back to the glass. "What else can I do?"

"A lot more than you know. But at least you know you are Fae. You might be more human at the moment, but I would say your powers will start to kick in pretty soon," replied Danielle.

Xanthia placed her hands in her lap and the glass of water fell on the floor. "Oops!"

"I can fetch you some books from the Gramaze coven's library, about the Fae. They really do help with mastering your powers and abilities," Danielle assured. Standing, she picked up the empty glass from the floor and placed it back on the side table.

"That would be great, Danielle. Thank you," said Xanthia, appreciative of any help.

"No problem. Just remember, you are not alone. If you need someone to chat with about being Fae, I'm your girl," stated Danielle.

Xanthia smiled, knowing she had someone else who would be able to help her through the adjustment, when it came.

"Knock, knock," said Albinus, as he stood in the doorway. "May I come in?"

"Of course, Father," said Xanthia, gesturing for him to enter the room. She patted her bed. "Come, sit."

Albinus walked into the room and sat at the foot of the bed.

Can you hear me, Xanthia? thought Danielle. *Nod if you can.*

Xanthia raised her eyebrows and nodded to Danielle.

Another one of your powers. I will leave you to chat with your father and come back later to show you where the library is, thought Danielle.

Okay! thought Xanthia. *Wow, this mind-talking thing is super cool.*

Yeah, it sure is, thought Danielle to Xanthia.

"Well, I need to get going," said Danielle. "I will see you later on, Xanthia. Bye, Albinus."

"Good night, dear," said Albinus.

"See you later, Danielle, and thank you," said Xanthia, smiling, as she watched Danielle walk through the doorway and close the door behind her.

"How are you doing, my girl?" asked Albinus, his brow furrowed from worry.

"Actually, never better," said Xanthia.

"That's good. Umm … there was something that I wanted to talk with you about," said Albinus.

"What's that, Father," asked Xanthia.

"Do you remember much about your mother?"

"How could I ever forget her. That's a silly question," said Xanthia.

"I believe that you have been given some news today, about yourself and the Fae world," said Albinus. He watched Xanthia's expression change.

"Yes," replied Xanthia, her brow furrowed.

I wonder how much father knows about the Fae? thought Xanthia.

"Can you tell me what happened today, once the creatures kidnapped you from Lycée?" asked Albinus.

"When Danielle and I were held captive by that disgusting creature, Eryndor, he told me that I was Fae. At first, I didn't know what he was talking about, but I think I have figured it out now. Was my mother Fae or are you Fae? Or was I adopted?" questioned Xanthia.

"Your mother was Fae, but she never joined the Fae Kingdom, and hardly ever used her powers," answered Albinus.

"If mother was Fae, well then that would make sense that I am Fae, too," stated Xanthia.

"Have you felt a difference in yourself since you have been told?" asked Albinus.

"Not really. I was talking to Danielle about it, and she said she is going to help me with this. Apparently, they have a library here at the Gramaze coven, that has a lot of Fae books and history. Did you know Danielle is part Fae?" asked Xanthia.

"No, I didn't know that. So, it looks like Danielle will be able to help you. That's if you want to follow the Fae path," said Albinus.

"Yes, Father. She told me she would help me, if I wanted it. But I'm not sure yet. It's a bit scary, and a lot more to deal with than what I ever expected in my life," stated Xanthia.

"It sure is. I'm sure you will make the right decision. You are a very intelligent woman, Xanthia, and I have every faith in you," said Albinus.

"Thank you, Father. Would you mind if I could have some time alone, to think?" asked Xanthia.

"Not at all, sweetheart. I am here if you need to talk," said Albinus, standing. "I'll see you tomorrow morning." He gave Xanthia a kiss on her forehead. "Night!"

"Thank you. Night, night," said Xanthia, as she watched her father head toward the doorway, closing the door behind him.

Life sure is going to be different from now on, thought Xanthia, as she refilled her glass with water and took a sip.

CHAPTER FORTY

William stood by the window, his fists clenched involuntarily, as he gazed out over the sprawling Gramaze property. The lush landscape, usually a source of tranquility, did little to ease his troubled mind. The phone call he'd just had with Garrick echoed in his thoughts, and the revelation of Eryndor's intentions and why he desired the Fae's Golden Ring weighed heavily on him. A sense of impending doom overshadowed his thoughts, as he tried to piece together a solution.

A soft creak of the door behind him broke his reverie. Turning, he noticed Renee walking toward him, her presence a comforting contrast to his feeling of unease.

"William, are you alright?" she asked gently, her brow furrowing with concern.

"Yes … why do you ask?" replied William, with his arms crossed over his chest.

"I feel from our Lepidoptera connection that you are worried, and this is making my stomach do somersaults," said Renee. "What is going on?"

"It's nothing for you to be worried about, my love," replied William, his brow furrowed.

"Whatever it is, we can figure it out together. Two heads are better than one," stated Renee as she stood beside him, placing her hand on his arm, trying to calm him with her Lepidoptera ability.

William looked at Renee and leaned in for a hug. As he slowly pulled away he said, "I rang Garrick earlier and told him that we have Hawk here with us, and that Eryndor had stolen Danielle's gold ring."

"And what did Garrick say?" asked Renee.

"Once the mind control has been taken from Hawk, he wants us to keep Hawk here to keep him safe from Eryndor."

"Well, that's a good thing. I think. Don't you?" asked Renee.

"I sure do. He is a real asset to the academy. I still need to speak with Talitha, to ask her to break Eryndor's mind control over Hawk."

"If that is all that is bothering you, then I can do this," stated Renee.

"It's not! Garrick told me that he knows why Eryndor wanted Danielle's ring. Eryndor is trying to end this world. Apparently, he requires three sacred items, and now he has all three of them. I fear our kind will be destroyed."

Renee's eyes widened and a cold shiver clawed its way down her spine. "Please tell me you've spoken to Talitha about this …"

"No, not yet."

"Hang on … you said Eryndor has all three sacred items."

"Yes, that's correct."

"But I thought that the chalice was still inside the book, and Stjernefrída was the only one who could extract it."

"Yes, that's true. But Garrick said he heard on the grapevine that Eryndor has propositioned the Fae Queen, Elyndra, and is promising her the world, if she can get the chalice out of the book. And what if she does?"

"I wouldn't count on that. You know how deceitful Fae can be, William. She has probably told Eryndor that she will do it for him, but in truth she can't. I think the only thing that you can do at this stage is talk with Talitha. She usually will have a solution to most problems."

"I think you are right, my love. Thank you for being my sounding board."

"You are welcome. That is one of the many things that life partners are for," said Renee, smiling up at William.

"There is a lot going on at the moment, and this is just another hindrance to get over. I will go and see Talitha now," said William, as he walked toward the doorway.

"Okay, my love. See you later, and no more worrying, please. My stomach cannot cope with the cartwheels," said Renee, smirking.

William walked back to Renee, kissed her quickly, and then ran toward Talitha's room.

* * *

"Hawk!" called Sully, as she stood at the dungeon doorway, peering through the door's small window.

There was no answer.

"What … I'm not good enough to talk to?" teased Sully. She noticed Hawk lying on the cold dungeon floor, chained down, with his back to the door.

Hawk sat up quickly. "Just fuck the hell off, you bitch." He pulled violently at the chains that bound him to the floor.

Sully noticed his glazed-over eyes. "I was not talking to you, asshole. Get the other Hawk."

"And what is my prize for letting Hawk surface?"

Sully opened the door with the metal key. "Me!" she teased, as she curtsied. *Fucking asshole, get out of Hawk's mind!*

The glazed-eyed creature smirked. "Now that is a prize I would like to get hold of."

"Well?" prompted Sully, standing an arm's length in front of him, with her arms folded over her chest.

The glazed-eyed creature grabbed the sides of his head, and his eyes rolled back into their sockets, before a clear-headed Hawk appeared.

"Sully, what are you doing in here. Please … be careful," said Hawk, knowing it would only be a matter of minutes, if not seconds, before the mind control took over again.

253

"I had to see you. I miss you. Are you okay?" stated Sully, as she knelt in front of him.

"I miss you, too," said Hawk. He leaned in to kiss her lips, and lingered for a few seconds, savoring her touch.

Sully leaned into his body, kissed his soft lips, and placed her arms around his shoulders. *Hmm, heaven!*

As Hawk slowly pulled away from their passionate embrace, he yanked at his chains and asked, "Can you get me out of these?"

Sully shook her head. "I don't have the strength. I believe you may have some visitors soon, who are coming to help you escape Eryndor's mind control. Then you'll be able to leave the dungeon."

"Is that right?" A glazed-eyed Hawk grabbed Sully by the throat and started to choke her.

"Hawk, stop. You're hurting me," her voice barely a whisper. Sully looked into his eyes and realized that he was no longer the Hawk she knew; instead, he was one of Eryndor's minions once again.

"Hawk is no longer here. Just I, bitch. Set me free, or you will die."

Sully struggled to breathe as Hawk's grip tightened around her throat, his fingers digging into her skin. Her vision blurred and she felt the strength draining from her body. Desperate, she summoned every ounce of her willpower, focusing on any chance she had to stop him.

"Hawk … let her go," demanded Grayson, as he entered the dungeon.

Hawk's glazed-over white eyes burned with a terrifying intensity, filled with a mad, murderous rage. They glowed eerily in the dim dungeon light, reflecting his desperate desire to kill, and to escape the chains that bound him.

"I said, let her go, fucker!" Without hesitation, Grayson rushed forward. and grabbed a nearby iron rod. With all his strength, he swung it at Hawk's arm, aiming to break his grip and free Sully from his deadly hold.

Gasping for breath, Sully broke free and crumpled to the ground, clutching her bruised throat.

"You will pay, Lepidoptera," yelled Hawk, clutching his arm.

With his Lepidoptera Vampire speed, Grayson collected Sully from the dungeon floor and pulled her away from Hawk's grasp. "Are you alright?" asked Grayson, placing Sully on the floor.

Sully nodded and pushed herself upright. As she glanced at Hawk, tears began to well in her eyes. "How could you?" she whispered.

"Remember … that is not Hawk you are talking to. It's one of Eryndor's minions," stated Grayson, as he looked from Sully to a glazed-eyed Hawk. "Come on, let's get out of here."

Sully nodded in agreement, as Grayson helped her to stand.

Hawk yanked at his chains, desperately trying to free himself, but it was to no avail.

I'm so sorry, Sully! thought Hawk, watching Grayson and Sully close the door and lock it. *I didn't mean to hurt you. Please, forgive me.*

Sully chose to dismiss his thoughts to her, as the tears spilled over onto her cheeks, and she continued up the stairs with Grayson.

"How's your throat?" asked Grayson, as he walked up the stairs.

"It's okay. I heal fast. My heart is another issue, though," replied Sully. She wiped the tears from her cheeks.

"I glad you're okay. Don't worry too much about Hawk. He will return to you soon enough," said Grayson.

"I'm so thankful that you came along when you did, otherwise I think Eryndor's minion would have killed me," said Sully.

"Definitely! I know it's hard being away from your life partner, but you need to remember that you won't be safe near Hawk until the mind control has been taken off him," explained Grayson.

"I know you're right. I couldn't help myself. I am so drawn to him," stated Sully.

"Don't worry, it will all be over soon, I promise." Grayson placed his arm around Sully's shoulder and they continued up the stairs.

CHAPTER FORTY-ONE

"How did you go with Talitha?" asked Renee, watching as William walked into their bedroom.

"Much better than I expected," William remarked, removing his shirt as he headed toward the connected bathroom. "She's visiting Hawk tonight, to lift the mind control. At least that's one thing sorted."

"And what about the three sacred objects that Eryndor has?" asked Renee, following William to the bathroom. She leaned on the doorframe and watched him take off his jeans.

William took a deep breath, his resolve hardening. "Essentially, I need to discover where Eryndor is hiding the three sacred artifacts, and where he's holed up. At first light tomorrow, we must gather everyone for a coven meeting to devise a plan to find them and counteract their power." He stepped into the shower and turned on the faucet. "It won't be easy, but if we fail and Eryndor wins, well, there won't be a world left to save," he stated matter-of-factly.

"We won't fail, William. We've faced worse than this before. We'll find those artifacts and stop Eryndor. Let's get some rest tonight and tackle this tomorrow."

"Agreed, my love," said William, as he lathered his body with a loofah covered with bodywash. "I'll need to call Garrick and Elara as well to discuss coordinating our resources."

"Good idea!" agreed Renee, as she discarded her clothes to the floor and stepped into the shower with William.

* * *

Hawk heard the cell door's lock click open and looked up to see Queen Talitha approaching. He sat up quickly. "What do you want?" his voice sharp and defiant.

"Well, well … I see you haven't changed much, minion," stated Talitha, as she stood in front of him and sneered.

Hawk met her sneer with a cold glare. "And I see that you're still the same arrogant Lepidoptera," he retorted. "What do you want this time, Talitha?"

"Humph!" Talitha waved her hand at Hawk sealing his lips closed.

Hawk pulled violently at the chains that bound him, his frustration mounting, as the metal dug into his wrists.

With a flick of her hand, Talitha conjured the ancient book of spells, which would help break Hawk's mental bond with Eryndor. Skimming through the pages, she found the spell again and began chanting the incantation.

> By the blood that flows through night,
> Within shadows, deep and tight,
> I command the chains to break,
> Free this mind, no more to take.

The atmosphere crackled with a mix of ancient magic and potent energy that permeated the room. Talitha's fingertips emitted a soft, ethereal glow, and with each gesture, she directed the arcane energies to unravel the threads of mind control that Eryndor had woven over Hawk.

Hawk's eyes blazed with fury and defiance, locked on Talitha with an intensity that spoke of his determination to resist her control. His body twitched involuntarily as the mystical forces began their delicate work.

As the last fragments from Eryndor's control began to dissipate, lucidity once again returned to Hawk.

"Welcome back!" said Talitha, watching as the oppressive darkness lifted and was replaced by a newfound clarity and awareness.

"Queen Talitha?" stated Hawk, recognizing her face.

"How are you feeling?" asked Talitha.

"A little groggy, but better," replied Hawk, pulling at his chains.

"Let me help you there, dear," said Talitha. She clicked her fingers to unshackle Hawk from his chains.

"Thank you," said Hawk, standing and rubbing his wrists.

"You are welcome," replied Talitha. "Now … let's get you sorted with a shower, clean clothes and some nourishment," said Talitha. "Come this way!" She gestured toward the cell doorway.

Hawk followed Queen Talitha out the door and up the concrete stairs to the Gramaze coven household.

* * *

"Thank you for this lovely meal, Lamiae," said Hawk, seated at the white marble island bench in the Gramaze kitchen, with his back to the doorway.

"You're welcome. Can I interest you in some fruit salad and ice cream for dessert?" asked Lamiae, collecting his plate from the bench and placing it in the dishwasher.

"That sounds awesome. Thanks, Lamiae. Do you have some ambrosia as well?" asked Hawk.

"Let me have a look." She opened the fridge and searched every shelf for it. "Nope, doesn't look like we have any. Sorry, Hawk," replied Lamiae, her French accent apparent.

"That's okay, I will be happy with the fruit salad and ice cream," replied Hawk.

"Awesome! Coming up," stated Lamiae, as she walked over to the freezer for the ice cream. "Where's that lovely partner of yours tonight?"

"I doubt if she would want to see me, at the moment. I do remember some of what happened between us, especially when I tried to strangle her," said Hawk, shaking his head.

"I am sure that she would have forgiven you by now, Hawk. Sully would have known that you were under mind control when you did that to her," replied Lamiae, placing the fruit salad in a dessert bowl.

"Humph! Forgiven me … I don't think so. I bet she never wants to see me again," stated Hawk.

"Here you go," said Lamiae, placing the bowl in front of him.

"Thanks," said Hawk.

Sully stood in the doorway to the kitchen and placed her pointer finger over her lips, winking at Lamiae.

Lamiae smiled knowingly and turned toward the sink to clear away the dishes.

Hawk suddenly felt hands gently cover his eyes.

"Guess who?" Sully's playful voice teased.

Hawk grinned as he reached up to remove the hands. Turning, he said warmly, "Hello!"

Sully leaned in and kissed him softly, her lips brushing against his with tender affection. Hawk's strong arms encircled her, pulling her closer, holding her as if he couldn't bear to let go.

I have missed this! thought Sully to Hawk.

Yeah, me too, Hawk replied silently, pulling back just enough to meet her gaze.

"So, what are you up to today?" Sully asked, curiosity in her voice.

"I asked William if I could return to training, but he said no. Apparently, I need a few more days to let my mind and body recover. So, I'm not sure. What about you?" Hawk responded.

"I've been assigned to guard Stjernefrída and Kura," Sully said, her eyes locking with his.

Stjernefrída and Kura, hmm. "In the ancient forest, or are they here at Gramaze mansion?" Hawk asked.

"They're staying at the mansion until Eryndor is dealt with," Sully explained.

"Oh, right!" said Hawk.

"And what about the Golden Chalice? Has it been removed from the book yet?" Hawk asked, recalling from his cultural lessons that Stjernefrída was the only one capable of retrieving it.

"From what I've heard, Eryndor now has the book, with the chalice still sealed inside. Apparently, he's approached Queen Elyndra of the Fae to extract it."

Hawk frowned. "And has Elyndra managed to do it?"

"I don't think so. Otherwise, we wouldn't be standing here right now. Eryndor has made it quite clear—once he possesses all three sacred objects, he'll destroy our world."

"Three sacred objects," Hawk frowned again. "What's the third one?"

Sully's expression darkened. "A few days ago, while you were under mind control, Eryndor stole Danielle's gold ring. It's apparently a priceless Fae family heirloom that's been passed down to her through generations. From what I've heard, once Eryndor collects all three sacred items, he plans to end the world—and everyone in it. Crazy, right?"

Hawk's expression remained neutral, though something flickered in his eyes—a shadow of conflict quickly hidden. He forced a casual shrug.

"Crazy is one way to put it," he said, his voice steady. "But who even knows if that's true? People love to twist stories when it comes to power and relics."

Sully's brow creased as she gave him a curious look.

Hawk held her gaze without faltering, his tone deliberately nonchalant. "Besides, if Eryndor really wanted to end the world, why hasn't he done it already? Maybe there's more to this than we're being told."

"Not sure," replied Sully.

"Anyways, let's forget about all that for the moment. When will I be able to see you?" asked Hawk.

"Not until late this evening, probably," answered Sully.

"That long? What about if I come and guard with you. Do you think that will be okay?" asked Hawk. "That way I can spend some more time with you."

"As much as that would be nice, I don't think William would be too happy about us hanging out, and me not taking my job seriously. After all, I am meant to guarding Stjernefrída and Kura."

"Right!" said a disheartened Hawk. "So … where in the Gramaze mansion are they being held?"

"I don't know."

"What … is it top secret or something?" asked Hawk.

"I think so. All I know is that I have to report to the operations room, and from there I will be taken to their room, where I will stand guard all day," replied Sully. She looked at the clock up on the wall in the kitchen. "I need to get moving. My shift starts in ten minutes, and I still need to get dressed."

"Oh, okay. Well, I hope it goes well. Let me know when you're finished, and we can meet somewhere; either at the academy or the mansion," said Hawk.

"Okay!" Sully leaned in to kiss his lips. Pulling away slowly, she said, "See ya!"

"I look forward to it," said Hawk, as he watched her walk toward the doorway.

"Looks like you had nothing to be worried about, Hawk," said Lamiae, as she wiped the island benchtop.

"Yeah, I sure am one lucky man," replied Hawk, a wide grin spreading across his face. "Well, I think I'll head back to the academy and get some rest. Catch you later, Lamiae."

"Take care, young man," Lamiae said softly, her gaze following Hawk as he walked toward the doorway.

CHAPTER FORTY-TWO

Hawk lay on his back with his hands tucked under his head on the pillow, staring up at the ceiling, his thoughts drifting to Sully and all the things they had been through together. A smile tugged at his lips as he pictured her beautiful face, wondering what the future would hold for them, especially as he was next in line to the throne in Norway.

Hawk!

Hawk jolted upright, his feet slamming against the ground as his wide, panicked eyes swept the room. That voice—it couldn't be. It was too familiar, too chilling. "Eryndor?" he whispered, the name catching in his throat. His heart pounded like a war drum, thundering in his chest. With a trembling hand, he raked his fingers through his shoulder-length blond hair, breath shallow as he strained to hear it again—the voice that haunted him.

Come now, Hawk ... you know exactly who it is.

Eryndor? Get the fuck out of my head, thought Hawk, his fists clenching as he stood tall.

You will do my bidding, brother ... or else, I will kill your delectable Sully. Or ... I could always have her for myself, thought Eryndor, a cruel smile playing on his lips, as he stood on the deck of another derelict ship, staring out over the North Atlantic Ocean.

You won't touch her. I will make damn sure of that, Eryndor, thought Hawk.

Enough of this, thought Eryndor, his patience wearing thin. He extended his shadowy hand in front of him, digging his talons into his palm, a grimace flickering across his face.

Hawk clutched his head as a sharp, searing pain tore through his skull—Eryndor was forcing his way into his mind again. The pressure mounted with every second, unbearable and relentless. "Aww, fuck!" he gasped, his vision swimming, knees threatening to buckle beneath him. Each time Eryndor invaded his thoughts, the psychic link between them grew stronger—despite the reinforced wards surrounding the Gramaze mansion. Hawk could feel him pushing deeper, more violently than ever before.

Are we clear now? Eryndor's voice echoed in Hawk's mind, cold and taunting.

Yes, Master, thought a semi-glazed-eyed Hawk, as he stood to attention.

I believe Stjernefrída is holed up at the Gramaze mansion. Is this correct? questioned Eryndor, who had been listening in to Hawk and Sully's earlier conversation.

I believe so. Hawk clutched at his head, desperate to break free from the mind control.

Well, is that a yes, or no? I need to know, NOW, yelled Eryndor into Hawk's mind.

Hawk's legs buckled beneath him, and he collapsed to the floor, clutching his head with both hands. A sharp, searing pain shot through his skull as Eryndor's control tightened around his mind, the darkness wrapping around his thoughts like a vise. His breathing grew erratic as he fought to retain control, his nails digging into his temples, desperately trying to push the foreign presence out.

No ... I won't ... he thought, but the words felt hollow, as Eryndor's will was stronger than his own. His vision blurred, the white film over his eyes returning, clouding his mind. "Stop ... please ..." Hawk gasped, his voice strained and weak. But the pressure only intensified, crushing his will further. His heart pounded a chaotic rhythm in his chest and then, as the last shred of resistance finally broke, he gave in.

The words tumbled from his lips before he could stop them. "Stjernefrída and Kura ... they're hiding at the

Gramaze mansion," Hawk muttered, his voice devoid of any fight. "They're guarded at all times …"

The words slipped out as though Eryndor had torn them from him, the final betrayal heavy in his chest. Hawk's gaze was vacant, his will completely surrendered to the darkness that had consumed him.

Humph! How the hell am I going to breach the wards around that building again? Eryndor mused to himself, his mind racing.

Hawk, until I come up with a plan, stay where you are. Blend in, and don't draw attention to yourself. Are we clear? Eryndor commanded, his thoughts cold and firm.

Yes, Master, thought Hawk. Without thinking, Hawk lay down on his bed and closed his eyes, his body tense and ready, anticipating his master's next command for their mission.

Eryndor clicked his fingers to create a portal to take him back to the Fae Kingdom.

* * *

"Elyndra … where are you?" shouted Eryndor, his voice echoing as the portal closed behind him.

"Ah, Eryndor … what compels you to call my name?" came Elyndra's voice from behind him, a soft question in the air.

Eryndor spun around, his gaze following her as she emerged from the depths of the forest. "Have you been able to retrieve the chalice from the book yet?"

"Come!" said Elyndra, her words almost melodic. She extended her regal hand out front for him to take. "I will lead you to it."

Eryndor placed his hand in hers and within moments they were standing in the heart of Elyndra's home library.

"What trickery is this?" Eryndor shot Elyndra a look of contempt.

Elyndra moved gracefully to the round table at the center of the room and waved her hand over the closed book. "No trickery," she replied, her voice calm.

"Well, where is it—the Golden Chalice you promised to retrieve?" Eryndor demanded, his patience wearing thin.

"I haven't been able to retrieve the Golden Chalice from this book." Her fingertips grazed the book with a delicate touch. "If you give me a few more days, I may be able to."

"A few more days … humph … that is not going to happen, Elyndra. You've had ample time," Eryndor snapped, stepping toward the book.

In a swift motion, Elyndra snatched the book from the table, clutching it tightly to her chest, her eyes narrowing. "You'll get it when I'm ready," she said, her tone firm, refusing to let it go.

Eryndor's eyes darkened as Elyndra clutched the book to her chest. "You think you can keep it from me?" he growled, taking a step closer. "You have no idea who you're dealing with, Fae. If you want to keep playing these games, be prepared for the consequences."

Elyndra's gaze remained steady, unflinching as Eryndor drew closer. She could feel the weight of the tension building, but her expression remained calm. With a soft yet defiant smile she slowly backed away, keeping the book pressed to her chest.

"I'm not afraid of your threats, Eryndor," Elyndra said, her voice cold and resolute. "If you want it, you'll have to earn it—*on my terms*."

With that, she turned and walked toward a nearby bookshelf, her movements graceful and deliberate, leaving Eryndor to stew in the growing frustration of his failed attempt to intimidate her.

Eryndor's patience had worn thin, and the sight of Elyndra walking away with the book pushed him to the edge. His eyes flickered with cold determination as he strode toward her, his movements sharp and deliberate.

"You've had your fun, Elyndra," he growled, his hand shooting out toward the book. "It's mine, and I will take it back."

Before she could react, his fingers wrapped around the edge of the book. But Elyndra, ever quick and calculating, spun around with surprising speed, pulling the book just out of his reach. She cradled it protectively against her chest once more, her gaze piercing.

"Do you really think I'd hand it over that easily?" she said, her voice dangerously calm, a mocking smile curling on her lips.

Eryndor's eyes flashed with fury. He reached for it again, this time more forcefully, but Elyndra stepped backward, maintaining a space between them. Eryndor made a sudden lunge forward, trying to overpower Elyndra, but she sidestepped, using her agility to stay just beyond his grasp.

Eryndor's talons dug into the palms of his hands, and with a flick of his wrist, he unleashed a bolt of searing light toward Elyndra. She screamed and her body jerked violently, before collapsing to the ground. The book slipped from her grasp as she fell unconscious.

"I warned you," Eryndor muttered, his voice cold and unforgiving. He stood over her lifeless form, the faintest trace of triumph in his eyes. With a deliberate motion he bent down and seized the book from the ground, holding it tightly as he stood once more. With a wave of his hand, Eryndor conjured a swirling portal, vanishing into its depths, leaving only a sharp crack of lightning still echoing in the air.

The Fae Queen's three sisters, alerted by the commotion, emerged from the surrounding halls, their senses sharp and on high alert.

Rushing into the room, their eyes widened in shock and horror as they found Elyndra lying motionless on the ground, her body cold and lifeless. The book was gone, and an eerie stillness had settled over the room.

Aevyressa, her face drained of color, dropped to her knees beside Elyndra's body. Her trembling fingers brushed against her sister's cold skin. "No … this can't be," she whispered, her voice breaking, as she felt for her pulse. "What has happened to her?"

Myrrathen stood tall, her eyes burning with fierce determination as she scanned the room. "Who did this? We will find the one responsible." Her gaze flickered to the place where the portal had once been, and a growing realization stirred within her. "Eryndor …" she muttered under her breath.

"He will pay for this," Thalara said, her voice choked with emotion, tears brimming in her eyes. "He will pay dearly, with his life."

Their hearts were heavy with a mix of rage and sorrow, and the sisters swore to avenge Elyndra's death. Her life would not be lost in vain; they would see justice done.

CHAPTER FORTY-THREE

Hawk's eyes opened slowly, then he jolted upright in bed. His breathing was ragged, his skin damp and clammy with sweat. As he scanned the dimly lit dorm room, his heart pounded wildly, as though he'd run for miles, and he remembered the phantom echo of a voice lingering in his mind—a whisper, sinister and familiar, from Eryndor.

You will do my bidding, brother, or else!

Hawk shivered despite the heat pulsing through him, every muscle tense as though they refused to believe he was awake. He scrubbed his hands over his face, inhaling sharply to ground himself. "Just a dream," he muttered to himself, his voice hoarse. *It had to be.*

Am I ever going to be able to get Eryndor out of my dreams or head? The thought struck hard, lingering as Hawk sat frozen in bed. *Was that a dream?* He scowled, his jaw tightening. *Don't be stupid. Eryndor can't get past the wards, so how would he be able to talk to me or control me?*

The room was still dark, and a pale silver glow from the pre-dawn crept through his curtains. He glanced at the clock. *Too early.* Still, sleep was no longer an option. Throwing the covers off, Hawk swung his legs to the floor, his bare feet landing on cool tiles.

Just a dream ... he told himself again as he rose, though the words felt hollow.

The bathroom was cool and silent, and Hawk wasted no time stepping into the shower. Steam curled around him as hot water cascaded down his body, chasing the sweat from his skin. He shut his eyes and tried to clear his mind, but the lingering shadow of Eryndor's presence clung like a second skin. It felt *too real*. Every word, every sensation—it had wrapped itself around him like chains.

"No!" Hawk growled under his breath, forcing his mind to focus. "He's gone. He's *gone*."

By the time he'd dried off and dressed, pulling on his usual fitted black shirt and denim jeans, Hawk felt marginally steadier, though the mirror reflected a version of himself he didn't quite recognize—with shadows beneath his eyes, and a weariness in his stance.

Shaking it off, Hawk leaned against the wall and reached out with his mind, his thoughts searching for a familiar, calming presence. *Sully!*

It took only seconds before her voice answered, soft but alert. *Hawk? You're up early.*

He closed his eyes briefly, the sound of her mind-voice easing something tight in his chest. *Yeah. Couldn't sleep. You busy?*

Just finished up. Stjernefrída and Kura are safe and sound. No disturbances tonight.

That's good. A flicker of warmth settled in his thoughts. *Let's meet up.*

Sure thing. I could use a break. Where? thought Sully

Hawk glanced out the window, the sky shifting from indigo to pale blue. *The cathedral tower?*

Perfect. Give me ten, thought Sully, as she walked toward her room to freshen up.

See you soon, thought Hawk.

For a moment he exhaled deeply, as though he'd been holding his breath this entire time. The dream—*if it was a dream*—clawed at the edges of his mind again, but Sully's voice had been an anchor, dragging him back to reality.

It was just a dream, Hawk thought again, as he grabbed his boots and headed for the door. *Nothing more.*

But somewhere deep inside an unease coiled tighter, whispering to him that this wasn't over—and it wasn't a dream at all.

* * *

Sully glanced at her watch, impatience tugging at her as she stood alone in the cathedral tower. "I've been here for thirty minutes. Where the hell is Hawk?" she muttered under her breath.

Hawk! thought Sully. *Are you still meeting up with me?*

There was no answer.

Hawk! she tried again, but still no response.

With frustration mounting, she turned her focus to her brother. *Samuel, have you seen or heard from Hawk in the last hour?*

There was no answer from Samuel either.

What the hell is going on? Sully wondered, a chill running down her spine. Something was wrong—she could feel it.

Suddenly, William's urgent voice cut through her mind, sharp and commanding.

Lepidopteras, be alert. We have a breach at the front gate. Wards are down. I repeat—wards are down. I want every one of you to protect the academy and our coven.

Sully bolted toward the Gramaze mansion, her movements a blur as she raced through the underground tunnel linking the academy to the mansion. The air felt heavy, pressing in on her as dread gnawed at the edges of her thoughts. *I wonder what is going on?*

Emerging into the mansion's dimly lit foyer, Sully skidded to a stop, her breath catching in her throat. There, just beyond the shadows, was Hawk—who had spent the last thirty minutes scouting every corner of the Gramaze mansion—now striding toward the front gates with an unconscious Stjernefrída limp in his arms.

Hawk! Sully's voice tore through their connection, sharp and desperate. *What are you doing?*

Her words hit him like a wall. Hawk froze mid-step, his body rigid, shoulders tensing as though fighting some unseen force. Slowly, he turned to face her. Sully's heart sank. His eyes—normally so sharp, so alive—were clouded over, empty, their familiar spark extinguished.

No ... she thought, horror creeping up her spine. *Shit! Eryndor must have gotten through to him somehow.*

The mansion seemed to darken around her as the weight of it hit—Hawk wasn't in control anymore.

You know what to do, Hawk. Eryndor's voice slithered through the air like poison, cold and commanding. *Hand Stjernefrída over to me and your Griffin half-breed bitch lives.*

Eryndor's words cut deep, dripping with malice, as if each syllable were a blade meant to slice through Hawk's resolve.

Hawk walked over to Eryndor and bowed his head slightly. "Yes, Master. Stjernefrída is yours," his voice flat and distant.

With unsettling care, he placed the unconscious Stjernefrída into Eryndor's waiting arms.

"Now ... follow me," Eryndor commanded, his tone laced with triumph as a swirling portal burst to life beside him.

Hawk turned, just for a moment, his gaze finding Sully. Her face was etched with raw disappointment—hurt and disbelief warring in her eyes. The sight pierced him deeper than any blade could.

I'm sorry, Hawk whispered into their connection, his voice trembling with guilt. *I don't have a choice.*

And then, without another word, he stepped through the portal. It rippled and snapped shut behind him, leaving only silence—and Sully standing in its wake, stunned and alone.

How in the hell did that happen? Sully's mind raced, her thoughts swirling in a storm of confusion and disbelief. Every part of her screamed that this couldn't be real, that there had to be another explanation. But the emptiness left in Hawk's wake told her everything she needed to know— he was Eryndor's minion once more, and there was nothing she could do to stop it.

"Good question," William's voice cut through the silence, his presence suddenly beside her. He had been listening to her thoughts. He looked as stunned as she felt, but his eyes were sharp, calculating.

Sully didn't turn to face him. She couldn't. Her focus was still on the spot where the portal had closed, where Hawk had vanished. "How could he—?" Her voice cracked, betraying the rawness of her shock.

William's gaze softened, just for a moment. "I don't know, but we need to figure it out."

With frustration and confusion mixing in her voice, Sully said, "I thought no one could penetrate the wards around the academy or the mansion."

"Usually, yes, that's correct. But it seems someone managed to turn the wards off—just enough for Eryndor and Hawk to slip through with Stjernefrída."

Sully's fists clenched at her sides. "Who could do that? Who has the power to breach our defenses like that?"

William's face hardened. "Someone on the inside, that's who." A picture of Hawk appeared in his mind.

"Sire, what would you like us to do?" asked Grayson, who was now standing beside William.

"I haven't been able to contact Talitha, Violette or Kura. I need you to see if they are alright. Take Michael, Shepherd and Christian with you," commanded William.

"Yes, Sire," answered Grayson. *Michael, Shepherd, Christian; you are coming with me. We need to check on our Queen, the Princess and Kura.*

Michael hadn't heard from Violette all morning, and their Lepidoptera connection offered no reassurance—he couldn't reach her or sense if she was okay.

They all answered 'Yes' and ran at Vampire speed toward the house with Grayson.

William stood before the open wrought-iron gates of his home, his gaze distant as he pondered Eryndor's next move, now that he had Stjernefrída. A deep sigh escaped him and he shook his head, the weight of responsibility heavy on his shoulders.

Lepidopteras ... we'll convene in the operations room in five minutes. Prepare for a meeting to discuss our plan of attack.

At his command, everyone sprinted toward the mansion, eager to learn the details of their next mission.

* * *

As Grayson, Michael, Shepherd and Christian hurried down the concrete stairs toward Talitha's room, they stumbled upon Kura, who was moving sluggishly, her hands gripping the walls for support.

"Kura … are you alright?" asked Grayson, concern etched into his voice, as his eyes fell on her bloodied head. Leaning in, he wrapped an arm around her back to steady her.

"I need some assistance. I have been attacked by Hawk and he has taken Stjernefrída," Kura replied, her voice strained as she leaned into his support.

"Yes, we know, Ma'am. Let's get you upstairs to our healer," Grayson said firmly.

"Thank you," Kura whispered faintly.

Heads are going to roll when I find out who was supposed to be guarding Kura and Stjernefrída. This should never have happened. How the fuck did they manage to take the wards down—again—and slip past our guards? Grayson seethed quietly to himself.

"You are welcome," Grayson replied, his tone steady. *Danielle, you are needed for a healing.*

Yes, Grayson. I will meet you in the infirmary, Danielle replied through the mind-link.

Grayson turned to the others. "Michael, Shepherd, Christian, you need to find Talitha and Violette, while I take Kura up to the infirmary."

The three Lepidopteras nodded in unison, and sprinted toward Talitha's room without hesitation.

* * *

As Michael, Shepherd and Christian approached Talitha's doorway, they stopped short, eyes widening at the sight of the door blasted clean off its hinges and two guards lying unconscious on the ground.

"Shepherd, take these guards up to Danielle so she can heal them," Michael said, gesturing to the two unconscious men lying beside Talitha's doorway.

"No problem," replied Shepherd, picking them up with ease and rushing toward the concrete stairs.

"Fuck!" Christian muttered sharply as he stepped into the room.

Inside, at the far end, the unconscious bodies of Violette and Talitha lay crumpled on the floor.

Michael and Christian rushed to their sides without hesitation.

"They're still breathing," Michael confirmed after a quick check, relief mixing with urgency. "Let's get them up to the infirmary. Move!"

Without wasting another moment, Michael scooped Violette into his arms and headed for the stairs, his steps quick and deliberate. Christian lifted Queen Talitha carefully, falling into step behind Michael, as they carried the two to safety.

"Two more for you, Danielle," Michael said, as he and Christian carefully placed the unconscious bodies onto infirmary beds.

Danielle's eyes widened in shock as she turned and saw her sister, Violette, and Queen Talitha lying motionless before her. "What happened?" she whispered, her voice trembling as she hurried to their sides, already assessing their injuries.

"Hawk and Eryndor, that's what," Grayson replied, his voice hard with barely contained anger. "They'll pay for what's happened here." He raked a hand through his hair, frustration evident. "Will you be alright if we leave them here for you to heal? We need to get upstairs to the meeting in the operations room."

"Yes, yes, go. I'm fine here," Danielle answered quickly, already focused on her task. She had finished healing Kura's head wound, and now turned her attention to Talitha and Violette, determination in her eyes.

"Thanks, Danielle," Grayson said with a nod. He turned to the others. "Let's go, guys. We're needed upstairs."

Without another word, Grayson, Michael, Shepherd, and Christian headed out, their footsteps quick and purposeful, as they disappeared toward the operations room.

CHAPTER FORTY-FOUR

"Quieten down, everyone," William said firmly, his sharp gaze sweeping across the room.

The room fell silent at once, each Lepidoptera turning their full attention to their leader.

"As you all know, we had a breach this morning here at the mansion," William began, his voice steady but edged with tension. "From what we've gathered so far, Eryndor and Hawk are responsible for the attack. And I regret to inform you that they have taken Stjernefrída."

A low murmur rippled through the room, but it was quickly broken by a voice.

"What about Violette and Talitha? Are they okay?" Adrian asked anxiously.

"They're a bit beaten up," William replied, his tone softening slightly, "but Danielle is with them now and has already begun healing their injuries."

Just as he finished speaking, the sliding doors to the operations room opened with a quiet hiss. Heads turned as the crowd instinctively parted, and into the room stepped Violette, Talitha and Kura. Though a little pale and bruised, they walked with purpose, their presence commanding as they moved to stand beside William at the front of the room.

How are you two holding up? William thought to Violette and Talitha.

A bit bruised and battered, but we'll survive, Talitha replied. *We've also reactivated the wards.*

Great. Thank you! William thought back, his relief palpable.

"Listen up," Queen Talitha said, her gaze sweeping the room. "What we didn't know—until now—is that Eryndor has been siphoning his own power into Hawk for hours, forging a dark link strong enough to override even the most reinforced wards. When Hawk attacked, he wasn't acting alone. He was under Eryndor's mind control, moving with unnatural precision and strength—Eryndor's strength. He took down the guards and stunned Violette, Kura, and me before we even had a chance to react."

The room erupted in hushed outrage and confusion.

"What is being done about the kidnapping of my granddaughter, Stjernefrída?" Kura interrupted, her voice sharp as she turned to William, worry etched across her brow.

"I can answer that, Sire," stated Brock, who was sitting at the operations room computer.

William nodded to Brock, motioning him to speak.

Standing, Brock pushed his chair back and addressed the crowd. "I am currently scanning the world, via satellite feed, for the whereabouts of not only Stjernefrída, but also Eryndor and Hawk. As of now, I haven't pinpointed their exact locations, but it's only a matter of time before I have a facial recognition match."

The room held its breath, waiting for more.

"And when we do find them," William continued, his voice resolute, "rescuing Stjernefrída will be our number one priority. As for Eryndor and Hawk … for their part in the abduction, I will make sure they face the consequences." He paused, his gaze sweeping the room, ensuring his message was clear to everyone present.

Slowly, murmurs rippled through the gathered Lepidopteras, a quiet agreement spreading among them.

Sully, who was standing quietly among the others, felt a complex mix of emotions as she listened to William's declaration about Eryndor and Hawk facing consequences for their actions. Though her loyalty to the mission and the need for justice was undeniable, a pang of concern tugged at her heart for Hawk.

Her hands twitched with indecision. Part of her wanted to speak out and defend him, but she knew the others saw the situation differently. After all, Hawk had still taken Stjernefrída, still helped cause harm, even if he wasn't in control of his actions. Her heart wavered between the loyalty to her family and the compassion she had for Hawk.

Hawk wasn't acting of his own will, Sully thought, a quiet voice of doubt rising in her mind. *He was a pawn in Eryndor's game. Can justice really be served if he's been controlled like that?*

William listened intently, his sharp senses picking up on Sully's conflicted thoughts. He had always been able to read the subtle shifts in her emotions, the way her heart and mind would wrestle with each other, when it came to matters of justice and mercy. He could feel her internal struggle—her deep sense of loyalty to her family, and her empathy for Hawk, despite his actions.

His gaze softened, his expression thoughtful as he regarded Sully from across the room. He knew her well enough to understand that she would never be fully at peace with Hawk facing the consequences for something he hadn't chosen to do. He had seen the bond they shared, the way Sully believed in redemption, in the ability of someone to change if given the right chance.

Sully, I know what you're thinking, his tone gentle but firm. *I understand your loyalty to him. But remember, we can't allow Eryndor and Hawk's actions to go unpunished. What they've done has consequences, not just for Stjernefrída, but for all of us.* He paused for a moment, letting the weight of his words settle in. *But if Hawk truly wasn't in control, if he was manipulated, we'll deal with that. We'll find a way to help him, to bring him back from this. But justice must still be served.*

Sully's gaze lifted, meeting his eyes, a silent understanding passing between them.

William didn't expect her to agree immediately, but he knew she would come to see that sometimes harsh decisions had to be made for the greater good. And, deep down, he hoped that Hawk would get the chance to redeem himself—on his own terms, when the time was right.

"Right!" William said, his voice steady as he scanned the room. "Get your battle gear on and make sure your weapons are ready." His gaze lingered on each face, ensuring they fully grasped the gravity of the task ahead. "We need to be fully prepared when we find them."

As William watched his coven leave the operations room one by one, he couldn't shake the weight of uncertainty that settled over him. Each figure disappearing into the halls, focused and determined, only deepened his sense of foreboding. What would the future hold for them all? The mission ahead was dire, but it was only one part of the puzzle.

His mind drifted to Eryndor—an unpredictable force whose ambition seemed limitless. If Eryndor managed to get his hands on the Golden Chalice … the consequences would be catastrophic. The three sacred objects held power beyond their understanding, a force that could alter the balance of their world and beyond. And if Eryndor wielded that power, who knew what horrors he might unleash.

A deep breath escaped William's lips as he turned away, the weight of responsibility pressing on his chest. The coming days would test them all—his coven, his leadership, and the fragile hope that they could stop Eryndor before it was too late. He didn't want to consider the possibility of failure, if they couldn't retrieve the three sacred objects, but the thought gnawed at him.

With a sharp shake of his head, William pushed the thought away, refocusing on the task at hand. There was no time for hesitation. He would make sure his coven stood strong, no matter what the future held.

Taking his mobile phone from his jacket pocket, William called Garrick and Elara Ironclaw to let them know what had transpired with their two sons, Eryndor and Hawk.

CHAPTER FORTY-FIVE

Stjernefrída's eyes fluttered open, then she sat up abruptly, her mind racing. Her first thought was of Hawk Ironclaw's visit at the Gramaze mansion, and then him threatening her, eventually knocking her unconscious.

Where am I? she wondered, her eyes scanning the darkness of the room. As she attempted to stand, she quickly realized her wrists were shackled to the floor, the chains holding her in place. Drawing on her celestial powers, she focused, manipulating the chains with a surge of energy until they snapped free from her wrists. Rubbing the sore skin where the chains had bitten into her, she pushed herself off the floor and made her way toward the door.

"Going somewhere?" Eryndor asked, his voice cold, as he appeared on the other side of the door just as Stjernefrída opened it.

Startled, Stjernefrída jumped and took a step back, narrowing her eyes. "Get out of my way." She thrust a hand forward, attempting to shove him aside with her power, but he didn't flinch.

Eryndor's lips curled into a sneer. "You think *that* will work on me? Pathetic!" His talons sparked with energy as he raised a hand, lightning crackling to life. "Let's skip the theatrics—I'm not in the mood."

Before she could react, he sent a searing bolt at her, dropping her to her knees in pain.

"Damn you," Stjernefrída hissed through clenched teeth, glaring up at him. "You'll regret this, Eryndor."

"Regret?" He laughed, low and dangerous. "The only thing I regret is wasting my time listening to your whining. Here's the deal." He tossed the ancient book onto the ground in front of her, his voice dripping with contempt. "Extract the Golden Chalice. Now!"

"Never!" she shot back defiantly, her hands trembling as she composed herself. "I won't help you desecrate that artifact. Do it yourself, if you're so powerful."

Eryndor's eyes darkened, his patience fracturing like glass. "Do you think I *asked* you? I don't need your permission, Stjernefrída. I need your *power*." He stepped closer, his shadow falling over her like a storm cloud. "So … you *will* extract the chalice, or I will make you *beg* to do it. Your choice."

"I'll die before I help you," Stjernefrída snapped, fire flashing in her eyes.

Eryndor growled, his temper flaring. "That can be arranged." Eryndor glared at Stjernefrída and his patience shredded. "This is your last chance. Extract the chalice. Now!"

Stjernefrída rose shakily to her feet, defiance burning in her gaze. "I already told you—I will *never* do it. Not for you, not for anyone."

Eryndor's jaw tightened, his talons sparking with deadly energy. "Do you think this is a game? You are nothing but an obstacle. An inconvenience." He stepped closer, his voice a menacing growl. "You *will* give me what I want."

"Go to hell, Eryndor," Stjernefrída spat, her voice unwavering even as pain lingered in her body. "I'd rather die than help you corrupt that power."

Eryndor stilled for a moment, his cold gaze locking onto hers. Then, he let out a low, humorless chuckle. "Then you shall have your wish."

Before Stjernefrída could react, his talons shot forward, lightning crackling in a blinding flash. The bolt struck her square in the chest, searing through her as her screams echoed off the dark walls.

Her body crumpled to the ground, unmoving. The air still hummed with residual energy as Eryndor looked down at her lifeless form, his expression devoid of remorse.

"Foolish girl," he muttered, his voice ice-cold. "Your sacrifice changes nothing. I *will* get what I want … one way or another."

He turned sharply, leaving the room in silence, and Stjernefrída's lifeless body crumpled in a heap on the cold, unforgiving floor.

Hawk!

Yes, Master, thought Hawk.

Who else can take the Golden Chalice out of the book, besides Stjernefrída? thought Eryndor, as he walked up the steps to the top deck of the derelict vessel.

I am not aware of any others, Master. Maybe Kura? Why do you ask? thought Hawk.

Because I just killed the bitch, thought Eryndor.

Hawk's thoughts faltered for a moment, stunned. *You … killed her?*

Yes, Eryndor replied coldly, reaching the top deck, his gaze fixed on the horizon. *She was useless to me the moment she refused. But now we have a problem.*

If no one else can extract the chalice, Hawk thought cautiously, *then what's your plan?*

Eryndor's eyes narrowed, the wind whipping around him as the derelict vessel creaked beneath his boots. *We'll find another way. Power like this doesn't stay buried forever.*

And Kura? Hawk pressed.

She's our next lead, Eryndor replied sharply. *If she knows how to unlock the chalice's secrets, we'll make her talk. One way or another.*

Hawk hesitated, something gnawing at the edges of his thoughts. *And if she doesn't?*

Eryndor's voice turned deadly. *Then we burn the world until we find someone who can.*

Hawk swallowed hard, the weight of Eryndor's words sinking in. He knew his master wasn't bluffing—Eryndor would stop at *nothing* to secure the Golden Chalice, even if it meant destroying everything in his path.

* * *

"Anything yet, Brock?" William asked as he walked into the operations room. Two days had passed since Stjernefrída had been taken by Eryndor and Hawk, but the computer's satellite facial recognition program had yet to turn up any trace of them.

"I was just about to call you, Sire," replied Brock, turning around. "The police are reporting that a body of a woman has been found. Apparently, a fisherman reported finding a body washed ashore after a storm, near the western inlet of Olden Fjord. I checked the satellite feedback, and it looks like the body of Stjernefrída. I can't be sure, though."

"Show me the footage you found," asked William.

Brock replayed the footage. "See … there." He pointed to the screen and zoomed in on her face.

"Shit, that is Stjernefrída. I am damn sure of it," said William, raking a hand through his hair in frustration. He thought carefully for a few seconds. "I need to give Garrick and Elara a call, to see what they want to do. Then I need to inform Kura. Leave it with me."

"Yes, Sire," Brock said.

* * *

William shut the door to his office and walked over to the window, contemplating his conversation with Garrick. Taking his mobile from his jacket pocket, he scrolled through his contacts, selected the Ironclaw's number, and waited for it to connect.

"Hello, my friend. Is there any news yet?" asked Garrick.

"I'm afraid it's not good news," William replied, his tone heavy. "Stjernefrída's body has been found … floating in Olden Fjord."

A hard gulp echoed over the line, followed by a long silence. "That … that is the last thing I expected," Garrick finally said, his voice strained. "Are you absolutely certain it's her?"

"Yes, I'm sure," William said solemnly. "What would you like us to do with her body?"

"I'll send someone to retrieve her," Garrick replied, his voice tight. He glanced up as Elara entered the room, concern etched on her face. "Have you told Kura yet?"

"Not yet," William admitted. "I wanted to call you first before breaking the news to her."

"Right …" Garrick let out a slow, heavy breath. "So, I'm guessing Stjernefrída refused to help Eryndor retrieve the chalice from the book. And for that … he killed her."

"It looks that way," William agreed grimly. "Would I be correct in assuming that Kura will be his next target?"

"It's possible," Garrick said, brow furrowing. "Eryndor might believe Kura knows how to extract the chalice, but he'd be wrong. To my knowledge, only Stjernefrída knew how—unless she had children. And according to history, she didn't. Kura will know for certain, though."

"Understood," William said. "I'll speak with her now and see what I can find out."

"Thank you, William. Let me know what she says." Garrick ended the call and set the phone down with a sigh, his face dark with worry.

Elara sat across from him, her eyes wide. "What's happened?"

"Stjernefrída is dead," Garrick said quietly, meeting her gaze. "I fear Eryndor killed her."

Elara's hand flew to her mouth. "No … are you sure?"

"Yes, we are sure." Garrick's expression hardened, his jaw tight. "This ends now, Elara. No matter what we promised Eryndor's parents, we can't let him continue. He's beyond saving."

Elara let out a heavy sigh, her shoulders slumping. "Yes, I agree. But how are we supposed to find him—let alone take his life?"

"Other than what William Gramaze is already doing—running scans through his satellite system—I'm not sure," Garrick admitted, his frustration evident. "Eryndor and Hawk are too good at covering their tracks."

Elara frowned, deep in thought. "There has to be another way. They can't stay hidden forever."

"Perhaps not," Garrick said, his gaze distant, "but time isn't on our side. The longer they're out there, the more damage they'll cause."

Elara's brows drew together. He was right. But the more she thought about it, the more unease settled in her chest. Eryndor had grown stronger—the dark, malevolent power now surged through him. Even if they found him … how were they supposed to end his life?

* * *

"Knock, knock." William's voice was soft, but his presence in the doorway was unmistakable—tall and well built, he filled the frame with quiet authority.

"Enter …" Kura replied, her eyes already drawn to him, sensing that something was terribly wrong, as she watched him approach.

"Good morning, Kura. I wish I could bring you better news, but there's something I must share with you." William's voice was calm as he sat beside her, his face a mix of sorrow and regret. "I'm afraid … I must tell you that your granddaughter, Stjernefrída … she has passed away."

Kura's breath caught in her throat. For a long moment, she didn't speak, her heart pounding. "No … no, you're wrong," she whispered, the words coming out almost like a plea. "She was just …" Her voice faltered, and then the tears began to fall, slow at first, then fast and uncontrollable, spilling down her cheeks.

William's hand gently rested on her shoulder. "I am so sorry for your loss, Kura," he said, his voice thick with sympathy. "Is there anything I can do for you?"

"My Stjernefrída …" Kura's words were barely a whisper, as the weight of the grief pressed down on her. She cradled her face in her hands, sobbing quietly as reality began to sink in. "She can't be gone. Not like this. Not my granddaughter …"

William offered her a tissue, his heart aching as he watched her unravel. "Can I get you anything?"

"Kura wiped her eyes, shaking her head, still in disbelief. "No … Thank you, but no. I … I just can't believe it. My only grandchild … she's gone." She stared at the tissue in her hands, the weight of her grief suffocating her. "What am I supposed to do now?"

William took a deep breath. "Once the authorities release her body, we can arrange for her funeral. If you need help with anything, just say the word."

"Released?" Kura's voice was hoarse as she looked up at him, her eyes filled with confusion and pain.

"Her body was found in the Olden Fjord this morning," William explained softly. "The police will hold it until a relative claims her. Are you able to do this? Or would you prefer I ask Garrick and Elara to handle it for you?"

Kura's heart pounded in her chest. "I'll go," she said firmly, her voice breaking with the force of her determination. "I have to prepare her body for the ancient burial rites. And I need to speak with the three guardians of the River of Whispers. I … I can't believe this is happening." Her voice trembled with emotion as she looked up at him. "Did Eryndor do this?"

"We're not entirely sure," William replied carefully, his tone grave. "But we suspect it was Eryndor. We believe he may have tried to persuade her to take the chalice from the book. When she refused … well, it's possible he killed her because of it."

Kura's eyes tightened with both sorrow and understanding. "That … that would make sense. Oh, my poor Stjernefrída. She was so brave." She clutched the tissue in her hands, her fingers trembling. "William … can I ask a favor?"

"Anything!" he said without hesitation.

"If I go to collect Stjernefrída's body from Olden, would you send some of your people with me? I'm afraid Eryndor will think I know how to unlock the chalice from the book, but I don't. Once I leave this place, he will likely be waiting for me." Her voice dropped to a whisper as the fear of the unknown began to creep in.

William nodded solemnly. "Of course, Kura. And you are welcome to stay with us for as long as you need."

"Thank you," Kura said quietly, her eyes meeting his with genuine gratitude. "I appreciate your kindness."

"Anytime," William replied, his voice kind but filled with a deep sense of loss. "When would you like to go and collect Stjernefrída's body?"

"I'm not sure. We might need to contact the Olden police for that," said Kura, still lost in the fog of grief.

"Okay. I hate to ask you this in this time of grief … Do you know if Stjernefrída has any children?" asked William.

"Why do you ask?" Kura's brow furrowed in concern.

"We think that if she did have a child," he said, his voice deepening with concern, "Eryndor might be after her next. Your family has a long history of passing down certain abilities—especially from mother to daughter. And as history shows, once the power is transferred, the previous bearer loses it completely."

Kura's heart skipped a beat. "Yes … she did have a daughter. Years ago. I never met her. Stjernefrída kept her hidden, and far from the dangers of our land." She paused, the realization dawning slowly. "But if Stjernefrída is dead

… then this child will soon come into her powers. William, we have to find her. She'll be terrified, not knowing what she's capable of. And I dread to think what will happen if Eryndor finds her."

William leaned forward. "Do you know where we can find her?"

"Yes," Kura answered, her voice steady despite the whirlwind of emotions. "She was adopted by a family in Australia."

"Do you know where in Australia?" William asked, urgency creeping into his voice.

"Somewhere in Western Australia, I think … a small town called Cowaramup. She would be around twenty-two by now."

William's expression hardened. "Do you know if she knows anything about her heritage? About the abilities she might possess?"

"No," Kura replied, her voice tinged with regret. "She doesn't know anything about us. But now … now that Stjernefrída is gone, this girl will come into her powers, and she will have no idea how to control them." Her eyes widened as panic set in. "We need to find her before Eryndor does. We need to protect her, William."

William nodded, determination setting in. "Do you know her name or have an address for her?"

Kura shook her head slowly, her thoughts racing. "I'm not sure. Stjernefrída may have kept some information about her in our home … but how do we get to it now, especially as Eryndor will probably be keeping an eye on our home?

"Leave that to me," William said, his voice firm, as he pushed his chair back. "I'll arrange for someone to go to your home and retrieve any information. You'll also need to inform the three guardians of the River of Whispers about our plans. They'll need to let us pass through safely."

Kura nodded, her resolve returning despite the weight of her grief. "I'll contact them immediately. They'll be heartbroken when they hear about Stjernefrída. But they'll understand." She watched William stand and push his chair under the table.

"Kura … I'll contact the Olden Fjord police and make the arrangements for you to collect Stjernefrída's body. I'll also send someone to your home to search for any address or documents that might lead us to her daughter. You'll have answers soon, I promise." His tone carried the confidence of a man who understood the gravity of the task ahead.

Kura looked up slowly, her red-rimmed eyes meeting his. "Thank you, William. I don't know what I'd do without your help."

"You won't have to do any of this alone," William replied firmly. "I'll be back soon with details—time, logistics, and whatever else you need. For now, try to rest if you can."

"Rest?" Kura's voice was bitter, the word almost a laugh. "How am I supposed to rest when my granddaughter's body is waiting in some morgue and my great-granddaughter's life could be in danger?"

William stepped closer, lowering his voice to something softer, more personal. "I know this is impossible right now, but you need your strength, Kura. When the time comes to face the guardians, to collect Stjernefrída, or to protect her child—you'll need to be ready. Don't let your grief rob you of that strength."

Kura stared at him, her expression torn between sorrow and understanding. "You're right."

"I know," William replied, his voice thick with sympathy. "But I swear to you, we'll find your great-granddaughter, and we'll keep her safe. Eryndor won't get to her. Not if I have anything to say about it."

She gave a small nod, a fragile acceptance.

William hesitated for a moment at the door, his hand hovering on the doorknob. "I'll return as soon as I have news. And if you need anything before then, send word—I'll come straight back."

"Thank you," Kura murmured, the faintest trace of gratitude in her broken voice.

With one final glance, William stepped out of the room, shutting the door behind him. The quiet seemed to linger for a moment, heavy and suffocating, before William exhaled sharply. Straightening his shoulders, he moved with purpose down the hallway, his mind already turning to what needed to be done.

First, the Olden Fjord police, William thought grimly. *Then we'll find that girl before Eryndor does. No matter the cost.*

As he disappeared into the corridor's shadows, the echo of his boots against the floor seemed to carry his unspoken vow: *I will not fail you, Kura. Or your great-granddaughter.*

SNEAK PEAK AT BOOK THREE

Coming in 2026

Balance Power & Protection

EMPIRE OF THE LEGACIES ACADEMY SERIES
BOOK THREE

CHAPTER ONE

"Alessia, are you ready to go?" TJ called, rummaging through her handbag for the car keys. "We're going to be late if you don't get a wriggle on."

"Yes, *Mother*," Alessia shouted from her bedroom, rolling her blue eyes with exaggerated frustration. "I'm almost done."

She shoved the last of her university books into her bag, zipped it shut, and slung it over her shoulder, before heading toward the kitchen.

"Did you sleep in again this morning?" TJ asked, as Alessia strolled into the kitchen.

"Yeah … I've been so exhausted lately," Alessia replied with a yawn. "And the weird dreams aren't helping. Things like celestial realms that I govern as a Goddess. And being able to communicate with animals and plants."

"That is strange. Sorry to hear that, sweetheart. Fortunately, they are only dreams." She handed Alessia a plate with two pieces of toast on it.

"Aww … thanks, Mum," Alessia said, taking the plate from her.

"No problem. You'll need the energy, especially with your end-of-year exams today," TJ replied.

"I'm not sure if I'm ready," Alessia admitted softly, her brow furrowing as doubt flickered in her eyes. "I've studied, I swear, but … it's overwhelming. Like there's just *too much* to hold on to, and I'm afraid I'll forget it all when it really matters."

"You'll be fine, I'm sure of it," TJ said gently, resting a reassuring hand on her daughter's shoulder. "You're smarter than you give yourself credit for. Now, come on—we'd better get going."

"Good luck today, sweetheart," Parker said, sitting at the kitchen island bench, glancing up from his newspaper.

"Thanks, Dad," Alessia replied. "I'm definitely going to need it."

"See you later, babe," TJ said, slipping her bag onto her shoulder. She walked over and kissed him on the cheek.

"I'll be here," Parker replied, leaning in to her kiss.

"See you this afternoon, Dad," said Alessia, as she walked toward the carport doorway.

"See you, sweetheart," said Parker, as he watched both of them head out.

* * *

The V8 cruiser hummed along softly, as TJ navigated the winding roads toward the university. Alessia sat quietly in the passenger seat, gazing out the window, her mind still buzzing with nerves.

"Did you dye some of your hair?" TJ asked, her gaze narrowing slightly, as she noticed a few strands of Alessia's hair had turned a striking shade of silver, when they pulled up in front of the university.

Alessia ran a hand through her dark brown hair, brushing the silver strands behind her ear. "No, it just kind of happened," she shrugged, a flicker of uncertainty in her eyes.

TJ leaned in a little, inspecting the silver strands more closely. "When did this start?"

"Just recently," Alessia replied. "I woke up a few days ago and they were there. It's weird, right?"

TJ's brow furrowed with concern, but she tried to mask it with a casual smile. "Well, I guess you're just getting more unique, huh?" She gave her daughter's shoulder a reassuring squeeze. "Nothing to worry about, just … keep an eye on it."

Alessia forced a smile, but inside a tiny seed of doubt began to sprout.

"Do you need anything before you go in?" TJ asked, her expression a mixture of concern and pride.

"I think I'm good," Alessia replied, with a small smile. "Just need to survive the next few hours, and then I'll be done for the year. Can't wait to get this PhD in astrophysics done and dusted."

TJ chuckled softly. "You've got this. Just remember to breathe, okay? It's only one day, one exam at a time."

Alessia nodded, trying to push the weight of the exams from her mind. Taking a deep breath, she hoped that she was ready to face whatever came next.

"I'll pick you up later," TJ said, as Alessia opened the door to get out.

"Thanks, Mum. See you soon." Alessia waved goodbye, as she made her way toward the entrance.

* * *

Alessia stood in front of a wooden door that had a sign pinned to it, that read:

EXAMS IN PROGRESS
PLEASE BE QUIET
9.30 am – 1.00 pm

Opening the door, Alessia stepped into the exam room and noticed rows upon rows of small tables, each paired with a chair. She quietly made her way to the back of the room, settled into a seat, and began reviewing her notes for the exam.

As a yawn escaped her, Alessia froze. Glowing runes and symbols flickered across her right forearm and hand, shimmering faintly, before spreading to her left. She frowned, shaking her head, and the strange markings vanished as quickly as they had appeared. *What the hell was that?*

Glancing around the room, she saw it had nearly filled with other students, all hunched over their notes, desperately cramming last-minute details. No one else seemed to have noticed anything out of the ordinary.

Her thoughts were interrupted as the examiner's voice rang out from the front of the room.

"Alright, quieten down, everyone," he said, his sharp gaze sweeping across the room as he waited for their attention.

"In a few minutes, I'll be handing out the exam papers. First, write your full name and today's date at the top of the page. Once the clock hits nine-thirty," he gestured to the large clock on the wall behind him, "you may begin. The exam will end promptly at one. At that time, all completed papers must be placed on my desk to be marked."

He paused briefly before continuing. "Results will be published in two weeks on the university website. You'll need your log-in ID and password to access them. Good luck to you all."

With that, he began walking between the rows of desks, placing an exam paper face down in front of each student.

When the exam began, Alessia, along with the rest of the students, turned over her paper and carefully wrote her name and the date at the top. Flipping to the first page of the questionnaire Alessia glanced at the first question. *Yep, I know this one*, she thought confidently as she scribbled down her answer.

For the next ten minutes, the pattern continued—question after question came easily to her, the answers flowing effortlessly. *Maybe I did study enough after all*, she mused with a small sense of relief.

But just as she started to settle into the rhythm, something strange happened. The glowing runes and symbols reappeared, flickering across her forearms and hands like living light. This time, however, they weren't just on her skin—they pulsed within her mind, vivid and insistent, as though they were trying to tell her something.

When the examiner's voice rang out, "Pens down," Alessia was startled back to reality. She blinked in surprise, unable to believe it was already over. Glancing around the room, she noticed other students had either finished early, or were now making their way to the front, placing their papers on the examiner's desk.

Shaking her head, she looked up at the clock. Sure enough, it read one p.m. *Far out, where did the time go?*

She glanced down at her hands and forearms, searching for the glowing symbols and runes she had seen earlier— but they were gone. *What the hell is going on?* Alessia wondered, her brow furrowing in confusion.

With a deep breath, she lowered her gaze back to the exam paper in front of her. Flipping through the pages, she realized, with surprise, that she had somehow completed the entire exam.

Alessia felt tingles of warmth coursing through her body, particularly in her hands and chest. She wondered whether it was anxiety or something else entirely—perhaps a sign of relief that her final exam had been done and dusted.

Slinging her bag over her shoulder, she walked over to the examiner and placed the paperwork on his desk.

"Ah, Miss McCrindle. How do you think you did on the exam?" asked the professor, his voice warm with curiosity. He had been a great mentor to her throughout the past year at university.

"I'm not sure," Alessia replied, a hint of uncertainty in her voice. "It's all a bit of a blur. I just hope I did well. I'd really love to get a job in astrophysics."

"I'm sure you did well, dear. As I said this morning, your results will be posted in about two weeks on the university website, so you will be able to check them then," said the professor.

"Thank you. Have a good holiday, professor, and thank you for all your help throughout the year."

"You're welcome! Hope you have a good holiday, too."

Alessia smiled and walked toward the doorway.

* * *

Did you enjoy reading some of the first chapter of book three? Keep an eye out on my social media or on my website **www.susanhoddy.com** for when book three of the Empire of the Legacies Academy series will be coming out in 2026.

CATCH UP ON ALL THE LATEST NEWS AND UPDATES FROM SUSAN HODDY

Facebook: Susan Hoddy–Author

Instagram: susanhoddy

LinkedIn: Susan Hoddy

TikTok: Susan Houston 478

Threads   Susan Houston (Hoddy) (@susanhoddy)

Website: https://www.susanhoddy.com/

All readings, discussions, signings or appearances are done by appointment only.

If any libraries, schools, daycares, bookstores or book clubs would like Susan to come along and do a reading of some chapters and/or a discussion about her books to their group of passionate readers, please don't hesitate to contact Susan via her website and fill in the **Contact Us** form.

https://susanhoddy.com/contact/

For rights availability inquiries, including film and television options, please inquire directly with the author using the **Contact Us** form at her website.

https://susanhoddy.com/contact/

ACKNOWLEDGMENTS

This book would not be here, resting in your hands or on your e-reader if it weren't for the following people. I owe all of them my deepest gratitude and love.

My book cover artist, Ammonia Book Covers, who worked tirelessly on the cover. Thank you, your cover is overwhelmingly beautiful, and I am so lucky to have found you.

My editor, Debbie Phillips from DP Plus, whose continued knowledge, advice and support has provided me with a much-needed calming strength to keep going. I am extremely grateful to you. Thank you, Debbie.

My formatter, Debbie Phillips from DP Plus. Thank you, Debbie, for a wonderful job of making my book look awesome on each page.

My wonderful husband, Michael, for putting up with me, when all I spoke about for months was the characters, plotlines and storyline of this book. Thank you for your patience and for everything you do for me.

My beautiful daughter, Samantha, who has always given me her advice, support and love. Thank you, Sam. As an avid reader, I think one day you, too, might become a writer.

My many friends and associates, for all their support, feedback and suggestions. I appreciated each and every one of you. Many thanks to you all.

ABOUT THE AUTHOR

Award-winning author Susan Hoddy is a multi-published fantasy, romance and young-adult fiction writer, best known for her Lepidoptera Vampire series and her other novel called *Security*. Recently, Susan has added to her writing skills, and one of her new adventures is a fully illustrated children's book series called *The Adventures of Georgia and Cash*.

Susan was born in Perth, Western Australia, in 1966, and enjoys a good chinwag with family and friends, road trips with her husband, cups of tea, daydreaming and writing.

Susan has always worked in many facets of an office during her life, but in 2012 she decided life was too short and she wanted to make a start on her passion—writing. After acquiring her novel writing diploma from the Australian College of Journalism, she continues to create her children's book series, and other worlds where fantasy and romance exist, with her books.

AWARDS

In 2022 Susan won two book awards for *Attraction* and *Awakened* in the Lepidoptera Vampire series.

***Attraction*, book one in the Lepidoptera Vampire series**, was chosen as the Silver Winner in the Fiction Romance category from MMH Press Book Awards.

***Awakened*, book two in the Lepidoptera Vampire series**, was chosen as the Bronze Winner in the Fiction Romance category from MMH Press Book Awards.

In 2019 Susan won two book awards for *Attraction* and *Awakened* in the Lepidoptera Vampire series.

***Attraction*, book one in the Lepidoptera Vampire series**, was chosen as the Official Selection Winner in the Young Adult General Fiction category from New Apple Literary Fifth Annual Indie Book Awards.

***Awakened*, book two in the Lepidoptera Vampire series**, was chosen as the solo Medalist Winner in the Young Adult General Fiction category from New Apple Literary Fifth Annual Indie Book Awards.

OTHER SUPERNATURAL FANTASY BOOKS WRITTEN BY SUSAN HODDY

The Lepidoptera Vampire Series

Keep an eye out for news on Susan Hoddy's social media or on her website www.susanhoddy.com for details on when her next book will be published.

Stories from the Faerie Queene

By

Mary Jane McLeod Bethune

First published in 1916

Published by Left of Brain Books

PUBLISHER'S PREFACE

About the Book

"Spenser's The Faerie Queene is one of the masterpieces of English poetry, and certainly part of the literary pedigree that culminated in Tolkien. However, the original text is very difficult to follow for modern readers because of the archaic language and spelling. To the rescue comes Mary Macleod. Her late Victorian retelling in straightforward modern English allows one to plow through Spenser's intricate and allegorical plot. If you are planning to read the Faerie Queene, or want to understand the narrative but don't have the time or patience to tangle with an epic poem in early modern English, you've come to the right place."

(Quote from sacred-texts.com)

About the Author

Mary Jane McLeod Bethune (1875 - 1955)

"Mary Jane McLeod Bethune (July 10, 1875(1875-07-10) - May 18, 1955) was born in Mayesville, South Carolina and died in Daytona Beach, Florida. A tireless educator born to former slaves, she is best known for founding a school in 1904 that later became part of Bethune-Cookman College in Daytona Beach. She was president of the college from 1923-42 and 1946-47, one of the few women in the world who served as a college president at that time. Bethune worked for the election of Franklin D. Roosevelt in 1932, and attempted to get him to support a proposed law against lynching. She was also a member of Roosevelt's Black Cabinet, among other leadership positions in organizations for women and African Americans. Upon her death, columnist Louis E. Martin said, "She gave out faith and hope as if they were pills and she some sort of doctor." Her house is preserved by the National Park Service as Mary McLeod Bethune Council House National Historic Site, and a sculpture of her is located in Lincoln Park in Washington, DC."

(Quote from wikipedia.org)

CONTENTS

INTRODUCTION

THE object of this volume is to excite interest in one of the greatest poems of English literature, which for all its greatness is but little read and known-- to excite this interest not only in young persons who are not yet able to read "The Faerie Queene," with its archaisms of language, its distant ways and habits of life and thought, its exquisite melodies that only a cultivated ear can catch and appreciate, but also in adults, who, not from the lack of ability, but because they shrink from a little effort, suffer the loss of such high and refined literary pleasure as the perusal of Spenser's masterpiece can certainly give.

Assuredly, when all that cavillers can say or do is said and done, "The Faerie Queene" is deservedly called one of the greatest poems of English literature. From the high place it took, and took with acclamation, when it first appeared, it has, in fact, never been deposed. It has many defects and imperfections, such as the crudest and most commonplace critic can discover, and has discovered with much self-complacency; but it has beauties and perfections that such critics very often fail to see; and, so far as the status of "The Faerie Queene" is concerned, it is enough for the ordinary reader to grasp the significant fact that Spenser has won specially for himself the famous title of "the poets' poet." Ever since his star appeared above the horizon, wise men from all parts have come to worship it; and amongst these devotees fellow-poets have thronged with a wonderful enthusiasm. In one point all the poetic schools of England have agreed together, viz., in admiration for Spenser. From Milton and Wordsworth on the one hand to Dryden and Pope--from the one extreme of English poetry to the other--has prevailed a perpetual reverence for Spenser. The lights in his temple, so to speak, have never been extinguished-never have there been wanting offerers of incense and of praise; and, to repeat in other words what has already been said, as it is what we wish to specially emphasise, amidst this faithful congregation have been many who already had or were some day to have temples of their own. We recognise amongst its members not only the great poets already mentioned, but many others of the divine brotherhood, some at least of whom rank with the greatest, such as Keats, Shelley, Sidney, Gray, Byron, the Fletchers, Henry More, Raleigh, Thomson, not to name Beattie, Shenstone, Warton, Barnefield, Peele, Campbell, Drayton, Cowley, Prior, Akenside, Roden Noel. To this long but by no means exhaustive list might be added many of high eminence in other departments of literature and of life, as Gibbon, Mackintosh, Hazlitt, Craik, Lowell, Ruskin, R. W. Church, and a hundred more.

Now, of course, the acceptance of a poet is and must be finally due to his own intrinsic merits. No amount of testimonials from ever so highly distinguished persons will make a writer permanently popular if he cannot make himself so-if his own works do not make him so. Of testimonials there is very naturally considerable distrust--very naturally, when we notice what second-rate penmen have been and are cried up to the skies. But in the present case the character of the testifiers is to be carefully considered; and, secondly, not only their words but their actions are to be taken into account. Many of our greatest poets have praised Spenser not only in formal phrases, but practically and decisively, by surrendering themselves to his influence, by sitting at his feet, by taking hints and suggestions from him. He has been their master not merely nominally but actually, and with obvious results. If all traces of Spenser's fascination and power could be removed from subsequent English literature, that literature would be a very different thing from what it is: there would be strange breaks and blanks in many a volume, hiatuses in many a line, an altered turning of many a sentence, a modification of many a conception and fancy. And we are convinced that the more Spenser is studied the more remarkable will his dominance and his dominion be found to be. To quote lines that have been quoted before in this connection--

"Hither, as to their fountain, other stars Repairing, in their urns draw golden light." "The Faerie Queene " is one of the great wellheads of English poetry; or, in other words, Spenser's Faerie Land has been and is a favourite haunt of all our highest poetic spirits.

And yet it is incontrovertible that this poem is very little known as a whole to most people. Everybody is familiar with the story of Una and the Lion, and with two or three stanzas of singular beauty in other parts of "The Faerie Queen," because these occur in most or all books of selections: in every anthology occur those fairest flowers. But the world at large is content to know no more. The size of the poem appals it. "A big book is a big evil," it thinks, and it shudders at the idea of perusing the six twelve-cantoed books in which Spenser's genius expressed itself--expressed itself only in an incomplete and fragmentary fashion, for many more books formed part of his enormous design. "Of the persons who read the first canto," says Macaulay in a famous Essay, "not one in ten reaches the end of the First Book, and not one in a hundred perseveres to the end of the poem. Very few and very weary are those who are in at the death of the Blatant Beast. If the last six books, which are said [without any authority] to have been destroyed in Ireland, had been preserved, we doubt whether any heart less stout than that of a commentator would have held out to the end." And Macaulay speaks truly as well as wittily. He is as accurate as Poins when Prince Hal asks him what he would think if the Prince wept because the King his father was sick. "I would think thee a most princely hypocrite," replies Poins. "It would be every man's thought," says the Prince: "and thou art a blessed fellow to think as every man thinks. Never a man's thought in the world keeps the roadway better than thine." Even so is Macaulay "a blessed fellow to think as every man thinks," and no doubt his blessedness in this respect is one of the characteristics--by no means the only one--that account for his widespread popularity. He not only states that people do not read "The Faerie Queen," but he shows that he himself, voracious reader--helluo librorum--as he was, had not done so, or had done so very carelessly; for, alas! the Blatant Beast, as at all events every student of the present volume will know, does not die; Sir Calidore only suppresses him for a time; he but temporarily ties and binds him in an iron chain, "and makes him follow him like a fearful dog;" and one day long afterwards the beast got loose again--

> "Ne ever could by any, more be brought
> Into like bands, ne maystred any more,
> Albe that, long time after Calidore,
> The good Sir Pelleas him tooke in hand,
> And after him Sir Lamoracke of yore,
> And all his brethren borne in Britaine land
> Yet none of them could ever bring him into band.
> So now he raungeth through the world againe,
> And rageth sore in each degree and state
> Ne any is that may him now restraine,
> He growen is so great and strong of late,
> Barking and biting all that him doe bate,
> Albe they worthy blame, or clear of crime
> Ne spareth he most learned wits to rate,
> Ne spareth he the gentle Poets rime;

But rends without regard of person or of time." And Spenser goes on to declare that even his "homely verse of many meanest" cannot hope to escape "his venemous despite;" for, in his own day, as often since, Spenser by no means found favour with everybody. Clearly even Macaulay's memory of the close of "The Faerie Queene" was sufficiently hazy. But even Milton, to whom Spenser was so congenial a spirit, and whom he acknowledged as his "poetical father," on one occasion at least forgets the details of the Spenserian story. When insisting in the Areopagitica that true virtue is not "a fugitive and cloistered virtue, unexercised and unbreathed, that never sallies out and sees her adversary," but a virtue that has been tried and tested, he remarks that this " was the reason why our sage and serious poet Spenser, whom I dare be known to think a better teacher than Scotus or Aquinas, describing true temperance under the person of Guion, brings him in with his Palmer through the cave of Mammon and the bower of earthly bliss, that he may see, and know, and yet abstain." But the Palmer was not with Sir Guyon in the Cave of Mammon, Phædria having declined to ferry him over to her floating island. See "The Faerie Queene," ii. 6, 19:--

> "Himselfe [Sir Guyon] she tooke aboord,
> But the Black Palmer suffred still to stond,
> Ne would for price or prayers once affoord
> To ferry that old man over the perlous foord.
> "Guyon was loath to leave his guide behind,
> Yet being entred might not back retyre;
> For the flitt barke, obeying to her mind,
> Forth launched quickly as she did desire,
> Ne gave him leave to bid that aged sire
> Adieu."

So Macaulay's lapse must not be regarded too severely, though, as may be seen, much more prominence is given by Spenser to the fact that the Blatant Beast was not killed, than to the absence of the Palmer from Guyon's side in Mammon's House. It seems probable, indeed, that Macaulay mixed up the fate of the Dragon in the eleventh canto of the First Book with that of the Blatant Beast in the twelfth of the Sixth. But we mention these things only to prevent any surprise at the general ignorance of Spenser, when such a confirmed book-lover as Macaulay, and such a devoted Spenserian as Milton, are found tripping in their allusions to his greatest work.

Now this ignorance, however explicable, is, we think, to be regretted. A poet of such splendid attributes, and with such a choice company of followers, surely deserves to be better known than he is by "the general reader"; and we trust that this volume may be of service in making the stories of "The Faerie Queene " more familiar, and so in tempting the general reader to turn to Spenser's own version of them, and to appreciate his amazing affluence of language, of melody, and of fancy.

Clearly, Spenser does not appeal to everybody at first; we mean that to enjoy him fully needs some little effort to begin with--some distinct effort to put ourselves in communication with him, so to speak; for he is far away from us in many respects. His costume and his accent are very different from ours. He does not seem to be of us or of our world. "His soul" is "like a star": it dwells "apart." We have, it would appear at first sight, nothing in common with him: he moves all alone in a separate sphere--he is not of our flesh and blood. What strikes us at first sight is a certain artificiality and elaborateness, as we think. We cannot put ourselves on confidential terms with him; he is too stately and point devise. His art rather asserts than conceals itself to persons who merely glance at him. But these impressions will be largely or altogether removed, if the reader will really read "The Faerie Queene." He will no longer think of its author as a mere phrase-monger, or only a dainty melodist, or the master of a superfine style. He will find himself in communion with a man of high intellect, of a noble nature--of great attraction, not only for his humanism, but for his humanity. To Spenser, Wordsworth's lines in "A Poet's Epitaph" may be applied with particular and profound truth

> "He is retired as noontide dew,
> Or fountain in a noonday grove;
> And you must love him ere to you
> He will seem worthy of your love."

The very opulence of Spenser's genius stands in the way of his due appraisement. There can scarcely be a doubt that if he could have restrained the redundant stream of his poetry, he might have been more worthily recognised. Had he written less, he would have been praised more; as it is, with many readers, mole ruit sua: they are overpowered and bewildered by the immense flood. The waters of Helicon seem a torrent deluge. We say his popularity would have been greater, if he could have restrained and controlled this amazing outflow; but, after all, we must take our great poets as we find them. In this very abundance, as in other ways, Spenser was a child of his age, and we must accept him with all his faults as well as with all his excellences. Both faults and excellences are closely inter-connected. Il a les défauts de ses qualités.

He said that Chaucer was his poetical master, and more than once he mentions Chaucer with the most generous admiration:-- And Chaucer too may be said to suffer from a very plethora of wealth. Chaucer is apt to be superabundant; but yet he was a model of self-restraint as compared with Spenser. One cannot say in this case, "Like master, like man," or, "Like father, like son." Their geniuses are entirely different--a fact which makes

Spenser's devotion to Chaucer all the more noticeable and interesting; and the art of the one is in sharp contrast with the art of the other. Chaucer is a masterly tale-teller: no one in all English poetry equals him in this faculty; he is as supreme in it as Shakespeare in the department of the drama. In his tales Chaucer is, "without o'erflowing, full." The conditions under which they were told beneficially bounded and limited them. Each is multum in parvo. They are very wonders of compression, and yet produce no sense of confinement or excision. Spenser could not possibly have set before himself a better exemplar; but yet he so set him in vain. The contrast between the two poets, considered merely as narrators or story-tellers, is vividly exhibited in the third canto of the Fourth Book of "The Faerie Queene," where, after a reverent obeisance to his great predecessor, he attempts to tell the other half of the half-told story. It is not without some misgiving that he adventures on such a daring task:--

> "Dan Chaucer, well of English undefyled,
> On Fames eternal beadroll worthy to be fyled."
> "That old Dan Geffrey, in whose gentle spright
> The pure well head of Poesie did dwell."
>
> "Of Cambuscan bold,
> Of Camball and of Algarsife,
> And who had Canace to wife,
> That owned the virtuous ring and glass,
> And of the wondrous horse of brass,
> On which the Tartar king did ride."
>
> "Then pardon, O most sacred happie Spirit
> That I thy labours lost [1] may thus revive,
> And steale from thee the meede of thy due merit,
> That none durst ever whilest thou wast alive,

---

[1] Spenser thought that the latter Part or Parts of the "Squire's Tale" had actually been written but been lost--been "quite devoured" by "cursed eld," and "brought to nought by little bits," as he quaintly expresses it. But it may be taken as certain Chaucer left the tale as we have it, that is, "half told." The closing lines of what we have are clearly unrevised. For some reason or another--trouble or sickness, or his growing infirmity--what would have been one of the most brilliant works of the Middle Ages was never completed, and, like "Christabel" and "Hyperion," remains only a glorious fragment.

> And being dead in vain yet many strive.
> Ne dare I like; but through infusion swete
> Of thine own Spirit which doth in me survive,
> I follow here the footing of thy feete,
> But with thy meaning so I may the rather meete."

But it can scarcely be allowed either that he follows the footing of his master's feet, or that he caught the breath of his master's spirit. There are "diversities of operations"; and Spenser's method and manner were not those of Chaucer, however sincere the allegiance he professed, and however sincere his intentions to tread in his footsteps and march along the same road. He wanted some gifts and some habits that are necessary for the perfect story-teller--gifts and habits which Chaucer, by nature or by discipline, possessed in a high degree, such as humour, concentration, realism. The very structure of "The Faerie Queene" is defective. It begins in the middle--at its opening it takes us in medias res, seemingly in accordance with the precedent of the Iliad or of the Æneid, but only seemingly, for both Homer and Virgil very soon finish the explanation of their opening initial scenes, and their readers know where they are, But the first six books of "The Faerie Queene" are very slightly connected together; and what the connection is meant to be we learn only from the later of the poet to Sir Walter Raleigh, which it was thought well to print with the first three books, no doubt in consequence of some complaints of obscurity and disattachment. This letter is significantly described as "expounding his" (the author's) "whole intention in the course of this work," and as "hereunto annexed, for that it giveth great light to the reader for the better under-standing." Certainly a story ought not to require a prose appendix to set forth its arrangement and its purpose, even if only a fourth of it is completed. The exact correlation of eleven books was to remain unre-vealed till the Twelfth Book appeared. In fact, had the poem ever been completed, we should have had to begin its perusal at the end! Thus "The Faerie Queene," as has often been remarked, lacks unity and cohesion. It is not so much one large and glorious mansion as a group of mansions. To use the metaphor of Professor Craik, to whom many subsequent writers on Spenser have been so considerably indebted, and often without any at all adequate acknowledgment, it is a street of fine houses, or, to use another metaphor of Professor Craik's, which also has been freely adopted by other critics, it is in parts a kind of wilderness--a wilderness of wonderful beauty and wealth, in. which it is a delight to wander, but yet a wilderness with paths and tracks dimly and faintly marked, often scarcely to be discerned.

Such was the abundance of Spenser's fancy, and so various and extensive was his learning, that he wrote, it would seem, with an amazing facility, never checked by any paucities of either knowledge or ideas. His pen could scarcely keep pace with his imagination. His material he drew from all accessible sources--from the Greek and Latin classics (his sympathetic acquaintance with Plato is one of his distinctions), from the Italian poets (not only from Ariosto and Tasso, but Berni, Boiardo, Pulci, and others), from the old Romances of Chivalry (especially the Arthurian in Malory's famous rendering, Bevis of Southampton, Amadis de Gaul), from what there was of modern English literature (above all, Chaucer's works, but also Hawes and other minor writers) and of modern French literature (especially Marot), from contemporary history (all the great personages of his time are brought before us in his pages): but all these diverse elements he combines and assimilates in his own fashion, and forms into a compound quite unique, and highly characteristic both of the hour and of the man. No wonder if the modern reader is at first somewhat perplexed and confused; no wonder if he often loses the thread of the story, and fails to comprehend such an astonishing prodigality of incident and of personification. Figure after figure flits before his eyes--the cry is still "They come"; one seems to be n the very birthplace and home of dreams, knights, ladies, monsters, wizards, and witches; all forms of good and evil throng by in quick succession, and we are apt to forget who is who and what is what. Probably some candid good-natured friend complained to Spenser of this complicatedness, which is certainly at its worst in the Third and Fourth Books; and in a certain passage in the Sixth he makes some sort of defence of himself for what might seem divisions or aberrations in the story of Sir Calidore. He compares himself to a ship that, by reason of counter-winds and tides, fails to go straight to its destination, but yet makes for it, and does not lose its compass; see VI. xii. I and 2.

We are sure that for all young readers such a version of Spenser's stories as is given in this volume may be truly serviceable in preparing them for the study of the poem itself. And with some older readers too--and it is to them this Introduction is mainly addressed--we would fain hope this volume may find a hearty welcome, as providing them with a clue to what seems an intricate maze. What we should like to picture to ourselves is young and old reading these stories together, and the elder students selecting for their own benefit, and for the benefit of the younger, a few stanzas here and there from "The Faerie Queene" by way of illustration. Of course we do not make this humble suggestion to the initiated, but to those--and their name is Legion--who at present know nothing or next to nothing of what is certainly one of the masterpieces of English literature.

JOHN W. HALES.

THE RED CROSS KNIGHT

THE COURT OF THE QUEEN

ONCE upon a time, in the days when there were still such things as giants and dragons, there lived a great Queen. She reigned over a rich and beautiful country, and because she was good and noble every one loved her, and tried also to be good. Her court was the most splendid one in the world, for all her knights were brave and gallant, and each one thought only of what heroic things he could do, and how best he could serve his royal lady.

The name of the Queen was Gloriana, and each of her twelve chief knights was known as the Champion of some virtue. Thus Sir Guyon was the representative of Temperance, Sir Artegall of Justice, Sir Calidore of Courtesy, and others took up the cause of Friendship, Constancy, and so on.

Every year the Queen held a great feast, which lasted twelve days. Once, on the first day of the feast, a stranger in poor clothes came to the court, and, falling before the Queen, begged a favour of her. It was always the custom at these feasts that the Queen should refuse nothing that was asked, so she bade the stranger say what it was he wished. Then he besought that, if any cause arose which called for knightly aid, the adventure might be entrusted to him.

When the Queen had given her promise he stood quietly on one side, and did not try to mix with the other guests who were feasting at the splendid tables. Although he was so brave, he was very gentle and modest, and he had never yet proved his valour in fight, therefore he did not think himself worthy of a place among the knights who had already won for themselves honour and renown.

Soon after this there rode into the city a fair lady on a white ass. Behind her came her servant, a dwarf, leading a warlike horse that bore the armour of a knight. The face of the lady was lovely, but it was very sorrowful.

Making her way to the palace, she fell before Queen Gloriana, and implored her help. She said that her name was Una; she was the daughter of a king and queen who formerly ruled over a mighty country; but, many years ago, a huge dragon came and wasted all the land, and shut the king and queen up in a brazen castle, from which they might never come out. The Lady Una therefore besought Queen Gloriana to grant her one of her knights to fight and kill this terrible dragon.

Then the stranger sprang forward, and reminded the Queen of the promise she had given. At first she was unwilling to consent, for the Knight was young, and, moreover, he had no armour of his own to fight with.

Then said the Lady Una to him, "Will you wear the armour that I bring you, for unless you do you will never succeed in the enterprise, nor kill the horrible monster of Evil? The armour is not new, it is scratched and dinted with many a hard-fought battle, but if you wear it rightly no armour that ever was made will serve you so well."

Then the stranger bade them bring the armour and put it on him, and Una said, "Stand, therefore, having your loins girt about with truth, and having on the breastplate of righteousness, and your feet shod with the preparation of the gospel of peace; above all taking the shield of faith, wherewith ye shall be able to quench all the fiery darts of the wicked, and take the helmet of salvation and the sword of the SPIRIT, which is the word of GOD."

And when the stranger had put off his own rough clothes and was clad in this armour, straightway he seemed the goodliest man in all that company, and the Lady Una was well pleased with her champion; and, because of the red cross which he wore on his breastplate and on his silver shield, henceforth he was known always as "the Red Cross Knight." But his real name was Holiness, and the name of the lady for whom he was to do battle was Truth.

So these two rode forth into the world together, while a little way behind followed their faithful attendant, Prudence. And now you shall hear some of the adventures that befell the Red Cross Knight and his two companions.

THE WOOD OF ERROR

THE first adventure happened in this way. Scarcely had the Red Cross Knight and the Lady Una started on their journey when the sky suddenly became overcast, and a great storm of rain beat down upon the earth. Looking about for shelter, they saw, not far away, a shady grove, which seemed just what they wanted. The trees here had great spreading branches, which grew so thickly overhead that no light could pierce the covering of leaves. Through this wood wide paths and alleys, well trodden, led in all directions. It seemed a truly pleasant place, and a safe shelter against the tempest, so they entered in at once.

At first, as they roamed along the winding paths they found nothing but pleasure. Deeper and deeper into the heart of the wood they went, hearing with joy the sweet singing of the birds, and filled with wonder to see so many different kinds of beautiful trees clustered in one spot. But by-and-by, when the storm was over and they wished to go forward on their journey, they found, to their sorrow, that they had lost their way. It was impossible to remember by which path they had come; every way now seemed strange and unknown. Here and there they wandered, backwards and forwards; there were so many turnings to be seen, so many paths, they knew not which to take to lead them out of the wood.

In this perplexity, at last they determined to go straight forward until they found some end, either in or out of the wood. Choosing for this purpose one of the broadest and most trodden paths, they came presently, in the thickest part of the wood, to a hollow cave. Then the Red Cross Knight dismounted from his steed, and gave his spear to the dwarf to hold.

> "Take heed," said the Lady Una, "lest you too rashly provoke mischief. This is a wild and unknown place, and peril is often without show. Hold back, therefore, till you know further if there is any danger hidden there."

"Ah, lady," said the Knight, "it were shame to go backward for fear of a hidden danger. Virtue herself gives light to lead through any darkness."

"Yes," said Una; "but I know better than you the peril of this place, though now it is too late to bid you go back like a coward. Yet wisdom warns you to stay your steps, before you are forced to retreat. This is the Wandering Wood, and that is the den of Error, a horrible monster, hated of all. Therefore, I advise you to be cautious."

"Fly, fly! this is no place for living men!" cried timid Prudence.

But the young Knight was full of eagerness and fiery courage, and nothing could stop him. Forth to the darksome hole he went, and looked in. His glittering armour made a little light, by which he could plainly see the ugly monster. Such a great, horrible thing it was, something like a snake, with a long tail twisted in knots, with stings all over it. And near this wicked big creature, whose other name was Falsehood, there were a thousand little ones, varying in shape, but every one bad and ugly; for you may be quite sure that wherever one of this horrible race is found, there will always be many others of the same family lurking near.

When the light shone into the cave all the little creatures fled to hide themselves, and the big parent Falsehood rushed out of her den in terror. But when she saw the shining armour of the Knight she tried to turn back, for she hated light as her deadliest foe, and she was always accustomed to live in darkness, where she could neither see plainly nor be seen.

When the Knight saw that she was trying to escape, he sprang after her as fierce as a lion, and then the great fight began. Though he strove valiantly, yet he was in sore peril, for suddenly the cunning creature flung her huge tail round and round him, so that he could stir neither hand nor foot.

Then the Lady Una cried out, to encourage him, "Now, now, Sir Knight, show what you are! Add faith unto your force, and be not faint! Kill her, or else she will surely kill you."

With that, fresh strength and courage came to the Knight. Gathering all his force, he got one hand free, and gripped the creature by the throat with so much pain that she was soon compelled to loosen her wicked hold. Then, seeing that she could not hope to conquer in this way, she suddenly tried to stifle the Knight by flinging over him a flood of poison. This made the Knight retreat a moment; then she called to her aid all the horrid little creeping and crawling monsters that he had seen before, and many others of the same kind, or worse. These came swarming and buzzing round the Knight like a cloud of teasing gnats, and tormented and confused him with their feeble stings. Enraged at this fresh attack, he made up his mind to end the matter one way or another, and, rushing at his foe, he killed her with one stroke of his sword.

Then Lady Una, who, from a distance, had watched all that passed, came near in haste to greet his victory.

> "Fair Knight," she said, "born under happy star! You are well worthy of that armour in which this day you have won great glory, and proved your strength against a strong enemy. This is your first battle. I pray that you will win many others in like manner."

THE KNIGHT DECEIVED BY THE MAGICIAN

AFTER his victory over Falsehood, the Red Cross Knight again mounted his steed, and he and the Lady Una went on their way. Keeping carefully to one path, and turning neither to the right hand nor the left, at last they found themselves safely out of the Wood of Error.

But now they were to fall into the power of a more dangerous and treacherous foe than even the hateful monster, Falsehood.

They had travelled a long way, and met with no fresh adventure, when at last they chanced to meet in the road an old man. He looked very wise and good. He was dressed in a long black gown, like a hermit, and had bare feet and a grey beard; he had a book hanging from his belt, as was the custom with scholars in those days. He seemed very quiet and sad, and kept his eyes fixed on the ground, and all the time, as he went along, he seemed to be saying prayers, and lamenting over his own wickedness.

When he saw the travellers he made a very humble salute to them. The Red Cross Knight returned the greeting with all courtesy, and asked him if he knew of any strange adventures that were then taking place.

> "Ah, my dear son!" said the hermit, "how should a simple old man, who lives in a lonely cell, and does nothing all day but sorrow for his own faults-how should such a man know any tidings of war or worldly trouble? It is not fitting for me to meddle with such matters. But, if indeed you desire to hear about danger and evil near at hand, I can tell you about a strange man who wastes all the surrounding country."

"That," said the Knight, "is what I chiefly ask about, and I will reward you well if you will guide me to the place where he dwells. For it is a disgrace to knighthood that such a creature should be allowed to live so long."

"His dwelling is far away from here, in the midst of a barren wilderness," answered the old man. "No living person may ever pass it without great danger and difficulty."

"Now," said the Lady Una, "night is drawing near, and I know well that you are wearied with your former fight. Therefore, take rest, and with the new day begin new work."

"You have been well advised, Sir Knight," said the old man. "Day is now spent; therefore take up your abode with me for this night."

The travellers were well content to do this, so they went with the apparently good old man to his home.

It was a little lowly hermitage, down in a dale by the side of a forest, far from the beaten track of travellers. A small chapel was built near, and close by a crystal stream gently welled forth from a never-failing fountain.

Arrived at the house, they neither expected nor found any entertainment; but rest was what they chiefly needed, and they were well satisfied, for the noblest mind is always the best contented. The old man had a good store of pleasing words, and knew well how to fit his talk to suit his visitors. The evening passed pleasantly, and then the hermit conducted his guests to the lodgings where they were to spend the night.

But when they were safely asleep a horrid change came over the old man, for in reality he was not good at all, although he pretended to be so. His heart was full of hatred, malice, and deceit. He called himself Archimago, which means a "Great Magician," but his real name was Hypocrisy. He knew that as long as Holiness and Truth kept together, no great harm could come to either of them; so he determined to do everything in his power to separate them. For this purpose he got out all his books of magic, and set to work to devise cunning schemes and spells. He was so clever and wily that he could deceive people much better and wiser than himself. He also had at his bidding many bad little spirits, who ran about and did his messages; these he used to help his friends and frighten his enemies, and he had the power of making them take any shape he wished.

Choosing out two of the worst of these, he sent one on a message to King Morpheus, who rules over the Land of Sleep. He bade him bring back with him a bad, false dream, which Archimago then carried to the sleeping Knight. So cunningly did he contrive the matter, that when the Knight awoke the next morning he never knew that it had only been a dream, but believed that all the things he had seen in his sleep had really happened.

In the meanwhile, Archimago dressed up the other bad spirit to look like Una, so that at a little distance it was impossible to tell any difference in the two figures. He knew that the only way to part Holiness and Truth was to make Holiness believe by some means that Truth was not as good as she appeared to be. He knew also that the Red Cross Knight would believe nothing against the Lady Una except what he saw with his own eyes. Therefore he laid his plans with the greatest care and guile.

Now we shall see how he succeeded in his wicked endeavour.

THE KNIGHT FORSAKES UNA

THE next morning at daybreak the Knight awoke, sad and unrested after the unpleasant dreams that had come to him in the night. He did not know he had been asleep; he thought the things that troubled him had really happened.

It was scarcely dawn when Archimago rushed up to him in a state of pretended sorrow and indignation.

"The Lady Una has left you," said this wicked mail. "She is not good as she pretends to be. She cares nothing at all for you, nor for the noble work on which you are bound, and she does not mean to go any farther with you on your toilsome journey."

The Red Cross Knight started up in anger. This was like his dream, and he knew not what was true nor what was false.

"Come," said Archimago, "see for yourself."

He pointed to a figure in the distance whom the Knight took to be Una. Then, indeed, he was forced to believe what the wicked magician told him. He now took for granted that Una had been deceiving him all along, and had seized this moment to escape. He forgot all her real sweetness and goodness and beauty; he only thought how false and unkind she was. He was filled with anger, and he never paused a moment to reflect if there could be any possibility of mistake. Calling his servant, he bade him bring his horse at once, and then these two immediately set forth again on their journey.

Here the Red Cross Knight was wrong, and we shall see presently into what perils and misfortunes he fell because of his hasty want of faith. If he had had a little patience he would soon have discovered that the figure he saw was only a dressed-up imitation. The real Lady Una all this time was sleeping quietly in her own bower.

When she awoke and found that her two companions had fled in the night and left her alone behind, she was filled with grief and dismay. She could not understand why they should do such a thing. Mounting her white ass, she rode after them with all the speed she could, but the Knight had urged on his steed so fast it was almost useless to try to follow. Yet she never stayed to rest her weary limbs, but went on seeking them over hill and dale, and through wood and plain, sorely grieved in her tender heart that the one she loved best should leave her with such ungentle discourtesy.

When the wicked Archimago saw that his cunning schemes had succeeded so well he was greatly pleased, and set to work to devise fresh mischief. It was Una whom he chiefly hated, and he took great pleasure in her many troubles, for hypocrisy always hates real goodness. He had the power of turning himself into any shape he chose--sometimes he would be a fowl, sometimes a fish, now like a fox, now like a dragon. On the present occasion, to suit his evil purpose, it seemed best to him to put on the appearance of the good knight whom he had so cruelly beguiled.

Therefore, Hypocrisy dressed himself up in imitation armour with a silver shield and everything exactly like the Red Cross Knight. When he sat upon his fiery charger he looked such a splendid warrior you would have thought it was St. George himself.

HOLINESS FIGHTS FAITHLESS, AND MAKES FRIENDS WITH FALSE RELIGION

THE true St. George, meanwhile, had wandered far away. Now that he had left the Lady Una, he bad nothing but his own will to guide him, and he no longer followed any fixed purpose.

Presently he saw coming to meet him another warrior, fully armed. He was a great, rough fellow, who cared nothing for GOD or man; across his shield, in gay letters, was written "Sans Foy," which means Faithless.

He had with him a companion, a handsome lady, dressed all in scarlet, trimmed with gold and rich pearls. She rode a beautiful palfrey, with gay trappings, and little gold bells tinkled on her bridle. The two came along laughing and talking, but when the lady saw the Red Cross Knight, she left off her mirth at once, and bade her companion attack him.

Then the two knights levelled their spears, and rushed at each other. But when Faithless saw the red cross graven on the breastplate of the other, he knew that he could never prevail against that safeguard. However, he fought with great fury, and the Red Cross Knight had a hard battle before he overcame him. At last he managed to kill him, and he told his servant to carry away the shield of Faithless in token of victory.

When the lady saw her champion fall, she fled in terror; but the Red Cross Knight hurried after her, and bade her stay, telling her that she had nothing now to fear. His brave and gentle heart was full of pity to see her in so great distress, and he asked her to tell him who she was, and who was the man that had been with her.

Melting into tears, she then told him the following sad story:--She said that she was the daughter of an emperor, and had been engaged to marry a wise and good prince. Before the wedding-day, however, the prince fell into the hands of his foes, and was cruelly slain. She went out to look for his dead body, and in the course of her wandering met the Saracen knight, who took her captive. "Sans Foy" was one of three bad brothers. The names of the others were "Sans Loy," which means Lawless, and "Sans Joy," which means Joyless. She further said that her own name was "Fidessa," or True Religion, and she besought the Knight to have compassion on her, because she was so friendless and unhappy.

> "Fair lady," said the Knight, "a heart of flint would grieve to hear of your sorrows. But henceforth rest safely assured that you have found a new friend to help you, and lost an old foe to hurt you. A new friend is better than an old foe."

Then the seemingly simple maiden pretended to look comforted, and the two rode on happily together.

But what the lady had told about herself was quite untrue. Her name was not "Fidessa" at all, but "Duessa," which means False Religion. If Una had still been with the Knight, he would never have been led astray; but when he parted from her he had nothing but his own feelings to guide him. He still meant to do right, but he was deceived by his false companion, who brought him into much trouble and danger.

UNA AND THE LION

ALL this while the Lady Una, lonely and forsaken, was roaming in search of her lost Knight. How sad was her fate! She, a King's daughter, so beautiful, so faithful, so true, who had done no wrong either in word or deed, was left sorrowful and deserted because of the cunning wiles of a wicked enchanter. Fearing nothing, she sought the Red Cross Knight through woods and lonely wilderness, but no tidings of him ever came to her.

One day, being weary, she alighted from her steed, and lay down on the grass to rest. It was in the midst of a thicket, far from the sight of any traveller. She lifted her veil, and put aside the black cloak which always covered her dress.

> "Her angel's face,
> As the great eye of Heaven shinèd bright,
> And made a sunshine in the shady place."

Suddenly, out of the wood there rushed a fierce lion, who, seeing Una, sprang at her to devour her; but, when he came nearer, he was amazed at the sight of her loveliness, and all his rage turned to pity. Instead of tearing her to pieces, he kissed her weary feet and licked her lily hand as if he knew how innocent and wronged she was. [1]

When Una saw the gentleness of this kingly creature, she could not help weeping.

Sad to see her sorrow, he stood gazing at her; all his angry mood changed to compassion, till at last Una mounted her snowy palfrey and once more set out to seek her lost companion.

The lion would not leave her desolate, but went with her as a strong guard and as a faithful companion. When she slept he kept watch, and when she

---

[1] The figure of the lion may be taken as the emblem of Honour, which always pays respect to Truth.

waked he waited diligently, ready to help her in any way he could. He always knew from her looks what she wanted.

Long she travelled thus through lonely places, where she thought her wandering Knight might pass, yet never found trace of living man. At length she came to the foot of a steep mountain, where the trodden grass showed that there was a path for people to go. This path she followed till at last she saw, slowly walking in the front of her, a damsel carrying a jar of water

The Lady Una called to her to ask if there were any dwelling-place near, but the rough-looking girl made no answer; she seemed not able to speak, nor hear, nor understand. But when she saw the lion standing beside her, she threw down her pitcher with sudden fear and fled away. Never before in that land had she seen the face of a fair lady, and the sight of the lion filled her with terror. Fast away she fled, and never looked behind till she came at last to her home, where her blind mother sat all day in darkness. Too frightened to speak, she caught hold of her mother with trembling hands, while the poor old woman, full of fear, ran to shut the door of their house.

By this time the weary Lady Una had arrived, and asked if she might come in; but, when no answer came to her request, the lion, with his strong claws, tore open the wicket-door and let her into the little hut. There she found the mother and daughter crouched up in a dark corner, nearly dead with fear.

The name of the poor old blind woman was Superstition. She tried to be good in a very mistaken way. She hid herself in her dark corner, and was quite content never to come out of it. When the beautiful Lady Una, who was all light and truth, came to the hut, the mother and daughter, instead of making her welcome, hated her, and would gladly have thrust her out.

Trying to soothe their needless dread, Una spoke gently to them, and begged that she might rest that night in their small cottage. To this they unwillingly agreed, and Una lay down with the faithful lion at her feet to keep watch. All night, instead of sleeping, she wept, still sorrowing for her lost Knight and longing for the morning.

In the middle of the night, when all the inmates of the little cottage were asleep, there came a furious knocking at the door. This was a wicked thief, called "Kirkrapine," or Church-robber, whose custom it was to go about stealing ornaments from churches, and clothes from clergymen, and robbing the alms-boxes of the poor. He used to share his spoils with the: daughter of the blind woman, and to-night he had come with a great sackful of stolen goods.

When he received no answer to his knocking, he got very angry indeed, and made a loud clamour at the door; but the women in the hut were too much afraid of the lion to rise and let him in. At last he burst open the door in a great rage and tried to enter, but the lion sprang upon him and tore him to pieces before he could even call for help. His terrified friends scarcely dared to weep or move in case they should share his fate.

When daylight came, Una rose and started again on her journey with the lion to seek the wandering Knight. As soon as they had left, the two frightened women came forth, and, finding Church-robber slain outside the cottage, they began to wail and lament; then they ran after Una, railing at her for being the cause of all their ill; they called after her evil wishes that mischief and misery might fall on her and follow her all the way, and that she might ever wander in endless error.

When they saw that their bad words were of no avail, they turned back, and there in the road they met a knight, clad in armour; but, though he looked such a grand warrior, it was really only the wicked enchanter, Hypocrisy, who was seeking Una, in order to work her fresh trouble. When he saw the old woman, Superstition, he asked if she could give him any tidings of the lady. Therewith her passion broke out anew; she told him what had just happened, blaming Una as the cause of all her distress. Archimago pretended to condole with her, and then, finding out the direction in which Una had gone, he followed as quickly as possible.

Before long he came up to where Una was slowly travelling; but seeing the noble lion at her side, he was afraid to go too near, and turned away to a hill at a little distance. When Una saw him, she thought, from his shield and armour, that it was her own true knight, and she rode up to him, and spoke meekly, half-frightened.

> "Ah, my lord," she said, "where have you been so long out of my sight? I feared that you hated me, or that I had done something to displease you, and that made everything seem dark and cheerless. But welcome now, welcome!"

> "My dearest lady," said false Hypocrisy, "you must not think I could so shame knighthood as to desert you. But the truth is, the reason why I left you so long was to seek adventure in a strange place, where Archimago said there was a mighty robber, who worked much mischief to many people. Now he will trouble no one further. This is the good reason why I left you. Pray believe it, and accept my faithful service, for I have vowed to defend you by land and sea. Let your grief be over."

When Una heard these sweet words it seemed to her that she was fully rewarded for all the trials she had gone through. One loving hour can make up for many years of sorrow. She forgot all that she had suffered; she spoke no more of the past. True love never looks back, but always forward. Before her stood her Knight, for whom she had toiled so sorely, and Una's heart was filled with joy.

IN THE HANDS OF THE ENEMY

UNA and the Magician (who was disguised as the Red Cross Knight) had not gone far when they saw some one riding swiftly towards them. The new-comer was on a fleet horse, and was fully armed; his look was stern, cruel, and revengeful. On his shield in bold letters was traced the name "Sans Loy," which means Lawless. He was one of the brothers of "Sans Foy," or Faithless, whom the real Red Cross Knight had slain, and he had made up his mind to avenge his brother's death.

When he saw the red cross graven on the shield which Hypocrisy carried, he thought that he had found the foe of whom he was in search, and, levelling his spear, he prepared for battle. Hypocrisy, who was a mean coward, and had never fought in his life, was nearly fainting with fear; but the Lady Una spoke such cheering words that he began to feel more hopeful. Lawless, however, rushed at him with such fury that he drove his lance right through the other's shield, and bore him to the ground. Leaping from his horse, he ran towards him, meaning to kill him, and exclaiming, "Lo, this is the worthy reward of him that slew Faithless!"

Una begged the cruel knight to have pity on his fallen foe, but her words were of no avail. Tearing off his helmet, Lawless would have slain him at once,